Everything Under the Sky

Also by Matilde Asensi

FICTION

The Last Cato

Everything Under the Sky

A NOVEL

Matilde Asensi

Translated from Spanish by Lisa Carter

HARPER

An Imprint of HarperCollinsPublishers

www.harpercollins.com

FIRST EDITION

Originally published in Spanish as *Todo bajo el Cielo* by Editorial
Planeta, S.A., in Spain in 2006.

Designed by Kathryn Parise

Library of Congress Cataloging-in-Publication Data is available
on request.

ISBN: 978-0-06-145841-5

08 09 10 11 12 WBC/RRD 10 9 8 7 6 5 4 3 2 1

For Pascual and Andres.
After all the long and hard negotiations, they win.
And on top of everything, I love them.

Everything Under the Sky

Chapter
I

One afternoon, amid the interminable seasickness and misery that overshadowed our crossing on the *André Lebon*, a surprising calm fell over the ship. I struggled to open my eyes at least partway, as if that would tell me why the packet boat had stopped pounding against the waves for the first time in six weeks. Six weeks! Forty dreadful days, out of which I remember being on deck just once or twice—and only after a great deal of effort. I never saw Port Said, Djibouti, or Singapore. I wasn't even able to rise enough to look out the porthole in my cabin as we crossed the Suez Canal or when we docked in Ceylon and Hong Kong. Nausea and fatigue had kept me flat out in that narrow bed in my second-class cabin ever since we left Marseille on the morning of Sunday, July 22. Neither the ginger infusions nor the stupefying whiffs of laudanum had alleviated my distress.

Oceans were not for me. I was born in Madrid, inland, on the Castilian plateau, far from the nearest beach. Boarding a ship to float halfway around the world, rocking to and fro, was not in my nature. I would much rather have made the trip by train, but Rémy always said it was too dangerous. Indeed, ever since the Bolshevik revolution in Russia, it was absolute madness to travel through Siberia. Thus I had no choice but to buy tickets on that elegant steamer operated by Compagnie des Messageries Maritimes. I just prayed the god of the sea would be compassionate and not feel some eccentric need to sink us into the ocean, where we'd be devoured by fish, our bones covered in sludge forever. There are some things we are simply not born to do, and I certainly had not come into this world with a seagoing spirit.

Once the disconcerting silence and calm had revived me, I gazed up at the familiar blades of the fan hanging from the ceiling. At some point on our journey, I swore that if I managed to set foot on solid ground again, I would paint that fan just as I had seen it under the effects of laudanum. Perhaps the art dealer Kahnweiler, who was so fond of the cubist works by my countrymen Picasso and Juan Gris, would want to buy it. But that foggy vision of the fan blades didn't explain why the ship had stopped. I was struck by a sense of foreboding when I didn't hear the usual commotion or the sound of passengers rushing up on deck that accompanied arrival at port. After all, we were on the perilous East China Sea, and even in that year of 1923, dangerous Asian pirates still boarded passenger ships to rob and kill. My heart pounded, and my hands began to sweat. Just then a sinister knock came at my door.

"May I, Auntie?" inquired the muted voice of the brand-new niece I had apparently won at a raffle, for which I'd never even bought a ticket.

"Come in," I murmured, holding back a mild wave of nausea. Since Fernanda came only to bring me the infusion for seasickness, my stomach turned whenever she arrived.

Her plump figure squeezed through the doorway. She held a large porcelain cup in one hand and her perennial black fan in the other. The girl never let go of that fan, just as she never let her hair out of the ponytail pulled tight at the nape of her neck. The robust youth of her seventeen years contrasted sharply with the deep mourning dress she always wore. Her outfit was outrageously old-fashioned, even for a young woman from Madrid, and completely inappropriate for the scorching heat in these parts. I had offered her some of my own clothing (chic, lighter blouses and a shorter skirt, cut to the knee as was fashionable in Paris). But, being the proud heiress of a dry, ungrateful personality, she flatly rejected my offer, crossing herself and staring down at her hands, categorically settling the matter once and for all.

"Why has the ship stopped?" I asked as I slowly sat up, catching a hint of the acrid potion that the cooks routinely prepared.

"We're no longer at sea," she explained, sitting on the edge of my bed and bringing the cup to my lips. "We're at a place called Woosung or Woosong, something like that, fourteen miles from Shanghai. The ship has to move slowly because we're heading upriver and there's the possibility we could hit bottom, but we should be there within a couple of hours."

"At last!" I exclaimed, noticing that mere proximity to Shanghai was much more soothing than the ginger tisane. Still, I wouldn't truly feel well until I was out of that awful, salty-smelling cabin.

Fernanda, who kept the cup at my lips no matter how far I leaned back, made a grimace that was supposed to be a smile. The poor thing was exactly like her mother, my insufferable sister Carmen, who had passed away five years earlier during the terrible flu epidemic of 1918. In addition to her personality, Fernanda had inherited her mother's big, round eyes and protruding chin. They also had the same nose, which ended in a funny little ball and gave them a somewhat comical look, despite their constant sour expressions. Fernanda had, however, inherited her size from her father, my brother-in-law Pedro, a man with an enormous paunch, his double chin so big that he'd grown a beard just to try to hide it. Pedro wasn't exactly the epitome of charming either, so it was no wonder the fruit of that unfortunate marriage was this serious young thing dressed in mourning and as sweet as lemons.

"You should gather your things, Auntie. Shall I help you pack?"

"If you wouldn't mind." I exhaled, falling back onto the hard old bed with an exaggerated display of suffering that, while absolutely real, did come off as rather affected. Still, the girl had offered to help. Why not let her?

As she rummaged through my trunks and cases, collecting the few things I'd used on that arduous voyage, I began to hear noises and happy-sounding voices in the passageway. The other second-class passengers were undoubtedly as impatient as I was to get off the water and back onto dry land with the rest of humanity. I was so cheered by this thought that, moaning and groaning, I struggled to rise and managed to sit on the edge of the bed with my feet on the floor. I was terribly weak, but even worse than the fatigue was the renewed sense of sadness, momentarily erased by the laudanum, that came flooding back.

I didn't know how long we'd have to stay in Shanghai to attend to Rémy's affairs. Still, even though the very thought of the return trip made my hair stand on end, I hoped our stay would be as brief as possible. In fact, in order to conclude matters as quickly as possible, I had sent a cable arranging to meet with the lawyer the very next morning. Rémy's death had been a terrible shock, and I was still trying to come to terms with it. Rémy, dead? How absurd! The idea was absolutely ridiculous, and yet the memory of the day I heard the news remained fresh in my mind. It was the same day Fernanda appeared at my door in Paris with her little leather suitcase, black overcoat, and that prissy bonnet so typical of well-to-do Spanish girls. I was still trying to adjust to the idea that this creature, a complete stranger to me, was my niece, the daughter of my sister and her recently deceased husband. Just then a gentleman from the Ministry of Foreign Affairs came to the door. He took off his hat and, offering his sincerest condolences, handed me an official dispatch attached to a cable announcing Rémy's death at the hands of thieves who'd broken in to his house in Shanghai.

What was I to do? According to the dispatch, I had to go to China to make arrangements for his body and settle his legal affairs. But now I was also guardian of this Fernanda (or Fernandina, as she preferred, though I refused to call her that), born a few years after I'd severed all ties with my family, in 1901, and moved to France to study art at the

Académie de la Grande Chaumière—the only school in Paris with no enrollment fees. There was no time to fall apart or feel sorry for myself. I left a few gold chains at the pawnshop, sold all the paintings in my studio for a song, and bought two very expensive tickets to Shanghai on the first boat sailing from Marseille the following Sunday. After all, apart from anything else, Rémy De Poulain was my closest friend. I felt a stabbing pain in the middle of my chest whenever I realized he was no longer in this world, laughing, smiling, walking, simply breathing.

"What hat would you like to wear to disembark, Auntie?" Fernanda's voice brought me back to reality.

"The one with the blue flowers," I murmured.

My niece remained still, watching me with the same opaque stare her mother had used when we were children. That inherited trait of hiding her thoughts was what I liked least about Fernanda, because you could still see what she was thinking. I'd played that game for many years with her mother and grandmother, so this young lady was no match for me.

"Wouldn't you rather the black one with the buttons? It would go well with one of your dresses."

"I'll wear the flowered one with my blue skirt and blouse."

Her expression remained the same. "You remember, don't you, that someone from the consulate will be here to meet us?"

"Precisely why I'm going to wear the outfit that suits me best. Oh, and the white shoes and purse, please!"

Once all my trunks had been closed and the clothes I asked for were laid out at the foot of my bed, Fernanda left without another word. By then I was feeling much better, thanks to the relative immobility of the ship. From what I could see out the porthole, we were slowly moving through heavy traffic. There were other boats as big as ours and a bevy of swift craft where solitary fishermen or entire families—including the elderly, women, and children—took shelter in the shade of enormous square sails.

I had hurriedly bought a Thomas Cook travel guide at the American bookstore Shakespeare and Company the day before we set sail. It said we were heading up the Huangpu River. The great city of Shanghai lay on its shores near the confluence with the mighty Yangtze, or Blue River, the longest in all of Asia, crossing the continent from west to east. As strange as it may seem, even though Rémy had lived in China for the past twenty years, I'd never been there. He'd never asked me to come, and I'd never been tempted to make such a journey.

The De Poulain family owned large silk factories in Lyon. Initially, Rémy's older brother, Arthème, sent the raw material from China, but he returned to France to take over the business after their father died. Rémy, who until then had only ever lived an idle, carefree life in Paris, was left no choice but to take up Arthème's post in Shanghai. So, at forty-five and never having done a day's work, he suddenly became representative and agent for the family's spinning mills in the richest, most important metropolis in Asia, the so-called Paris of the Far East. I was twenty-five at the time and, in all sincerity, relieved when he left. I became mistress of my own house, free to do whatever I wanted—exactly what he'd been doing while I studied at the Académie. Of course, from that moment on I had to rely solely on my own meager income, but time and distance healed our topsy-turvy relationship. Finally Rémy and I became the best of friends. We wrote often, told one another everything, and there's no doubt that without his prompt financial assistance I'd have found myself in a real predicament more than once.

By the time I finished dressing, there was a considerable amount of hubbub on the ship. From the light coming into the cabin, I guessed it was approximately four in the afternoon and, based on the noise, that we must be docking at the shipping company's wharf in Shanghai. If the trip had gone as planned, it should be Thursday, August 30. Before leaving my cabin to go up on deck, I added one final, outrageous touch to the summery outfit I, a forty-something widow, was wearing. Undoing the ties on my blouse, I knotted around my neck a beautiful soft white silk foulard embroidered with flowers. The one Rémy had given me in 1914 when he was back in Paris as a result of the war.

I picked up my purse and stood in front of the mirror, placing the hat firmly on my short *à la garçon* hair. I touched up my makeup, applying a little rouge to detract from my pallor and the dark circles under my eyes—luckily, pallid tones were in that year—and walked unsteadily toward the door. And the unknown. I was in Shanghai: the most dynamic, opulent city in the Far East, famous all over the world for its unbridled passion for pleasures of any kind.

From the deck I could see Fernanda striding down the gangway. She was wearing that terrible black bonnet and looked exactly like a crow in a field of flowers. The uproar was tremendous: Hundreds of people were crowding to disembark from the ship while thousands more were gathered on the wharf among the sheds, customs buildings, and offices flying the French tricolor. Bundles and luggage were being unloaded, cars offered for rent, and rickshaws for hire. Many were simply waiting for friends and family arriving, like us, on the *André Lebon*. Policemen dressed in yellow with cone-shaped hats and stripes down their pant legs were attempting to bring order to the chaos by brutally caning Chinese vendors. Barefoot, half-naked men carried oscillating bamboo poles across their shoulders with woven baskets on either end containing food or cups of tea they sold to Westerners. The poor coolies' cries were drowned out by all that human clamor, but you could see them run from the rod only to stop a few feet farther on and continue their sales.

Fernanda was perfectly visible in that crowd. All the colorful hats in the world, all the bright Chinese parasols, all the canopies on all the rickshaws in Shanghai wouldn't have been able to hide that plump, black-robed figure charging through like a German tank on its way to Verdun. I couldn't imagine what had caused her to leave the ship with such determination, but I was too busy trying not to get trampled by the other passengers to worry. Fernanda had received an education befitting a Spanish señorita from a family of means—French, sewing, religion, a little painting, and a little piano—however, the girl was big enough to trounce a couple of little Chinese men with pigtails in the blink of an eye.

As I walked down the gangway, the pungent odor of putrefaction and filth rising up from the wharf made me feel sick all over again. Thankfully, we were moving very slowly, so I had time to put a few drops of cologne on my fine linen handkerchief, which I held over my nose and mouth. Other ladies around me quickly followed suit, while poker-faced gentlemen resigned themselves to inhaling the overpowering fecal stench. At the time I assumed that the smell came from the dirty waters of the Huangpu, given the additional aromas of fish and burned oil. Only later did I discover that this was the usual smell of Shanghai, something you eventually had to get used to. And so I stepped onto Chinese soil for the very first time, my face hidden behind a perfumed mask that revealed only my eyes. Surprisingly, my diligent niece was right there at the bottom of the gangway, accompanied by an elegant gentleman who courteously broke in to kind greetings after offering his condolences on the death of my husband. It was Monsieur Favez, attaché to the consul general of France in Shanghai, Auguste H. Wilden. He had the great pleasure of inviting me to lunch the following day at his official residence if, naturally, I did not have other plans and was sufficiently recovered from the trip.

I had only just arrived, and my calendar was already filling up: a meeting with Rémy's lawyer in the morning and lunch with the consul general of France at noon. I felt as if it would take me a few lifetimes to feel steady on solid ground again. For some reason Fernanda looked fresh, rested, and in top form. Never, in the month and a half that I'd known her, had I seen my niece exude anything so akin to happiness. Could it be the stench of Shanghai or perhaps the crowds that had changed her? Whatever the reason, the girl's chubby cheeks were flushed and her sour grimace had sweetened immensely, not to mention the courage and determination she'd shown by setting out on her own through that crowd to find the consular attaché (who was, in fact, glancing at her with a not-at-all-diplomatic look of astonishment on his face). However, that pleasant impression was as ephemeral as a ray of sunshine in a storm. As M. Favez helped us with our paperwork in the Compagnie offices, Fernanda reverted to her habitual stone face and leaden personality.

In no time at all, a handful of coolies had loaded our things into the trunk of M. Favez's car—a splendid white convertible Voisin with a rear spare tire and a silver starting crank. Without further ado we left the wharf in a lovely screech of tires that caused me to exclaim in delight and put a satisfied smile on the attaché's face as he drove down the left-hand side of the Bund, that beautiful avenue on the western shore of the Huangpu. I know I didn't look at all like a widow who'd arrived in Shanghai to make arrangements for her husband's body, but I couldn't have cared less. It would have been worse to feign proper mourning, especially when the entire French colony had to know perfectly well that Rémy and I had lived apart for twenty years. In all likelihood, they were very aware of his hundreds, even thousands, of amorous affairs. Rémy and I had a marriage of convenience: I married for security and a roof over my head in a foreign country, he to have a lawful wife and thus gain access to the considerable inheritance from his mother. The poor woman had died desperate to see her libertine son settle down. Having fulfilled its objectives, our marriage grew into a beautiful friendship. Only I knew how much it hurt me to lose Rémy, and I was certainly not about to display that pain in public.

As my eyes leaped from one strange character to another on that busy street, M. Favez explained that the majority of people in Shanghai were Celestials and yet it was an international city controlled by Westerners.

"Celestials?" I interrupted.

"That's what we call the Chinese. They consider themselves subjects of the Son of Heaven's Empire. The last emperor, the young Puyi,[1] still lives in the Forbidden City in Peking, although he hasn't held power since 1911, when Dr. Sun Yat-sen overthrew the monarchy and established the republic. Many Chinese still believe they are superior to Westerners, whom they cal *yang kwei* or 'foreign devils' in return, so we sarcastically call them Celestials. Or yellows. We also call them yellows," he stated with a smile.

"And doesn't that seem a little insulting?" I asked, surprised.

"Insulting? No, not any more than when they call us barbarians or 'big noses.' Quid pro quo, don't you think?"

There were three major territorial and political divisions in Shanghai, the attaché explained as he drove full speed, honking the horn for people and vehicles to move out of his way. First, there was the French Concession, where we were, an elongated strip of land that included the wharf on the Bund at which the *André Lebon* had docked. Second, there was the old Chinese city of Nantao, an almost-circular space south of the French Concession. It was surrounded by a beautiful boulevard built on the remains of ancient walls that were demolished after the republican revolution of 1911. Finally, there was the much larger International Concession to the north, which was governed by the consuls from every country with diplomatic representation.

"And they all have equal power?" I asked, holding the foulard against my chest to keep it from blowing up in my face.

"Monsieur Wilden has full authority in the French colony, madame. In the International area, most political and economic weight is held by England and the United States—the strongest nations in China—but there are Greek, Belgian, Portuguese, Jewish, Italian, German, and Scandinavian colonies. Even Spanish," he emphasized. I was French by marriage, but my accent, my name, my rich brown hair and brown eyes were obvious signs of my heritage. "And these days," he continued, gripping the wheel, "Shanghai has many Russians, Bolsheviks who live in the consulate and surrounding areas, and White Russians who fled the revolution. Mostly the latter."

"The same thing has happened in Paris."

M. Favez turned to look at me for an instant, laughed, and then quickly looked back at the road. He honked and skillfully avoided a streetcar so packed with Celestials wearing hats and long Chinese garments that some even clung to bars on the outside of the car. All the streetcars in Shanghai were painted green and silver and displayed bright, colorful advertisements written in Chinese characters.

"Yes, madame," he conceded, "but wealthy Russians, the czarist aristocracy, went to Paris. Only the poor have come here. In any event, the most dangerous race, if I may put it that way, is the Nipponese. They've been trying to take control of Shanghai for years. In fact, they've created their own city within the International Concession. Japanese imperialists have great ambitions for China, and, what's worse, they also have a very powerful army." M. Favez suddenly realized that perhaps he was saying too much and smiled with concern. "Did you know, Mme De Poulain, that two million people live in this beautiful city, the second-busiest port in the world and the largest market in the Orient? Only fifty thousand of those are foreigners, and the rest are yellows. Nothing is simple in Shanghai, as you'll no doubt find out for yourself."

M. Favez suddenly turned left onto boulevard Edouard VII. It was a shame we saw only the short bit of the Bund belonging to France that first day. I'd have liked to have seen the architectural marvels along Shanghai's most impressive street: the most luxurious hotels and sumptuous clubs, the tallest buildings, and the most important consulates, offices, and banks—all in front of the dirty, stinking waters of the Huangpu.

I was pleasantly surprised by the French Concession. I'd been afraid the neighborhoods would have narrow streets and houses with those upturned roofs, but it was a delightful place. It had the same residential feel as the quarters in Paris, full of lovely whitewashed villas and gardens with exquisite lilacs, rosebushes, and privets. There were tennis clubs, cabarets, little plazas bordered by sycamore trees, public parks where mothers sat sewing next to their baby carriages, libraries, a movie house, bakeries, restaurants, clothing and cosmetic stores. I could have been in Montmartre, in the pavilions of the Bois, or in the Latin Quarter and not have known the difference. Every now and then, here or there, you could see a Chinese-style house with its red doors and windows, but they were the exception in those clean, pleasant French neighborhoods. Thus, when M. Favez stopped in front of a wooden gate outside one of the Oriental homes, I was slightly taken aback.

"Here we are," he declared happily as he turned off the motor and got out of the car.

Underneath one of two red paper lanterns, adorned with Chinese characters, hanging on either side of the door was a chain coming out through a hole in the wall. M. Favez pulled on it energetically and then returned to open my door and gallantly help me from the car. Although his hand remained outstretched, waiting, a sudden and devastating paralysis took hold of me, and I was unable to move. Not once in twenty years had Rémy mentioned that he lived in a Chinese-style house.

"Are you all right, Mme De Poulain?"

The large doors opened slowly, without a sound, and three or four servants, including one woman, came out into the street. They were bowing and murmuring phrases that must have been greetings, in their unfamiliar language. The first movement I was able to make was not to take the patient hand M. Favez extended, but to turn toward the back seat and look at my niece in search of a little understanding and complicity. Indeed, Fernanda's eyes were as big as saucers, expressing the same horrified surprise that I felt.

"What's wrong?" the attaché asked, leaning in with concern.

I recovered from my confusion as best I could and finally put my hand in M. Favez's. I had nothing against Chinese houses, of course; it was simply not what I expected of Rémy. He'd been such a refined bon vivant, so French, always on the alert for comforts and European good taste. How he had managed to live in a vulgar old Celestial house escaped me.

The female servant was as tiny and thin as a reed, and it was impossible to determine her age—you could just as easily have guessed fifty as seventy. She ceased giving orders to the three men who were carrying our luggage and bowed down so low before me that her lips nearly kissed the ground.

"My name is Mrs. Zhong, *tai-tai*,"[2] she said in perfect French. "Welcome to your late husband's house."

Mrs. Zhong, wearing a short jacket with a high collar and wide pants the same color blue it seemed all Chinese wore, bowed ceremoniously again. Her jet-black hair was pulled into a ponytail like Fernanda's, although that's where the similarity ended. It would have taken two or three Mrs. Zhongs to fill the physical space occupied by my niece, who remained sitting in the car, hesitant to leave.

"Come on, Fernanda," I encouraged. "We have to go in."

"Everyone in Spain calls me Fernandina, Auntie," she replied coldly in Spanish.

"Watch your manners in front of M. Favez and Mrs. Zhong. They don't speak our language. Out of the car, please."

"I'll say good-bye now, madame, mademoiselle," the attaché said, elegantly adjusting his cravat. "I'll go by the consulate to confirm your lunch with M. Wilden tomorrow."

"Leaving already, M. Favez?" I asked, alarmed.

As Fernanda got out of the Voisin, the attaché leaned over and took my hand, raising it lightly to his lips in farewell.

"Don't worry, madame," he whispered. "Mrs. Zhong is absolutely reliable. She worked for your late husband for years and can help you with anything you need." He straightened up and smiled. "I'll pick you up at twelve-thirty tomorrow, then?"

I nodded, and the diplomat turned toward my niece, who'd come to stand by my side.

"Good-bye, mademoiselle. It was a pleasure to meet you. I hope you enjoy your stay in Shanghai."

Fernanda gestured vaguely with her head, tilting it I'm not sure how, and suddenly an image of her grandmother, my mother, came to mind. I could picture her sitting in the parlor of the old family home on calle

Don Ramón de la Cruz in Madrid, wrapped in her beautiful Manila shawl to receive visitors on Thursday afternoons.

The Voisin sped down the street and disappeared. Fernanda and I turned toward the house with as little joy as if we'd been condemned to the garrote. Mrs. Zhong held one of the large doors open to allow us to pass. I don't know why, but just then she looked so like a Spanish civil guard that it unsettled me. Perhaps I'd mistaken her hair for a three-cornered hat; they were the same color and had the same lacquered shine. It was odd to be remembering things from Spain that I hadn't thought of in the last twenty years. No doubt this was due to the presence of that sullen, scowling child who'd brought my past back to me in her suitcase.

We walked onto an enormous patio with lush flower borders, blue-green ponds adorned with rock gardens, and enormous, hundred-year-old trees unlike any I had seen before. Some were so tall I'd noticed their branches above the wall from the street outside. A wide path in the shape of a cross led from the gate to three rectangular one-story buildings. Broad stone staircases ascended to porches filled with plants. Each building was painted white and had large, wooden windows carved with geometric shapes. The roofs had those horrible upturned corners of glazed pottery, painted such a vibrant green they shone brightly in the late-afternoon light.

With mincing steps Mrs. Zhong led the way to the main building directly in front of us. Watching her, I wondered why she didn't have those deformed feet that everyone who'd ever been to China always talked about. Rémy once told me that it was a Chinese custom to bind girls' feet starting at the age of two or three, so that the four smaller toes would curl under the sole of the foot. In a monstrous ritual of tears, screams, and pain that led to the death of some unlucky girls, the bandage was tightened a little more every day, for years, to prevent the extremity from growing. These poor women were forever condemned to walk with a swaying motion because they could use only what was left of the heel and the big toe, having to extend their arms and stick out their buttocks to keep their balance. Such horrific feet, called "Golden Lotus" or "Golden Lilies," caused the victim pain for the rest of her life and incomprehensibly provoked the most passionate desire in Chinese men. Rémy had also told me that the custom of foot binding had been banned since the end of the empire—that is, ever since Dr. Sun Yat-sen toppled the monarchy. But that had been only eleven years earlier, and Mrs. Zhong was more than old enough to have been subjected to the torture.

However, there she went, her small but healthy feet stuffed into white socks and the strangest flat black felt slippers, leading the way to the house that was now mine—as long as there were no more surprises during my meeting with Rémy's lawyer. I intended to sell it, of course, along with all the contents, and thus obtain some sorely needed income. I was also counting on the fact that Rémy would have left me a little money, not much, but enough to allow me to live comfortably for a few years until cubism, dadaism, constructivism, and so on went out of fashion and my paintings would fetch a better price. I admired Marcel Duchamp's innovation, Mondrian's geometry, and Picasso's genius, but as an art dealer had once told me, my paintings were too literal and too accessible. I'd never be considered one of the greats. No matter; I didn't care. All I wanted was to capture the surprising movement of a head, the perfection in a face, the harmony of the human body. I derived inspiration from beauty, wherever I found it, and wanted to express that magic on canvas, conveying the same power and emotion it evoked in me. I wanted whoever viewed my work to feel the pleasure, to be imbued with the same flavor and aroma. Unfortunately, because this wasn't in style, I was barely able to make ends meet. I was sure that Rémy, who knew all this, would have left me a tidy little sum in his will. The thought of inheriting his entire estate never even crossed my mind. The powerful De Poulain family would never allow a poor foreign painter to become co-owner of their silk factories. But the house, yes—it would have been crass even for the De Poulains to deprive a widow of her husband's home.

"Please come in," Mrs. Zhong invited as she pushed open the beautiful carved double doors to the main building.

It was much bigger inside than I expected. Large rooms stretched out to the left and right of the entrance, separated by wooden panels carved with geometric shapes, like the windows, and similarly covered from behind with a fine white paper that let an orangish, amber light through. Strangest of all were the doors in the center of the panels—if these round openings, these large holes in the shape of full moons, could be called doors. I have to admit that the furnishings were truly beautiful, inlaid and carved, lacquered in shades ranging from bright red to dark brown so that they stood out against the white walls and light-colored tile floor. The room Mrs. Zhong took us to—the last on the right—was filled with tables of all kinds, shapes, and sizes. Exquisite porcelain vases and bronze dragons, tigers, turtles, and birds sat on some; others were covered in flowerpots; on still others, red candles, wide at the top and narrow at the bottom, with no plate or candleholder underneath. I realized that all the decorations in this and the other rooms we'd passed through were curiously symmetrical—very strange to my Western eyes. And yet this harmony was deliberately split, by certain pictures or calligraphies on the walls, or a sideboard covered in ceramic bowls that looked out of place, almost accidental. It would take some time before I discovered that Celestials thought of each piece of furniture as a work of art, and its placement in a room had nothing to do with chance or mere aesthetics. A complex, thousand-year-old philosophy lay behind domestic décor. At the time, however, I thought Rémy's house looked like a museum of Oriental curiosities, and while such chinoiseries were still very much in style in Europe, I found the sheer profusion dizzying.

A servant with a mortarboard hat suddenly appeared carrying a tray of pretty white cups with lids and a red clay teapot. Moving as if sleepwalking, he set it on a large pedestal table in the center of the room. Mrs. Zhong pointed to a couch along one wall and then bent over to lift a squat, square table off the floor. She set it in the middle of the couch, exactly where I'd been about to sit, so that Fernanda and I were separated by it. As Mrs. Zhong poured us a cup of tea, the aroma drifting up from it awoke my poor gastric juices, making me feel suddenly famished. Unfortunately, however, the Chinese don't serve cookies with their tea, nor do they add milk or sugar, so I was left no choice but to simply rinse my stomach with that hot liquid.

"*Tai-tai*," Mrs. Zhong addressed me, bowing respectfully, "what should I call the young miss?"

"My niece?" I replied, looking over at the girl as she stared in confusion at her cup. "Call her by her name, Mrs. Zhong: Fernanda."

"My name is Fernandina," my niece objected as she continued to search in vain for the handle.

"Listen, Fernanda," I said gravely. "Spaniards have the habit of using the diminutive of a person's name: Lolita, Juanito, Alfonsito, Bernardino, Pepita, Isabelita . . . but elsewhere it's considered silly, do you understand?"

"I don't care," she replied, in Spanish to anger me even more. I ignored her.

"Mrs. Zhong, call the girl Fernanda, despite what she might tell you."

The servant bowed again, accepting my order.

"Your luggage has been taken to monsieur's room, *tai-tai*, but if you prefer otherwise, please let me know. I've put Mlle Fernanda in the bedroom next to yours."

"That sounds fine, Mrs. Zhong. Thank you so much for your help."

"Oh, *tai-tai*, a letter came for you today," she added, taking a small step forward and pulling an elongated envelope out of her pants pocket.

"For me?" I couldn't believe it. Who could possibly have written to me at Rémy's in Shanghai?

The envelope was imprinted with an important-looking emblem, and the note inside was written on fine paper. Fernanda and I were invited to dinner on Friday, August 31, at the home of Mr. Julio Palencia y

Tubau, consul general of Spain, where he and his wife, along with the most distinguished members of the small Spanish community in Shanghai, would be delighted to make our acquaintance.

My social obligations were beginning to overwhelm me. After I spoke to his lawyer, I'd planned on visiting the French cemetery where Rémy was temporarily buried. However, that didn't look as if it'd be possible, since the consuls of my native and adoptive countries were determined to meet me right away. Why the hurry?

"We'll have to reply one way or another," I murmured, setting the envelope on a corner of the little table and lifting the lid off my tea to take a sip.

Fernanda reached out and took the note. A smile—this time a genuine smile—came over her face, and she looked at me expectantly. "We'll go, won't we?"

When I looked at her, I realized that the girl was suffering from the malady that all of us feel who are forced out of our country for a prolonged period of time: the yearning for a familiar place and language.

"I suppose," I said. The tea was really very good, even without sugar. The contrast between the white porcelain and the lovely bright red infusion was absolutely inspiring. I wished I'd had my palette and paintbrushes at hand.

"We can't say no to an invitation from the Spanish consul."

"I know, but I have a lot to do tomorrow, and I'll be exhausted by evening, Fernanda. Try to understand. It's not that I don't want to go, I just don't know whether I'll have the energy."

"Dinner will be ready in an hour," Mrs. Zhong announced.

"Let me remind you, Auntie, that duty—"

"Comes before pleasure, I know," I interrupted, finishing the old saying.

"If you're tired, just have a nice cup of hot chocolate and—"

"I'll be as good as new, because chocolate can bring the dead back to life, right? Isn't that what you were going to say?"

"Yes."

I sighed deeply and set my cup on its saucer.

"As difficult as it might be to believe, Fernanda, we come from the same family. We were both raised with the same ideas, the same customs, and the same ridiculous clichés. So just remember that I've heard it all before. Okay? Oh, and one more thing. As Spanish as it might be to drink a cup of hot chocolate to recover your strength, that could be rather difficult in China. You'd better get used to tea."

"Very well, but no matter how you might be feeling tomorrow evening, Auntie, we must go to the Spanish consulate," she stubbornly insisted with a scowl.

I fixed my gaze on a beautiful bronze tiger with its jaws open wide, its sharp teeth bared, front claws raised and ready to attack. For a second I felt as if I'd become that animal and looked at my niece through its eyes. . . . Then I took another deep breath and drank my tea.

A ghostly-looking Mrs. Zhong carrying a candle came to wake me the next morning. The house was equipped with gas lighting, and Rémy had a powerful electric chandelier with a large fan installed in his office in one of the other buildings. While his study may have been impressive with its colossal almondwood desk and bronze fittings, shelves filled with strange Chinese folding books—no covers, just bound paper—and his collection of writing brushes and calligraphies adorning the walls, his bedroom was even more extraordinary. There was a deep red wardrobe inlaid with mother-of-pearl, a chest of drawers decorated with exotic bolts and hinges, and a monumental folding lacquered screen painted with a rural scene at the back of the room. The screen hid a tin bathtub and what Mrs. Zhong called a *ma-t'ung*—nothing more than a seat over a chamber pot. The enormous four-poster bed was enclosed by panels so finely wrought they looked like lace, and each one had a large circular opening covered by lovely silk curtains. The fabric was so fine that it let the night breeze through and acted as a magnificent mosquito net, allowing me to rest at last without being bothered by the pesky things. Being able to sleep, however, was quite a different matter. My mind morbidly recalled far-off times, causing a terribly current pain. My youth had been left behind, and gone, too, was the enchanting Rémy I had married, that fun-loving man I'd had to lead to bed each morning when he'd come home drunk on Pernod, Champagne, and Cointreau, the smell of tobacco and perfume clinging to his clothes from who knows which turn-of-the-century Parisian music hall or cabaret. When morning came, I was still awake, my eyes brimming with tears.

Fernanda joined me for breakfast. Her habitual sullenness had abated somewhat, and she was eager to know our plans before M. Favez came to pick me up at twelve-thirty. I told her I had personal matters to discuss with Rémy's lawyer and was going out on my own. She asked whether she could use the morning to look for a Catholic church in the French Concession where she could attend Mass while we were in Shanghai. I agreed, on the condition that Mrs. Zhong or one of the other trusted servants go with her. I also recommended she read something from Rémy's library. I hadn't seen her so much as touch a book since we met (missal and prayer book aside). Her reaction was outrageous.

"French books!"

"French, English, Spanish, German—what does it matter! Just read. You're old enough to appreciate the works and thoughts of people who've seen the world from a different point of view. It's important to taste life, Fernanda, or you'll lose out on so many enjoyable, interesting things."

Surprisingly, my words seemed to truly affect her, as if she'd never heard anything like that before. Truth be told, the poor thing had grown up in a very narrow-minded, shortsighted environment. Perhaps she just needed to be taught to appreciate freedom. "I must be off," I remarked, pushing my chair back and standing up. "My meeting's in half an hour. Good luck finding the church. You can tell me all about it later."

I was wearing a light cotton skirt, a sleeveless summer blouse, and a white picture hat to protect me from the bright sun beating down on Shanghai. As I crossed the garden on my way to the street, I could see a small rickshaw through the open gates. Mrs. Zhong stood next to it, speaking to the barefoot coolie in Chinese. As soon as they saw me, Mrs. Zhong's voice became shrill and hurried. The coolie rushed to take his place, ready to transport me to rue Millot, where Rémy's lawyer and executor, André Julliard, had his office.

I said good-bye to Mrs. Zhong and asked her to please look after Fernanda until I returned. As we set out on that frenetic trip through the streets of the French Concession, I stared at the coolie's sweaty, skeletal back, his head shaven except for a ring of spiky hair—likely what was left of a queue—listening to his labored breathing and the slapping of his bare soles on pavement. Cars, rickshaws, bicycles, and buses wove in and out around one another as the occupants delighted—in spite of the *lovely* smell of Shanghai—in the sights of pretty villas and little shops lining both sides of the street.

Short, narrow rue Millot was next to the old Chinese city of Nantao, and M. Julliard's office was located in a dark building that smelled of musty paper and rotting wood. The lawyer, who appeared to be about fifty and was wearing the wrinkliest linen jacket in the world, kindly met me at the door and led me into his office, asking his secretary to bring us tea. It was a small, glassed-in room from which you could see the other offices, the desks where his typists sat, and young Chinese clerks milling about. In his strong accent from the south of France (exaggerating the r's, like they do in Spanish), he offered me a seat and walked behind a large desk covered in cigarette burns. Without further ado he pulled a thick file from a drawer and opened it somberly.

"Mme De Poulain," he began, "I'm afraid the news is not good."

He smoothed his gray mustache, yellowed by nicotine, and set on the bridge of his nose a pair of small, round, wire-rimmed glasses that had surely seen better days. My heart pounded in my chest.

"Here's a copy of the will," he said, handing me a sheaf of papers that I took and began to flip through. "Your late husband, madame, was a dear friend of mine. It pains me to tell you that he was not a prudent man. I repeatedly told him to put his finances in order, but you know how things are. Moreover, you know what Rémy was like."

"What was he like, M. Julliard?" I asked in a wisp of a voice.

"Pardon me, madame?"

"I asked you what Rémy was like. I'm beginning to think I don't know much of anything. I'm completely taken aback by what you just said. I always thought Rémy was a good, intelligent man who was decidedly well-off."

"True, true. He was a good, intelligent man. But he was not well-off, Mme De Poulain, or rather he had less and less money that he spent more and more wantonly. I don't like to speak of my old friend this way, you understand, but I do have to tell you so that . . . Well, Rémy left nothing but debts."

I stared at him with incomprehension written all over my face. He placed both hands on the file and looked at me compassionately.

"I'm very sorry, madame, but as Rémy's wife you are now responsible for a series of debts that come to an amount so large I almost daren't mention it."

"What . . . what are you talking about?" I stammered, feeling an enormous weight in the middle of my chest.

M. Julliard sighed deeply, as if overwhelmed.

"Mme De Poulain, ever since Rémy returned from France, his financial situation was, shall we say, problematic. He incurred very large debts that he couldn't repay, so he took bank loans and advances from the silk factory that also went unpaid. In addition, he handed out promissory notes for exorbitant amounts. While it's true that everything in Shanghai can be arranged with a signature and that even a cocktail can be paid for in installments, Rémy went far beyond that. The situation became so serious that his family sent an accountant from Lyon to look into his finances. As a result, Rémy's brother, Arthème, had no choice but to send another representative to take over the business. He wanted Rémy to return to France, but given your husband's . . . poor health, madame, this was impossible. In the end, in order to help Rémy and prevent further damage, Arthème removed his brother from the family business and gave him a monthly stipend to live out with dignity what time was left to him."

What on earth was the man saying? What was he talking about? Hadn't Rémy been killed by thieves? I felt as if I could no longer hear him; his voice had become muted, and a muffled, buzzing noise began in my head. I was frightened: These were the first signs of one of my anxiety attacks. I'd always been intrepid in terms of thoughts and ambitions, but exceedingly cowardly when faced with physical or emotional pain. I felt as though something terrible was about to happen. My pulse raced, and I thought I'd have a heart attack. Calm down, Elvira, calm down, I said to myself.

"In fact," the lawyer continued, "Arthème paid many of Rémy's debts but ultimately he refused to cover them all. Your husband, madame, continued to go further into debt until the day he died."

"You said . . . What was wrong with Rémy? How was his health?"

M. Julliard looked at me with a mixture of worry and pity.

"Oh, madame!" he exclaimed, taking a rather dirty handkerchief out of a pocket in his blazer and running it over his face. "Rémy was very ill, madame. His health had seriously deteriorated. This will is ten years old, and in it he names you beneficiary of all his assets, except for his share in the family silk mills, for reasons I'm sure you understand. The situation was very different then, of course, but things changed, and Rémy never updated his will despite my suggestions in this regard. He was very ill, madame. According to French law, you do inherit his estate, that's true, but you also inherit his outstanding debts."

"But why?" I nearly shrieked.

"That's what the law says. You were his wife."

"No, I'm not talking about that! I mean why didn't I know all this? Why didn't he ever tell me he was sick, that he was in debt? Wasn't he murdered by thieves who broke in to his house? You've been talking in circles without actually telling me anything!"

The legal adviser leaned back in his chair and remained still for a few minutes, staring straight through me, not blinking, lost in thought. Finally, after repeatedly twisting the ends of his mustache, he leaned on the desk and gazed at me over his spectacles with great sadness in his eyes.

"When the band of thieves broke into his house, madame, Rémy was *nghien*. That's why they were able to do what they did."

"*Nghien?*" I repeated with difficulty.

"In a state of need . . . needing opium, that is. Rémy was addicted to opium."

"Addicted to opium? Rémy?"

"Yes, madame. I hate to be the one to tell you, but in the last few years your husband squandered his fortune on opium, gambling, and brothels. I beg you not to think ill of Rémy. He was an excellent man, as you know. These three passions tend to corrupt all men in Shanghai, whether they're Chinese or Westerners. Very few escape. It's this city. . . . This damn city is at fault. This is what life here consists of, madame, this and getting rich if there's enough time. Everyone here spends lavishly, on gambling most of all. I've seen many prominent men fall and more than one fortune disappear. I've been in Shanghai so long that nothing surprises me anymore. It was a foregone conclusion with Rémy, if you'll forgive me for saying so. I'm sure you understand. You could see it coming before the war, and after it . . . well, he lost control. That was the end."

I ran my hand over my forehead and noticed that my palms were cold and clammy. My anxiety attack hadn't materialized; perhaps it was staved off by the enormous sorrow I felt. Really, if I was honest with myself, Rémy had come to the only end possible. I wasn't referring to his violent death, which was unjust no matter how you looked at it, but to his plummet into self-destruction. He was the nicest, most entertaining, elegant man in the world, but he was also weak, and fate had unfortunately placed him in the most inappropriate place. If he'd disappeared for days in Paris, arriving home in a sorry state, what must have hap-

pened in Shanghai where it seemed that overindulgence was both common and easy? A man like Rémy wouldn't be able to resist. What I still
didn't understand, however, was where he'd gotten the money he sent
me every now and then through the Crédit Lyonnais. The salary I earned
working for Paul Ranson's widow as a teacher at her Académie didn't
allow many luxuries, so on occasion I would write to Rémy for help.
Nearly as fast as the return post, a generous sum would be waiting for
me at the Crédit branch on boulevard des Italiens.

M. Julliard interrupted my train of thought.

"Now, Mme De Poulain, you will have to settle Rémy's debts or face
lawsuits and seizures. In fact, there are already cases in progress that
won't stop as a result of his death."

"What about his brother? I don't have any money."

"As I told you, madame, Arthème paid off most of Rémy's debts a few
years ago. The company lawyers and Monsieur Voillis, the new representative, have advised me that the family washes its hands of any problem with respect to Rémy or to you. They asked me to relay the message
that you not ask them for any assistance or make any claim against
them."

My pride made me square my shoulders.

"Tell them not to worry. They don't exist as far as I'm concerned.
But I repeat, M. Julliard, I don't have any money. I can't make those payments."

I once again felt my heart race, and no air seemed to reach my
lungs.

"I know, madame, I know, and you can't imagine how sorry I am,"
the lawyer murmured. "If you'll allow me, I can propose a few solutions
that I've been considering in order to tackle this problem."

He began to rummage through the file so vigorously that the papers
scattered all over his desk.

"And the servants, M. Julliard?" I asked. "How am I going to pay the
servants?"

"Oh, don't worry about that!" he exclaimed, distracted. "Servants work for room and board. That's the way things are here. There's a great deal of poverty and hunger, madame. Rémy may have given Mrs. Zhong a little money now and then because he was very fond of her, but you're not required to— Ah, here it is!" he interrupted himself, pulling a page out of the disorganized pile. "So, let's see. . . . First of all, madame, you'll have to sell both houses: the one here and the one in Paris. Do you have any other property we can include?"

"No."

"Nothing? Are you sure?" The poor man didn't know how to insist, and I could barely breathe. "Any property in Spain? A house, a piece of land, a business . . . ?"

"I . . . no." A slight whistle escaped my throat, and I held on desperately to the edge of my seat. "My family disowned me, and now my niece has inherited it all. But I can't . . ."

"Would you like a glass of water, madame? The tea!" he suddenly remembered. M. Julliard bolted up and ran to the door. A few moments later, I had in my hand a beautiful Chinese cup with a lid, and the aroma that rose up from it was divine. I took small sips until I felt better. The lawyer was truly worried and had come to stand by my side.

"M. Julliard," I implored, "I have nothing I can draw on in Europe, and I'm not going to ask my niece for help. It doesn't seem right."

"Very well, madame, as you wish. Perhaps, with a bit of luck, we can get enough from both houses and the contents."

"But I can't lose the house in Paris! It's my home, the only one I have!"

Was I going to have to start all over again at forty-something years of age? No. Impossible. I was young when I left Spain and had the drive and energy to face poverty, but I wasn't that person anymore. The years had dulled my shine, and I didn't think I could live in some filthy, attic apartment in a bad neighborhood.

"Calm down, Mme De Poulain. I promise I'll do everything I can to help you, but the houses will have to be sold. There's no other way. Unless you can come up with three hundred thousand francs in the next few weeks."

How much did he say? No. Three hundred thousand?

"Three hundred thousand francs!" I shrieked, horrified. I earned only seventy-five francs a month at the Académie! How was I going to get my hands on that much money? Besides, life in Paris had become intolerably expensive after the war. It had been ages since anyone had been able to shop in places like Le Louvre or Au Bon Marché. People had to be extremely frugal just to survive, and the few who still had money had seen their income severely reduced.

"Don't worry. We'll sell the houses and organize an auction. Rémy was a great collector of Chinese art. Surely we'll be able to get almost the full amount."

"My house in Paris isn't very big," I whispered. "It might be worth four or five thousand francs at most, and that's only because it's near L'École de Médecine."

"Would you like me to contact a colleague so he can take care of the sale?"

"No!" I exclaimed with what little energy I had left. "I will not sell my house in Paris."

"Madame . . . !"

"Absolutely not!"

M. Julliard backed off, greatly distressed. "Very well, Mme De Poulain, whatever you say. But we're going to be in trouble. We might be able to get a hundred thousand francs for Rémy's house and another thirty or forty thousand from the auction, if all goes well. That still leaves a huge amount outstanding."

I had to get out of that office. I had to get out into the street so I could breathe. I couldn't stay a minute longer unless I wanted the lawyer to witness one of my spells.

"Give me a few days, monsieur," I said, standing up, gripping my purse. "I'll think of something."

"As you wish, madame," the lawyer replied, kindly opening the door to his office. "I'll wait to hear from you, but please don't take too long. Could you sign the papers now so I can begin organizing the sale and auction?"

I couldn't wait another second.

"Some other day, M. Julliard."

"Very well, madame."

Once outside, I had to lean against the wall to keep my legs from buckling. The rickshaw coolie stopped dozing in the seat the moment he saw me and slipped out to take hold of the poles, ready to go, but I couldn't walk, couldn't cross the few feet between us. I was frightened, completely distraught. It felt as if the earth were sinking beneath my feet; my entire life was on shaky ground. I was about to lose everything. I could stay with friends for a while or find a cheap rooming house in Montparnasse, support myself from the sale of my paintings and with my job at the Académie, but I wouldn't be able to afford another house. I covered my eyes and began to silently cry. The thought of losing that beautiful, three-bedroom house, where strong light streamed in from the southeast and contributed to the purity of line and color in my paintings, caused me enormous distress and unbearable fear. Everything Rémy had given me in life he had taken from me in death. I was back where I'd been twenty years earlier, before I'd ever met him.

I finally came undone amid endless sobs on the way home. Nothing was going to be easy over the next few weeks, and going back to Paris had become another nightmare. In addition, I suddenly realized there was a problem I hadn't even considered: Accustomed to being on my own, to only ever thinking about myself, I'd forgotten that I was now responsible for my niece. She would have to follow me wherever I went until she came of age; I would have to support her while she was under my care. It felt as if life were out to get me, had decided to bury me in the mud, stomping on me with an iron boot. How could all these problems arise at once? Who had put this curse on me? Wasn't dealing with financial ruin enough?

I got back to the house in time to change my clothes and head out again. I had to evade Mrs. Zhong and Fernanda, both of whom popped up in my path like shadows. Despite my best efforts, I think my niece realized that something was wrong. I locked myself in Rémy's room and, after washing my face with cold water, changed into a green muslin dress and matching picture hat more appropriate for afternoon. I'd have given anything not to go out, to crawl into bed and stay there forever, let the world fall apart, but touching up my makeup and lipstick did more for me than escaping reality ever could. The consul general of France was expecting me for lunch, and maybe, just maybe, M. Wilden would be able to help. A consul always has power, information, and the resources to face awkward situations abroad. I was a French widow in a real predicament in China; perhaps he would be able to think of something.

M. Favez arrived behind the wheel of his marvelous Voisin convertible at twelve-thirty sharp.

"You don't look well, Mme De Poulain," he commented worriedly as he helped me into the car. "Are you all right?"

"I didn't sleep well, monsieur. I found my husband's Chinese bed terribly uncomfortable."

The attaché let out a happy chuckle.

"There's nothing like a soft European bed, is there, madame?"

Actually, there was nothing like a lot of money in the bank so as not to worry about the gambling, opium, and brothel debts of a good-for-nothing like Rémy. I began to deeply resent that merrymaking scoundrel I'd always found so amusing. He was an utter idiot, a brainless imbecile incapable of self-control. I wasn't the least bit surprised his brother had removed him from the business; Rémy would surely have bankrupted the company through mismanagement and embezzlement. There is a fine line between having fun, even excessive fun, and causing irreparable damage to your life, your work, and your family: Rémy couldn't see that line. Whatever his body wanted came first, second, and even third. Alcohol? Alcohol. Women? Women. Gambling? Gambling. Opium? Opium. The man indulged in it all to excess, until he'd collapse, exhausted.

M. Wilden and his wife, the charming Jeanne, were really very nice to me. About my age, the consul was an intelligent, elegant man, well versed in Chinese culture. They'd been in the country for eighteen years and had lived in cities with names as exotic as Tchong-king, Tcheng-tou, and Yunnan. He and Jeanne tried their best to console me when, in tears, I explained what I'd learned from Rémy's lawyer that morning. Their relationship with my husband had always been cordial, they said. Since their arrival in Shanghai, in 1917, they'd seen him on numerous occasions at consulate celebrations for French national holidays and Christmases. Jeanne had laughed a great deal with Rémy, given his talent for telling a joke or making a witty remark at just the right moment. Yes, of course they knew about his financial problems. Shanghai wasn't very big, and nothing remained secret for long. Rémy's situation—and his was not the only one—was often a topic of conversation among his many friends. He had gone to great lengths to maintain his social circle and was always willing to help anyone in need. Hundreds of people had attended his funeral, the Wildens said, and the entire French colony was very sorry to hear of his death, especially because of the manner in which it occurred.

"Have you been given the details?" Jeanne inquired with a certain amount of worry in her voice.

"I was hoping to hear them from you."

The consul and his wife were so refined that they never once mentioned Rémy's state on the night of the tragedy. They didn't mention the word "opium"; they simply narrated the facts in the kindest possible way. It seems that ten thugs from the miserable Pootung area—located on the other side of the river, across from the Bund—slipped into the French Concession. When they saw Rémy's Chinese-style house, they likely thought it would be easier to break in to and move about without waking the occupants, who should have been sound asleep at that time of night, around three in the morning. All of this was in the Concession police report, which the consul was willing to copy for me if I so desired. Unfortunately, Rémy was still awake in his office. He may have been studying one of the Chinese objets d'art he was so fond of, because various pieces from his collection were scattered all over the floor. Rémy must have bravely stood up to them, because the office was left looking like a battlefield. Awakened by the noise, his servants came armed with sticks and knives, but the thieves ran in all directions, leaving Rémy dead on the floor. The housekeeper, Mrs. Zhong, swore that nothing had been taken, that nothing in her master's house was missing. Rémy had managed to defend his home and property after all.

"What would you like to do with Rémy's remains, Mme De Poulain?" Consul Wilden suddenly asked, though not without tact. "Would you like to take them to France, or do you wish to leave them here in Shanghai?"

I looked at him rather disconcerted. Until that very morning, I had intended to bury Rémy in Lyon, in his family's vault, but by then I wasn't so sure. Transportation would cost a fortune, and this was no time for idle expenses, so perhaps it would be best to leave him where he was.

"Rémy's plot in the Concession cemetery is owned by the French government, madame," M. Wilden clarified with gesture of remorse. "You would have to purchase it."

"I'm not in a position to do so, as you can imagine," I stated, taking a drink of the coffee that had been served after lunch. "My financial situation has me bound hand and foot. Perhaps you might be able to help me, Mr. Consul General. Can you think of any way out of this predicament? What do you suggest I do?"

Auguste Wilden and his wife glanced surreptitiously at one another.

"The consulate could give you the burial plot," he commented, "but it would have to be justified as a gesture from our country to the prestigious De Poulain family."

"Thank you, monsieur."

"With respect to the financial difficulties you find yourself in, madame, I don't know what to say. I think your lawyer has given you good, sensible advice."

"Why don't you ask your late husband's family for help, dear?" Jeanne inquired, setting her cup on the saucer.

"Their lawyers have made it very clear that help would not be forthcoming."

"Pity!" Consul Wilden exclaimed. "I'm very sorry, Mme De Poulain. We would truly like to help you, but as consul of France I'm not in a position to do anything more. I hope you understand. Purchasing Rémy's plot is a gesture I can allow myself, because he was a prominent member of our colony and a notable citizen of our country. Anything else, however, would be outside my scope and could be misinterpreted by the embassy in Peking, the Ministry of Foreign Affairs, and certainly by the French community in Shanghai. Good luck to you, madame. Jeanne and I wish you the very best, and if there's anything else we can do to help, please don't hesitate to ask."

I strode out of the old mansion that housed the consulate, feigning a strength I didn't possess. Once the Wildens had shown that they were unable to do anything beyond what was politically appropriate, I didn't want them to see my trembling hands or weak knees. Riding in the rickshaw that was taking me back for the second time that day to the house that had turned out to be an ephemeral property that was to bring me nothing but sorrow, I began to think I was entering a dark alley that seemed to be a dead end, and worst of all I would have to suppress my anguish for several more hours. Fernanda and I were expected at the Spanish consulate that evening, and I couldn't even begin to imagine what the devil I'd lost.

I didn't want any of the snacks Mrs. Zhong prepared midafternoon, nor did I want to leave my room or see anyone until it was time to prepare for dinner. I didn't feel well, and the effort to speak was simply too much. I tried to think of ways to obtain the 150,000 francs still needed to pay off Rémy's debts, but I couldn't come up with a single solution.

The only really good idea I had—to escape to Spain and hide in some far-off village—wasn't feasible no matter how you looked at it. Only big cities like Madrid or Barcelona were up to European standards in terms of hygiene and culture, while the rest languished in hunger, filth, and ignorance. And besides, where could a single woman go there? Women had taken on a new role in the rest of the civilized world, much more free and independent, but in Spain they continued to be objects, adornment at best, dominated by church and husband. My wings would be clipped, the air would be too oppressive to breathe, and the very thing that had driven me out twenty years earlier would finish me off once and for all. A woman painter? María Blanchard and I, Elvira Aranda, personified what women painters in Spain could do: leave.

My niece came in at around seven to remind me it was time to go. I got out of bed under her scrutinizing stare and began to get ready. Fernanda stood immobile in the doorway, following me with her eyes until I couldn't take it anymore.

"Don't you have to get changed?" I asked brusquely.

"I'm all ready," she replied. I looked her over carefully but didn't notice anything different. She looked the same as ever in that old-fashioned black dress, her hair in a ponytail, and that perennial fan in her hand.

"Are you waiting for something?"

"No."

"Well, go on, then. Get."

She seemed to hesitate for a moment and finally left. Looking back, I think she might have been worried about me, but at the time I was so overcome with sorrow I couldn't respond properly to anything.

After curling my hair and perfuming it with Quelques Fleurs, I put on a delightful, brown silk evening dress with large tulle bows on both sides. The result in the mirror was spectacular. Why deny it? After all, it was my best dress, a copy of a Chanel made from a piece of silk Rémy had given me. Satisfied, I adjusted the thin straps on my bare shoulders, put on my bisque-colored shoes, and straightened the seam up the backs of my stockings. It was strange to think about everything that had happened that day as I examined my reflection. Primping certainly does wonders for your constitution. I felt much better by the time I held the wave over my forehead in place with a delicate multicolored barrette shaped like a dragonfly.

We left the French Concession for the first time that night, passing through the border post in two rickshaws and entering the International Concession. Huge new cars—mostly American models—sped through the streets with their headlights on. I should point out that they drive on the left in Shanghai, like the English, and that it's the impressive Sikh police, sent by the British from their colony in India, who direct traffic. These subjects of the English Crown, with bulging red turbans and thick, dark beards, use long batons to do their job— batons that become lethal weapons in their hands should the need arise.

The Spanish consulate wasn't far. In no time we found ourselves in front of a modern, Mediterranean-style villa with a lush garden, lit up like one of those bright Chinese lanterns. The national flag fluttered from a pole on the second floor. Two or three luxury cars were parked to one side, a sign that other guests had already arrived. Strangely enough, my niece was a bundle of nerves, repeatedly snapping her fan open and closed, chattering uncontrollably in our native language as soon as she stepped out of the rickshaw. I had to smile realizing that the silliest little things could still lift my spirits, even on a day as awful as this.

The consul, Julio Palencia y Tubau, was an extraordinary man[3] with a wonderful personality and the warmest of manners. Not only was he the son of the actress María Tubau and the playwright Ceferino Palencia, but his brother, also named Ceferino, was married to Isabel de Oyarzábal,[4] my favorite author. I'd had the great pleasure of meeting her two years prior during a fascinating conference she gave in Paris. One of Isabel's many commendable positions was as president of the National Association of Spanish Women, an organization fighting for equal rights in our extremely difficult country. She was extremely cultured and firmly believed it was possible to change the world. I was thrilled to discover she was related to the consul and immediately liked him and his wife, an elegant lady of Greek origin. While I was conversing with them and a few of the guests (Spanish businessmen who'd made their fortunes in Shanghai, along with their wives), Fernanda was having a lovely time in the company of a priest with a quixotic beard and an enormous bald head. The seating arrangement at the table was such that the two were able to continue talking uninterrupted. I learned that he was Father Castrillo, superior of the Augustinian mission from El Escorial monastery and a distinguished businessman. He'd known how to put his community's money to good use, buying land in Shanghai when it was worthless and then selling it for a fortune in later years. In this way the Augustinians had come to own many of the city's principal buildings.

Another peculiar character in attendance was a bald Irishman in his fifties who hovered around me most of the night. His name was Patrick Tichborne, and the consul introduced him as a distant relation of his wife's. Tichborne had a great potbelly and the bronzed skin of a country man. A journalist, he worked for various English papers, primarily the Royal Geographic Society's *Journal*. He followed me all night, milling about nearby and awkwardly looking away whenever our eyes met. He was so annoying that I started to feel uncomfortable and was about to mention it to the consul.

I'd just finished a very interesting chat with the wife of a Mr. Ramos, wealthy owner of six of the best movie houses in Shanghai, when Tichborne dashed over to speak to me. All the other guests were occupied in conversations; fearing the worst, I adopted a surly expression.

"Might I speak with you for a moment, Mme De Poulain?" he mumbled in French, his breath reeking of alcohol.

"Go ahead," I replied, looking displeased.

"Thank you. I must be quick. No one else can hear what I'm about to tell you."

Oh, dear! This Irishman was really starting off on the wrong foot.

"A friend of your husband's needs to speak with you urgently."

"I don't understand all the secrecy, Mr. Tichborne. He can leave his card at my house if he'd like to see me."

He began to grow nervous, glancing furtively left and right.

"Mr. Jiang can't go to your house, madame. You're being watched day and night."

"What?" I asked indignantly. I was no stranger to the various ways a man can approach a woman, but this was really ridiculous. "I think, Mr. Tichborne, that you've had too much to drink."

"Listen!" he exclaimed, gripping my arm urgently. I pulled away sharply and tried to walk toward the consul, but Tichborne grabbed me again, forcing me to look at him. "Don't be a fool, madame. You're in danger! Listen to me!"

"If you dare touch me again," I warned him coldly, "I will inform the consul at once."

"Look, I don't have time for silly games," he declared, letting me go. "Your husband wasn't killed by thieves, Mme De Poulain, but by hired assassins from the Green Gang, the most dangerous mafia in Shanghai. They broke into your house in search of something very important. When they didn't find it, they tortured your husband to make him confess. But Rémy was *nghien*, madame, and couldn't tell them anything. Now they're after you. They've been following you since you disembarked yesterday. You can be certain they'll try again, so your life and your niece's life are in grave danger."

"What are you talking about?"

"If you don't believe me," he said haughtily, "interrogate your servants. Don't accept the official story without investigating first. Get to the truth with a sturdy rod; yellows won't talk unless they're afraid. The Green Gang is extremely powerful."

"But what about the police? The French consul told me today that the police report—"

The Irishman let out a guffaw.

"Do you know who's in charge of the French Concession police force, madame? Huang Jin Rong, better known as 'Pockmarked Huang' because of the smallpox scars on his face. Pockmarked Huang is also the boss of the Green Gang. He controls the traffic of opium, prostitution, and gambling, as well as the police who're watching your house and wrote the report concerning your husband's death. You have no idea what things are like in Shanghai, madame, but you'll have to learn quickly if you want to survive."

The anguish I'd felt since speaking with Rémy's lawyer that morning suddenly returned with a vengeance. I had heart palpitations and felt as if I were suffocating all over again.

"Are you serious, Mr. Tichborne?"

"Look, madame, I never joke unless I'm drunk. You should meet Mr. Jiang. He's a respectable antiquarian from Nanking Road who was a good friend of your husband's for many years. Since you're being followed, Mr. Jiang can't go to your house and you can't go to his shop. You'll have to meet somewhere the Chinese aren't allowed. That way your pursuers will have to remain outside, like now."

"But if the Chinese aren't allowed in, Mr. Jiang won't be either."

"He will if I bring him in through the back door. I'm speaking of my club, the Shanghai Club, on the Bund. I live there, in the hotel, in one of two rooms the Royal Geographical Society keeps for members who travel to this part of the Orient. Mr. Jiang will come to my room through the kitchen, and you'll come in normally, through the front door. Let me warn you that it's an all-male club, so you won't be able to go into the parlors or the bar. You'll have to come to my room on the pretense of bringing me this book." He surreptitiously pulled a small, leather-bound volume out of his jacket pocket. Luckily, it just fit into my purse. "Say you're coming to have me sign this book I wrote. Hotel guests receive all sorts of female visitors—secretaries, American businesswomen, Russian jewelry merchants—so you won't arouse too much suspicion or endanger your reputation, especially since we met here tonight. Don't even think of bringing anything the Green Gang assassins might mistake for a piece of art. Mr. Jiang is convinced they're looking for something like that. They would kill you in plain sight just to get their hands on it."

I tried to reflect on that flood of information but still didn't under-stand what this Mr. Jiang could want with me.

"Mr. Jiang is convinced that if you can discover what the Green Gang wants and give it to them, then you and your niece will no lon-ger be in danger," Tichborne hurriedly explained, staring fixedly over my shoulder. The expression on his face was clear: Someone was ap-proaching. "He has a few ideas in this regard. . . . Of course I can sign my book for you, madame!" he exclaimed, suddenly sounding happy. The consul's smiling wife entered my field of view. "Come by my hotel tomorrow at noon, and I'd be delighted to dedicate your copy."

"I've come to rescue you, Elvira," Julio Palencia's elegant wife de-clared in her slightly accented Spanish, giving me a wink. "Patrick can be rather annoying at times." Then, in English, she asked him to bring her a glass of champagne.

"She's read my book, darling. That's what we were talking about," he said snidely in French.

The consul's wife was wise enough not to ask questions as she kindly led me to the largest group of guests, who were discussing the threat of a military uprising in our country. I'd always followed events in Spain with a certain amount of interest, such as the opening of the first big department stores or the construction of the first subway line in Madrid. I'd never been very interested in politics, perhaps because it was so confusing and problematic that I didn't quite understand it. I had, however, been very worried by the recent attacks and riots. I sim-ply couldn't imagine that the military would once again attempt to take power. Consul Palencia maintained an impartial silence as Antonio Ra-mos, owner of the movie houses, and Lafuente, an architect from Ma-drid, expressed worry about an imminent coup.

"The king won't allow it," Ramos offered hesitantly.

"The king, my dear friend, backs the military," Lafuente objected. "Moreover, he backs General Primo de Rivera."

The consul's wife intervened to bring the thorny conversation to an end. "What do you say we play some Raquel Meller on the gramophone?" she asked out loud, with that slight accent of hers.

That was all it took. Enthusiasm rippled through the guests, who exclaimed jubilantly and rushed moments later to dance enthusiastically. It was then I began to feel tired—exhausted, in fact. I was suddenly so worn out I could hardly stand. Thus, when "La Violetera" came on and everyone began to sing the refrain *"Llévelo usted, señorito, que no vale más que un real"* at the top of their lungs, I decided it was time to leave. I collected Fernanda, who was still chatting with Father Castrillo, and we said good-bye to the consul and his wife, thanking them for everything and assuring them we'd visit again before we left China.

As we crossed the garden on our way to the street, I began to worry about what Tichborne had said. Were the Green Gang's henchmen really out there? It was a frightening thought. Once we were through the gates, I glanced all around but saw only a couple of slender, ragged women bent under the weight of the baskets they were carrying and a few coolies dozing in their vehicles as they waited for their patrons. Everyone else was European. In any event, that night I would have every single one of the servants stand guard once they'd secured the doors.

Fernanda and I got into the rickshaws as Meller's piercing voice drifted out the consulate windows; it was a truly extravagant experience in that Oriental setting. Much later, after I'd heard the intolerable caterwauling that Celestials consider the most exquisite of operatic songs, I realized that Meller actually had a very beautiful voice.

Chapter

2

I was so exhausted I slept deeply all night long and woke feeling completely rested. What I needed most that morning was the time and tranquillity to organize my thoughts. It would have done me good to sit and sketch for a while, take a few notes in the garden, and regain the clarity I'd lost due to nerves the day before. My head was filled with noise. Fleeting images and bits of the conversations I'd had with M. Julliard, M. Wilden, Consul Palencia and his wife, and especially Tichborne sped through my mind, out of control. The fear of ruin weighed on my soul like a stone. I was usually quick and efficient at making decisions—the result of living alone for so long and having had to stand on my own when I was just a girl. And yet these problems that had come crashing down on me rendered me dim-witted, slow; they aggravated my panic attacks. I resignedly told myself that even if I couldn't sketch, I should at least try to get out of bed and make an effort to rally.

I had breakfast with Fernanda, from whom I had to pry a short summary of her very long conversation with Father Castrillo. It seems the two had become quite friendly, as strange as a friendship between an elderly expatriate priest and a seventeen-year-old orphan might seem. Father Castrillo had invited her to attend church on Sundays and to visit the institutions that the El Escorial Augustinians ran in Shanghai. At the orphanage there was a young boy who spoke perfect Spanish and could serve as Fernanda's servant and interpreter. The girl wanted to head over as soon as breakfast was finished, but I was obliged to ruin her plans, telling her she had to accompany me on the strange visit I was to pay Tichborne at the Shanghai Club. I preferred to take a chaperone just in case the risk to my reputation was more than he had so blithely said.

After breakfast I led Fernanda into the office and whispered the Irishman's bizarre story to her. She did not believe a word and remained completely impassive upon learning we were in the very room where Rémy had been tortured and killed. The only minor apprehension she expressed was when she found out we weren't going to a public place but to the journalist's rooms at the hotel. Deprived of her complicity, I was left no choice but to call Mrs. Zhong into the office. If she confirmed Tichborne's tale, the girl would have to believe me. But Mrs. Zhong turned out to be a hard nut to crack. She denied the accusations over and over again with increasingly exaggerated displays of emotion, culminating in a note of hysteria in defense of her honor and the honor of the other servants. Since I didn't plan on using the rod to get her to confess—I was horrified by the thought of actually hitting and causing another human being pain—I finally had to resort to other, slightly more civilized measures. I threatened to throw her out, send her packing, and fire the rest of the staff as well, condemning them to a life of hunger roaming the streets. Through Mrs. Zhong's pleas, I learned she had a daughter and three grandchildren in the squalid district of Pootung—the very same area Rémy's murderers were from—whom she supported with some of the leftovers from this house. That broke my heart, but I had to maintain my harsh, inflexible image no matter how callous I felt. The ruse worked, and the old servant finally spoke.

"Your husband stayed up very late that night," she explained, kneeling reverently before us as if we were sacred Buddhas. "All of us servants had gone to bed except Wu, who opens the door and takes out the garbage. Master Rémy had run out of medicine and sent him for more."

"Opium," I murmured.

"Yes, opium," Mrs. Zhong reluctantly admitted. "When he got back, a group of thugs were waiting to get inside. It's not his fault, *tai-tai*. Wu just opened the door, and they attacked, leaving him hurt in the garden. The rest of us were awakened by the noise. Tse-hu, the cook, crept up to see what was happening in the office. When he came back, he told us they were beating your husband with sticks."

My stomach churned and tears stung my eyes as I imagined how poor Rémy must have suffered.

"A little while later, when everything went quiet," Mrs. Zhong continued, "I ran to help your husband, *tai-tai*, but there was nothing I could do."

Her eyes turned to the floor, between the window and the desk, as if she could see Rémy's body just as she had found it that night.

"Tell me about the murderers, Mrs. Zhong," I said.

She shuddered and looked at me anxiously. "Please don't ask me that, *tai-tai*. The less you know, the better."

"Mrs. Zhong . . ." I admonished, reminding her of my threats.

The old servant shook her head sadly. "They were from the Green Gang," she finally admitted. "Filthy murderers from the Green Gang."

"How do you know?" Fernanda asked in disbelief.

"Everyone in Shanghai knows them," she murmured. "They're very powerful. Besides, Master Rémy bore the mark of what's known as 'hamstringing.' The Green Gang severs the tendons in their victims' legs before killing them."

"Oh, God!" I exclaimed, bringing my hands to my face.

"And why did they want to kill M. De Poulain?" Fernanda inquired, less skeptical now.

"I don't know, mademoiselle," Mrs. Zhong replied, wiping her cheeks with the tails of her blouse. "This office was destroyed. The table and chairs were overturned, books were on the floor, and the expensive art-work was strewn all around. It took me two days to clean this room and put it back in order. I didn't want any of the other servants to help me."

"Did they take anything, Mrs. Zhong?"

"No, *tai-tai*. I was familiar with everything your husband had in here. Some of the pieces were very valuable, so I was the only one al-lowed to do the cleaning."

Rémy was not a brave man, I thought, letting my eyes wander over the beautiful furniture and bookcases. There was no way he could have withstood physical pain without giving in to their questioning. Since he was too old to be called to active duty during the war, he went to work for the French government's Welfare Service. They had to assign him an office job because he couldn't stand the sight of blood, not to mention how his hands would shake and his face would turn white every time the air-raid sirens sounded for a German zeppelin attack. I wasn't sure what it meant to be *nghien*, but surely it would have given Rémy suffi-cient reason to talk, to tell those heartless swine whatever they wanted to know.

"Mrs. Zhong, my husband stayed up late that night because he was nervous, wasn't he? He needed opium."

"Yes, but he wasn't in need when they attacked. He sent Wu to buy more because he'd smoked the last pipeful."

Oh, so Rémy had been dazed, asleep!

"Had he smoked very much?"

Mrs. Zhong stood with surprising ease for someone her age and walked toward the shelves crammed with piles of Rémy's Chinese books. She pulled a couple of the stacks out, revealing bare wall behind. With a soft knock of her fist, a square piece swiveled on a central axis, revealing a sort of cupboard. She pulled out a painted wooden tray that held several antique objects: a long stick with a jade adornment on the end, some-thing that looked like a little oil lamp, a small gold-colored box, a paper wrapper, and a saucer made of copper. It was all very beautiful at first

glance. Mrs. Zhong brought the tray over and set it on my lap, then
moved back and humbly knelt again. I stared perplexed at the objects
and was overcome with repugnance and a desire to push them away as
soon as I realized what they were. As if in a dream, I saw Fernanda's
hand rise up and head resolutely toward the opium pipe I had initially
thought was nothing more than a stick. I couldn't resist the instinct to
grab her wrist.

"Don't touch a thing, Fernanda," I said without averting my eyes.

"As you can see, *tai-tai*, your husband had smoked several pipes that
night. The box of opium balls is empty."

"Yes, quite right," I said, opening it and examining the inside. "But
how many were there?"

"As many as are in the paper wrapper. Wu had gone to buy them
that afternoon. Master only wanted the purest 'foreign mud,' the best
quality, and only Wu knew where to get it."

"And he went out again that night?" I asked, astonished. I carefully
unfolded the wrapper and saw three strange black balls inside.

Mrs. Zhong seemed bothered by my question.

"Your husband liked to have a supply of opium in the *bishachu* in
case he felt like smoking several pipes."

"The *bishachu*?" I repeated with difficulty. Everything in that strange
language seemed to consist of sibilant *s*'s and explosive *ch*'s.

She pointed to the secret cupboard.

"That is a *bishachu*," she explained. "It means 'green silk cupboard,'
and it can be as small as this one or as big as a room. The name is very
old. Master Rémy didn't like his opium pipe out in view. He said it was
vulgar, and since these items called for discretion, he had the *bishachu*
built."

"And that night he had smoked so much he couldn't say a word, isn't
that right, Mrs. Zhong?"

She leaned forward until her forehead touched the floor and remained there in silence. A pair of narrow sticks crossed through her
black ponytail.

"So he was completely drugged when the Green Gang thugs arrived," I reflected out loud as I held the tray in both hands and stood up to set it on the table. "And so, even though they beat and tortured him, they didn't get the information they were looking for, because Rémy couldn't speak. He was in no shape to confess. Perhaps that's why they were so brutal. . . ." I instinctively walked toward the *bishachu*. According to Tichborne, the murderers had come looking for something of great importance but didn't find it. Also according to Tichborne, Mr. Jiang, the antiquarian, was convinced that the Green Gang was looking for a piece of art. Furthermore, Mrs. Zhong had said that the assassins had torn through everything in the office on the night of the murder, making a terrible mess. Whatever they were after was valuable enough to kill for. Rémy may have been many things—including foolish—but he wouldn't have left something like that out in plain sight.

I leaned over the bookshelf to look inside the cupboard; the empty shelf that had held the tray was at eye level. When I tried to move it, I found that it was loose and lifted it very slowly. The light coming in from the room outlined a barely visible rectangular shape down below, in a deep, dark hollow. I reached in carefully until my fingertips brushed against it. It felt rough, and a soft aroma of sandalwood drifted up. I pulled my arm out and put the shelf back in its place. I turned toward my niece, who was watching me silently with a furrowed brow, and signaled that she was not to say a word.

"Thank you, Mrs. Zhong," I said kindly to the old servant, who remained with her forehead on the floor. "I need time to think about everything you've told us. This is all very difficult for me. You can go; please leave me alone with my niece."

"Do I still have work with you, *tai-tai?*" she asked fearfully.

I leaned over, smiling, and helped her up.

"Don't worry, Mrs. Zhong. No one will be fired." No, I wouldn't throw anyone out. I'd just sell the house and leave them to the mercy of the new owner. "Don't forget that in about an hour Fernanda and I will be going to visit a friend who lives on the Bund."

"Thank you, *tai-tai*," she exclaimed, and crossed through the full-moon door of Rémy's office, much calmer now, bowing with both hands together in front of her face.

"You were right, Auntie," Fernanda reluctantly admitted as soon as Mrs. Zhong had stepped into the garden. "The story that Englishman—"

"Irishman."

"—told you was true. They really are watching us. Do you think it's wise to go to this meeting?"

I didn't reply but walked back to the *bishachu* and lifted the shelf again. I could now bring the object out and examine it carefully. It took a bit of work, because the cupboard had been designed for a longer arm than mine, but I was finally able to get a hold of the wooden object that felt like a small jewelry or sewing box. As soon as it was out in the light, I was surprised to discover a chest, a beautiful Chinese chest that was so old I thought the simple pressure of my fingers might destroy it.

Fernanda jumped up and rushed to my side, filled with curiosity. "What is it?" she asked.

"I haven't the faintest idea," I replied, setting the chest on the desk next to a small stand that held Rémy's calligraphy brushes. There was an exquisite, gold-colored dragon contorted into spirals on the lid. I couldn't believe how beautiful the piece was, the myriad of details in the drawings, the strange strips of yellow paper with red ink characters that must have sealed it at one time and now hung softly off both ends, the smell of sandalwood it still exuded. It was absolutely perfect! I was astounded by the artisan's meticulousness, the patience he must have had to make such a thing. Just then, without the slightest consideration, Fernanda opened it with those chubby paws of hers. Good Lord, the girl was completely lacking in artistic sensibility!

"Look, Auntie, it's full of little boxes."

When the chest was opened, it unfolded like a staircase into a series of steps that were divided into dozens of small pigeonholes, each of which contained a lovely tiny little object. My niece and I began to pick each one up and examine them carefully, unable to believe our eyes. There was a small porcelain vase that could only have been made under a powerful magnifying glass; a miniature edition of a Chinese book that unfolded just like the big ones and appeared to contain a complete work of literature; an exquisite ball of incredibly carved ivory; a black jade stamp; a small gold tiger cut lengthwise in half with a row of inscriptions on its back; a peach pit on which we saw nothing at first, but then, when we held it up against the light, discovered that it was completely covered in Chinese characters no bigger than half a grain of rice— characters that also appeared on a handful of pumpkin seeds in another of the pigeonholes; a round, bronze coin with a square hole in the middle; a little horse also made of bronze; a silk scarf that I didn't dare unfold in case it fell to pieces; a green jade ring; a gold ring; pearls of various sizes and colors; earrings; strips of paper rolled up on fine wooden spools that, when unrolled, contained ink drawings of incredible landscapes. . . . In short, it's impossible to describe everything we saw, much less our astonishment at seeing such treasures.

I may have already mentioned that I was never very fond of Chinese artifacts, despite the fervor they aroused all over Europe, but I had to admit I'd never seen anything like what lay before me, a thousand times more exquisite and beautiful than any of the expensive but crude trinkets sold in Paris, Madrid, or London. I'm a staunch believer in sensitive understanding: understanding through one's senses and feelings. How else can we enjoy a picture, a book, or a piece of music? Art that doesn't move you, that doesn't speak to you, isn't art, it's fashion. Each one of the tiny objects in the chest contained the magic of a thousand sensations that combined like the colored glass in a kaleidoscope to form a unique, breathtaking image.

"What are you going to do with all of this, Auntie?"

Do? What was I going to do? Well, sell it, of course. I desperately needed the money.

"We'll see," I murmured, starting to place the little treasures back in their places. "For the moment I'll put it back where it was. Keep this a secret, do you hear me? Don't say a word to anyone, not to Father Castrillo or Mrs. Zhong."

We left for the Bund a short while later, each of us in a rickshaw. The midday heat was stifling. A haze floated in the air, distorting the streets and buildings, the asphalt seeming to melt like gum under the poor sweaty coolies' bare feet, and no one was safe from attacks by fat, iridescent flies. Municipal employees continuously threw buckets of water on the tram tracks, while the doors and windows of houses were covered by bamboo blinds and rice-paper mats to shield the interiors from the high temperatures. What had Tichborne been thinking to arrange a meeting at such an impossible time! The only thing that made me smile was the wicked thought that our pursuers, whoever they might be, were being deep-fried right along with us.

We passed through the wire fence bordering the French Concession and reached the international Bund within ten or fifteen minutes. It was then that we saw the shimmering waters of the filthy Huangpu, spoiling the incredible majesty of that grand avenue crowded with half-naked Celestials and Europeans in shirtsleeves and cork pith helmets. The rickshaws came to a stop. The coolies set the poles down in front of an impressive marble staircase guarded by typically British doormen in red flannel livery and top hats bearing the Shanghai Club emblem. In this heat the club's nod to tradition seemed a bit cruel.

Fernanda and I went up the stairs and into the luxurious entrance hall dominated by a bust of King George V. The cool air (nearly frozen compared to outside) smelled of loose tobacco. I took a lovely, deep breath of it and walked over to the concierge to ask for Mr. Tichborne's room number. He interrogated me tactfully, to which I replied pleasantly, showing him the book the Irishman had given me the day before. I don't know whether the concierge actually believed me or just pretended to, but in any event he advised the journalist that we had arrived and asked us to please take a seat in the leather armchairs nearby. Indeed, from what I could tell during the short wait for our host, there weren't any women there at all. Various shops and offices, including a barber's, opened up off both sides of the hall, and an exclusively male crowd wandered silently in and out, with pipes in mouths and newspapers under arms. All men, no women: so typical of misogynistic English clubs.

The fat, bald Irishman suddenly appeared from behind a column and came to greet us. He was very polite to Fernanda, treating her with the respect afforded an adult woman. He then whispered to me that the girl couldn't stay on her own in the entrance hall and would thus have to accompany us, as if this were inconceivable and would ruin our meeting. I tilted my head in assent, letting on without further explanation that that was precisely my intention. A wide white marble staircase curved around behind the majestic iron elevator the three of us took up to the journalist's room. By the looks of it, Rémy's antiquarian friend Mr. Jiang was already waiting for us there.

I had seen a good number of Celestials since my arrival in Shanghai. Not only was the French Concession full of them, but there were also the servants at the house and the clerks in Western clothing at M. Julliard's office. I had not encountered an authentic mandarin, a Chinese gentleman in old-style clothing, a shopkeeper I would have mistaken for an aristocrat had I seen him on the street. Mr. Jiang, who leaned on a light bamboo cane, was wearing a full-length black silk tunic with a shiny black damask vest over top, done up to the neck with small dark green jade buttons. A white goatee, round tortoiseshell glasses, and a skullcap rounded off the image, with a curved gold nail on each pinkie as the final decorative touch. His gaze was like that of an eagle, all-seeing without appearing to move, and the smile that danced on his lips made his prominent cheekbones even more pronounced. This, then, was Mr. Jiang, the antiquarian, whose bearing radiated strength and distinction, though I couldn't have said whether he was attractive or not, I was so unfamiliar with Celestials' facial features, in terms of both beauty and age. His cane and white beard were obvious signs that he was older, but how much so was impossible to say.

"*Ni hao*,[5] Mme De Poulain. Delighted to meet you," he murmured in excellent French, bowing his head in greeting. He didn't have the slightest accent, speaking the language better than Tichborne, who mumbled, swallowing most of the vowels.

"Likewise," I replied, lifting my right hand so he could take it, then pausing when I realized how absurd the gesture was: Chinese men never touch women, not even for a polite Western greeting. I quickly lowered my arm and remained quiet, feeling slightly awkward.

"This must be your niece," he said, looking at her but not bowing his head.

"Yes, Fernanda, my sister's daughter."

"My name is Fernandina," she rushed to clarify, before realizing that Mr. Jiang had already looked away and was ignoring her. He didn't look at her again the whole time we were there, and in the weeks to come, my niece simply didn't exist as far as he was concerned. Women are of little importance to Chinese men, and girls even less; Fernanda had to swallow her outrage and accept the fact that Mr. Jiang probably wouldn't even see or hear her if she were drowning and screaming for help.

As we sat in easy chairs crowded around a coffee table, the antiquarian told me that his family name was Jiang, his given name Longyan, and his courtesy name Da Teh, that his friends called him Lao Jiang, and that Westerners knew him as Mr. Jiang. Naturally, I thought it was some sort of a joke that I didn't quite understand, so I laughed out loud. But this was another serious blunder: Tichborne raised his eyebrows at me to stop. Then, in a superior tone, he explained that it was polite for Chinese people to introduce themselves by giving their full name— reversing the order and putting family name first, since one's given name is extremely personal and reserved solely for family—then their courtesy name, which only men of higher learning and a certain social class were allowed to use, and then the name given to them by friends in informal situations, which was formed by placing the word *Lao*, "Old," or *Xiao*, "Young," before the family name. There were many other names, Tichborne said—baby name, school name, generation name, even a posthumous name—but as a general rule only the three that Mr. Jiang had mentioned were used during introductions. The antiquarian remained silent but animated, listening to our conversation. Then, as if doing us a great honor, the Irishman told Fernanda and me that Jiang meant "Jade Case" and Da Teh meant "Great Virtue."

"And don't forget my given name," the antiquarian added humorously. "Longyan means 'Dragon Eyes.' My father thought it suited the son of a merchant, who must always pay attention to the value of things."

At that point, it would seem, it was all right for us to laugh.

"Well then, Mme De Poulain," Mr. Jiang went on—and I must say the name "Dragon Eyes" fit him like a glove—"has everything gone well since you arrived in Shanghai? Has anything untoward happened to you since you spoke with Paddy last night at the consulate?"

"With whom?" I asked, surprised.

"With me," Tichborne clarified. "Paddy is the diminutive of Patrick."

Fernanda shot me a look of reproach that bore an unmistakable message: So he can call himself Paddy, but I can't call myself Fernandina? I followed the antiquarian's lead and simply ignored her.

"No, Mr. Jiang, nothing untoward has happened to us. I left all the servants on guard to watch the house last night."

"Good idea. Do the same tonight. We're running out of time."

"Time for what?" I asked worriedly.

"Did you find a small chest among the pieces in Rémy's collection, Mme De Poulain?" he suddenly asked, catching me off guard. My silence gave me away. "Ah, I see that you have! Well, good. Marvelous. You must give it to me so I can resolve this matter."

Just a moment. Stop right there. No, none of that. Who was this Mr. Jiang for me to simply hand over a very valuable piece that could help me escape ruin? What did I know about Mr. Jiang apart from what Tichborne had told me? And who was Tichborne? Had I unwittingly brought my niece into the lion's den? Could these two colorful characters be members of the very Green Gang that was supposedly threatening our lives? My sudden nervousness must have been obvious, because my niece placed a reassuring hand on my arm and turned to the journalist.

"Tell Mr. Jiang that my aunt's not going to give him a thing. We have no idea who the two of you really are," she declared.

That's it, they're going to kill us now, I said to myself. The Irishman would pull out a gun and threaten our lives if we didn't hand over the chest, and then the antiquarian would sever the tendons in our knees.

Mr. Jiang stretched his lips into a mocking smile—had my fear been that obvious?—and quietly said:

"Exactly two months ago, Mme De Poulain, the chest you found in your home came to me from Peking with the imperial seals intact. It was one of several objects bought just outside the Forbidden City by my agent in the capital. The court of the last Qing[6] monarch is collapsing, madame. My great country and our ancestral culture are being destroyed not only by foreign invaders but also, and above all, by this weak, outdated dynasty that has left power in the hands of warlords. The pathetic young Emperor Puyi can't even control the theft of his own treasures. Everyone from the highest dignitary to the lowliest eunuch unscrupulously steals items of inestimable worth, all of which can be found a few hours later in the antiquities markets that have recently sprung up in the streets around the Forbidden City. In a vain attempt to stop this, Puyi decreed that a complete inventory be taken of all valuables. Unsurprisingly, the first in a terrible series of fires erupted a short while later in the street stalls where antiquities were being sold. To be more precise, according to the papers, the first fire occurred in the Palace of Established Happiness on June twenty-seventh, and just three days later I received the hundred-treasure chest that you found in your home, leaving no doubt as to its origin."

"I didn't know any of this!" Tichborne stammered angrily. Was he really upset, or was he just pretending? True, all he had mentioned the night before at the consulate was "something very important" and "a piece of art." Had the antiquarian kept this from him until now? Didn't he trust him?

" 'Hundred-treasure chest'?" I asked, curious, pretending to ignore the Irishman's discontent.

Mr. Jiang remained impassive. "It's an old Chinese tradition. The name comes from the fact that they contain exactly one hundred objects of value. Believe me, Mme De Poulain, many hundred-treasure chests like ours have come out of the Forbidden City since June twenty-seventh."

"And what is so special about *ours*, Mr. Jiang?" I asked sarcastically.

"That's precisely the problem, madame: We don't know. Some of the objects must be truly priceless, because the following week, the first week of July, three notable gentlemen from Peking appeared in my shop. They wanted to buy the chest and were willing to pay however many silver taels I asked."

"And you didn't sell it?" I asked in surprise.

"I couldn't, madame. I had offered it to Rémy the same day the lot arrived on the Shanghai Express, and he bought it, naturally. The chest was no longer in my possession, and that's what I told those honorable gentlemen from Peking. They were not at all pleased by the news and insisted I tell them who owned it. I refused, of course."

"How do you know they were from Peking?" I objected suspiciously. "They could have been members of the Green Gang in disguise."

The antiquarian Jiang smiled so broadly his eyes disappeared in the folds of his Oriental eyelids.

"No, no," he replied happily. "The Green Gang appeared a week later, accompanied by a couple of Dwarf Invaders—Japanese, that is."

"Japanese!" I exclaimed. I immediately called to mind what M. Favez had told us about the Nipponese: They were dangerous imperialists with a large army and had been trying to take control of Shanghai and China for years.

"Let me continue, madame," Mr. Jiang begged. "You're making me lose the thread of my story."

"Sorry," I murmured, surprised to see how that rotund Paddy smiled in satisfaction at the reprimand I had just received.

"The distinguished visitors from Peking were very upset when they left my shop, and I was certain they'd be back or would at least try to find whoever owned the chest. Their attitude and words made it abundantly clear that they intended to get what they wanted, by fair means or foul. I knew that the object now in Rémy's hands was an excellent piece, an original from the reign of the first Qing emperor, Shun Zhi, who ruled China from 1644 to 1661, but why such interest? There are thousands of Qing objects on the market—many more since the fire of June twenty-seventh. I could have understood if it had been a Song, Tang, or Ming[7] piece, but Qing? In any event, so that you will fully understand my surprise, let me just tell you that at first I paid no attention to the shrill falsettos these obstinate customers used. Then, as they left my store, I noticed the short little steps they took, with their legs close together and bodies leaning forward. I could no longer ignore the fact that these were Old Roosters."

"Old Roosters?" I asked. "What are you talking about?"

"Eunuchs, Mme De Poulain. Eunuchs!" Paddy Tichborne burst out with a guffaw.

"And where are there eunuchs in China?" Mr. Jiang asked rhetorically. "In the imperial court, madame. Only in the imperial court in the Forbidden City. That's why I told you the gentlemen were from Peking."

"I wouldn't exactly call them gentlemen. . . ." the Irishman commented disagreeably.

"What are eunuchs, Auntie?" Fernanda wanted to know. For a moment I wondered whether or not to answer; the girl was old enough to learn certain things. Strangely, though, I immediately decided not to tell her.

"They're servants to the Chinese emperor and his family."

My niece looked at me as if waiting for further explanation, but I was done.

"And because they're the emperor's servants, they speak in falsettos and walk with their legs together?" she insisted.

"Different customs, Fernanda, can be a mystery to outsiders."

Mr. Jiang interrupted our brief dialogue. "I hope, madame, that you can understand how frightened I was when I realized just who my fellow countrymen in Western clothing were as they stormed out the door. I had dinner with Rémy that night and told him what had happened, warning him that the hundred-treasure chest could be dangerous. I thought it best to advise him to give it back to me so I could then sell it to the Old Roosters, getting us both out of a difficult situation, but he paid absolutely no attention to me. Since he hadn't yet paid for the chest, he thought I simply wanted to obtain a better price and so refused to return it. I tried to make him understand that someone very powerful from the imperial court, perhaps the emperor himself, wanted the chest back and that such people were used to getting their way. Until recently they could have killed us for it and not broken a single law. However, madame, you know what Rémy was like." The antiquarian carefully adjusted his glasses, a serious look on his face. "He assured me he'd put the chest in a safe place and that if the eunuchs returned, he would personally come to my shop to tell them he wasn't interested in selling."

"And he didn't change his mind after the Japanese and the Green Gang came to see you?" I couldn't believe how irresponsible Rémy had been; although, come to think of it, why was I surprised?

"No, he didn't change his mind. Not even when I told him that Huang Jin Rong himself, head of the Green Gang and the French Concession Police, warned me there might be an unfortunate accident if we didn't deliver the chest within a week."

"They knew Rémy had the chest?"

"They knew everything, madame. Pockmarked Huang has spies everywhere. You may not know this, but Huang is the most dangerous man in Shanghai."

"M. Tichborne told me about him last night."

At the mention of his name, the journalist crossed and uncrossed his legs.

"Believe me when I tell you," the antiquarian went on, "that I was truly afraid when I saw him walk through the door of my shop. Certain individuals don't deserve to be sons of this noble, honorable land called China, but there's nothing we can do about it. They are the result of the bad luck that plagues my country. Pockmarked Huang doesn't usually come in person, so the situation suddenly became much more dire than I had previously thought."

"And what do the Japanese have to do with all this?"

"The answer to your question may be inside the chest, madame. In a way, I'm sorry I didn't hold on to it a while longer before offering it to Rémy. I didn't even examine it. Breaking the yellow imperial seals would have diminished its value, you see. But if I had, I might have a better understanding of what's happening today. I might understand why Pockmarked Huang came to my store with his deputy, Du Yu Shen, 'Big Ears' Du, and those two Dwarf Invaders who stood quietly by and stared at me with contempt."

Mr. Jiang had by then succeeded in frightening me. I began to feel the uneasiness in my stomach that heralded heart palpitations. How could I not panic? I was in possession of this damn chest that was wanted by the imperial eunuchs, Japanese colonialists, and that Pockmarked Huang from the Green Gang!

"H-how can I get it to you?" I stuttered.

"Don't worry, madame. I'll send a completely trustworthy fish vendor. Wrap the chest up well in dry cloths and have a servant set it in one of the baskets while pretending to buy something for dinner."

It was a good idea. Since wealthy women couldn't go out in public because tradition forbade it—and they obviously couldn't walk on those horrible, mutilated feet called "Golden Lilies" or "Golden Lotus Feet"— there were always vendors at the door, coming right in to the patio off the kitchen with fruit, vegetables, meat, spices, needles, thread, pots, or other household items for sale. Mr. Jiang's fish vendor would go completely unnoticed amid all the comings and goings.

When he finished speaking, the antiquarian stood up gracefully, and although he seemed to lean wearily on his bamboo cane, I noted that he rose with the same astonishing flexibility as displayed by Mrs. Zhong. It was odd the way the Chinese moved, as if their muscles required no effort and the older they got, the more flexible they were. Such was not the case with the much-younger Fernanda and Paddy Tichborne, both of whom had to push themselves up out of their seats. I also had a time standing, though not for the same reason. In my case it was the trembling in my legs that made it hard for me to move.

"When can I expect the fish vendor to come?" I asked.

"This afternoon," Mr. Jiang said, "at about four. How does that sound?"

"Will it all be over then?"

"I hope so, madame," the antiquarian hurried to say. "This nightmare has already cost one life, that of your husband and my friend, Rémy De Poulain."

"Isn't it strange," I murmured, walking toward the door, followed by Tichborne and Fernanda, "that they haven't tried to get into the house again? No one but the servants was there for over a month, and it's not as if they're exactly threatening."

"They didn't find anything that first day, madame, so why go back? That's the reason I'm worried about your safety now. They're likely waiting for *you* to find the chest, and then they'll force you to hand it over. The Green Gang knows the financial situation Rémy left you in, and they know that sooner or later you'll have to get rid of everything you own to settle those debts. Logically, you'll take stock, or someone will on your behalf. You'll go through cabinets and cupboards, dump out all of the drawers, and sell off anything valuable. It's just a matter of time. As soon as they suspect that you have the chest, they'll come after you."

The antiquarian remained standing in front of his chair in the living room, and we were almost at the door when suddenly the bottom dropped out of my world. I looked at my niece and saw her watching me intently, her eyes wide with surprise at hearing about Rémy's financial situation. I looked at Jiang the antiquarian and saw in his face sincere concern for our lives. Then I looked at Tichborne, and the Irishman pretended to be trying to find something in the pocket of his rumpled jacket. What was happening to me? Where was the painter from Paris who lived what now seemed like a carefree life, who taught classes and walked along the Seine on Sunday mornings? I had gone from being a completely normal person, faced with the usual difficulties that any struggling artist faces, to being financially ruined, my life in danger, and caught up in a terrifying conspiracy that could involve the very emperor of China himself. I could only think that these things didn't happen in real life, that no one I knew had ever been involved in anything as mad as this, so why me? And now, on top of it all, I would have to explain Rémy's debts to my niece, something I wanted to avoid at all costs.

"We're unlikely to see one another again, Mme De Poulain," the antiquarian said as we were leaving Tichborne's rooms. "It was a pleasure to meet you. Remember to leave your servants on guard at night. And I'm truly sorry you're getting such a bad impression of China. It wasn't always like this."

I gave a slight nod of my head and turned back around. I was more worried about breathing and staying upright than saying good-bye.

The hands on the clock in the Shanghai Club entrance hall said one-thirty when Fernanda and I, smiling spectacularly, bade good-bye to the stout journalist. My meeting with the antiquarian had lasted only half an hour, but it had been one of the worst half hours of my life. Why on earth had I decided to come to China to put Rémy's affairs in order, I wondered, letting myself collapse despondently into the rickshaw. If I'd known what to expect, there's no way I would have boarded that damn *André Lebon*. The hot air along the Bund only intensified my feeling of suffocation, and the trip back to the house was absolute hell.

❧

The afternoon sped past. While I wrote a note to M. Julliard, the lawyer, telling him to begin the necessary paperwork to sell the house and auction off the contents, Fernanda, much to my displeasure, insisted on visiting Father Castrillo, despite the danger involved in going out. The fish vendor came at the agreed-upon time to take the bundle Mrs. Zhong gave him.

It was the evening of Saturday, September 1, and I was in Shanghai. Perhaps I could have done something—I don't know, drawn or read—but I didn't feel very well. So, sitting on a bench in the garden, I watched the sun go down behind the walls surrounding the house and gazed at the flower beds and the soft, waving branches on the trees. A couple of servants attempted to keep the ground cool using water-soaked brooms. In truth, despite my apparent calm, inside I was waging all-out war against despair and anxiety. Everything seemed unreal, and not only because this house and this country were new to me. There are times when circumstances are so far from normal that the world becomes unfamiliar and it feels as if you'll never return to the life you once led. I couldn't quite orient myself in space or time, and I had the oppressive feeling of being lost, all alone in a vast silence. Staring at the white rhododendrons, I decided to leave Shanghai as soon as possible. I had to get back to Europe, leave this strange land behind and regain my sanity, get back to normal. I would go to the Compagnie des Messageries Maritimes offices on Monday to buy return tickets on the first ship to sail for Marseille. I didn't want to remain a minute longer than necessary in this country that had brought me nothing but misfortune.

Given the late hour, I was beginning to wonder where Fernanda was when Mrs. Zhong burst through one of the doors, running toward me and shaking a newspaper in the air.

"*Tai-tai!*" she shouted as she ran. "An enormous earthquake has destroyed Japan!"

I looked at her in confusion and snatched the paper out of the air as soon as she was near. It was the evening edition of *L'Écho de Chine*, and the front page bore an enormous headline announcing the worst earthquake in the history of Japan. According to preliminary reports, it seemed the number of dead in Tokyo and Yokohama was estimated at over a hundred thousand. Both cities were still engulfed in flames. It was proving impossible to extinguish the terrible fires caused by the quake because horrific hurricane-force winds were assailing the cities at nearly three hundred feet per second[8] and water supplies had been affected by the catastrophe. The news was awful.

"People are taking to the streets, *tai-tai!* The vendors say they're all heading to the Dwarf Invaders' colony. Huge waves of refugees will start arriving in Shanghai soon, and that's not good, *tai-tai.* That's not good at all. . . ." Then she lowered her voice. "The boy who sells newspapers door-to-door brought you a letter from Mr. Jiang, the antiquarian from Nanking Road."

I looked at her in surprise but said nothing. I had just seen my rather sizable niece come into the garden, and she was not alone: A very tall, very thin Chinese boy dressed in faded blue pants and shirt followed a bit behind, glancing around curiously but confidently. The two could not have looked more different, geometrically speaking.

"I'm back, Auntie," Fernanda said, opening her black fan with a lovely, typically Spanish flick of her wrist.

"Here, *tai-tai,*" Mrs. Zhong insisted, placing the envelope in my hand before giving one of her exaggerated bows and heading back to the main building.

Though I hadn't moved a muscle, I was once again as taut as a violin string. The letter from Mr. Jiang was completely unexpected and burned in my hands. He was supposed to have given the Green Gang the chest. What could have happened in the last three hours for the antiquarian to feel the need—dangerous by any reckoning—to write me? Something must have gone wrong.

"Auntie, this is Biao," my niece announced in Spanish, sitting down beside me on the bench, "the servant Father Castrillo found for me." The tall, thin boy held both hands in front of his forehead and gave a respectful bow, although a hint of mockery seemed to belie the gesture. He looked like a street urchin, a crafty little ragamuffin. He was quite handsome; his eyes were big and round, only slightly almond-shaped, and his hair was cut European style, with a part down one side. I didn't entirely dislike him.

"*Ni hao*, señora. At your service," Biao greeted me in his macaronic Spanish, bowing again. The Chinese must have iron backs, I thought, although this one was too young to suffer from such things.

"Do you know what Biao means in Chinese, Auntie?" my niece asked with a smile, fanning herself vigorously. " 'Little Tiger.' Father Castrillo told me he'll work for me as long as I like. He's thirteen and knows how to serve tea."

"Ah . . . very good," I murmured absentmindedly. I needed to read that letter from Mr. Jiang. I was scared.

"With all due respect, Auntie," Fernanda said, snapping her fan closed against her palm, "I think we need to talk."

"Not now, Fernanda."

"When did you plan on telling me about the financial trouble Mr. Jiang mentioned?"

I stood up slowly, resting my hands on my knees as if I were an old woman, and slid the antiquarian's letter into my skirt pocket.

"I'm not going to discuss the matter with you, Fernanda. Please don't ask me about it again. It doesn't concern you."

"But I have money, Auntie," she protested. At times my niece awoke something akin to tenderness in me, but it passed as soon as I looked at her: She was the spitting image of my sister Carmen.

"Your money is in trust until you turn twenty-three, child. Neither you nor I can touch it, so forget the entire matter," I said as I headed toward the building that housed our rooms.

"You mean I'm going to suffer hardship and poverty for six years even though I have the inheritance from my parents?"

Now, that was more like it. There was the daughter and granddaughter who must have made them so proud.

Still walking away, I grimaced and replied, "It will only serve to make you a better person, Fernanda."

I was not at all surprised to hear a dry thump as she stomped her foot on the ground. That was another well-known sound in our family.

Sitting at last in that Chinese bed, shielded from the world by those lovely silk curtains that let the lamplight through, with trembling hands I opened the envelope from the antiquarian, a shiver of fear running up my arms and legs. Yet the letter contained only a note, and a brief one at that: "Please come to the Shanghai Club as soon as possible." It was signed by Mr. Jiang and written in an elegant, old-fashioned French script that could only be his. . . . Well, unless it were a forgery and the Green Gang had sent it, a possibility I considered carefully as I hurried to dress and asked Mrs. Zhong to give Fernanda her dinner. I was so terrified that, in all honesty, I was unable to judge anything clearly. The most absurd things were happening as if they were normal; the extraordinary had become part of the ordinary. Here I was on a Saturday night in China, heading for the second time that day—as if it were the most natural thing in the world—to a meeting that could put my life in real danger. This was merely the beginning, I supposed, of a mad spiral into insanity. Even if Pockmarked Huang, the imperial eunuchs, and the imperialist Japanese might be waiting for me in Tichborne's room, it was best that I go in case it really *was* the antiquarian who summoned me there. Something might have happened when the chest was being delivered, and so, at the risk of having the tendons in my knees severed, I went to the Shanghai Club.

The concierge grinned smugly as soon as he recognized me, thinking the fat Irishman and I had started some sort of intimate relationship. He maintained that arrogant attitude even when I stared coldly back at him as I got into the elevator. You can be sure he wouldn't have aired his suspicions like that if I'd been a man. Since Tichborne hadn't come down to meet me, I crossed the long carpeted hallway to his room on my own, frightened half to death. I was so nervous that when Paddy smiled as he opened the door, I thought I saw a crowd of people behind him. Luckily, the image disappeared after a quick blink. In reality, no one other than Mr. Jiang was there, dressed in his splendid black silk tunic and shiny damask vest. He was smiling, too; a sense of euphoria seemed to float in the air. This was very different indeed from what I'd expected, and it calmed my nerves almost immediately. The hundred-treasure chest with that marvelous, gold-colored dragon on the lid sat on the coffee table, next to a tea set and a bottle of scotch.

"Come in, Mme De Poulain," the antiquarian urged as he leaned on his bamboo cane. If I hadn't seen him move as sprightly as a cat that afternoon, I'd have thought he was an old man on his last legs. "We have some monumental news to share."

"Was there a problem with the chest?" I asked anxiously as the three of us sat in the easy chairs.

"Not at all!" Tichborne burst out happily. There was an empty glass in front of him and only an inch of whiskey left in the bottle, leaving no doubt as to the cause of his merriment. "Wonderful news, madame! We now know what the Green Gang wants. This little box is the key!"

I turned to look at the antiquarian and saw he was smiling so widely his eyes had almost disappeared in a sea of wrinkles.

"True, very true," he confirmed, falling comfortably against the back of his chair.

"And this will save my life and my niece's life?"

"Oh, madame, please!" the fat Irishman protested. "Don't be so melodramatic!"

Before I could offer an appropriate reply to such rudeness, Mr. Jiang gestured to get my attention, the curved gold nail on his little finger dancing in front of my eyes.

"I doubt, Mme De Poulain," he began as he bent over the table to pour a nearly transparent tea into the two Chinese cups on the table, "that you've ever heard the legend of the Prince of Gui. In this great country that we, the sons of Han, call *Zhongguo*, 'the Middle Kingdom,' or *Tianxia*, Everything Under the Sky, children fall asleep at night listening to the story of the prince who became the last and most forgotten of the Ming emperors and who saved the secret regarding the tomb of Shih Huang-ti, the first emperor of China. It's a beautiful tale that helps revive our pride in this immense nation of four hundred million inhabitants."

He held a cup of tea out for me, but I refused with a slight wave of my hand.

"No?"

"It's too hot out."

Mr. Jiang smiled. "There's nothing better for the heat, madame, than a nice hot cup of tea. It'll leave you feeling refreshed in no time, you'll see," he insisted, passing the cup to me. I took it, and he settled back in the chair with his own. "When I was a boy, we used to act out the tragedy of the Prince of Gui. The neighbors would always give my brother, my friends, and me a few coins after our street performances, even if we'd done a really bad job." He laughed silently, remembering. "I must say, though, that in time we became quite good."

"Get to the point, Lao Jiang!" the Irishman exclaimed. I couldn't help but wonder what two such different men had in common. Luckily, the antiquarian didn't seem bothered by the interruption and continued his story as I took a sip of my tea, surprised by the lovely, fruity flavor. I immediately started to perspire, of course, but quickly the sweat cooled, leaving me feeling fresh all over. The Chinese were quite intelligent, and they did drink some excellent herbal teas.

"Before you hear the legend of the Prince of Gui, there are a few things you need to know about a very important part of our history, Mme De Poulain. A little over two thousand years ago, the Middle Kingdom as we know it today did not exist. Our territory was divided into various kingdoms that fought bitterly; that time is thus known as the Warring States Period. According to historical records, the man who would become the first emperor of a unified China was born in the year 259 B.C. His name was Yi Zheng, and he ruled over the kingdom of Qin.[9] After coming to power, Prince Zheng began a series of glorious battles that led him to take over the kingdoms of Han, Zhao, Wei, Chu, Yin, and Qi in just ten years, thus founding the country of Zhongguo or the Middle Kingdom, so called because it is situated in the middle of the world. In turn, the prince adopted the title Huang Ti or 'August Sovereign,' which is how we address our emperors to this day. People added the modifier Shi, which means 'First,' so the name he was known by throughout history was Shi Huang Ti or 'First Emperor.' His enemies, however, called him the 'Tiger of Qin.' " As he said this, Mr. Jiang opened the hundred-treasure chest, took out the half a gold tiger with inscriptions along its back that Fernanda and I had been examining that morning, and set it on the table. "Since he liked the name, he adopted the tiger as his military insignia. It was not a compliment, however; in reality his adversaries called him that because of his ferociousness, his ruthless heart. As soon as Shi Huang Ti had all of China under his absolute control, he initiated a series of important economic and administrative reforms, such as standardizing weights, measures, and currency," Mr. Jiang said as he placed the round piece of bronze with a square hole in the middle on the table, "the adoption of a single writing system— the one we still use today"—he set the minuscule Chinese book, the peach pit, and the pumpkin seeds with ideograms on them next to the coin—"a centralized system of canals and roads," he continued, placing a small cart drawn by three bronze horses on the table, "and, most important of all, he began construction on the Great Wall."

"Quit beating around the bush, Lao Jiang!" Paddy shouted impolitely. I looked over at him with absolute contempt. His manners were unbelievable!

"In short, Mme De Poulain, insofar as we are concerned," Mr. Jiang went on, "Shi Huang Ti was not only the first emperor of China but also one of the richest, most important, powerful men in the world."

"And this is where the little chest comes in," the Irishman pointed out with a grin.

"Not yet, but we're getting there. When Prince Zheng came to the throne, he ordered that work start on his royal mausoleum. This was normal practice at the time. Once he was no longer the prince of a small kingdom but Shi Huang Ti, the great emperor, that initial project was enlarged until it attained massive proportions: Over seven hundred thousand workers were sent from all over the country to make it the biggest, most luxurious, most magnificent burial tomb ever. Millions of treasures were buried with Shi Huang Ti upon his death, as well as thousands of living people: hundreds of childless imperial concubines and the seven hundred thousand workers who'd been involved in construction. Everyone who knew where the mausoleum was located was buried alive, and the place was shrouded in secrecy and mystery for the next two thousand years. An artificial hill with trees and grass was built over the tomb, which was forgotten, and this whole story became part of the legend."

Mr. Jiang stopped in order to softly set his empty cup on the table.

"Excuse me, Mr. Jiang," I murmured, confused, "but what does the first emperor of China have to do with this chest?"

"Now let me tell you the story of the Prince of Gui," the antiquarian replied. Paddy Tichborne snorted, bored, and tossed back the last of the whiskey he had emptied into his glass. "During the fourth moon of the year 1644, Emperor Chongzen, the last emperor of the Ming dynasty, was being hounded by his enemies and hanged himself from a tree in Meishan, Coal Hill, north of the imperial palace in Peking. This brought an official end to the Ming dynasty and gave rise to the current dynasty, the Ch'ing, of Manchu origin. The country was in chaos, the public treasury in ruins, the army disorganized, and the Chinese people divided between the old and new ruling houses. However, not every Ming had been exterminated. There was one last legitimate heir to the throne: the young Prince of Gui, who had managed to flee south with what remained of a small army of followers. At the end of 1646, the Prince of Gui was proclaimed emperor in Zhaoqing, province of Canton, and given the name Yongli. The chronicles have very little to say about this last Ming emperor, but we know that from the moment he took the throne, he was constantly on the run from Ch'ing troops until finally, in 1661, he had to ask the king of Burma, Pyé Min, for exile. The king reluctantly agreed and then humiliatingly treated him like a prisoner. One year later, General Wu Sangui's troops set up along the Burmese border, ready to invade if Pyé Min didn't hand over Yongli and his entire family. The Burmese king didn't hesitate, and General Wu Sangui took Yongli to Yunnan, where he was executed along with his entire family during the third moon of the year 1662."

"And you, madame," Paddy Tichborne interrupted, slurring, "will be wondering how the first emperor of China and the last Ming emperor are connected."

"Well, yes," I admitted, "but what I'm really wondering is how all this is connected to the hundred-treasure chest."

"You needed to know both stories," the antiquarian indicated, "in order to comprehend the importance of our discovery. As I said, the old legend of the Prince of Gui, also known as Emperor Yongli, which is told to children from the time they're born, the same one I acted out with my friends for a few copper coins, is a part of Chinese culture. Legend has it that the Ming possessed an ancient document indicating where to find the mausoleum built by the first emperor, Shi Huang Ti, as well as how to get inside without falling into the traps set for tomb raiders. That document, a beautiful *jiance*, was secretly passed from emperor to emperor as the state's most valuable object."

"What's a *jiance*?" I asked.

"A book, madame, a book made of bamboo slats bound with string. Until the first century A.D., here in China we wrote on shells, rocks, bones, bamboo slats, or pieces of silk. Then, around this time, we invented paper made of plant fiber, but *jiances* and silk were still used for a while longer. In any event, according to the legend of the Prince of Gui, on the night the prince was proclaimed emperor, a mysterious man arrived in Zhaoqing. An imperial messenger had come from Peking to deliver the *jiance*. The new emperor had to swear to protect it with his life or destroy it before it could fall into the hands of the new reigning dynasty, the Qing."

"And why didn't they want it to fall into Qing hands?"

"Because they're not Chinese, madame. The Qing are Manchus, Tartars. They come from the north, on the other side of the Great Wall. As usurpers of the divine throne, possessing the secret of the

First Emperor's tomb and seizing the most important treasures and objects would undoubtedly have legitimized them in the eyes of the people and the nobility, who were not so easily persuaded. In fact—and pay close attention to what I'm about to say, madame—a similar discovery even today would be so crucial, if it were to occur, that it could result in the end of Dr. Sun Yat-sen's Republic and the restoration of the imperial system. Do you see what I'm trying to say?"

I frowned in an attempt to concentrate and grasp the magnitude of what Mr. Jiang was saying, but it was difficult to do as a European ignorant of the history and mentality of the so-called Middle Kingdom. Certainly the China I barely knew, the China of Shanghai with its Western way of life, its love of money and pleasure, didn't seem likely to take up arms against the Republic in order to return to a feudal past under young Emperor Puyi's absolutist government. And yet it was reasonable to assume that Shanghai was the exception rather than the rule with regard to Chinese life, culture, ancestral customs, and traditions. Outside of this Westernized port city, there was surely a vast country, as big as a continent, still anchored to the old imperial values. After all, it was highly unlikely after two thousand years of living a certain way that things would have changed in just a decade.

"I do, Mr. Jiang. And I gather that possibility has become a reality due to something related to the hundred-treasure chest, correct?"

Paddy Tichborne stumbled up to get another bottle of scotch off the bar. I drank the last of my tea, tepid by then, and set the cup on the table.

"Precisely, madame." The antiquarian nodded, smiling. "You've touched on the last and most important point I wanted to make. Now is when the plot truly thickens. According to the legend of the Prince of Gui, on the night before the king of Burma handed Yongli and his entire family over to General Wu Sangui, the last Ming emperor invited his three closest friends to dinner: Wan the scholar, Yao the physician, and Yue Ling the geomancer and fortune-teller. He said to them, 'My friends, since I am going to be killed and the Ming lineage ends forever once I and my young son and heir are dead, I must give you a very important document. The three of you are to protect it on my behalf. The night I was enthroned as Lord of Ten Thousand Years, I swore that should a time like this come, I would destroy an important *jiance* that has been in my family's possession for many years and contains the secret of the First Emperor's tomb. I do not know how we came to possess it, but I do know that I am not going to keep the promise I made. One day a new, legitimate Chinese dynasty must regain the Dragon Throne and expel the Manchu usurpers from our country. And so I give you these.' Taking the *jiance* and a knife," the antiquarian continued narrating, "he cut the silk threads that held the bamboo slats together, creating three pieces, and gave one to each of his friends. Before parting company with them forever, he told the men, 'Disguise yourselves. Assume other identities. Go north; leave General Wu Sangui's armies behind until you reach the Yangtze. Hide the pieces in different places along the length of the river so that no one can unite the three parts until a time comes when the sons of Han can retake the Dragon Throne.'"

"Well, he certainly made it difficult!" I exclaimed, startling Tichborne, who had remained standing with a full glass once again in his hand. "If no one else knew where the Prince of Gui's three friends hid the pieces, they could never be put back together. What madness!"

The antiquarian nodded. "That's why it was a legend. Legends are lovely stories that everyone believes are false, tales told to children, a script for the theater. No one would ever have thought to look for three sets of bamboo slats that are over two thousand years old all along the shores of a river like the Yangtze, which is some four thousand miles long from its source in the Kunlun Mountains of central Asia to the estuary here in Shanghai. But—"

"Fortunately, there's always a but," the Irishman added before taking a noisy slurp of whiskey.

"—the story is true, madame, and the three of us know where the Prince of Gui's friends hid those pieces."

"What? We do?"

"We do, madame. Here in this chest is an invaluable document that recounts the well-known legend of the Prince of Gui, with a few important differences from the popular version." Reaching out his right arm, the antiquarian placed the hand with one gold nail on the miniature edition of the Chinese book and pushed it toward me, separating it from the other objects he'd taken out of the chest earlier in our conversation. "For example, it clearly mentions where the prince told his three friends to hide the slats, and the choice is certainly very logical from the Ming point of view."

"But what if it's false?" I objected. "What if it's just another version of the legend?"

"If it were false, madame, what other object in this chest could have motivated three imperial eunuchs to come here from Peking? What else could bring two menacing Japanese dignitaries to my store accompanied by Pockmarked Huang? Remember, Japan still has a powerful emperor on the throne who is unquestioned by his people and has demonstrated more than once that he's willing to back an imperial restoration by becoming militarily involved in China. In fact, for years he's provided millions of yen to certain princes loyal to the Qing in order to maintain Manchu and Mongol armies that continue to harry the Republic. The Mikado wants to make that fool Puyi a puppet emperor under his control and thus take over all of China in a single, masterful move. You can be absolutely sure that uncovering the tomb of the First Emperor of China would be the definitive blow. All Puyi would have to do is claim it as a divine sign, say that Shi Huang Ti blesses him from heaven and recognizes him as his son or some such thing in order for hundreds of millions of poor peasants to humbly throw themselves at his feet. People here are very superstitious, madame; they still believe in mystical events like that. And you foreigners, the Yang-kwei, would undoubtedly be massacred and expelled from China before you could ask yourselves what was happening."

"Yes, but, Mr. Jiang, you're forgetting one minor detail," I protested, feeling somewhat offended that the antiquarian had used the pejorative expression Yang-kwei, or "foreign devils," to refer to me as well. "You told me the chest came from the Forbidden City. Your agent in Peking acquired it after the first fire at the Palace of Established Happiness. I remember because I liked that name; it seemed so poetic. If Puyi could do everything you say with help from the Japanese if the chest were in his possession, why hasn't he done it already? Unless I was misinformed, Puyi lost power over China in 1911."

"In 1911, madame, Puyi was six years old. He's now eighteen and recently married, which means he has come of age. If the revolution hadn't occurred, this would have meant the end of his father's regency, that ignorant Prince Chun, and Puyi's rise to power as Son of Heaven. It would have been absurd to think about the restoration before now. Indeed, there have been attempts in the intervening years, all of which amounted to ridiculous failures, as ridiculous as the very fact that four million Manchus want to continue governing four hundred million sons of Han. The Qing court lives in the past, maintaining the old customs and ancient rituals behind the high walls of the Forbidden City, and doesn't realize there's no longer any place for True Dragons or Sons of Heaven in this country. Puyi dreams of a kingdom full of Qing queues,[10] a time that will fortunately never return. Unless, of course, a miracle should occur, such as the divine discovery of the lost tomb of Shi Huang Ti, the first great emperor of China. The common man is fed up with power struggles, military governors who become warlords with private armies, and internal disputes throughout the Republic, not to mention that there is a strong pro-monarchist party, spurred on by the Japanese, the Dwarf Invaders, that sympathizes with the military because it disagrees with the current political system. If, madame, you combine Puyi's recent age of majority and his open desire to regain the throne with the discovery of Shi Huang Ti's sacred mausoleum, you'll see that conditions are ripe for a monarchical restoration."

I was moved by Mr. Jiang's words and, above all, by the zeal with which he spoke. Without realizing it, I may have looked at him more intently than decorum allowed. If my first impression of him had been that of an authentic mandarin, an aristocrat, I was now discovering a man passionately devoted to his thousand-year-old race, heartbroken by the decline of his people and his culture, and full of disdain for the Manchus who had governed his country for nearly three hundred years.

Tichborne had remained very quiet, busy filling his glass only to quickly empty it again. So unsteady on his feet that he'd been leaning against the living-room wall for the last few minutes, he let out a thunderous guffaw.

"Puyi must have got quite the fright when he discovered he'd lost the chest that could have given him back the throne—all because he ordered an inventory of his treasures!"

"Now I'm more certain than ever," Mr. Jiang interjected, "that the Old Roosters who came to my store hired the Green Gang and sought assistance from the Japanese consulate when they discovered that it wasn't so easy to recover the document containing the true story of the Prince of Gui."

"So what are we going to do?" I inquired anxiously.

The Irishman pushed himself off the wall, smiling all the while, as the antiquarian narrowed his eyes to study me closely.

"What would you do, madame, if in your current financial situation there was a way for you to get a few million francs?" he asked. "Note I said millions, not thousands."

"Not only would I be enormously rich," Paddy jabbered, "I'd get the feature story of my life. What am I saying? I'd get the book of my life! And our friend Lao Jiang would become the most renowned antiquarian in the world. What do you think, Mme De Poulain?"

"More important, madame, we would prevent the Manchu dynasty from returning to power, averting what would be a historical and political catastrophe for my country."

Millions of francs, my tired mind repeated. Millions of francs. I could settle Rémy's debts, keep my house in Paris, and provide for my niece, do nothing but paint for the rest of my life and not have to worry about teaching for seventy-five paltry francs a month. What must it feel like to be rich? I had counted my pennies for so long, worked wonders to afford food, canvas, paints, and kerosene, that I couldn't imagine what it would mean to have millions of francs in my pocket. It was crazy.

"How would we evade the eunuchs from the Forbidden City? Actually, how would we evade the truly dangerous ones, the Green Gang assassins?"

"Well, we haven't done too badly so far, don't you think, madame?" Mr. Jiang smiled. "Go home and wait for my instructions. Be ready to leave at any moment."

"Leave? Leave for where?" I asked, suddenly alarmed.

The antiquarian and the journalist exchanged a complicit glance, but it was Paddy, his tongue loosened by alcohol, who told me what was on both of their minds.

"The three pieces of the *jiance* are hidden in three places that were very important during the Ming dynasty. Two of them are many hundreds of miles up the Yangtze. We'll have to travel to the interior of China to get there."

By boat? Stuck inside another boat for days and days, heading up a Chinese river that was thousands of miles long, this time being pursued by eunuchs, the Japanese, and gangsters? This was insane!

"And do I have to go?" I worried. Perhaps it wasn't necessary. "Remember, I'm responsible for my niece and can't abandon her. Besides, what use will I be?"

Tichborne burst out with another unpleasant guffaw. "Well, stay if you trust us! But I personally can't guarantee I'll be willing to share my cut once we're back. In fact, I don't even want you to be part of this expedition! I already told Lao Jiang there was no reason for you to find out any of this, but he insisted."

"Listen, madame," the antiquarian hastened to say, leaning forward, "don't pay any attention to Paddy. He's had too much to drink. The man is a wealth of knowledge when he's sober. I myself often consult him. Unfortunately, his hangovers tend to last several days," he said as Tichborne laughed again. Mr. Jiang gripped the handle of his cane as if trying to keep it from whacking the Irishman of its own accord. "It's your lives, Madame, yours and your niece's, that are in danger, not Paddy's or mine. And we mustn't forget that the chest belonged to Rémy. You therefore have the same right as we do to a share in whatever we find in the mausoleum, but that means you must come with us. No one will be able to guarantee your safety if you stay in Shanghai. As soon as the Green Gang discovers that Paddy and I have disappeared, they'll come after us. They're not stupid. You and your niece will then be their victims, and you know what they're capable of. This chest is very valuable. Do you think they'll chase after us and leave you alone? I wouldn't count on it, madame. The sensible thing is for the three of us to go, to escape Shanghai together and try not to get caught until we find the mausoleum. Once our discovery is made public, Puyi and the Dwarf Invaders won't be able to do a thing. They'll have to seek restoration some other way. Please listen to me, madame. Paddy and I will take care of the details. Prepare your sister's young daughter as well. She can't stay behind in Shanghai. She'll have to come, too."

"It's going to be awfully dangerous," I murmured. It's a good thing I was already sitting down, because I'm not sure I'd have been able to remain standing.

"Yes, madame, it will, but with a little luck and intelligence we'll succeed. Your financial difficulties will be over forever. In fact, of the three of us, I think you have the most reason to embark on this adventure and thus be able to return to Paris safe and sound. The Green Gang is connected to other secret Chinese societies, such as White Lotus and the Triad—both of which have spread beyond our country's borders, especially to Meiguo[11] and Faguo."[12]

"The United States and France," Tichborne clarified for me.

"What I'm trying to say is that you can't even escape to France in peace. Unless you resolve this matter in China, they'll find a way to kill you there. You have no idea how powerful the secret societies are."

"All right! All right! We'll go!" I exclaimed.

Fear choked me. How could I involve my niece in such a perilous situation? I'd never forgive myself if anything happened to her. Mr. Jiang was right: She would be in danger in Shanghai or in Faguo, too. Fernanda had fallen into a death trap because of me, and the very thought made me feel just awful.

"And now, to cheer you up a bit, listen to this, madame," the antiquarian jovially proposed. Picking the miniature book up off the table, he took a second pair of glasses out of his vest pocket and used them like a magnifying glass in order to see the tiny little characters in the minute paper accordion. "Where was it . . . ? Ah, yes! Here, this is it. Listen closely. We're in Burma, at the Prince of Gui's dinner with his friends the night before he's handed over to the Qing general. Let's see, then. . . . The prince says to his friends, 'Put on disguises and assume another's identity in order to cross Wu Sangui's army lines without endangering your lives. Go north, toward the central plains of China, until you reach the Yangtze. Once there, you, Scholar Wan, go east until you reach the river delta. Find Tung-ka-tow, in the county of Songjiang, and look for the beautiful Ming gardens that are exact replicas of the imperial gardens in Peking. Hide your piece of the *jiance* there. The best place is undoubtedly beneath the famous zigzag bridge. You, Physician Yao, go to Nanking,[13] the Southern Capital, where the tombs of my forefathers who governed China from that city are located. In Jubao Gate, find the mark of the artisan Wei from the region of Xin'an, province of Chekiang,[14] and leave your fragment there. And you, Master Geomancer Yue Ling, do not allow them to find you until you reach the small fishing port of Hankow. There you will set out on the long, difficult walk west that will lead you to the Qin Ling Mountains and, once there, to the honorable monastery of Wudang. Ask the abbot to keep your piece of the book. After safeguarding the *jiance*, escape to save your lives. The Qing will not be satisfied with killing nine generations of my family; they will execute all of our friends as well.' "

The Prince of Gui's message must have made complete sense to Mr. Jiang and Tichborne, because as soon as the antiquarian stopped reading, both of them smiled so happily, so exuberantly, that they looked like small children with a new toy.

"Do you understand, madame?" the Irishman jabbered. "We know exactly where the pieces of the *jiance* are hidden and can go after them whenever we want."

"Well, to be quite honest, I didn't understand much of the message, but I gather that the two of you do."

"Indeed, Mme De Poulain," the antiquarian concluded. "And the first fragment, the one that Wan the scholar hid, is right here in Shanghai."

"Go on!"

"According to the message in this book, Wan's fragment is underneath a bridge that zigzags in some Ming-style gardens in a place called Tung-ka-tow, at the Yangtze delta. We're at the delta. Tung-ka-tow was the name of the old Chinese citadel that gave rise to what is now Shanghai and still exists within what is known as Nantao, the old Chinese city. In the heart of Nantao, in what was Tung-ka-tow, there are indeed some old, abandoned, trash-filled gardens, Yuyuan Gardens, which they say were built by a Ming official to imitate the imperial gardens of Peking. There's almost nothing left of them now. They're in a very poor, dangerous area, and only a few curious *Yang-kweis* ever visit the teahouse on an island in the center of what must have been a beautiful lake."

"And can you guess what the bridge that leads to that island is like, madame?" Paddy asked.

"It zigzags?"

"Precisely!"

"How lucky the first piece is here in Shanghai," I pointed out. "That way, if we don't find it, it means the text isn't true and there'll be no need to take that trip, right?"

The two of them exchanged another complicit glance, clearly unwilling to give credence to my assertion. But another, more worrying thought was filling my head by the time they turned back toward me.

"How am I going to slip past the Green Gang's lookouts? If they really are following me everywhere, I'll never escape without their noticing. It's one thing to leave them waiting at the door, like now, and another to depart Shanghai right under their noses."

"You're right, madame," Mr. Jiang admitted. He remained lost in thought for a few moments, then looked back at me with a gleam in his eyes. "I know what we'll do. Talk to Mrs. Zhong and ask her to discreetly find some Chinese clothing for you and your niece. It shouldn't be too difficult for her to get a few things from the other servants. Your big feet will go a long way to making you both look the part. Try to do your hair in the Chinese style, although that may be difficult with your short, wavy hair, and be sure to make yourselves up so your Western eyes aren't too obvious. Finally, leave the house in a crowd of servants so you'll blend in with the group. If you do all this, I'm certain you won't be discovered."

I must admit, I wasn't a bit pleased with the idea of dressing as a servant, but I kept my tongue.

"What do you say we end this meeting?" the fat Irishman bellowed from deep in his seat. "It's nine o'clock, and none of us have had dinner yet."

He was right. I tended to follow the Spanish custom of eating late (never having gotten used to the European way), and I was getting hungry, so they must have been famished.

"Expect to hear from me, madame," Mr. Jiang concluded, standing up energetically. "We've a great journey ahead of us."

A journey of thousands of miles through an unknown country, I thought. A bitter smile appeared unbidden as I remembered my plan to buy our tickets on the first ship to sail from Shanghai in the coming days. I could still hardly wait to leave China, but if everything worked out, I'd be able to settle Rémy's debts and forever go back to my quiet life in Paris, my Sunday walks along the Left Bank. Fernanda's safety was what worried me most. When she found out she'd have to dress as a Chinese servant to travel by boat up the Yangtze in order to recover pieces of an old book, fleeing the same murderers who'd killed Rémy, she would protest vigorously, and rightly so. What could I say to

convince her that she'd be in much more danger if she stayed in Shanghai? Then I suddenly thought of a solution: She could stay with Father
Castrillo at the Augustinian mission while I was gone! It was perfect.

"Oh, no! Never!" she exclaimed, offended, when I proposed this to
her. We were in the small study next to Rémy's office (there, as elsewhere in the house, everything was symmetrical and balanced), sitting
in two chairs with high, slightly curved backs beside a folding screen
that hid a ma-t'ung. I had gotten her out of bed when I arrived, and she
was wearing a horrid nightgown under an even more hideous robe, her
hair out of its usual ponytail. She looked like a specter from hell in the
candlelight. As I ate a piece of duck quiche with mushrooms and kite
eggs on the side, I outlined the legend of the Prince of Gui and the secret of the First Emperor's tomb, leaving out all those complicated Chinese names.

"There's nothing more to say," I replied resolutely. "You'll stay at the
mission under Father Castrillo's protection. I'll go to Mass with you
tomorrow morning and ask him to do me this favor."

"I'm going with you."

"I said no, Fernanda. This discussion is over."

"And I said I'm going with you."

"Insist all you like, but I've made up my mind, and we're not going to
spend the whole night arguing about it. I'm exhausted. I've had only one
moment of peace since we disembarked, and that was this afternoon in
the garden. I'm ready to drop, Fernanda, so let's not fight."

She jumped up and stomped out of the building, her eyes filled with
tears of rage, but I'd made my decision. I couldn't carry that weight on
my conscience. The girl would stay in Shanghai with Father Castrillo.
However, with a run of bad luck like I was having, I should have known
that everything would change just so I wouldn't be given a moment's
rest. My plan was ruined at five o'clock that morning when I was awo-
ken by the light of a candle glowing in Mrs. Zhong's hands. The fish
vendor had just arrived with the first catch of the day, and he brought an
urgent message from Mr. Jiang:

"'At the hour of the Dragon at the North Gate in Nantao.'"

I sighed, sliding my feet out of bed. "What is the hour of the Dragon, Mrs. Zhong?"

"At seven A.M.," she whispered, using her hand to shield the flame and leaving me in the most ominous darkness, "at the old northern gate to the Chinese city."

"And where's that?"

"Not far from here. I'll explain how to get there as you dress. Here's the clothing you asked me for last night. I'll go wake Mademoiselle Fernanda while you wash."

I could hardly believe my eyes half an hour later when I looked at myself in the mirror: Wearing old pants, a faded blue cotton blouse, and a pair of light felt shoes, I looked like a complete stranger. Thanks to newly straightened bangs, cheekbones emphasized by makeup, and eyes lined using fine cotton swabs dipped in ink, I could easily have passed as a native servant or peasant. Mrs. Zhong added a few colorful necklaces that were actually amulets and brightened my pale face a little. I had an even harder time believing the vision of that robust Chinese girl who slipped into my room, similarly dressed and made up, although with a long ponytail down her back and canvas sandals on her feet. Fernanda's face shone with satisfaction, just as it had when we disembarked from the *André Lebon*. It was obvious that the girl truly needed freedom and excitement. My sister Carmen and I may have been opposite sides of the same family coin as far as temperament was concerned, but her daughter had most certainly inherited some of each.

We left the house at six-thirty that morning in the middle of a group of servants that Mrs. Zhong sent to the Chinese city to shop. We carried large, empty baskets on our shoulders to hide us even further in case anyone was watching. The street seemed deserted, although early-morning sounds could be heard from the nearby boulevard de Montigny. Strangely enough, I thought I saw the same slender, ragged old women who had been outside the Spanish consulate the night of the reception. It scared the living daylights out of me: Were *they* the Green

Gang spies? If those were the same women—and they seemed to be—there was no doubt of it. I became increasingly nervous but didn't say a word to Fernanda, who was walking next to her lanky servant Biao, the boy who spoke Spanish. I didn't want her to do anything that might attract the old women's attention. Until we reached L'École Franco-Chinoise on the corner of Montigny and Ningpo, I kept casually turning my head to see whether they were following us, but I didn't see them again. We'd done it.

Soon we were in front of what used to be the so-called North Gate—that is, the rear entrance to the old walled Chinese city. Celestials believe that south is the principal cardinal point (the direction in which their compasses point, unlike ours), and thus the front doors of their houses and cities face that direction. The north, therefore, is the back in the Chinese concept of space. There was no gate anymore, nor were there any walls; it was simply a slightly wider street that led into Nantao but kept the old name. To one side, similarly dressed as humble Celestial serfs, were the nearly unrecognizable Lao Jiang and Paddy Tichborne, the latter wearing a broad, cone-shaped hat. I recognized them only because of the intent way they were looking at us. I later learned they didn't know us either. It was no wonder!

The servants from the house left without making a fuss or saying good-bye, taking the baskets from our hands and passing us the bundles containing our belongings, calmly continuing on through the narrow, humid, winding streets of the old city. That was when I realized that Biao was still standing next to Fernanda.

"What's he doing here?" I barked at my niece.

"He's coming with us, Auntie," she calmly explained.

"Send him back to the house right now."

"Biao is my servant, and he'll go wherever I go."

"Fernanda!" I exclaimed, raising my voice.

"Don't shout, madame," Mr. Jiang said as he started down the street. It was odd to see him without his gold nails or his lovely bamboo cane, dressed in that shabby beige tunic and Western hat.

"Fernanda!" I whispered, following the antiquarian as I held my niece by the arm so I could give her a pinch she wouldn't soon forget.

"I'm sorry, Auntie," she whispered back without even flinching, "but he's coming with us."

One day I would kill that girl and happily dance over her dead body. Right then, however, there was nothing I could do but apologize to Mr. Jiang and Paddy Tichborne.

"Don't worry, madame," Lao Jiang calmly replied, surreptitiously scanning in all directions. "A servant who knows how to make tea will come in handy."

Biao said something in Chinese that I couldn't understand. To me, Chinese phrases sounded just like the shriek of a butcher's steel as it passed over the teeth of a saw: a bunch of monosyllables that rose and fell and rose again in pitch and intonation, creating a strange tune made of conflicting notes.

Lao Jiang replied in his excellent French, "Very well, Little Tiger. You'll make the tea and serve the meals. You'll help your young mistress, obey orders from us all, and remain humble and silent. Is that understood?"

"Yes, venerable one."

"Let's go, then. Yuyuan Gardens are just over there."

We moved on, elbowing our way through the crowded, smelly streets filled with miserable little shops that sold everything imaginable: birdcages, used clothing, bicycles, goldfish, unrecognizable meat, chamber pots, spittoons, fresh bread, aromatic herbs, and so much more. I saw a couple of workshops that made both lovely furniture and coffins. Beggars, lepers without hands or noses, merchants, street musicians, tightrope walkers, peddlers, and regular customers haggled, begged, sang, or shouted, resulting in an awful pandemonium beneath the bright, colorful, vertical signs that hung down from on high with gold, vermilion, and black Chinese ideograms. I listened as Tichborne amused himself by translating the signs out loud: "Serpent Potions . . . Benevolent Pills . . . Tiger Tonic . . . Four Literary Treasures."

The high walls of Yuyuan Gardens suddenly appeared as we rounded a corner. Two large dragons with open jaws and twisting mustaches protected the door, which was open and almost off its hinges. It was not until I passed through the entrance, right underneath them, that I discovered that they didn't have mustaches but in fact it was smoke billowing from their nostrils.

There were no longer any gardens inside. The land had been taken over by squalid little houses, huts made of sticks and cloth, crammed one next to another until not an inch of space was left. Dirty, naked children ran back and forth while women bent over to sweep the ground in front of their homes using bundles of straw. The smell was nauseating, and swarms of black flies buzzed frantically in the heat above piles of dung in the nooks and crannies. Everyone looked at us curiously, but no one seemed to realize that three of the five in our group were Big Noses, foreign devils.

"You *Yang-kwei* call this the Mandarin's Garden," Lao Jiang commented as he walked confidently down sidewalks littered with garbage. "Did you know that the word 'mandarin' doesn't exist in Chinese? When the Portuguese arrived on our shores a few centuries ago, they used this derogatory word to refer to the local authorities, the government employees in charge, and the nickname mandarin has stuck ever since. But we sons of Han don't use it."

"Still," I pointed out, "Mandarin's Garden is a very pretty name."

"Not to us, madame. To us the Chinese name Yuyuan is much prettier. It means 'Garden of Peace and Health.'"

"Well, it doesn't seem very peaceful or healthy anymore," Tichborne grumbled, kicking a dead rat onto a pile of garbage. Fernanda put her hand over her mouth to stifle a yelp of disgust.

"Pan Yunduan, the Ming official who ordered its construction four centuries ago," the antiquarian proudly continued, "wanted to give his aging parents a garden just as beautiful as the imperial gardens of Peking, where they could enjoy peace and health in their final years. It became famous throughout the Middle Kingdom."

"If you say so," the journalist replied disagreeably, "but it's a disgusting garbage dump now."

"Now," Lao Jiang objected, "it's where the poorest of my people live."

That phrase reminded me of the rousing Marxist speeches during the Bolshevik revolution, but I refrained from commenting. It was best not to get involved in politics, because it seemed people in both China and Europe had become quite sensitive since the events in Russia. Even in Spain, as far as I knew, the powerful, uncompromising, landholding oligarchy, consisting mostly of the noble class, was allowing small improvements in their tenant farmers' living conditions in an effort to prevent worse problems. When your neighbor's house is on fire, throw water on your own, they must have been saying. I thought a certain amount of panic was good; maybe then things would start to change a little.

"The lake!" Paddy suddenly shouted. Before there was time to react, a threatening roar rose up out of four or five throats behind us. I barely had time to turn around when I saw a group of assassins flying through the air toward us with their feet outstretched.

What happened next was one of the most extraordinary sights I've ever seen. With lightning speed, Mr. Jiang pulled a large fan, at least double the usual size, out of his tunic and hurled Fernanda, Biao, Tichborne, and me onto the ground, a good distance away. The force was the same as if we'd been hit by a Parisian bus—luckily, we weren't hurt. The most incredible thing of all was that by the time we hit the ground, Mr. Jiang was already fighting all five thugs at once, barely moving, his left arm held casually behind his back as if he were having a pleasant conversation with friends. One of the assassins lifted his leg to kick Mr. Jiang. With the fan held calmly against his stomach, the antiquarian kicked back so that the assassin's leg rebounded, hitting one of his cohorts straight on and throwing him against a pile of garbage. The one at the rear of the group must have been knocked unconscious, because he didn't move, while the first had been thrown off balance and tumbled through the air, waving his arms until he crashed against a large rock, his head bouncing off it like a ball. Meanwhile, a third henchman had picked up speed and was attempting to kick Mr. Jiang on the left in midstride. But the antiquarian, who remained calm, stopped the kick by smashing his fan into the henchman's instep. I hope I'm getting this right, because it all happened so quickly I could barely follow it (I was still trying to get on my feet again). In any event, I believe that right then, as the henchman was pulling his leg back, he reached out to punch Lao Jiang in the stomach. Mr. Jiang calmly hit his wrist with the fan, then moved it up to strike him in the face. The man let out a horrible cry as his left cheek began to bleed profusely, his right hand and foot hanging limp, like the limbs of the slaughtered animals we'd seen on hooks in the butcher shops. Meanwhile, two other assassins ran toward Lao Jiang with fists outstretched. Mr. Jiang's fan caught the first in the ribs with a tremendous blow, winding him, and the second was struck on his upraised arm, such that both men faltered for a moment. Mr. Jiang took advantage of those brief seconds to crack one on the head with his fan, making him collapse like a rag doll, while brutally kicking the other in the stomach, catapulting him backward folded in two. All the assassins were incapacitated.

"Come. Hurry," the antiquarian urged, turning back toward us. We were all on our feet again, frozen with astonishment.

Biao was the first to react. Leaping like a cat, he confronted the two thugs who were moaning on the ground, causing them to flee, staggering weakly. At the same time, Mr. Jiang leaned over the three who were still unconscious, his fingers dancing quickly over their necks, pressing mysteriously. Then he stood with a satisfied sigh and smiled.

Fernanda, Tichborne, and I remained statues. It had all happened in less than a minute.

"You . . . you never told me you'd mastered the secret arts, Lao Jiang," the journalist stammered, pushing his unruly mop of gray hair back and setting the straw hat firmly on his head.

"As Sun Tzu[15] says, Paddy, 'The art of war teaches us to rely not on the likelihood of the enemy not coming, but on our own readiness to receive him; not on the chance of his not attacking, but rather on the fact that we have made our position unassailable.'"

I wanted to know more about what I'd just seen but my mouth refused to move. I was so perplexed, so shocked, that I couldn't react.

"Come, madame," the antiquarian prompted as he walked toward the lake.

Fernanda had remained just as immobile and silent as I. When Biao came back over, sporting one of those dazzling, contagious smiles so typical of the Chinese, my niece held him by the arm.

"What just happened?" she breathlessly asked in Spanish. "What kind of fight was that?"

"Well, it might have been what they call Shaolin, Young Mistress. I'm not sure. All I know is that's how the monks in the sacred mountains fight."

"Mr. Jiang is a monk?" Fernanda asked in astonishment.

"No, Young Mistress. Monks shave their heads and wear robes." Biao didn't seem entirely sure about the latter, despite the assurance in his voice. "Mr. Jiang must have been taught by an itinerant master. They say there are masters who travel incognito throughout the country."

"And they use fans as weapons?" my niece asked, even more astonished, pulling hers out of one of the many pockets in her Chinese pants, looking at it as if for the first time.

"They use anything, Young Mistress. They're known all over China for their skill. People say they have mental powers that make them invincible. But Mr. Jiang's fan isn't like yours. His is made of steel, and the ribs are sharpened blades. I saw one once when I was little."

I couldn't help but smile at this last comment. Did Biao think he was already a grown man? In any event, I watched the antiquarian with renewed interest as we walked toward a lake with murky green waters and a large, two-story building with a black roof and exaggerated upturned eaves set on a man-made island. Mr. Jiang had just stepped onto a strange zigzag bridge, followed by Paddy, who bent his head slightly to examine the floor, made of solid blocks of granite. The antiquarian looked ahead at the lone, run-down kiosk. My eyes had begun to get used to Chinese forms, and I could see how original this structure was. There was a certain beauty to it, something deeply sensual and harmonious, as elegant as the antiquarian himself.

"This bridge has four corners, Lao Jiang!" Tichborne shouted so we could all hear.

"No. You're wrong. It has seven."

"Seven?"

"It continues on the other side of the island."

"It's so long!" the Irishman complained. "How will we know where to look?"

Shortly after that, the five of us walked up and down the footbridge in search of anything that might catch our eye. A few elderly men and women watched us from the balustrades of nearby houses, while two or three people had gone over to the unconscious assassins and were laughing at them. I wondered what Mr. Jiang had done to their necks. Finally, we all met in front of the building's closed doors and had to admit there was nothing out of the ordinary along the bridge except for the large number of shiny carp whose backs rose up out of the greenish water underneath. Some were as long as my arm and as fat as a barrel, and there white, yellow, orangish, even black ones, all of them sparkling like diamonds.

"Why would they build a bridge like this?" I asked. "It takes much longer to walk from one end to the other."

"Because of the spirits!" Biao exclaimed, a frightened look on his face.

"The Chinese believe that bad spirits can only go in a straight line." Paddy grunted, walking back toward the bridge on the right.

"We'll have to go into the water to check under the bridge," Lao Jiang announced. "As Prince Gui said, 'The best place is undoubtedly beneath the famous zigzag bridge.'"

"Is he crazy?" I turned in horror to ask my niece, who'd been stand-ing beside me just a moment before. But along with Lao Jiang and her servant, Biao, Fernanda was already walking toward land, apparently with every intention of going into that green lake. Paddy was on his way back from the other end and looked at me with tired eyes.

"I hoped it wouldn't come to this. Maybe he wants us to jump in from here?" he asked ironically, following the three lunatics who were now walking onto the island.

I didn't move. There was absolutely no chance I was setting foot in that filthy water full of fish bigger than a toddler. Who knows how many microbes they hosted, how many illnesses you could catch in there? Dying of some fever was most certainly not part of my plan.

"Fernanda!" I yelled. "Come here right now, Fernanda!"

However, while my shout caused an entire neighborhood of almond-eyed locals to come out onto their balconies to see what was happening, my niece turned a deaf ear.

"Fernanda! Fernanda!"

I knew she could hear me, and so, with an ache in my heart, I was left no choice but to capitulate. One day, I told myself with a smile, one day I would hang that tubby body of hers from a meat hook.

"Fernandina!"

She stopped and turned to look at me. "What is it, Auntie?" she asked. If looks could kill, the girl would have dropped dead that instant.

"Come here!"

"Why?"

"Because I don't want you to go into that noxious lake. It could make you sick."

Just then there was the sound of a body hitting the water. Biao, liv-ing up to his name, had jumped into that verdant soup without a second thought. After the antiquarian took off his tortoiseshell glasses and set them on the ground, he walked down a few small steps carved into the rock and was soon up to his knees. His beige tunic floated up around him. The two were either crazy or ignorant fools. Countless people had died from drinking contaminated water during the war, and doctors had tried to keep the terrible epidemics in check by requiring that liquids be boiled before consumption.

"Don't worry, Mme De Poulain!" Lao Jiang shouted as he continued to wade in up to his neck. "We'll be fine!"

"I wouldn't be so sure, Mr. Jiang."

"Then stay where you are."

"My niece will be staying here, too."

Fernanda, obedient in spite of it all, stood beside the lake, watching Biao swim from side to side. After taking off his oiled hat, Tichborne went down the steps and followed the antiquarian, who was calmly walking toward the underside of the bridge. At some point he stopped wading and started swimming. Soon all three were paddling beneath me. Seeing that I was in a better position to watch the goings-on, Fernanda came and stood next to me, and we looked down over the railing.

"See anything, Lao Jiang?" we heard Paddy ask, huffing and puffing.

"No."

"And you, Biao?"

"No, me either, but the carp are trying to bite me."

The boy was over by the rocky island, and we saw him jump out of the water, pursued by bulldoglike orange and black carp.

"Fish don't bite, Biao. Their mouths are too small," Paddy commented, his breath once again calm. "We'd better examine the other side, the one with three corners."

Fernanda and I followed them from above and waited patiently as they finished inspecting each and every one of the stone pillars that supported the bridge.

"I don't think there's anything here, Mr. Jiang," Biao said, sputtering as his head came up out of the water. A green twig hung from his hair.

The antiquarian seemed quite angry; from up above I could clearly see the scowl on his face.

"It has to be here. It has to be here. . . ." he droned, and plunged back into the soupy lake.

Little Tiger lifted his head until he could see Fernanda, giving her a doubtful look, then disappearing again.

Paddy swam wearily toward the steps. It was obvious he was worn out and had conceded defeat. He emerged from the water with his clothes plastered to his body and flipped back two locks of wet hair—actually, long strands on either side that he used to cover his bald dome. As soon as he was up and out, he flopped down on to the ground and waved at us without moving another muscle.

Lao Jiang and Biao continued to search under the bridge. The sun was rising higher in the sky, and the light was getting stronger, whiter. The antiquarian and the boy passed near the rocks that formed the base of the artificial island several times, and every time they did, a shoal of fierce-looking carp rammed into them until they moved away. The third time this happened, Lao Jiang stopped. Fernanda and I couldn't see him, but the expression on Biao's face as he swam away like a mouse being chased by a pack of wild cats made it clear something bad was happening.

Fernanda couldn't contain herself. "What about Mr. Jiang, Biao?"

The boy shook the water off his head and looked in the antiquarian's direction.

"He's in among the carp!" he shouted in fear. By then the fish that had followed Biao had turned back to join the ones that were smashing into Lao Jiang. "He's not moving!"

"What do you mean, he's not moving?" I asked, startled. Had something happened to him? Was he drowning? "Help him! Get him out of there!"

"*Bu! Bu!*[16] I can't. But it's okay. I think he's okay. He's just not moving."

Startled by all the shouting, Tichborne had gotten up and was running as fast as he could to get down the steps and into the water.

"He's gesturing at me with his hands," the boy explained.

"What's he saying?" I screeched, on the verge of a nervous breakdown.

"He's telling us to be quiet," Biao explained, still treading water. "He's telling us not to make any noise."

I looked questioningly at Fernanda.

"Don't ask me, Auntie. I don't understand what's going on either. But if he's telling us to be quiet, we'd better listen."

The next few minutes were truly worrisome. Together, Biao and Tichborne watched the scene that was unfolding outside our field of vision, under the bridge, near the rocks. Neither spoke nor moved except to stay afloat. After what seemed like an eternity, they swam back a few feet, not taking their eyes off what was happening in front of them. Just then the antiquarian's head—more precisely, his head and a hand with something in it—appeared calmly in the middle of a ring of fish that moved along with him, crowded so close he hardly had room to breathe. The school was like a besieging army that wasn't about to let the enemy escape. The antiquarian glided very slowly, and the fish glided along with him. The Irishman and the boy began to swim furiously toward the steps, racing away from what was bearing down on them, while Fernanda and I held back a shriek of horror as we watched the hair-raising spectacle. We ran to where Paddy and the boy were coming out of the water, pushed by the horde of carp still surrounding Mr. Jiang as he moved ever so slowly toward the stairs. The water began to boil as soon as he put his foot on the first step. The fish began thrashing about, charging Lao Jiang as if they were bulls, but the antiquarian impassively continued his ascent until he was finally out, smiling triumphantly. He, Tichborne, and Biao stank, but I was undoubtedly getting used to the putrid smells in Shanghai, because I wasn't too bothered by it. Lao Jiang happily displayed an old bronze box covered in verdigris.

"Voilà!" he burst out contentedly, stamping in the pool of water forming at his feet. "We've got it!"

"Why did the carp attack you?" Fernanda inquired, wrinkling her nose when Biao came to stand next to her.

Mr. Jiang ignored her, so it was Paddy who answered.

"Carp are very nervous fish. They immediately feel threatened when you enter their territory and become extremely fierce if it's spawning season. Wan the scholar chose well: these carp have kept curious swimmers away from the box for centuries. He was a very intelligent man, that Wan."

"We should have known right away that the carp were part of his trick," Lao Jiang added as he put on his glasses.

"Why?" Tichborne asked, seemingly offended.

"Because carp are the Chinese symbol for literary merit, applying oneself to one's studies, having passed an exam with an excellent mark. . . . That is, they're the very symbol of Scholar Wan himself."

"Let's open it!" I exclaimed.

"No, madame, not yet. First we must leave Shanghai." The antiquarian lifted his eyes to the sky and looked for the sun. "It's late. We've got to go right now, or we'll miss our train."

Our train?

"Our train?" I asked, perplexed. All this time I'd been sure we'd escape up the Yangtze by boat.

"Yes, madame, the Nanking Express, which leaves the North Station at twelve-thirty."

"But I thought . . ." I stammered.

"The Green Gang will expect we've escaped by hiding on a river sampan, and they will search every boat on the water in the Yangtze delta over the next few days. By now the two thugs who ran off after the fight will have told them what happened. The Green Gang will already know we've started our search and that if they don't catch us now, they'll have to chase us all over the country."

We walked back toward the exit. The assassins whose necks Lao Jiang had touched were still in the same position, motionless, although their eyes were bulging and darting from side to side. The antiquarian didn't show even a flicker of expression.

"What's wrong with them?" I asked, examining them apprehensively from afar.

"They're locked inside their own bodies," Biao confirmed fearfully.

"Indeed."

"Will they die?" Fernanda asked, but Mr. Jiang remained silent, still walking toward the exit.

"My niece asked whether they'll die, Lao Jiang."

"No, madame. They'll be able to move in a couple of Chinese hours—that is, four of your hours. Life, all life, is to be respected, even ones as unworthy as these. You'll never achieve Tao if you've unnecessary deaths on your conscience. A fighter must not abuse his power, even if he's superior to his opponent."

The antiquarian was speaking like a philosopher now, and I knew he must be a compassionate man. What I didn't understand was that bit about Tao, but there would be time to ask the hundreds of questions piling up in my throat. Our priority was to escape, to leave Shanghai as soon as possible, because, as the antiquarian had said, the Green Gang would know that the five of us had visited Yuyuan Gardens first thing that morning and they would know that we hadn't been sightseeing.

"Do the imperial eunuchs know the real story of the legend of the Prince of Gui?" I then asked.

"Who can say?" Tichborne replied, wringing out the long tails of his tunic. "But we can assume they don't. Otherwise why would they need the chest?"

"They most likely knew of its existence," Lao Jiang sensibly observed. "Someone may have read it once and then kept it in a safe place in order to use the text when the time came. Puyi's stupidity was once again revealed when he ordered that inventory without calculating the consequences. Logically, the eunuchs and officers who'd been getting rich off the thefts were going to make sure they didn't get caught. The easiest solution was to burn the evidence, start the fires so there'd be no way ever to know how much had been stolen."

"But someone might remember what the text said," I objected.

"Whatever the case, madame, it doesn't matter whether Puyi and his Manchus knew where the pieces of the *jiance* were hidden—though this is highly unlikely given the absolute lack of intelligence shown by members of the imperial family and the old court. What really matters is that there's no way they can allow anyone else to have that information. Think carefully. Any warlord, any noble Han, any high-ranking, ambitious, erudite Hanlin could be just as interested in discovering the First Emperor's tomb, and for the same reasons as Puyi. That's why they need to get the chest back whatever the cost, and we are the ones who have it."

Tichborne burst out laughing. "Do you want to be emperor, Lao Jiang?" he asked.

"I thought you were deeply nationalistic," I mused, ignoring the Irishman.

"I am, madame, but I also believe that China can't keep turning its back on the world, reverting to the past. We have to make progress so that one day we can be a world power like Meiguo and Faguo, even like your country, Big Luzon, which is struggling to fit in with modern democracies."

"I'm from Spain, Mr. Jiang," I objected.

"That's what I said, madame. Big Luzon. Spain."

He had a time pronouncing the name of the country in Spanish. It turns out that Chinese merchants had been doing business with Manila, capital of the island of Luzon, for three hundred years. To them Spain was "Big Luzon," the far-off country that bought and sold products through its colony in the Philippines. They didn't have the slightest idea where it was or what it was like, and they didn't really care. I therefore once again agreed with Mr. Jiang: China had to open itself up to the world and stop living in the Middle Ages. What they needed was not more feudal emperors, whether Manchu or Han, but political parties and a modern, republican parliamentary party system that would bring it into the twentieth century.

We had come out into the narrow streets of Nantao again and were attracting a lot of attention, because all three men were soaking wet. The morning heat would soon dry their clothes, but in the meantime we needed to get to the railway station as quickly and inconspicuously as possible to board the Nanking Express.

We moved swiftly through the noisy crowd that filled streets lined with shops. There was no time to lose, but as we drew closer to the North Gate of Nantao, it became increasingly difficult to get through the ever more dense mass of Shanghaiese. A melon vendor struggled to get the wheels of his cart out of a ditch, while a half-naked coolie, arms outstretched, pushed from behind. Both had their heads down, tense with effort, sweaty, and oblivious to the holdup they were causing. There was no passing through.

"I know a way," Biao said, looking at Lao Jiang.

"Then we'll follow you," the antiquarian replied.

The boy turned and ran toward a narrow alley that twisted to the right. We all followed, trying not to fall behind. We raced through streets no wider than a handkerchief, the ground soft with filth. At times the smell was nauseating. After a short while, Fernanda was puffing like a set of bellows.

"Are you going to be all right?" I asked, turning to look at her.

She nodded, and we continued on until we realized we had left Nantao and were running down boulevard des Deux Républiques, that grand avenue that circles the old Chinese city on top of what used to be a defensive moat that had been filled in when the old walls were destroyed.

"Rickshaws!" Tichborne shouted, pointing to a group of coolies playing cards on the road next to their vehicles.

We quickly rented four and climbed into them as soon as Lao Jiang had paid our fares. Because Biao and I were the smallest in the group, we shared a rickshaw.

"How am I going to get on the *huoche* with you?" he turned to ask worriedly.

"I don't know what you just said, child."

"The *huoche* . . . The fire car . . . The train."

The poor boy could hardly pronounce the Spanish word. I never would have guessed that *ferrocarril* was so difficult, but those double *r*'s and the *l* were torture for the Chinese.

"Well, I suppose you'll get on just like the rest of us," I confirmed as we sped through the French Concession following Lao Jiang's directions. He seemed to want to take a particular route, away from the big avenues and boulevards.

"But who'll pay my fare?"

I suspected I'd be responsible for lanky Biao's expenses, because as far as I knew, Fernanda hadn't brought any money with her. In truth, I had only a handful of heavy Mexican silver dollars that I'd found in a chest of drawers in Rémy's room. Although the franc could be used without too much trouble in the French Concession, the official currency in Shanghai was the Mexican silver dollar, still the worldwide monetary standard since many countries refused to accept the gold standard (including Spain). When I took the money from Rémy's, I calculated that it would be a considerable sum once exchanged for Chinese taels, the currency we would most likely use during our trip into the interior.

"Don't you worry about a thing," I said to the boy without looking at him. "You're with Fernanda and me, and all you should worry about is doing a good job. We'll take care of the rest."

"But what if Father Castrillo finds out I've left Shanghai?"

Oh, I hadn't thought of that. That irresponsible Fernanda had made a decision that could get us into hot water. How could we justify Biao's disappearance from the orphanage and the city? It seemed the boy had more brains than my foolish niece.

"I told you not to worry about a thing. Now be quiet, you're making my head spin."

We had no trouble leaving the French Concession through one of the border posts after Lao Jiang had a chat with the head guard, who seemed to be a friend. Once inside the International Concession, the antiquarian's rickshaw pulled up beside Tichborne's and then moved over beside mine as we continued on our way.

"Can you hear me, madame?" he asked, speaking very quietly.

"Yes."

"The French police are looking for us. All concession border posts received the arrest warrant issued by Pockmarked Huang just a few minutes ago," he explained, laughing.

"And what's so funny?" I replied. I had become a criminal sought by the Shanghai French police. How long before the consul general of France, Auguste Wilden, found out, and what would the charming consul general of Spain, Julio Palencia, think?

A black coupé sped past us, causing my rickshaw coolie to yelp loudly.

"The race has begun, madame," Lao Jiang exclaimed.

"You'd better make sure that box from the lake isn't empty before we take this madness any further!"

"I already have." His wrinkled Chinese face expressed a happiness bordering on fanaticism. "There's a beautiful fragment of an ancient bamboo slat book inside."

I suppose his enthusiasm must have been contagious, because I was conscious of the sudden change in my own facial expression, from unease to the most I had smiled in some time. Trust was not my strong suit, but the piece of the *jiance* cut by the last, forgotten Ming emperor and hidden by the scholar Wan hundreds of years ago was in that black box stained with verdigris sitting on Lao Jiang's lap. The millions of francs that would settle Rémy's debts and make me rich just might exist: They were real, and above all they were a little bit closer, more within reach.

Lao Jiang's rickshaw moved off once again to lead our retinue to the station via streets and roads. It gave me scant opportunity to enjoy my second trip through the International Concession. I did, however, notice that the French feel of the neighborhoods had given way to a more Anglo-Saxon, more American setting, where the women wore light, fresh designs and no stockings, the men spit on the sidewalks with shocking calm and wore impeccably cut summer suits with double-breasted jackets and their hair shone with brilliantine. But I didn't see a single skyscraper, not a single avenue with illuminated signs, not even, what I most hoped to see, one of those big, modern, North American automobiles. We moved on through the outskirts heading north, avoiding the most inhabited, busiest streets, hidden inside our rickshaws even though Pockmarked Huang couldn't do a thing to us here because we were no longer in French territory.

At ten to twelve, we finally arrived at the big Shanghai North Railway Station building. With our bundles we looked like a Chinese family on our way home after a short stay in Shanghai. I was worried that the ink used to make my eyes look Oriental could have been smeared by sweat or humidity, but my reflection in the station windows confirmed that it was still intact. The same was true for Fernanda and Tichborne, who kept his parasol-shaped straw hat on at all costs.

Lao Jiang didn't say a word about the price of the trip. He left us under the station clock and marched off toward the crowded counters, coming back with five tickets a few minutes later. I managed to catch only a few words of what he said to Tichborne, something about a friend of his being the stationmaster. The man was turning out to be a veritable wealth of resources, and, truth be told, it was coming in very handy.

Not far from the enormous black locomotive that spewed soot and clouds of gray steam, a large group of foreigners stood on the platform, fenced off from the loud mass of Chinese we were among. When the whistle blew, they climbed into elegant cars painted a bright, dark blue, while the Celestials' cars were little more than rusty old crates with splintered wooden seats and floors covered in spit and garbage.

Shortly after we clattered off, a never-ending flood of vendors knocked on the compartment doors, offering a variety of foods. We bought noodles, rice pap, and meat-and-mushroom dumplings, all accompanied by green tea. An old woman poured the hot water while a young boy who must have been her grandson set a few leaves in the cup just long enough to give the brew a bit of color and then reused them in the next one. This was the first time Fernanda and I had been faced with the difficult task of trying to pick up and hold on to food with those thin sticks that Celestials use instead of cutlery. It was a good thing we were alone, because our cover wouldn't have lasted long with that display of extreme incompetence: Food flew, sauces splattered, and the chopsticks slipped out of our fingers or got tangled up in them. My niece quickly became quite adept; I, unfortunately, was having a little more trouble. Poor Biao wasn't used to the rocking motion of the train, and our lunch didn't sit so well with him; he vomited everything he had wolfed down, and more, into one of the spittoons.

During the first three hours of our trip, Lao Jiang and Paddy chatted about the antiquities business; Biao, embarrassed, had disappeared after vomiting; and Fernanda, bored, stared out the window. Even more bored, I wound up following her lead. I would much rather have read a good book (the trip to Nanking took twelve to fifteen hours), but it was an unnecessary weight to carry in my bundle. Outside the window huge fields and rice paddies separated small, thatched-roof villages. I didn't see a single inch of uncultivated land other than roads and the many large clusters of graves that were everywhere. I remember thinking that in a country with 400 million inhabitants, where ancestral tombs are never forgotten, the graves of the dead could one day take over all the land that supported the living. I had a feeling that thousands of years of tradition in a primarily agricultural people who still followed their ancient customs were going to be far too steep a mountain for Sun Ya-sen's fragile young Republic to climb.

Four hours after we left Shanghai, the train pulled in to the station in Suchow with a long screeching of brakes. Lao Jiang stood up.

"We're here," he announced. "It's time to disembark."

"But weren't we going to Nanking?" I protested. There was a priceless look of surprise on Tichborne's face as well.

"Indeed, that is where we're going. A sampan's waiting for us."

"You're crazy, Lao Jiang!" the Irishman bellowed, grabbing his bundle.

"I'm prudent, Paddy. As Sun-tzu says, 'Let your rapidity be that of the wind, your compactness that of the forest. In raiding and plundering be like fire, in immovability like a mountain.'"

Biao, who it seemed had spent the whole time sitting on the floor just outside the compartment, opened the doors and looked at us in astonishment.

"Fetch the bags," Fernanda ordered with mistressly determination. "We're getting off here."

There were no rickshaws in Suchow, so we had to rent litters. Once inside mine, I pulled the curtains and steeled myself to spend the next while bouncing around in that confessional-shaped box. Oh, how comfortable the rickshaws in Shanghai now seemed! We didn't go into the city of Suchow itself but skirted around the north until we came to a river I initially thought must be the Yangtze. Its perfectly straight banks did seem odd, however, and it turned out to be the Grand Canal. Construction on this, the world's oldest and longest man-made waterway, which crossed the entire country from north to south and was nearly two thousand kilometers long, began in the sixth century B.C. By the looks of it, our train had veered south, and we now had to go back north to continue our journey to Nanking.

I think it was on the Grand Canal, shortly after we boarded the flat-bottomed barge where we would spend the next three days, that I realized just how crazy our undertaking was. We were on one of a row of boats held together with thick ropes, transporting salt and other products to Nanking. Enormous water buffalo hauled the whole convoy as dozens of men toiled in front of them to clear any sediment that may have accumulated to impede their progress. And all the while, insane hordes of mosquitoes sucked our blood twenty-four hours a day, without respite even during the cool nighttime hours. Fernanda and I slept on the last boat, the one that swung from side to side the most. At times the canal seemed to sink into the earth, so high were its artificial banks. The food was disgusting, the sailors' shouts unbearable as they ran from bow to stern of the caravan all day and night, the smell nauseating, and the hygiene nonexistent. Not one of those hardships seemed to make any sense at the time. What were we doing there? What god had disrupted the natural of order of things such that my niece and I, born into the bosom of a good family from Madrid, had smeared our eyes with ink to make them look oblique and sat hour after hour on a smelly boat heading up the Grand Canal as mosquitoes bled us dry and passed on who knew what fatal illnesses?

Since I couldn't cry unless I wanted to ruin my disguise, just before we came to Chinkiang (where the Grand Canal and the Yangtze meet) on the second day of our trip, I decided that the only way to stay sane would be to draw. I took out a small Moleskine notebook and a red hematite pencil and jotted down everything I saw: the barge's wooden planks— the knots, the joints, the cracks—the water buffalo, the sailors working, and the piles of raw material. Fernanda used her time to torture poor Biao with tedious Spanish and French lessons. Tichborne went on a rice-wine binge that honestly lasted from the first night until the very day we arrived in Nanking. Lao Jiang, meanwhile, sat strangely still, contemplating the water unless it was time to eat or sleep and every morning when he did these strange, slow exercises. I was quite impressed as I secretly watched him: Completely absorbed, he would lift his arms as he picked up one leg and turn very slowly, in perfect balance. The whole thing took little more than half an hour and was really quite funny.

"They're tai chi exercises," Biao explained very seriously. "They help your chi, your life force."

"What nonsense!" Fernanda burst out contemptuously.

"It's not nonsense at all, Young Mistress!" the boy exclaimed nervously. "Wise men say chi is the energy that keeps us alive. Animals have chi. Rocks have chi. The sky has chi. Plants have chi," he chanted passionately. "The very earth and the stars have chi, the same chi is in every one of us."

Fernanda was not so easily persuaded.

"That's just silly superstition. If Father Castrillo heard you, he'd give you a good whipping!"

A shadow of fear crossed Little Tiger's face, and he immediately fell silent. I felt sorry for the boy and thought I should defend him.

"Every religion has its beliefs, Fernanda. You should respect Biao's."

Lao Jiang, who hadn't seemed to be listening as he did his strange tai chi dance, slowly lowered his arms, put on his glasses, and stood still, looking at us.

"The Tao is not a religion, madame," he finally declared. "It's a way of life. You people have a hard time understanding the difference between our philosophy and your theology. Taoism was not invented by Lao Tzu. It has existed for a very long time. Four thousand six hundred years ago, the Yellow Emperor wrote the famous *Huang Ti Nei Ching Su Wen*, the most important Chinese medical treatise on human energy still in use today. In this treatise the Yellow Emperor says you are to go outdoors when you rise in the morning, let your hair down, relax, and move your body slowly, with attention. In this way you will attain health and longevity. That is Taoism: meditation in movement. The external is dynamic, while the internal remains static. Yin and yang. Would you consider that a religious practice?"

"Of course not," I replied respectfully, while inside I was thinking, Looks like I've followed the Yellow Emperor's advice my whole life, because all I can do when I get up in the morning is slowly drag myself around for a good long while!

Lao Jiang waved his hand as if to say he was done with his tai chi that morning and certainly done explaining Taoism to a couple of foreign women.

"I think now is a good time," he said, "to finally take a look at our piece of the *jiance*. What do you think?"

What did we think! Sadly, Paddy was sleeping off a hangover under a straw roof two boats ahead, but Lao Jiang didn't seem to care. He strode over to his bag and carefully pulled out the box we had found in the lake, then came and sat down in front of me. (Fernanda was beside me and Biao to her right, a little ways off, but as far as the antiquarian was concerned, neither warranted widening the circle to include them.)

He lifted the heavy, rust-encrusted lid. A beautiful bright yellow silk scarf was wrapped protectively around a bundle of six fine bamboo slats, about eight inches long, held together by two faded green threads.

Lao Jiang pulled off the yellow cloth and set it back in the box after carefully studying it. He held the bamboo pieces in the palm of his hand with the utmost reverence and attention, using his body to protect them from the sun. Then he unrolled the bundle and set it on the tails of his tunic over his lap. He looked at it impassively for a minute and then, perplexed, turned it around so I could examine it, too. The three slats on the right were covered in Chinese characters. The other three, however, simply looked dirty, as if the scribe had shaken an ink-soaked brush over them. With a long, bony finger, Mr. Jiang pointed to the ones with writing on them.

"It's a letter and quite hard to read because it's written in a very complex form of classical Chinese. The old *zhuan* style, as I told you in Shanghai, was used until the First Emperor ordered that the writing system be standardized across the empire. Luckily, I have a good deal of experience working with ancient documents, so unless I'm mistaken, it's a personal message from a father to his son."

"And what does it say?"

Lao Jiang turned the pieces back to face him and began to read out loud:

" 'I, Sai Wu, send greetings to my young son, Sai Shi Gu'er' "—The antiquarian paused. "There's something very strange here. Sai Shi Gu'er, the son's name, literally means 'orphan of the Sai clan,' so Sai Wu, the writer, must have been either very ill or condemned to death. There's no other explanation. Further, the words 'orphan of the clan' suggest that the Sai lineage is ending, that only the boy is left."

"What a shame."

" 'I, Sai Wu, send greetings to my young son, Sai Shi Gu'er, wishing him health and longevity. By the time you read this letter' "—Lao Jiang stopped yet again, lifted his head, and looked at me desolately. "These characters are very hard to read, especially because some of them are smudged."

"Do the best you can." I was too curious to accept the fact that the antiquarian might not be able to translate the message.

"'By the time you read this letter,'" he continued, "'many summers and winters, many years, will have passed.'"

"All that is written on those three bamboo slats?" I asked in disbelief.

"No, madame, just in these first few characters," he said, pointing halfway down the first slat. It was obvious that the Chinese wrote from top to bottom and from right to left (two thousand years ago, at least) and that their ideograms expressed much more than our words. "'You are a man now, Sai Shi Gu'er, and I grieve that I will never know you, my son.'"

"The father was going to die."

"Most certainly. 'All three hundred members of the Sai clan will soon cross the Jade Gates and journey beyond the Yellow Springs because of me. Only you will be left, Sai Shi Gu'er, and you must avenge us. I am thus sending you to safety with a trusted servant, to far-off Chaoxian[17] and the home of my old friend Hen Zu. He recently lost a son your age, and you will take his place in the family until you reach adulthood.'"

"I gather that to 'cross the Jade Gates' and 'journey beyond the Yellow Springs' means they're all going to die?" I asked, horrified. "Three hundred family members? How can that be?"

"It was common practice in China until not that long ago, madame. Remember what the Prince of Gui said in the legend: Eighteen hundred years after this letter was written, the Ch'ing dynasty had nine generations of the Ming family murdered. The number of dead could have been similar, or even higher. Not only would a criminal be killed in punishment, but also every last one of his relatives, no matter how distant. A clan would thus be pulled out at the root, like a bad weed, preventing new shoots from springing up."

"And what crime had this father, Sai Wu, committed to warrant such punishment? You just said he felt responsible for this misfortune."

"Patience, madame."

I was an adult and could contain myself, but Fernanda and Biao, their eyes popping out, weren't going to wait much longer before pouncing on Lao Jiang and demanding that he continue reading. My niece was about to burst with impatience. I think the only reason she held back was that the antiquarian frightened her a little. If I'd been the one reading, she would have already clawed my eyes out.

"'According to a good friend of the unfortunate General Meng Tian, the eunuch Zhao Gao said that Hu Hai, the new Ch'in emperor, intends to bury every one of us who worked on the Original Dragon's mausoleum now that he has crossed the Jade Gates. I, Sai Wu, was responsible for this magnificent, far-off project for thirty-six years, ever since Minister Lü Buwei charged me with this task. My entire clan must therefore die in order to keep the greatest secret of all, the one I will reveal to you now so you can avenge your family, your relatives. Our ancestors will not rest in peace until justice is served. My son, what torments me most at this time of adversity is that I will not even be afforded the consolation of resting in the family vault.'"

Mr. Jiang paused. Not one of us said a word. The extent of the punishment imposed on an innocent family because one of its members had faithfully served the First Emperor was unbelievable.

"You must be almost at the end, aren't you?" I finally asked. I was still stunned by how much could be written in such a small space using those strange Chinese characters.

"This piece is very revealing," the antiquarian mused, ignoring me. "On the one hand, it mentions Meng Tian. He was a very important general in Shi Huang Ti's court, responsible for many of his military victories, and the First Emperor placed him in charge of building the Great Wall. The general and his entire family were sentenced to death in a will forged by the powerful eunuch Zhao Gao, who is also mentioned in the letter. Zhao Gao had worked for the First Emperor and wanted to take control when he died. This same forgery also forced Shi Huang Ti's oldest son to commit suicide and named Hu Hai, the weaker second son, as emperor. As you can see, our *jiance* must have been written at the end of 210 B.C., when Shi Huang Ti, otherwise known as the Original Dragon, died."

"So it's"—I did a quick mental calculation—"a little over two thousand one hundred years old."

"Two thousand one hundred and thirty-three, to be precise."

"Then what happened to Sai Wu?"

"Don't you remember what I told you in Shanghai about Shi Huang Ti's royal mausoleum? I said that everyone who knew where the mausoleum was located was buried alive with him: hundreds of childless imperial concubines and the seven hundred thousand workers who'd been involved in construction. This is confirmed by Sima Qian, the most important Chinese historian of all time.[18] All the more reason, then, for the man who was foreman on that great project to die. Sai Wu was the very person responsible for thirty-six years, as he explained to his son."

"Which makes Sai Wu the best engineer and architect of his time."

It was Fernanda who blurted out this comment, surprising us all. However, before I had time to respond, Mr. Jiang was speaking again. What he had to say was not very nice at all.

"Too much knowledge in girls is pernicious," he declared. "It ruins their chances of finding a good husband. You should teach your niece to be quiet, madame, especially in the presence of adults."

I opened my mouth to tell the antiquarian in no uncertain terms how absurd his assertions were, but—

"Auntie Elvira, please be so kind as to tell Mr. Jiang on my behalf," Fernanda said, her voice dripping with resentment, "that if he would like his traditions to be respected, he must also respect the traditions of others, especially as regards women."

"I agree with my niece, Mr. Jiang," I added, staring straight at him.

"We're not used to the way you treat the other half of your population,
those two hundred million women who aren't allowed to speak. Fernanda didn't mean to offend you. She simply made a valid contribution
to the conversation we were having, exactly as she would have done in
Europe."

"*Pa luen.*[19] I'm not going to discuss this matter with you, madame,"
the antiquarian declared, so coldly that the blood froze in my veins. He
immediately rolled up the bamboo slats, wrapped them in the yellow
silk scarf, and placed them back in the box. Then he stood with his
usual agility and walked away. It was unbelievably rude.

"Well, Biao," I said, standing up as well, though not quite as easily
as the antiquarian, "what's to be done in a situation like this, where two
cultures have unintentionally offended one another?"

Biao looked at me forlornly, more like a small child than ever.

"I don't know, *tai-tai*," he replied, apparently unwilling to take a
stand.

"I didn't do anything wrong!" Fernanda fumed.

"Calm down. I know you didn't. Mr. Jiang is going to have to get
used to us, whether he wants to or not."

I'd had a magnificent idea once when I was young. I was sketching a
little vase the teacher had set on a table as a lesson in how to work with
light and shadow, when I suddenly decided that I not only wanted to be
a painter when I grew up, but I wanted my own life to be a work of art.
Yes, that's exactly what I thought: I want to make my life a work of art.
Much water had passed under the bridge since then, and when I looked
back on that childish goal, I was proud of myself for having achieved it.
True, I didn't earn much as a painter, and I was still far from realizing
my dream; my marriage hadn't exactly been exemplary, because, like
Rémy, I wasn't predisposed to married life; I had never been close to my
family; the men in my life had always been deplorable (Alain, that idiot
of a pianist; Noël, the opportunistic student; Théophile, my lying colleague); and, above all, my youthful courage had disappeared with age,
leaving me defenseless when faced with the simplest of setbacks. But

regardless of these many deficiencies, I was still proud of myself. My life was different from that of most women of my generation. I had learned how to make difficult decisions. I lived in Paris, in my very own home, and painted in my studio, where the perfect southeast light streamed in the windows. I had pulled myself out of many a slump and had known how to preserve my friendships. When all is said and done, if that wasn't creating a little work of art, let God come down and judge for himself. I was confident it was. Looking on the bright side, perhaps this miserable trip through China was just another brushstroke in a picture that was acquiring beauty, errors, pentimenti, and all. At least that's how I felt the morning of the day we arrived in Nanking, as the breeze off the Yangtze caressed my face and fishermen dressed in black sent their cormorants out to explore the river.

The Chinese have a very unusual way of fishing, without poles or nets. They train those big aquatic birds with vibrant necks to catch the fish and regurgitate them into baskets on the boat, alive and undamaged. That morning I painted several cormorants along the margins and in the corners of already used pages in my notebook, intending to include them in the picture I wanted to paint of the whirring fan blades in my cabin on the *André Lebon*. I hadn't yet decided on all the elements for the composition, but I knew there would be cormorants and fans.

We arrived in Nanking before sunset on the afternoon of Wednesday, September 5. By this time I could hardly believe I'd been in China for only a week. It was as if I'd been there for months, and my departure from Paris began to feel like a distant memory. New experiences and journeys can exert a powerful, amnesiac influence on you, like painting one color over another, making a third that's even more vivid than its predecessors.

The Yangtze was so wide in Nanking that it could easily have been mistaken for an ocean. At some point we lost sight of the northern shore and never saw it again. The slow passing of muddy water in one direction was the only indication that this endless expanse was actually a river. Massive steamers, cargo ships, tugs, and gunboats moved up and down the river or remained docked, while barge caravans like ours and hundreds of family sampans—true houseboats—filled with men, women, and scantily clad children amassed, tacking back and forth in search of a clear stretch of water. The smell of fried fish was overpowering.

We left the river, crossed a wharf crowded with people, boxes, baskets, ducks and geese in cages, and headed into the city. We needed to find somewhere to stay that night and, though I didn't say it, somewhere to bathe as well—some of us stank like oxen. But Nanking was no Shanghai, with its modern hotels and night lights. It was a city in ruins; a big city yes, but in ruins. Nothing remained of its former splendor as the old Southern Capital (which is what Nanking means, as opposed to Peking, which means "Northern Capital"), founded in the fourteenth century by the first emperor of the Ming dynasty. The crumbling walls of the old city were visible here and there as we walked through wide, filthy streets in search of an inn. Paddy stumbled along with puffy, red eyes, waking up slightly in the somewhat-less-than-torrid night air.

Mr. Jiang walked confidently, happily ahead. Nanking brought back good memories of his youth; it was here he had taken his literary exam and gotten the highest possible mark. It seems the Southern Capital was a little like one of our European university cities, and scholars who studied here were viewed in much higher regard than were those who studied anywhere else in China. There were still huge Ming monuments in the city, mostly on the outskirts, since it had once been a metropolis of considerable political and economic importance with a large, educated population.

"Nanking," the antiquarian proudly commented, "is where the most beautiful books in the Middle Kingdom are published. The quality of the ink and paper made here are unrivaled."

"Chinese ink?" Fernanda asked distractedly as she stared at the poverty and desolation on the streets.

"Well, we're not in India," Paddy replied disagreeably, obviously still suffering from a hangover.

We finally found lodging in a sad *lü kuan* (a sort of cheap hotel) between the Catholic Mission and the Confucius Temple in the western part of the city. It was nothing more than a square patio that looked as if it had once been a pigsty, partially covered by a thatched overhang with rooms around four sides. In the back, faintly lit by lanterns and oil lamps, was a dining area crammed with tables full of people eating or playing a strange board game I'd never seen before.

Mr. Jiang soon struck up a conversation with the owner, a stocky, young Celestial with a high forehead and an old-fashioned Qing queue. The antiquarian stood next to a big wood-fired stove gathering information from the owner in an attempt to supplement what little we knew about where the physician Yao had hidden the second piece of Sai Wu's *jiance* over three hundred years ago. Meanwhile, the rest of us ate rolls stuffed with shrimp and pieces of seasoned meat, and a dish of sweet and sour pork. I had gotten much better at using chopsticks, *kuaizi*, over the last few days on the barge, and it was as if Fernanda had never eaten with anything else in her life. Just as we were finishing, the owner of the *lü kuan* said good-bye to Lao Jiang with a nervous smile, and the antiquarian came back over.

"What if he tells the Green Gang we're here?" I asked anxiously as Mr. Jiang sat down and picked up a big piece of pork with his chopsticks.

"Oh, I don't doubt he will," he replied pleasantly. "But not tonight; not now. So let's calmly have our tea, and I'll tell you what I found out."

Biao, who had eaten in a back patio with the other servants, still dirty and smelly, appeared with a pot of hot water for tea. Everyone seemed content that night. Perhaps I was worrying too much.

A blind old Chinese man came in and sat down next to a pillar. He set a case on the ground and pulled out a sort of small violin with a long neck and a sound box made from a turtle shell. Holding it vertically, he pulled a bow across the strings and began to sing a strange, melancholy song in a shrill falsetto. Some of the diners banged the table in time to the music, delighted with the entertainment. Both the antiquarian and the Irishman had big, happy smiles on their faces as they watched the musician.

"Here's the situation," Lao Jiang began, demanding our attention. "The names of most of the gates in the old Ming wall that circles the city have changed since they were built. That's why I didn't remember any Jubao Gate, as it's called in the Prince of Gui's message. The inn-keeper doesn't know of one either, but he's sure it must be *Nan-men*, the City Gate, also known as Zhonghua Gate or Zhonghua Men. It's the oldest gate in all of China, and there's a small mountain called Jubao in front, across the Qinhuai River that used to be the moat around the wall. It would have been the main gate into the old city of Nanking, the south gate, built during the second half of the fourteenth century by order of the first Ming emperor, Zhu Yuan Zhang."

"How many gates are there?" Tichborne asked.

"Originally, there were over twenty. During the Ming era, Nanking was the largest fortified city in the country, and there were two walls, the interior and the exterior. Nothing remains of the exterior wall. The interior wall, the one we're talking about, was almost sixty-eight *li*,[20] or twenty-three miles, long, of which only about thirteen remain. Just seven or eight gates are left. There were still twelve when I took my exams, but recent riots and uprisings damaged several of them. Zhonghua Men, however, is in perfect condition."

"But we're not sure this Zhonghua Men is Jubao Gate, are we?"

"It must be, madame. The fact that it's across from a mountain called Jubao is very significant."

"And what, exactly, did the Prince of Gui's message say? I'm sorry, but I don't remember."

Paddy snorted. His face was pale, and he had big black bags under his puffy red eyes.

"The Prince told Physician Yao to 'find the mark of the artisan Wei from the region of Xin'an, province of Chekiang' in order to hide his fragment there. In China, bricks are the most common building mate-rial after wood, and the artisans who manufactured them for the government were required to write their name and province of origin on them. That way they could be found and punished if their bricks weren't of good quality."

"And the Prince of Gui knew all the suppliers?" I asked in disbelief. "It seems strange that of the many artisans who must have manufactured bricks for the walls and gates in Nanking, the last Ming emperor would know this anonymous laborer Wei from the region of Xin'an, dead three hundred years before."

"Obviously there's more here than meets the eye, madame," Lao Jiang replied. "Let's not get ahead of ourselves. Everything will become clear once we solve the riddle. Right now it's important for you to learn to identify the Chinese characters for Wei, Xin'an, and Chekiang. We sons of Han use the same syllables to name many different things. Only our intonation differentiates them. That's why the *yang kwei* say our language has such an unusual musical quality to it: If they pronounce a syllable-word with the wrong intonation, the word means something entirely different from what was intended. The only way we can be precise is in writing; there is a different ideogram for every concept. We can understand one another in writing even if we're from different regions in the Middle Kingdom. We can even understand the Japanese and the Koreans, though they speak different languages, because they adopted our writing system many centuries ago."

"That was quite the oration!" Tichborne mocked. "It took me three years to speak your damn language and learn what few characters I know."

The antiquarian set our dinner bowls to one side and reached into his pocket for a small rectangular box covered in red silk, containing a smaller version of what Celestials call the "Four Literary Treasures": animal-hair brushes, a block of ink, a mixing bowl, and paper. He unfurled the little roll of rice paper and secured each corner with one of our dinner bowls, then rolled up his sleeves and poured a few drops of water from the kettle into the mixing bowl. Next he took the block of ink and methodically rubbed it until the bright black emulsion

acquired the appropriate density. Then he held the brush upright
with all five fingers of his right hand. With his left he pulled his right
sleeve back to keep it from dragging over the strokes and smudging
them. He dipped the brush in the ink and held it over the white surface. Oh, the unction in his every move! It was as if he were a priest
performing a sacred ritual. What he drew looked something like this:

"This is the character Wei," he said, lifting his head and handing
the brush to Paddy, who prepared to quickly copy it next to Lao
Jiang's—though with much less confidence and grace. "Wei is our artisan's last name. It means 'surround,' 'encircle,' 'enclose,' which you can
see by its shape. Memorize it. Drawing will help you to remember it
better. In any event, I'll show the character to you again, tomorrow, before we leave for Jubao Gate."

I pulled out my Moleskine and copied it using my red hematite pencil. Fernanda watched me with a certain amount of envy.

"May I have a sheet of paper, Auntie?" she asked humbly. She knew
that it was my only sketchbook and that she was asking me to make a
great sacrifice.

"Here," I said, pulling a sheet out gently, carefully, from top to bottom. "And here's a pencil as well. What about you, Biao? Do you want a
piece of paper and a pencil?"

Little Tiger looked away. "No, thank you," he replied. "I've already
memorized it."

Something provoked Lao Jiang, because he turned to look at the boy
suspiciously.

"Do you know how to write Chinese?" he challenged. "How many
characters do you know?"

The boy started. "They only teach us foreign handwriting at the
orphanage."

Sparks and flashes of lightning flew from Lao Jiang's eyes. He set the writing implements down in order to place his palms flat on the table, as if about to crush it.

"You don't know a single character in your own language?" he demanded. I had never seen the antiquarian so furious.

"I know this one," poor Biao murmured, pointing to the artisan's last name.

Paddy placed a calming hand on Mr. Jiang's shoulder. "Leave him be. It's not worth it," he said. "Teach him, and let that be the end of it."

The antiquarian inhaled deeply and exhaled very slowly through his mouth. With a look that instilled fear, he again held the brush in that elegant vertical manner and dipped it in the ink. His face immediately changed and became serene. It was as if he couldn't write if he were angry, as if he had to remain calm in order to concentrate on those complicated ideograms that required slow strokes and fast, short and long ones, gentle and vigorous. Watching him, it was easy to understand why the Chinese had made their calligraphy an art form and, similarly, why we hadn't.

"This is how you write the name Xin'an," he said, satisfied, "and this is how you write the province of Chekiang. Chekiang still goes by the same name, but Xin'an is now known as Quzhou. In any event, we have to look for its old name; that's the one that interests us. These two characters I've just drawn must be on the bricks along with the character for Wei."

The four of us pupils in that impromptu school studiously bent our heads to diligently copy the new strokes. Even Biao, who had at first refused my offer of pencil and paper, now toiled with genuine interest. I felt sorry for Little Tiger. He was just a poor thirteen-year-old orphan caught between two cultures, East and West, that had been in conflict for ages. To him they were represented by Father Castrillo and Mr. Jiang, both of whom he feared.

Much to my delight, I was finally able to take a hot bath after our lesson. An old servant brought steaming buckets of water from the kitchen and poured them over my head, filling the big wooden washtub that also served as a bathtub. Luckily, the soap wasn't too horrible, despite its unpleasant appearance and the fact that it left my skin quite dry. And the rags they brought for me to dry myself with were clean—unlike my clothes, which went right back onto my body, dirt and all, for a few more days. Although much too short for my liking (the others were falling asleep waiting their turn), the bath left me feeling fresh and revitalized. My good mood quickly vanished, however, as soon as I saw the miserable room where Fernanda and I were to sleep. The ceiling was so low you could touch it with your hands, and the adobe walls were dirty and peeling, to say nothing of the squalid bamboo *k'ang* set on top of a brick oven—luckily, not lit—where I was to sleep.

Still, I was so tired I didn't even notice when my niece came back from her bath, and the night passed in the blink of an eye. Suddenly I was opening my eyes, wide awake, listening to the soft rustling of cloth on the patio. I got up carefully (it was still pitch dark) and half opened the wooden door, my heart beating madly, ready to scream like a banshee as soon as I saw the Green Gang assassins. But that's not who it was. That dark shadow was Lao Jiang, doing his tai chi exercises by the light of a small Chinese lantern hanging from a beam. I don't know what made me approach instead of going back to my *k'ang*, but I did. Not only that, I also suddenly heard myself say, "Could you teach me, Mr. Jiang?"

The antiquarian stopped and smiled. "You'd like to learn tai chi?"

"If you wouldn't mind . . ."

"Women can also practice tai chi if they want," he murmured to himself.

"Will you teach me?"

"Not today, madame. It's late. We'll have our first class tomorrow morning."

So there I stayed, sitting on a bench, watching Lao Jiang slowly move and turn until he finished the day's session. There was truly great harmony in that strange dance, a mysterious beauty. I felt it all the more because someone so much older could move so agilely and so slowly as well, making it all the more difficult. That tai chi must have been the secret to how amazingly flexible the Chinese people were, and I wanted to learn it. I was approaching fifty with dizzying speed and definitely did not want to end up like my mother and grandmother, sitting in an armchair all day, full of aches and pains.

We left the inn a short while later. Biao led the way, carrying a long pole with a lantern dancing on the end, projecting a faint circle of light. It was dawn. Roosters could be heard crowing on patios, and a few shop-keepers were sweeping the ground in front of their stores. We walked only a few blocks. Soon we crossed an arched bridge over a canal and were in front of Zhonghua Men. I couldn't imagine what it must have looked like from afar, but it was certainly impressive—overwhelming, even—up close. What enemy would have dared to so much as dream of taking that colossal fortress, which actually consisted of four consecu-tive gates, each one as impregnable as the last? In fact, according to what Mr. Jiang told us, Zhonghua Men had never been attacked. Invading armies preferred to try to storm Nanking from anywhere else rather than be massacred at that defensive post truly worthy of Goliath.

"The complex measures forty-five *ren* from east to west and forty-eight from south to north," Mr. Jiang proudly told us.

"About three hundred and ninety feet long by four hundred and twenty feet wide," Paddy clarified after some thought. "The *ren* is an ancient measurement of length equal to a little over eight feet."

"It's enormous!" my niece blurted out, her head tilted back to take in the whole monstrosity. "How will we ever find Wei's bricks? There must be millions of them! And look at these walls—they've got to be fifty or sixty feet high!"

"We'll go to where the soldiers hid," Lao Jiang proposed as he walked toward the hulking mass. "If I wanted to hide something behind a brick, I'd try to find somewhere as far away from people as possible, somewhere discreet, and as you can see, there is nothing discreet about these walls and gates."

"Can't you just picture the physician Yao up on a ladder or hanging down from some ropes, removing a brick and hiding something behind it?" Biao asked before bursting out laughing.

The antiquarian turned and smiled at him.

"You're absolutely right, young man. That's why I think the under-ground tunnels in Zhonghua Men are the best place to start. Up to seven thousand soldiers could be hidden there, as well as food and weapons."

Biao lit up like a lightbulb. I was furious at the way Lao Jiang ignored my niece yet didn't hide the fact that he'd taken a shine to Little Tiger. It wasn't fair. I was getting tired of the old man's derogatory attitude toward women.

"There are twenty-seven underground rooms in the Zhonghua Men complex," Mr. Jiang continued as we followed him through a strange door in the wall, shaped like a squat little cross. "We'll have to examine them all. How many candles do we have, Paddy?"

"Don't worry, we've got plenty. I brought a good handful."

"Give us each one, please. Biao's lantern doesn't give off quite enough light."

Despite the pleasant morning temperature outside, it was terribly cold inside. Both the walls and the stairs leading down into the bowels of the earth were covered in a slick mold that could cause us to lose our footing if we weren't extremely careful.

With our candles lit, we started the slippery descent in single file, watching every step the person in front of us took. Tichborne snorted every now and then, Fernanda whimpered as we slowly descended, and I tried to contain the claustrophobia that was beginning to constrict my throat. Suddenly a happy thought lifted my spirits: How many days had it been since I'd had an anxiety attack? I could have sworn I hadn't had one since we left Shanghai. It was wonderful!

"Snakes!" Biao howled, raining on my parade. I thought I might die.

"Quiet!" Tichborne shouted rudely.

"Let me out of here!" Fernanda begged, turning to leave. I was left no choice but to give her a good pinch as soon as she came near.

"Calm down and be quiet," I whispered to her in Spanish. "Or do you want Lao Jiang to look down on you even more? Let's show them we're not damsels in distress who faint because of a little snake."

"But, Auntie . . . !"

"Keep going or I'll send you back to Shanghai on the first boat to leave Nanking."

Fernanda had a very strong sense of pride and didn't say another word. Rubbing her arm to ease the pain where I'd pinched her, she swallowed her fear and her tears. Together, one after the other, the two of us continued descending until at last we reached the first of many long tunnels carved out in the basement of Jubao Gate. Now, this was more like it. Despite the extraordinary dimensions, the walls were normal height, so it and the ceiling, also made of bricks, could be examined without too much difficulty.

"Let's not waste any time," Lao Jiang said.

The five of us quickly began to inspect every inch of that tunnel. The bricks were all quite different in terms of color (black, white, red, brown, yellowish, orangish, and gray), likely because of the different materials used to produce them. The ones on the floor were worn to varying degrees, having been stepped on by thousands of soldiers over the centuries. All of them, however, were exactly the same shape and size (about sixteen inches long by eight inches wide). I carried my notebook in one hand and the candle in the other, straining my eyes so as not to get confused by the jumble of characters that identified each brick. Although they all had long inscriptions that looked like chicken scratches engraved in the clay before it was baked, none of them contained the characters Wei, Xin'an, and Chekiang.

We didn't find those characters in the second tunnel or in the third, not even in the fourth or fifth. The morning passed without success, and it was coming on noon when we were in the fifteenth tunnel. One of the smallest and best preserved, it looked as though it had been used more as a storeroom than a hiding place for soldiers.

Suddenly Paddy Tichborne cried out jubilantly. "Here! Here!" he shouted, hoisting his candle like a flag to get our attention.

Luckily, no one else was in those abandoned galleries.

"Here!" the Irishman kept shouting, even though we were all by his side, looking down at the bricks he was pointing to on the floor. "There are tons of them!"

He was right. Underneath our feet were ten, a hundred, a hundred and fifty, two hundred—exactly 282 bricks bearing the mark of the artisan Wei and his place of origin, Xin'an in Chekiang.

"They're the only black and white bricks on the floor," Paddy remarked, running his hand over the smooth skin on his head.

Lao Jiang startled, as if he'd had a sudden revelation.

"It can't be. . . ." he murmured, walking into the center of the room. "That would be crazy. Bring all the candles! Look at this, Paddy. It's a game of Wei-ch'i!"[21]

"What?" Tichborne exclaimed, moving to join the antiquarian. Fernanda, Biao, and I rushed to bring light to the places Mr. Jiang indicated.

"Take a good look!" Mr. Jiang implored, more excited than we'd seen him thus far. "Nineteen rows by nineteen columns of bricks . . . no doubt about it, the floor is the board. Now look only at the black and white ones. It's a game! Each player has already made over two hundred moves."

"Not so fast, Lao Jiang!" the Irishman objected, holding him by the arm. "It could be just a coincidence. The bricks might be laid randomly, that's all."

The antiquarian turned and stared at him with a frozen expression.

"I've been playing Wei-ch'i my whole life. I recognize a game when I see one. I taught you, or did you forget? And in case you hadn't noticed, the name of the Prince of Gui's physician friend is Yao, the same as the wise emperor who invented Wei-ch'i to teach the slowest of his sons, and the name of the brick manufacturer is Wei, 'surround.' It all makes sense."

I had no idea what this Wei-ch'i they were talking about was. I thought the floor looked more like a huge game of checkers or chess with its black and white squares (although there were many other colors of brick there as well). It was unlike any sort of board game I'd ever seen. To begin with, there were many more squares than necessary, in the neighborhood of two or three hundred. What I didn't know was that the white and black ones weren't squares but the game pieces themselves.

"Don't you know what Wei-ch'i is, Young Mistress?" I clearly heard Biao whisper to my niece not far away. "Really?" The boy sounded so incredulous I was about to turn and remind him that my niece and I were from the other side of the world, but Paddy Tichborne had heard him, too.

"Outside China," the Irishman began, trying to escape the antiquarian's cold stare, "Wei-ch'i is known as Go. The Japanese call it Igo, and they were the ones who exported it to the West, not the Chinese."

"But it's a Chinese game," Lao Jiang qualified, turning back to look at the floor.

"Yes, it's a truly Chinese game. According to legend, it was invented by Emperor Yao, who ruled around the year 2300 B.C."

"Everything in this country is over four thousand years old," I said.

"In reality, madame, it may be much older, but written records only begin at about that time."

"In any event, I've never heard of Go either," I added.

"Do you know the rules, Biao?" the antiquarian asked.

"Yes, Lao Jiang."

"Then explain them to Mme De Poulain, so she doesn't get bored while Paddy and I study this game. And bring more light, please."

We lit a few more candles, and Lao Jiang had us set them on the bricks that were not black or white. By the looks of it, those two were the only ones that counted.

"All right, then, mistress," Little Tiger began, nervous at being given such an important task. Fernanda stood by my side and was listening, too. "Imagine that the board is a battlefield. The winner is the one who has taken the most territory at the end. One player uses white stones, and the other uses black stones. Each one takes a turn and puts a stone on one of the three hundred and sixty-one points where the nineteen vertical and nineteen horizontal lines intersect. That's how they mark out their territory."

That's why I saw so many squares! Three hundred sixty-one no less! You'd have to invent eleven new chess pieces to play on a board like that.

"And how many pieces does each player have?" Fernanda asked.

"White has one hundred eighty. Black, which always begins the game, has one hundred eighty-one," he said. "Now, Wei-ch'i doesn't have many rules. It's easy to learn and a lot of fun. All you have to do is gain territory. The way you take it from your opponent is by getting his stones off the board, surrounding them with your stones. Of course, that's the hard part"—he grinned—"because your enemy tries to stop you. But once a stone or a group of stones has been surrounded, it's dead and taken off the board."

"And since that space is surrounded," my intelligent niece commented pensively, "it doesn't make sense for the loser to put pieces back inside."

"Exactly. That territory belongs to the player who surrounded it. That's where the name Wei-ch'i comes from. *Wei*, as Lao Jiang said, means 'surround' or 'encircle.'"

"And *ch'i*?" I wanted to know.

"*Ch'i* is any kind of game, mistress. Wei-ch'i, pronounced like that, the way I just said it, means 'Surrounding Game.'"

A short distance away, Mr. Jiang and Paddy were having a much less amicable conversation.

"But what if it's black's turn?" Paddy asked angrily, his cheeks and ears as red as if they were on fire.

"It can't be. The legend says it's white's turn."

"What legend?" I asked, raising my voice so they'd hear.

"Ah, madame!" Tichborne replied, turning toward me with great affectation. "This damn shopkeeper swears that the game at our feet is an old Wei-ch'i problem known as 'The Legend of Lanke Mountain.' But how can he be sure? There are two hundred eighty-two pieces on the board! Could someone really remember the exact position of each one? And even if that were the case, whose turn is next—black or white? That could completely change the outcome of the game."

"Sometimes, Paddy," Lao Jiang said, coldly emphasizing each sylla-ble, "you're like a monkey that shrieks when it's been bitten by a flea and doesn't know enough to scratch. Keep banging your head against the bars to see if that gets rid of your itch. Listen, madame, one of the most famous Wei-ch'i legends, one every good player knows,[22] tells of a great mountain located in the province of Chekiang—note that here we find another clue with respect to the artisan Wei and the Prince of Gui's message. As I was saying, on this mountain in Chekiang, around 500 B.C., there lived a young woodcutter named Wang Zhi. One day he walked higher than usual looking for wood and came upon a couple of old men playing Wei-ch'i. Since he was a great enthusiast, he placed his ax on the ground and sat down to watch them. It was a very interesting match, and time flew by, but just before the game was about to end, one of the old men turned to him and said, 'Why don't you go home? Or are you going to stay here forever?' Wang Zhi was embarrassed and stood up to leave, but when he reached for his ax, he was surprised to see the wooden handle fall apart in his hands. When he got back to his village, no one recognized him and he didn't recognize anyone either. His fam-ily had disappeared, and his house was a pile of rubble. Astonished, he came to realize that over a hundred years had passed since he left to look for wood and that those old men must have been two of the immortals who secretly live in the mountains of China. Wang Zhi retained the entire game in his mind. Like the good player he was, he could remember each and every one of the moves. Unfortunately, he hadn't seen the end, so he didn't know who won, but he did know it was the white's turn to move next. This is known as 'The Legend of Lanke Mountain,' because *lanke* means 'rotten handle,' just like the handle on Wang Zhi's ax. The layout of the game has been reproduced in various old collections of Wei-ch'i games and is exactly the one represented by the bricks here."

"And no one has been able to solve the problem in the last twenty-five hundred years?" Fernanda asked innocently.

"Exactly!" Paddy burst out with a laugh. "Besides, Lao Jiang, how many times have you seen the famous Lanke diagram[23] to know for sure this is it?"

Mr. Jiang placed one knee on the ground and leaned over a group of black bricks. "Not often, that's true," he admitted without moving. "Once or twice at most. But just as I know the legend, I know that Lanke Mountain from the story is located in what is now Quzhou, formerly Xin'an, province of Chekiang. I suspect that a Ming hiding place was built right here under our feet when the Jubao walls and gates were built. Every member of the Ming family must have known about it and used it as needed. When the Prince of Gui gave the second piece of the *jiance* to his friend Yao the physician, the fact that he had the same name as the emperor who invented Wei-ch'i must have reminded the prince that this place existed. That's why he sent Yao here. He probably told him which bricks to move, even though that isn't in the document we found in the hundred-treasure chest."

"So what do we do now?" I asked.

"We think, madame," Paddy replied. "This game can be devilishly subtle, just like the Chinese themselves."

"But, Mr. Tichborne," Biao protested in a voice that suddenly became serious, "it's not difficult at all."

As the boy cleared his throat, Lao Jiang crossed the distance between them in an instant and grabbed him by the scruff of the neck—though he had to lift his arm to do so, because Biao and he were the same height.

"Show us," he demanded, pushing the boy into the middle of the room. Little Tiger seemed like more of a cub than ever, poor thing.

"I'm sorry, Lao Jiang. I don't know what I was saying," he squealed, intimidated, and began to beg and plead in Chinese. Though we couldn't understand a word, we knew exactly what he was saying.

"Don't speak unless you're capable of following through," the antiquarian chastised, letting him go.

Biao fell and mumbled something inaudible.

"What? What did you say?"

"If it's white's turn to play . . ." the boy said in a wisp of a voice. "I . . . I don't know who's going to win, but white's next move has to be to eliminate the two black stones in *jiao chi* between the southwest corner and the south side."

"*Jiao chi?*" Fernanda repeated. The girl's Chinese accent wasn't all that bad.

"In *atari*,[24] in check . . ." Paddy Tichborne tried unsuccessfully to explain. "When the next move threatens to capture stones that are surrounded everywhere but the spot that's about to be taken—"

"Enough, Paddy!" Lao Jiang exclaimed. "We can't waste any more time. Biao's right. Look."

Paddy politely ignored the antiquarian.

"What I mean is, the stones that are about to be surrounded are in *jiao chi*; that is, they're about to die. That doesn't mean the end of the game, of course. It's just that those stones are definitely going to be taken off the board."

"And as Biao said," Mr. Jiang concluded, kneeling next to the southern wall of the tunnel, just in front of the stairs we'd come down, "these two black stones are in fact in *jiao chi*, so I'm going to take them out of the game this instant."

"How are you going to get them out?" I asked in surprise. "Those stones . . . I mean, those bricks have been there for six hundred years."

"No, madame," the antiquarian reminded me. "Physician Yao was here in 1662 or 1663 by order of the last Ming emperor. If we're right, they were taken out and put back just two hundred sixty years ago."

"Besides," Paddy interjected condescendingly, "for thousands of years the Chinese have made their mortar out of a mixture of rice, sorghum, lime, and oil. It won't be hard to remove."

"Their buildings have certainly stood up well over the centuries!" Fernanda commented with an ironic smile. Was it my impression, or had the girl lost weight? I shook my head to erase the optical illusion: Chinese clothing could be very deceiving.

By then Lao Jiang was using the handle of his steel fan to scrape around the bricks. The resulting dust formed a gray cloud lit by a ray of midday sun coming obliquely down the gloomy stairwell. We all watched in silence, eager to see what would happen next.

The bricks came loose without his having to dig very much at all. The two were actually one long piece, joined on their shortest sides and set over a worm-eaten wooden board that was also easy to remove. When it was gone, and even though we were blocking the light as all of us tried to see at once, we discovered a sort of *bishachu* like the one in Rémy's office. It was very deep, and the sides cut into the granite were perfectly smooth. Paddy brought a candle closer, and way at the bottom we saw an old bronze box covered in green rust, exactly like the one we took out of Yuyuan Lake in Shanghai. There was also a metal cylinder with pale gold decorations. According to Lao Jiang, this was a Ming document case that would be worth a fortune on the antiquities market. He took the case out first, but apart from its being truly beautiful, there was absolutely nothing inside. Not so with the bronze box. There was the second piece of our *jiance*, with its old green threads and six bamboo slats. I couldn't see very well, but it didn't look like there were written characters on it, just seemingly meaningless drops of ink. Lao Jiang, however, let out a happy whoop.

"It's the missing piece of the map!"

"We'd better go," Paddy commented, standing up with a groan. "There's not enough light in here. Oh, my knees!"

"Let's put everything back in its place," the antiquarian said. "First the wood and then the bricks. We'll put what's left of the mortar back along the joints. It won't be perfect, but with the humidity it'll hardly be noticeable in a few days."

"Come on, let's get out of here," the journalist insisted. "I'm starving."

Suddenly the light coming down through the stairwell disappeared. Unconsciously, we all turned to look, but the light from the candles didn't reach that far; that area was completely in shadow. Lao Jiang passed the bronze box to Paddy.

"Get back," he whispered. "Move over into that corner."

"The Green Gang?" I stammered, obeying his order.

The antiquarian didn't have time to answer. Less than a second later, ten or fifteen thugs with knives and guns had slipped into the tunnel and were threatening us, shouting hysterically and gesturing aggressively. A terrible thought crossed my mind: There were too many of them. This time Lao Jiang wouldn't be able to handle them alone. A single gunshot could finish off any of us in an instant. We were easy prey. The ringleader was screaming more than anyone else. He walked quickly over to Lao Jiang and seemed to be demanding the box. The antiquarian remained calm and spoke without getting upset. The others pointed their guns at us. I could feel my niece sidling up to me. I lifted my arm very slowly, so as not to provoke anyone, and wrapped it around her shoulders. Lao Jiang and the Chinese thug continued conversing, one speaking quietly and the other shouting. On my left I could feel Biao also moving closer in search of protection, so I put my left arm around him and pulled the two of them close to calm them down. The strangest thing of all was that I wasn't scared. I really wasn't afraid. Instead of gasping for air and having heart palpitations, I had a clear mind, and the only thing worrying me was that something could happen to Fernanda or Biao. I felt them shaking, but I was strong, and it felt wonderful. Hadn't the very idea of death terrified me for years? Now that it was staring me right in the face, how was it that I couldn't have cared less? As the antiquarian and the assassin continued talking, I

realized how much of my life I had wasted worrying about this moment, when in reality it made me feel more alive than ever, stronger and
more secure than I'd felt in ages. If only I could have gone back in time
and told myself how silly my anxiety was! Distracted by such happy
thoughts, I hadn't realized that Mr. Jiang was speaking to us.

"Get down on the ground as soon as I tell you to," he said calmly,
and then continued speaking to the ringleader. The men looked like
nothing more than simple, shirtless coolies in dirty, threadbare, blue
linen pants, with shaved heads and fierce expressions. I imagined that
some of them must have been involved in Rémy's murder.

"Now!" the antiquarian suddenly yelled. The children and I threw
ourselves down on the ground, and I could tell by the mass of flesh
pressed against my head that Paddy had put himself in front to protect
us. There wasn't time to think of much else. A volley of gunfire burst
through the tunnel, and bullets began smashing into the walls right
next to us. The echo down there in the basement made it sound like an
extravagant fireworks display. Great shivers were rocking Biao, so I
pulled him tighter. If we were going to die, let it be together. Just then a
terrible spasm rippled through the Irishman's body, and he cried out.

"What's wrong, Mr. Tichborne?" I shouted.

"I've been hit!" he moaned.

I let go of the children and carefully started to lift my head to check
on the Irishman, but bullets were zipping through the air past my ears,
so I was left no choice but to duck back behind the injured man's great
belly. Fortunately, the bursts of gunfire began to die down and stopped
just a short while later. A sudden, deafening silence took hold.

"You can get up now," Lao Jiang advised.

The children and I slowly stood. I was completely perplexed by what I
saw farther along the tunnel: A handful of inert bodies lay on the ground,
and past them, on the other side of the Wei-ch'i board, through a thick
cloud of gunpowder, I could see several waxed-paper lanterns illuminating
a squad of soldiers carrying rifles with fixed bayonets. What was going on
there? Who were those soldiers? Why was Lao Jiang happily greeting the

one with a long saber on his belt (so ridiculously long that it scraped the floor)? A moan from Tichborne brought me back to reality.

"Mr. Tichborne," I called, trying to turn him over so I could see how badly he was hurt. "Are you all right, Mr. Tichborne?"

The journalist's face was contorted in pain as he gripped one leg that was bleeding profusely. Blood was the most plentiful thing in that room: a stream of it from the dead assassins was seeping in between the bricks on the floor—the Wei-ch'i stones—and filling the air with the strange smell of hot iron mixed with gunpowder. This was no time to get dizzy, I told myself. First I needed to see how the Irishman was, and then the children. I leaned over Tichborne and examined him: He was severely hurt. The bullet had shattered his right knee, and he was in urgent need of medical attention. Fernanda was as white as a sheet, her eyes sunken and brimming with tears. Biao, who'd been shaking uncontrollably, was now sweating copiously, fat drops of perspiration sliding down his face and falling to the ground like tears. The two had been frightened beyond belief and hadn't yet woken from the nightmare.

"How are you, Mme De Poulain?" Lao Jiang asked, startling me half to death. I had thought he was still talking to the soldier.

"The children and I are fine," I replied in a gravelly voice that didn't sound like mine. "Tichborne's been shot in the leg."

"Is it serious?"

"I think so, but I'm no nurse. We need to get him to a hospital."

"The soldiers will take care of that," he said, turning back to the captain with the saber and saying a few words to him.

Four or five armed young men—none of whom looked much better than the Green Gang thugs—immediately came over, set their rifles on the ground, and took charge of Tichborne. They carried him outside, laughing uproariously at the journalist's screams of pain.

"I owe you an explanation, Mme De Poulain."

"And I've been waiting for one, Mr. Jiang," I asserted, confronting him.

Some of the soldiers began to hoist the dead bandits over their shoulders without a second thought, while others got started throwing sand on the floor to soak up the blood.

"I've been a member of the Chinese Nationalist Party, the Kuomintang, since 1911, when it was founded by Dr. Sun Yat-sen, a man I'm honored to know and consider a good friend. He is financing this expedition and placed this battalion of soldiers from the Army of the South at our disposal here in Nanking to protect us from the Green Gang. Captain Song," he said, nodding at the man with the saber, who was standing a respectful distance away while his subordinates cleaned up, "knew of our arrival as soon as we disembarked yesterday and has kept us under discreet surveillance in order to help us if necessary."

I couldn't believe what I was hearing. I was having trouble understanding that this crazy adventure had been politically motivated from the very start.

"Do you mean to say, Mr. Jiang, that the Kuomintang knows what we're looking for?"

"Of course, madame. As soon as I learned what was in the hundred-treasure chest and guessed at the scope of the Qing and Japanese imperial restoration project, I immediately called Dr. Sun Yat-sen in Canton and explained the situation. Dr. Sun was equally alarmed and ordered me to secretly continue searching for Shi Huang Ti's lost mausoleum. However, there is no need to worry: My part of the treasure will undoubtedly go to the Kuomintang, but the rest of you will get what was agreed upon. My party simply wants to avoid the folly of a monarchical restoration any way we can."

One group of soldiers was sweeping the blood-soaked sand into baskets, while another came behind, throwing buckets of water over the areas that had already been swept, so as to finish putting the tunnel back in order. Soon the only sign of what had happened here would be the bullet holes in the walls. But no, not even those would remain. A couple of young men wearing military caps and bearing a small blue flag with a white sun in the middle[25] began to fill the holes with mud. This was obviously a very well-organized cover-up operation. What were we going to do now that Tichborne was out of commission?

"We have to carry on, madame. We can't stop now. The Green Gang is nipping at our heels, but just like the Kuomintang, they don't want this whole affair to come to light. It would be a national scandal with unimaginable repercussions. China cannot allow that. Western powers would try to take control of the discovery and exploit it in their favor or in favor of whoever they most wanted to keep bleeding this country dry. There is much at stake, and remember, we still need to find the lost mausoleum. Let's do this right, wouldn't you say, madame?"

"But what about Tichborne?"

"He knows nothing of the Kuomintang. He'll stay here for now and can follow us if he recovers quickly. In the meantime he'll be well looked after by Captain Song."

"Does Captain Song know anything about all this?"

"No, madame. He had orders to watch us from a distance and intervene if we were attacked. That's all. Dr. Sun and the two of us are the only ones who know."

"And the Emperor Puyi, and the imperial eunuchs, and the Japanese, and the Green Gang . . ."

Lao Jiang smiled. "Yes, but we have the *jiance*."

"Actually, Mr. Jiang, *I* have the *jiance*," I corrected him, leaning down to pick up the bronze box that Tichborne had dropped when he was wounded and that now lay by Fernanda's feet.

Mr. Jiang smiled even wider.

"I just have one last question. Do the Green Gang and everyone else know that the Kuomintang is involved?"

"I hope not. Dr. Sun doesn't want the party officially connected to this."

"He's afraid of ridicule, isn't he?"

"Yes, something like that. He believes that the Kuomintang is in a delicate situation, madame. We don't have the support of foreign imperialist powers. They think we're endangering their economic interests. They know that if we unite China under a single flag, we'll take away all the abusive commercial prerogatives they acquired by means of trickery over the last hundred years. Dr. Sun's Three Principles of the People—Nationalism, Democracy, and the People's Livelihood—mean the end of their huge economic benefits. If all this came to light . . . well, they might destroy the Kuomintang."

"And who's going to protect us on the rest of our trip? I don't need to remind you that not only are we being followed by the Green Gang, but we're about to go into areas that are controlled by warlords."

"I still have to sort that out."

"Well, make it quick," I advised, taking the still-terrified Fernanda and Biao by the hand. "These children are frightened to death. You deceived us, Mr. Jiang, by hiding an important aspect, *une affaire politique*, with respect to this dangerous journey. I don't think you're as honest as you try to appear. In my opinion you're putting your political interests above all else and are simply using us. I admired you up until now, Mr. Jiang. I thought you were an honorable defender of your people. Now I'm beginning to think that, like all politicians, you're a greedy materialist who doesn't consider the personal consequences of your decisions."

I don't know why I said all that. I was really very angry with the antiquarian, but I wasn't entirely sure if it was for the reasons I had listed or because I was so frightened. In any event, I'd just been through the most terrifying experience of my life and had actually come out of it with grace, feeling stronger than ever. I was beginning to note great changes inside. Still, there was nothing wrong with chastising Lao Jiang. He appeared livid, and I think my words had truly hurt him. I felt a little guilty but then immediately thought, He lied to us! And I no longer felt bad.

"I'm sorry to hear that," he said. "I'm simply trying to save my country, madame. You may be right, and up to now I may have been using you. I will meditate on it and give you a more satisfactory explanation. If I need to apologize, I will."

We left Jubao Gate and climbed into the back of an old truck that bounced over the cobblestones through the devastated streets of Nanking to Kuomintang headquarters, an ugly building painted the colors of the party's undulating flag and protected by tall barbed-wire fences. Inside, the soldiers on guard were playing cards and smoking. We were given something to eat and allowed to wash up. Tichborne lay on a cot in a dark, smelly little room, bleeding profusely, until a doctor in Western clothing arrived and began to treat him. By then someone had brought our things from the inn, and Biao, calmer now, told Fernanda and me that in the next room Lao Jiang and Captain Song were making arrangements for us to leave that night. I couldn't remember what our next stop was and therefore had no idea where we'd be heading. I did, however, have in my possession, safe and sound, the little box we'd removed from beneath the bricks at Jubao Gate. Since we were alone and no one was paying the least bit of attention to us, I decided it was the perfect time for the children and me to take another look at what was inside.

"You're going to open it, Auntie?" Fernanda asked, quite shocked. "What about Lao Jiang?"

"He can look at it later," I replied, lifting the greenish bronze lid. The little bundle of bamboo slats with the tiny spots of ink was still inside. Biao leaned curiously over it as soon as I held it out on my open palms. There was electricity in the Kuomintang barracks, and thus the little marks were clearly visible. "Mr. Jiang said it was a map, Biao. What do you think?"

I don't know what inspired me to put such faith in that wiry-haired young man. If he'd been bright enough to solve the Wei-ch'i problem all on his own, why wouldn't he be able to see something I couldn't because of my Western education?

"Yes, it's got to be a map, *tai-tai*," he confirmed after looking at it for a while. "I don't know what these tiny little characters next to the rivers and mountains say, but the drawings are quite clear."

"All I see are lines and dots," Fernanda said, jealous of her servant's important role. "A small round dot here, a square over there . . ."

"These dotted lines are rivers," Little Tiger explained to her. "Can't you see by the way they're shaped, Young Mistress? And these lines are mountains. The circles must be lakes, because they're on the dotted lines or near them, and this square here might be a house or a monastery. There's something written inside, but I don't know what it says."

"Would you like to be able to read in your own language, Biao?" I asked.

He thought for a moment, then shook his head and snorted, "Too much work!"

It was the answer any school-aged child in the world would have given, I thought as I hid a smile. I felt for Biao, but Lao Jiang wasn't about to let another day go by without teaching him more of the ideograms in their thousand-year-old writing system. So, between the French that Fernanda was teaching him and the Chinese calligraphy Lao Jiang would surely teach him, Little Tiger was in for a very busy trip.

"Do you know what we could do while we're waiting for Mr. Jiang?" I cheerfully asked the children. "We could play Wei-ch'i."

"But we don't have any stones," Fernanda objected, brightening up nonetheless. She'd been very withdrawn ever since the firefight in the tunnel, and I'd been worried.

Biao had jumped up and was running to the door.

"I saw a board!" he exclaimed, beaming. "I'll ask if we can use it."

He came back with a rectangular wooden board under his arm and two soup bowls filled with black and white stones.

"The soldiers loaned it to me," he explained. "They'd rather play Western cards," he added disparagingly.

Well, I thought to myself, some of the antiquarian's ideas were taking hold.

Shortly after they brought us dinner, Mr. Jiang finally appeared with a smile that became even more affable when he saw the three of us completely absorbed in the Wei-ch'i board. In all truth, such an exquisitely difficult game wasn't my cup of tea but Fernanda caught on right away.

Biao surrounded my stones easily and with amazing speed, devouring entire large groups while I was focused on some ridiculous attack I never managed to carry out. Fernanda was better at defending herself and at least didn't let him massacre her as he had me. Over the next nine days, as we headed up the Yangtze to Hankow on board a sampan, mistress and servant spent many an hour bent over the board (Lao Jiang got the soldiers to give us the game), caught up in fierce battles that began right after the morning classes and sometimes lasted until dark.

We weren't able to say good-bye to Tichborne, because the doctor was still operating on him when we left the barracks. Not much of his right knee remained, we were told. Even if it healed, he'd always limp. I had the impression it was extremely unlikely that he'd meet up with us later on our trip; his situation seemed quite dire. In any event, and even though I had always found him repulsive, I had to admit he'd been very brave during the confrontation, and the children and I would always be thankful for his protective gesture.

Our sampan was an authentic houseboat that, compared to the barge we'd taken to Nanking, could almost be considered a luxury hotel: It was big and wide, with two enormous sails that opened like fans, a couple of rooms inside the cabin—covered by a beautiful red roof made of sagging, woven bamboo—and a deck flat enough for Lao Jiang and me to do our tai chi. The only problem was the river current, which at times was quite rough. The skipper was a member of the Kuomintang, and the sailors under his command were two of Captain Song's soldiers, charged with looking after us until we reached Hankow. There, another military detachment would take care of our security. Lao Jiang was afraid the Green Gang might attack us on the river, so he had the soldiers watch the riverbanks day and night while he studied all the boats we passed, whether Chinese or Western, with an eagle eye. He hoped that heavy traffic on the river would make us invisible or that Pockmarked Huang's men would have thought we'd taken the Nanking-Hankow Express. For my part, whenever we passed a large city, I was afraid he'd say, "Let your rapidity be that of the wind, your compactness that of the forest. In raiding and plundering be like fire, in immovability like a mountain," and off we'd go, carrying our bundles, leaving the sampan to take some other, much less comfortable, means of transportation. But days passed, and we arrived in Hankow without any difficulty.

I remember one night of that trip in particular as I sat in the bow, engulfed by the incense the skipper used to ward off mosquitoes, watching the oil lamps sway to the rhythm of the current. In the distance you could hear the water as it lapped up on shore. I suddenly realized I was tired. My Western life seemed far, far away, and everything of value there seemed absurd here. Traveling has that magic power over time and reason, I thought, forcing us to break the habits and fears that have become thick chains around our necks without our even noticing. I wouldn't have wanted to be anywhere else right then, nor would I have exchanged the breeze off the Yangtze for the air in Europe. It was as if the earth were calling out to me, as if, all of a sudden, the immensity of the planet was begging me to explore it, to not lock myself up again in that petty little circle of trickery, ambition, and jealousy that is the world of painters, gallery owners, and art dealers in Paris. What did I have to do with all that? Now they were mandarins in the original sense of the word: pedantic officials who decided what was art and what wasn't, what was modern and what wasn't, what the public should like and what it shouldn't. I was sick of it. I just wanted to paint, and I could do that anywhere, without competing with other artists or having to fawn over gallery owners and critics. I would search for the First Emperor's tomb in order to settle Rémy's debts, but if it all turned out to be nothing more than madness and we were unsuccessful, I would never be afraid again. I would start all over with nothing. Surely the nouveau riche in Shanghai, so snobbish and chic, would pay well for a Western painting.

That very special night for me was September 13. Two days later we arrived in the port of Hankow. Shortly after disembarking, Fernanda and I learned from the international cables they received at Kuomintang headquarters that General Primo de Rivera had led a coup d'état in Spain on that day. Backed by the far right and with King Alfonso XIII's blessing, he had dissolved the democratically elected constituent assemblies and declared a military dictatorship. Martial law, censorship, political and ideological persecution now reigned in our home country.

Chapter

3

We hadn't even arrived, and the antiquarian was already anxious to leave Hankow. He said that it was a dangerous, violent city and we weren't safe there. Indeed, not only were there sampans, junks, tugs, and merchant steamships crowding the river, there were also a good number of huge warships from various countries, a sight that both terrified me and also convinced me we had to leave as soon as possible. However, it seemed we had to wait until the Kuomintang provided us with a detail of soldiers for protection. The captain of our sampan was clearly nervous, gripping the wheel and maneuvering through the fog, steering clear of those enormous metallic hulls.

Hankow,[26] located at the confluence of the Yangtze and one of its largest tributaries, the Han-Shui, was the last port upriver from Shanghai, over nine hundred miles away, before the great Blue River became impassable. For commercial reasons, Western powers declared the city a free port and built magnificent Concessions. Unfortunately, these had experienced nothing but bad luck: The city was practically razed to the ground during the 1911 revolution to overthrow Emperor Puyi, and just seven months before we arrived, there had been serious clashes and killings between members of the Kuomintang, the Kungchantang (the Communist Party, founded just two years prior in Shanghai), and the military troops that controlled the area.

The two soldiers who had accompanied us from Nanking, dressed as sailors, ran barefoot alongside our rickshaws to Kuomintang headquarters, their hands on the revolvers hidden beneath their clothes. I was beginning to dislike being in the hands of a militarized party more than attacks by the Green Gang and would much rather have found lodging in some insipid *lü kuan*. Still, I was well aware that we needed their protection. Now that we were back on dry land in Hankow, how much longer until the thugs who'd had been chasing us since Shanghai attacked again?

We passed crumbling old walls and were leaving the once-elegant British Concession when a superb Victorian building caught my eye, its façade destroyed as if by gunfire. This beautiful, Colonial-style architecture was everywhere, and everywhere it had been blanketed in an unfathomable destructive hate. As had happened in Europe not that long ago, the war in China had forced people to revert to vandalism, vulgarity, and barbarism. Hankow was a powder keg. We definitely needed to leave this place as soon as possible.

Luckily, everything was already prepared at the barracks. The commander had received a telegram, and our transportation, gear, and escorts had been ready and waiting for several days. It was then we heard of the coup in Spain, and I had to explain the scope of the disaster to my ignorant niece. Seeing that there was a phone, Mr. Jiang asked if he could call headquarters in Nanking to check on Paddy Tichborne. Unfortunately, the news was not good.

"There's gangrene in his right leg, and they're going to have to amputate," Mr. Jiang said when he joined us in the back patio, where the horses were stabled. "They transferred him to a hospital in Shanghai just yesterday, because he refused to be operated on in Nanking. It seems he created quite a ruckus when they gave him the news."

"That's awful," I murmured, deeply saddened.

"Let me give you your first lesson in Taoism, madame: Learn to see the good in the bad and the bad in the good. They're both the same thing, like yin and yang. Don't worry about Paddy," he recommended with a smile. "He'll have to forgo alcohol for a while, and later, when he's better, he can write about the experience in one of those insufferable books of his, and it will do very well. Europeans love stories about the dangerous Orient."

He was right. I loved them, too, especially the ones by Emilio Salgari.

"But what if he says something he shouldn't about the First Emperor's tomb?"

Lao Jiang narrowed his eyes and smiled mysteriously. "We still don't have the third piece of the *jiance*, and no one really knows where the mausoleum is. Besides, our friend Paddy has many months of painful recovery before he can even begin to think about writing," he added. "Are you ready, madame? We've a long journey ahead of us overland to the Qin Ling Mountains and the ancient Taoist monastery of Wudang. I estimate it'll take about a month and a half to cover the eight hundred *li* between here and there."

A month and a half? How long was a *li*? I wondered. A mile? Half a mile?

"It's about two hundred and fifty miles from Hankow to Wudang, heading westnorth,"[27] the antiquarian clarified, reading my thoughts. "But it's not an easy route, madame. We'll cross a valley for several days and then have to climb to the top of Wudang Shan.[28] That's where the Prince of Gui sent his third friend, the master geomancer Yue Ling, with the last piece of the *jiance*, remember?"

Unexpectedly then, the antiquarian wrapped the fist of one hand in his other, held it at face height, and bowed low before me.

"However, madame, I must apologize before we leave," he declared, remaining in that humble pose. "You were right in Nanking when you said I was using you to achieve my goals. Please forgive me. Nevertheless, I would also like to take this opportunity to ask your forgiveness in advance, since this is something I will continue to do. I appreciate your company, your Western point of view, and the things you are trying to teach me."

Despite my doubts about his sincerity, "I accept your apology," I replied, imitating both hands and bow, "and I thank you for all that you are teaching me. However, I would also like to take this opportunity to ask you to rise above your disdain for women and treat my niece with the same consideration you give our young servant. This is very important to us and would place you in a position more befitting the world we live in today."

Lao Jiang gave no indication of being upset by this—just the contrary, perhaps. We thus left Hankow in good spirits, with a new understanding that ultimately made the long, grueling trip a little less disagreeable.

Our convoy consisted of ten horses and mules loaded with boxes and bags, five soldiers dressed as peasants, and the four of us who walked alongside. Neither Fernanda, Biao, nor I knew how to ride, and Lao Jiang did but preferred to walk. Walking, he said, increased your energy, blood flow, and resistance to illness. It also allowed you to study the elegant, internal architecture of nature up close, and therefore study the Tao. While they were not the same, one was a reflection of the other. We had just left Hankow through Ta-tche Men Gate when I realized that my niece was no longer the chubby, unattractive girl in a prissy black bonnet who'd shown up at my house in Paris that day. She was swimming in her blue servant's outfit and now wore a Chinese hat. Fernanda had lost several pounds, and her figure, though hard to discern under the cotton clothing, seemed much more girlish. Just like her mother's and grandmother's, Fernanda's weight was a result of gluttony, a sin she was completely safe from on the trip, because our Chinese meals were quite frugal. The sun had also darkened her face, giving it a healthy glow and making her disguise that much more believable.

Not wanting to draw attention to ourselves, we took everything we needed in the boxes loaded onto the horses and mules: dried food, bricks of pressed tea, barley for the animals, fur hats, heavy coats for the mountains, woven soft bamboo mats for sleeping, blankets, rice wine, something called "tiger liquor" for the cold, and spare canvas sandals. There was also a first-aid kit—a Chinese first-aid kit! It of course contained nothing known in the West, but instead things like ginseng, reed tisanes, roots, leaves, dried begonias for the lungs and respiratory problems, Six Harmonies pills to fortify the organs, and an elixir called the Three Immortals to treat stomach and indigestion ailments. We hoped we could avoid the towns along the way, skirting all of them by means of endless detours. The Green Gang had presumably lost our trail after being defeated in Nanking, and we were unlikely to see them again, but it was best to go as covertly as possible, just in case. There was always a chance they might already know our next destination and be there, waiting to attack as soon as we reached the monastery. Mr. Jiang was convinced we'd be out of danger as soon as we reached Wu Tang: There wasn't an army in China that would dare attack a group of Taoist monks who were masters in the martial arts.

"Shaolin?" I asked the antiquarian as we walked on a wide embankment between terraced plots one afternoon, the setting sun in front of us. We were approaching a little village called Mao-ch'en-tu in the middle of a small valley.

"No, madame. Shaolin is a very aggressive, external style of Buddhist martial art. The monks in Wudang practice internal, Taoist styles intended for defense. These are much more powerful and secret, based on strength and flexibility in the torso and legs. The two techniques are completely different. According to tradition, the tai chi they practice at Wudang Monastery—"

"They practice tai chi in Wudang?" I interrupted excitedly. I'd been studying these exercises with Lao Jiang over the last few weeks while my niece played Wei-ch'i with Biao. Not only had I discovered a love for it, but the required concentration calmed my nerves and the physical effort was conditioning my poor, out-of-shape muscles. The slow, gentle, fluid movements—which had names as exotic as "Grasp Bird's Tail," "Strum the Pei Pa" or "Wild Stork Spreads Wings"—were much more exhausting than any normal exercise. What I found most difficult, however, was the strange philosophy surrounding each and every one of the movements and the breathing techniques that went along with them.

"In fact," Lao Jiang explained, "tai chi as we know it today originated in Wudang with Zhang Sanfeng, one of its most famous monks."

"So then it didn't come from the Yellow Emperor?"

Lao Jiang smiled, holding on tightly to his horse's reins. "All tai chi comes from the Yellow Emperor, madame. He gave us the Thirteen Essential Postures that Zhang Sanfeng worked on at Wudang Monastery in the thirteenth century. Legend has it that one day Zhang was meditating out in the countryside when he suddenly saw a heron and a snake begin to fight. The heron was futilely trying to impale the snake with its beak while the snake was unsuccessfully trying to strike the heron with its tail. Time passed, and neither of the two exhausted creatures had managed to vanquish the other, so they each went their separate ways. Zhang realized that flexibility was the greatest strength and could be beaten by gentleness. As you know, the wind cannot break the grass. As of that moment, Zhang Sanfeng devoted himself to applying this discovery to the martial arts and dedicated his life as a monk to developing the Tao, achieving incredible martial and healing abilities. He studied the Five Elements, the Eight Trigrams, the Nine Stars, and the *I Ching* in depth, all of which allowed him to understand how human energy works and how to attain health, longevity, and immortality."

I was stunned into silence. Had I heard properly, or had the gurgling stream running alongside confused me? Had Lao Jiang just said "immortality"?

"You're not going to tell me that Zhang Sanfeng is still alive, are you?"

"Well, he began studying at Wudang when he was seventy years old, and the chronicles say he died when he was a hundred and thirty.

That is what we, the Chinese, call immortality: a long life in which to perfect ourselves and attain Tao, true immortality. Of course, that's how we've characterized it in the last millennium or millennium and a half. Before that, emperors were often poisoned by the immortality pills their alchemists prepared for them. In fact, the First Emperor, Shi Huang Ti was obsessed with discovering the secret to eternal life and went to great lengths to find it."

"And here I thought the so-called immortality pills, the elixir of eternal youth, and the transmutation of mercury into gold were cooked up in medieval European pots."

"No, madame. As with many things, alchemy was born in China and is thousands of years older than that in your medieval Europe—which is nothing more than a cheap imitation, if I may say so."

❧

That night we camped on the outskirts of Mao-ch'en-tu. We'd been traveling for three days, and the children—as well as those of us who weren't such children—were growing tired. However, Lao Jiang insisted we were going too slowly and needed to pick up the pace. He repeated, "Let your rapidity be that of the wind, your compactness that of the forest. In raiding and plundering be like fire, in immovability like a mountain," more than once, but Fernanda, Biao, and I grew increasingly battered from sleeping on the ground. Our feet were blistered, and our legs ached at the end of a long day. It was too difficult a trek for inexperienced hikers such as we. Some nights we stayed with peasants whose houses appeared all alone in the middle of nowhere, but my niece and I found we much preferred sleeping out under the stars with the snakes and lizards, rather than subjecting ourselves to the torture of fleas, rats, cockroaches, and the unbearable smells in houses where people and animals shared the same room, covered in the owners' gobs of spit and pig and chicken excrement. China is a country of smells. You'd have to grow up there not to suffer as Fernanda and I suffered. Luckily, there was plenty of water throughout Hubei province, and we were able to wash ourselves and our clothes quite regularly.

It soon became obvious we were not the only group traveling through the vast Chinese countryside with a long journey ahead. Whole families and entire small villages moved as slowly as a death caravan along the same paths, fleeing hunger and war. It was shockingly sad to see parents carrying their sick, malnourished children, plus old men and women piled into handcarts along with the furniture, bundles, and objects that must have been all the meager family possessions that hadn't been sold. One day a man offered his young daughter to us in exchange for a few copper coins. I was horrified, even more so when I learned that this was commonplace, because daughters, unlike sons, are not valued very highly within the family. My heart broken, I wanted to buy and feed the poor, hungry girl but Lao Jiang angrily forbade it. He said we'd only encourage human trafficking if we participated in it and that furthermore, as soon as word got out, we'd be hounded by hundreds of parents, all with the same aspirations. The antiquarian explained that people had begun to emigrate to Manchuria, fleeing banditry, famines due to droughts or floods, as well as the abusive taxes and murders by military leaders indifferent to the people's misery. Manchuria had been an autonomous state since 1921, governed by the dictator Chang Tso-lin,[29] a former warlord. Economic activity was possible given the relative peace there, and the poor were thus arriving en masse.

Immersed in this river of humanity, we continued our journey to Wudang, passing villages that had recently been plundered and burned, the ruins still smoldering amid fields strewn with graves. We often came across regiments of mean-looking soldiers who shot anyone that resisted their thieving and violence. We luckily never suffered anything of the sort. On days we'd seen someone die, or bodies dumped by the side of the road, Fernanda and Biao couldn't sleep or would startle awake. It said a great deal, Lao Jiang commented, that the living would abandon their dead in strange lands without a proper burial in a country where ancestors and family are of the utmost importance.

Fifteen days after we left Hankow—and exactly one month after Fernanda and I had arrived in China—near a place called Yang-chia-fan a group of armed, dirty, ragged-looking young men planted themselves in our way and refused to let us pass. While the soldiers quickly took aim, the children and I, frightened half to death, sought cover behind the horses. One strapping young man walked toward Lao Jiang and, after wiping his hands on his threadbare pants, held out a medium-size folder. The antiquarian opened and carefully examined it. They then began to talk. Both seemed quite calm, and Lao Jiang gave no indication of danger. Though I was dying of curiosity, I didn't ask Biao what they were saying. I was afraid it might unnerve the rest of the group still standing behind their leader and didn't want them to begin firing on us or severing the tendons in our knees. The antiquarian came back a few minutes later. He said something to the soldier in charge, and they all lowered their weapons but remained looking stern. I couldn't help but notice an extreme expression of displeasure cross one of their faces.

"Don't be alarmed," Lao Jiang said, resting a hand on the saddle of the horse we were hiding behind. "They're young peasant members of the Kungchantang, the Communist Party's revolutionary army."

"And what do they want?" I whispered.

Lao Jiang furrowed his brow before answering. "It seems, madame, that someone from the Kuomintang let the cat out of the bag."

"What? How can that be?"

"Calm down," he entreated, looking worried. "I don't want to believe it was Dr. Sun Yat-sen himself, but he is an old friend of Chicherin, minister of foreign affairs for the Soviet Union," he reflected out loud. "In any event, the Nationalists and the Communists have been on good terms to date, so it's not going to be easy to discover where the leak occurred."

"So they know the whole story of the First Emperor's tomb?"

"No. They just know it has something to do with money, with riches. That's all. The Kungchantang, of course, now wants its share. These young men will join our soldiers to help protect us from the

Green Gang and the imperialists. That is their mission. The one I was talking to is their leader. His name is Shao."

That Shao wouldn't take his eyes off Fernanda, and I didn't like it one bit.

"Tell them to stay away from my niece," I declared.

Political relations between the Kuomintang and the Kungchantang may well have been good, but during our entire strange journey neither the five Nationalist soldiers nor the Communist Shao and his six men said a word to one another, unless it was to argue at the top of their lungs. I think they might have killed one another if they could have, and if *I* could have, I'd have sent them all to some far-off village. Things were not that simple, however: Every now and then, when least expected, shots and shouting in the distance would make our hair stand on end. Our twelve champions, despite their political differences, would draw their weapons and surround us, hurry us off the trail and hide us behind a nearby mound or hill, protecting us until they were certain the danger had passed. Even so, coexistence had become quite uncomfortable, and by the time we reached the Qin Ling Mountains in mid-October—a month after we'd left the Yangtze in Hankow—I couldn't wait to walk through the monastery door. Unfortunately, the hardest part of our journey was still ahead; our ascent into the mountains would coincide with the start of winter. The stunning green landscapes bathed in white mist took our breath away. It even took our horses' breath away, although our supplies had dwindled and they were only carrying barely enough food and replacement sandals to last us. We were now wearing coats with enormous, long sleeves—called "sleeves that stop the wind"—and fur hats, but Shao's young peasants braved frigid nights and glacial winds in the same clothes they'd been wearing in Yang-chia-fan. I waited in vain for them to leave, to refuse to travel farther, but the first snowfalls only made them laugh uproariously, and a small fire was enough for them to survive the icy nights. It was clear they were used to the harshness of life.

We finally reached a town called Junzhou.[30] Located between Mount

Wudang and the Han-Shui, that very same tributary of the Yangtze we'd left behind in Hankow a month and a half earlier, Junzhou was home to the immense, crumbling Jingle Palace. It was an ancient villa that had belonged to Zhu Di,[31] third Ming emperor and a devout Taoist, who built almost all the temples in Wudang in the early fifteenth century. We decided it would be a good place to spend the night. Since it was a remote, deserted, and decaying mountain village, there were no inns, of course, so we had to stay with a well-off family. After receiving a considerable sum in payment, they allowed us to use their stables and provided us with a huge pot of a stew made of meat, cabbage, turnip, chestnuts, and ginger. The children and I had water, but, to my dismay, the rest drank a nasty sorghum liquor that warmed their blood and kept them up most of the night, amid passionate political speeches, party hymns, and boisterous arguments. I didn't see the antiquarian when the children and I curled up next to the animals for warmth, on the smelly straw and blankets. But there he was the next morning before sunrise, silently doing his tai chi before he'd even had his usual cup of hot water for breakfast. Careful not to wake Fernanda and Biao, frozen to the bone, I joined in the exercises, watching the first morning light illuminate a perfectly blue sky and enormous sheer peaks covered in forest, the green hue changing without ever losing any of its intensity.

Lao Jiang turned to me as soon as we'd finished the closing movement.

"The soldiers won't be able to accompany us to the monastery," he said very seriously.

"I'm so happy to hear that!" I burst out. A lovely warmth was spreading through me despite the cold morning air. Tai chi had an odd way of bringing the body to just the right temperature. According to Lao Jiang, once you'd reached a state of relaxation, your mind and internal energy adjusted to one another like yin and yang. Even though the water in the pots was frozen, I felt splendid, as I did every morning after tai chi. It was no wonder I'd survived a trek of nearly 250 miles after years and years of total inactivity.

"The Green Gang could infiltrate Wudang Monastery, madame."

"Then let the soldiers come with us."

"I'm not sure you understand, Elvira," he replied. I was completely taken aback by his use of my name for the very first time and looked at the antiquarian as if he'd lost his mind, but he paid no attention and continued speaking. "The Kuomintang soldiers could, perhaps, stay in the vicinity of the monastery with special permission from the abbot. The Kungchantang, however, oppose anything they consider superstition and doctrine that goes against the interests of the people. They could use rifle butts and bullets to take their beliefs out on the sacred images, palaces, and temples there. We can't have one and not the other. If the Communists stay, so do the Nationalists."

"Then what about our security?"

"Will over five hundred monks and nuns who are experts in the martial arts be enough?" he asked ironically.

"Oh, my!" I replied, quite relieved. "Nuns as well? So Wudang is a mixed monastery? You didn't tell us that."

The antiquarian turned around and ignored me, as was his habit when something annoyed him. However, I was beginning to understand that his actions weren't as rude as I'd first thought; they were simply the awkward reaction of someone who doesn't know what to say or do and therefore keeps quiet, avoiding the situation. The antiquarian was human, too, though it might not seem so at times.

Thus our militiamen remained in Junzhou, after serious protests by the Kuomintang lieutenant and Shao, the Communist leader. I felt most sorry for the village people who were going to have to put up with them until we returned. However, Lao Jiang's order was unequivocal and his reasons logical: We had to respect the monks of Wudang. It would not be in our best interest to arrive with armed soldiers. Such a show of force was a mistake we could not make, especially because this time we weren't going to find a hidden *jiance*. As indicated in the Prince of Gui's message, we were to humbly ask the abbot of Wudang if he'd be so kind as to give us the old piece that had been in the monastery's possession for centuries, ever since it was left there by a mysterious master geomancer named Yue Ling. I didn't say a word to anyone, of course, but I seriously doubted the success of our mission. I honestly wondered why the abbot of Wudang would ever agree to something like that.

The antiquarian, the children, and I headed toward the first of the monastery gates, still accompanied by our twelve guardian warriors. Xuanyue Men means "Gate to the Mysterious Mountain," of all things, and this worried me right from the start. Mysterious Mountain? That didn't sound good—almost as bad as putting a gate on a mountain. Was there anything more absurd? However, Xuanyue Men was actually just a sort of commemorative stone arch some sixty-five feet high, the tops of its four columns and five tiered roofs lost in the forest canopy. It was certainly beautiful and didn't inspire the distrust its name suggested. There we said good-bye to the soldiers, who returned to Junzhou. Bundles in hand, we began our climb to the top, walking up the wide stone steps of a single ancient staircase that Lao Jiang called the "Divine Corridor" after he'd read the name carved into the rock. The first temple we came to was called Yuzhen Gong;[32] it was colossal but empty. All we could make out from the door was an enormous silver-plated statue of Zhang Sanfeng, the great tai chi master, in the main hall.

We climbed until night fell. At times the staircase was a steep trail and at others a narrow pass alongside a stunning precipice. I never lost my nerve or trembled in fear at the thought of falling. Life had become so much simpler now that I faced real danger. Since the Mysterious Mountain was a Taoist pilgrimage site, there was on it a humble inn that attended to the faithful. We were thus able to have an adequate dinner and sleep on warm, bamboo k'angs. We resumed our climb the next morning, looking out over beautiful pine forests lost in a sea of clouds as we headed toward the peak. We could now make out several strange buildings, dotted here and there with red walls and curved green roofs from which glittering gold reflections shot up into the clean, clear morning air. There was a symmetrical, ordered, harmonious look to the scene, like at Rémy's house, as if each building had been placed in the exact spot destined for it from the beginning of time. My legs, much stronger than before, carried me at a good pace, and I didn't tire. I could feel my muscles flex as I firmly set one foot in front of the other. In the sunlight the many grasses and bushes carpeting the ground exhaled new fragrances that heightened my senses, and the screeching, howling monkeys living on the Mysterious Mountain lent a real sense of adventure to our climb. Where had all my pathetic neuroses gone? Where were all my ailments? Was I the same busy, worried Elvira of Paris and Shanghai? I had almost decided I wasn't when I was distracted by an ugly insect that flittered next to the stone staircase and gave off the most incredible incandescent sparkles.

We finally reached the first inhabited monastic buildings of Wudang. Lao Jiang hit a bell with a piece of wood that was hanging down on a chain. A short while later, two monks came out of the gong—out of the temple, that is—wearing typical blue Chinese outfits but with strange little black hats and white gaiters up to their knees. Both smiled politely and bowed in greeting several times. Their faces were wrinkled and weathered by the sun and mountain air. So these were the great masters in martial arts? I wouldn't have guessed it in ten thousand years—the magical Chinese number that symbolizes eternity.

Lao Jiang approached courteously and spoke to them for quite some time.

"He's introduced himself and asked to speak privately with the abbot about a very important matter regarding the old master geomancer Yue Ling," Biao explained. If Fernanda had lost a minimum of twenty pounds, Little Tiger had grown four inches or more since we left Shanghai. He was already taller than me and it wouldn't be long before he was taller than the antiquarian. He'd soon be a giant! Unfortunately, his newly acquired height made him clumsy, with an awkward gait, hunched shoulders, and bones that seemed to be disjointed.

"He didn't introduce anyone but himself," Fernanda observed, annoyed. "Are you sure he didn't say anything about us?"

"No, Young Mistress."

Fernanda snorted and turned her back, as if to look out at the view. The sky was beginning to cloud over, and rain was on its way.

Lao Jiang came back a moment later, and one of the monks began running up the Divine Corridor as if the steep staircase were nothing more than a gentle slope.

"We're to wait here until I'm called by the abbot, Xu Benshan."[33]

"Until *we're* called?" I asked pointedly.

"What do you mean?"

"I'd like to meet with the abbot as well."

A look of annoyance crossed the antiquarian's face. "But you don't speak Chinese," he objected.

"I know quite a few words and can understand much of what's being said," I replied haughtily. "I'd like to be there when we're received by the abbot. Biao can explain anything I don't understand."

Silence was his only reply, but I couldn't have cared less. Lao Jiang and I were now the adults responsible for this journey, and even though being a Westerner put me in an uncomfortable and not terribly useful position, I was not about to become a silent pawn who existed only to serve the antiquarian's political interests.

The rain began to pour down before the abbot's messenger returned, and we were forced to take shelter in Tazi Gong. As we sat on reed mats, two young novices dressed in white served us some lovely tea. It was my niece who noticed that one of them was a nun about her age.

"Look, Auntie!" she exclaimed, pointing out the female novice with her eyes.

I smiled. I was beginning to like Wudang.

Suddenly Fernanda turned to the antiquarian. "Did you notice, Lao Jiang, that one of them is a young girl?"

I didn't have time to silence her with a pinch and was stunned when the antiquarian turned his head toward her and replied, with absolute calm, "Yes, Fernanda, I did."

Good Lord in heaven! Lao Jiang was speaking directly to my niece!

How had such a miracle occurred? He'd called me by my first name the day before, and now he was talking to Fernanda after having ignored her for nearly two months, as if it were absolutely normal. Either there was a prudent waiting period for these things according to protocol or the antiquarian had taken heed of our gibes and comments (which seemed highly unlikely). Whatever the reason, the miracle had occurred, and we couldn't allow it to go unnoticed.

"Thank you, Lao Jiang," I said with a bow.

"What for?" he asked with a smile, obviously well aware of what I meant.

"For using my name and speaking to my niece. Thank you for the trust you've shown in us."

"Haven't you been using my friendship name for months now?"

After a few seconds of surprise, I realized it was true. Both the children and I had inappropriately been using that form of address (Lao Jiang, "Old Jiang") because that's what Paddy Tichborne called him. I smiled to myself and continued to drink my tea. Fernanda, unaware of our conversation, was still watching the young nun. My niece's curiosity had been piqued by their similar ages and their cultural differences.

About an hour later, the messenger monk returned with news that the honorable Xu Benshan, abbot of Wudang, would receive us immediately in the Library Pavilion of Zixiao Gong, Purple Cloud Palace. Elegant litters with latticework windows were placed at our disposal to shelter us from the rain, which was now really pouring down, and this is how we traversed the final stretch into the very heart of the Mysterious Mountain.

Purple Cloud Palace was enormous, similar in size to a medieval walled city. We crossed a stone bridge over a moat before arriving at the main temple, raised up on three terraces carved into the side of a mountain and made of red lacquered wood with bright green ceramic roof tiles edged in gold. The litters stopped, and we got out in front of a high stone staircase. Although the porters didn't say a word, it seemed obvious we were to climb those stairs in order to meet Xu Benshan. The place was extraordinary, majestic, I might even say imperial, although the relentless rain gave us little opportunity for quiet contemplation. Splashing through the puddles, our sandals and hats soaked, we hurried up the stairs as a few monks dressed like those from Tazi Gong came down toward us carrying waxed straw umbrellas. Both groups met on a landing between two sets of stairs, next to a gigantic three-legged black iron pot. Gesturing kindly, the monks sheltered us from the deluge and accompanied us into the pavilion, where, with all the simplicity and magnificence of such an important Taoist abbot, Xu Benshan was waiting for us, seated at the end of a room lit by torches. All along both walls lay hundreds, perhaps even thousands, of ancient bamboo slat *jiances*. It was breathtaking but hardly seemed the place to receive a visit from strangers. Unless, of course, the abbot knew why we were there and what we were looking for; I surmised that Lao Jiang's message including the name of the old master geomancer Yue Ling had been an arrow that had hit its target.

Imitating the monks ahead of us, we approached the abbot in short, ceremonious steps. Once in front of him, we all bowed deeply. The abbot had no beard or mustache, and his hair was covered by a hat that looked like an upside-down pie. There was nothing to help me guess his age. He was wearing a sumptuous flowing brocade tunic with a black-and-white motif, and his hands were hidden inside his long "sleeves that stop the wind." One thing I did notice when I bowed were his black velvet shoes, and they had me absolutely perplexed: The raised leather soles were nearly four inches high. How could he walk on them? Or didn't he walk? In any event, despite his undeniably aristocratic bearing, Xu was otherwise a very normal man. Actually quite small and thin, he had a pleasant face and jet-black, almond-shaped eyes. He looked nothing like a dangerous warrior—no one in the monastery did, and yet this was their most famous trait.

"Who are you?" he inquired, and I was ecstatic when I realized I'd understood him. To our surprise, Lao Jiang responded with the truth, telling him all about Fernanda and me, including our full names in

Spanish. Biao acted as interpreter, because my niece was determined not to learn a single word of Chinese. I found it helpful, since I still didn't know many words and expressions, and there were times when I couldn't correctly identify the musical tone that made a word mean one thing or another.

"And what is this matter regarding the master geomancer Yue Ling that you wish to speak to me about?" the abbot asked after the introductions.

Lao Jiang took a deep breath before answering. "The abbots of this great monastery of Wudang have had a piece of an old *jiance* in their possession for two hundred sixty years. It was entrusted to them for safekeeping by the master geomancer Yue Ling, close friend of the Prince of Gui, known as Emperor Yongli, last Son of Heaven of the Ming dynasty."

"You are not the first to come to Wudang demanding such piece," the abbot replied after a moment's reflection. "But, as I told the emissaries sent by the current Emperor Hsuan Tung of the Great Qing, I must advise you that we know nothing of this matter."

"Puyi's imperial eunuchs have been here?" Lao Jiang asked worriedly.

The abbot was surprised. "I see you know they were eunuchs from the imperial palace. Indeed, Chief Eunuch Chang Chien-Ho and his assistant the vice-eunuch general came to Wudang just two moons ago."

Such silence fell over the hall that we could hear the faint rattling of the bamboo slats and the soft crackling of the flames in the torches. Our conversation had come to a dead stop.

"What happened when you told them you knew nothing about the *jiance*?"

"I don't think that is any concern of yours, Antiquarian."

"But were they furious? Did they attack?"

"I repeat: That is none of your concern."

"I must tell you, Abbot, that they've been pursuing us since Shanghai. The Green Gang, the most powerful mafia in the Yangtze delta—"

"I know the gang you speak of," Xu Benshan murmured.

"—was hired by the eunuchs and the Japanese imperialists to attack us in Yuyuan Gardens, where we found the first piece of the ancient book. They then attacked in Nanking as soon as we found the second piece. We made the trek here, traveling in stealth over eight hundred *li*, to ask you for the last piece so we can complete our journey."

The abbot remained silent. Something Lao Jiang said had given him pause.

"Do you have those two pieces of the *jiance* here with you?" he asked at last.

Lao Jiang's eagle eyes sparkled. They were entering his territory now: it was time to negotiate. "Do you have the third piece in Wu-dang?"

Xu Benshan smiled. "Give me your half of the *bufu*, the insignia."

Lao Jiang was taken aback. "What insignia do you mean?"

"If you cannot give me your half of the *bufu*, I cannot give you the third and final piece of the *jiance*."

"But, Abbot, I have no idea what you're referring to," Mr. Jiang replied. "So how can I give it to you?"

Xu Benshan sighed. "Listen, Antiquarian. Though you may be in possession of the first two pieces of the *jiance*, obtaining the third will do you no good if you do not have, or do not know you have, the indispensable objects that will allow you to achieve your goals. Note that at no time have I asked you about the purpose of your journey, and my only interest is in helping you. I believe that your words are sincere and that you have the first two pieces of the ancient letter from the foreman. But I must not disobey the Prince of Gui's instructions, which were brought to us by Master Yue Ling. The third piece is the most important, and it bears special protections."

Lao Jiang's face was a mask of astonishment. I could practically hear the wheels turning as he tried to recall anything about an insignia from the Prince of Gui relating to the *jiance*. I was also racking my brain, calling up every word from the scene in the original text of the miniaturized book where the prince spoke with his three friends. But if memory served me correctly, no one mentioned any sort of insignia there. No insignia, no emblem, no badge of any kind. Perhaps it was in the *jiance* itself, in the very letter from Sai Wu to his son Sai Shi Gu'er, on the bamboo slats. But no, because as far as I remembered from what Lao Jiang read when we were on the barge on the Grand Canal, there was no reference to any such object there either. It was completely absurd. The only insignia we'd seen and actually held in our hands since this crazy story of royal treasures and imperial tombs began was in the hundred-treasure chest, and that had nothing to do with the Prince of Gui or the *jiance*. It was that thing . . . that half a gold tiger. My thoughts came to a sudden halt. The half a tiger. It was then I understood: The gold tiger and the Tiger of Qin!

"Lao Jiang," I called out in a small voice, my heart racing. "Lao Jiang."

"Yes?" he replied without turning around.

"Lao Jiang, do you remember that gold figurine we saw in the hundred-treasure chest? The one of half a tiger, its back covered in ideograms? I think that's what the abbot's referring to."

"What are you talking about?" he asked angrily.

" 'The Tiger of Qin,' Lao Jiang. Don't you remember? Shi Huang Ti's military insignia."

The antiquarian's eyes grew wide in understanding. "Biao!" he thundered.

"Yes, Lao Jiang," the boy replied in a frightened voice.

"Bring me my bag. Immediately!"

We had left our bundles at the entrance, so Biao dashed off. In the meantime the abbot stuck up a conversation with me.

"Mme De Poulain, what motivates a foreigner like you to make such a dangerous journey through an unknown country?"

Lao Jiang translated the question for me and gestured to indicate that I should speak freely. "Financial difficulties, *monsieur l'abbé*. I'm a widow, and my husband left me with debts I'm unable to pay."

"Do you mean it is out of necessity?"

"*Exactement.*"

The abbot remained silent for a few seconds, during which time Biao returned and handed Lao Jiang his travel bag.

The antiquarian began to dig around inside and, completely distracted, mumbled, "The abbot has asked me to translate these lines from the *Tao Te Ching*[34] by Lao-tzu: 'Because one is moderate, one may be said to follow the way from the start. / Following the way from the start, one may be said to accumulate an abundance of virtue. / Accumulating an abundance of virtue, there is nothing one cannot overcome. / When there is nothing one cannot overcome, no one knows his own limits.'"

"Please thank the abbot very much," I replied, trying to memorize the long Taoist thought Xu Benshan had just given me. It was truly beautiful.

Lao Jiang pulled out the lovely hundred-treasure chest, wrapped in silk. He'd carried it with him the whole time, and I hadn't even thought to wonder what had happened to it, whether the antiquarian had hidden it well before we left Shanghai or whether he had it with him. I felt completely irresponsible, foolish—and it wasn't the first time. The little gold tiger cut lengthwise in half shone in the antiquarian's hand, his face an inscrutable mask as he approached the abbot. We could be wrong, of course; it was far too early to celebrate.

But Xu Benshan, abbot of Wudang Monastery on the Mysterious Mountain, smiled broadly when he saw what Mr. Jiang was holding. Reaching into his wide left sleeve with his right hand, he pulled out something that he kept concealed in his fist until the antiquarian handed him our half of the tiger from the hundred-treasure chest. Then, with great satisfaction, he joined the two pieces and showed the figurine to us.

"This *hufu* belonged to the First Emperor, Shi Huang Ti," he explained. "It was used to guarantee the transmission of orders to his generals, since both pieces had to fit perfectly. The calligraphy along its back is written in the ancient *zhuan* style, so this tiger predates the decree to unify the writing system and is therefore over two thousand years old. It reads, 'Insignia in two parts for the army. The right one is held by Meng Tian. The left comes from the Imperial Palace.'"

Where had I heard the name Meng Tian before? Was he the general Shi Huang Ti had given the task of building the Great Wall?

"Will you give us the third piece of the *jiance* now?" the antiquarian barked in what I considered a completely inappropriate tone. The good abbot was only fulfilling the Prince of Gui's instructions and seemed very willing to help us however he could. Where exactly did that attitude come from? Lao Jiang was impatient—an unlikely mistake for such a good negotiator.

"Not yet, Antiquarian. I told you the third piece of the *jiance* bears special protections. There is still one left."

He gestured to the two monks who had remained at attention by the door at the end of the hall, and both rushed out. They returned moments later, walking unsteadily, carrying a thick bamboo pole on their shoulders. Four big square stone slabs were hanging down from the pole, swinging in the air. Once the monks reached the front of the hall, they set the stones down carefully, untied them, and stood them up in a row, facing us. Each contained one beautifully carved Chinese ideogram. The abbot began to speak, but young Biao was so spellbound by the stones—and likely exhausted from the effort his work as volunteer interpreter required—that he forgot to do his job. My sweet niece, all kindness and understanding, snapped a few brusque words at him, and the poor boy was immediately brought back to the harsh reality of his life.

"Emperor Yongle ordered that these four fundamental characters from Wudang Taoism be carved into our beautiful Nanyan Palace," the abbot was saying. "Do you know how to put them in order?"

Of course Lao Jiang would know, I thought. "The first one on the left is the ideogram *shou*, which means 'longevity,' " the antiquarian began explaining to us. It was a very complicated ideogram, with seven horizontal lines of differing lengths. "The next is the character *an*, the principal meaning of which is 'peace.'" Luckily, *an* was much simpler and looked like a young man dancing the fox-trot, knees bent and crossed, arms outstretched. "Next is *fu*, the character that represents 'happiness.'" The ideogram for happiness was quite peculiar: two arrows in a row, pointing to the right in the upper part and underneath them, two squares and a sort of hammer with arms hanging down. "And, finally, the ideogram *k'ang*, which sounds similar to 'bed' but means 'health.'" I quickly memorized the shape of a man with a trident through him, a whip held out in his left hand and five twisted legs.

"And what exactly do we have to put in order?" I asked, puzzled.

"We'll talk about it later," Lao Jiang muttered, tight-lipped.

"Give it some thought," the abbot concluded as he got to his feet. "Take your time. There are twenty-four possibilities, but you will have only one opportunity. You are welcome to stay in Wudang as long as you like. You'll be safe here. In any event, the rainy season has begun, and it's dangerous to leave the monastery in such weather."

We were given a house with a small inner patio adorned with flowers and rooms arranged around it. Lao Jiang took the largest, Fernanda and I the middle one, and Biao the smallest, which was also where visitors were received. The dining room and study were on the second floor, off a narrow wooden latticework balcony that looked out over the puddles that filled the patio due to the endless downpour. The walls were painted with gorgeous frescoes of Taoist immortals, and everywhere was the penetrating smell of the perfumed oil that was burned in the lamps, the incense from the little altars, and what wafted out from the heavy old curtains that covered each of the doorways. It was the best lodging we'd had in nearly two months. In the coming days, two or three young children would appear at various times to bring us food and do the cleaning—although the house always seemed dirty with all that mud and rain.

That night, after we'd spoken with the abbot and as we ate a magnificent soup similar to minestrone, Lao Jiang set out the problem of the four stone characters in a way that we could understand.

"What is most important to a Taoist from Wudang?" he asked, staring at us. "Longevity or perhaps attaining peace, inner peace?"

"Inner peace," Fernanda was quick to say.

"Are you sure?" the antiquarian inquired. "How can you have inner peace if you suffer from a painful illness?"

"Health, then?" I suggested. "In Spain we say that health, money, and love are the three most desirable things."

"But there was no 'money' or 'love' in the four ideograms we were shown," my niece objected.

"Those concepts aren't important to Taoists," the antiquarian said.

"Which ones are?" Biao asked, gulping down a chunk of bread he'd dipped in his soup.

"That's precisely what the abbot has asked us," Lao Jiang replied, doing the same.

"So then we have to put the Taoist objectives of longevity, peace, happiness, and health in order of importance," I concluded.

"Exactly."

"Well, there are only twenty-four possibilities," Fernanda snapped. "How hard can it be?"

"I think we should use the time we'll be here because of the rains to talk to the monks and get the information that way," I said. "It shouldn't be too difficult. All we have to do is find someone willing to tell us."

"That's true!" Biao smiled. "We might even have the answer tomorrow!"

"I hope you're right," Lao Jiang replied, lifting his bowl to drink the last of his soup, "but I'm afraid it won't be that easy. You've got to understand the subtlety and depth of Chinese thought in order to solve this deceptively simple problem. I think the books, those *jiances* that filled the room where we met Xu Benshan, might also be a good source of information."

"But you're the only one who knows how to read Chinese," I noted.

"True. And of the three of you, only Biao knows how to speak the language. I propose the following: I'll look for the information in the monastery libraries, and you, Elvira, with Biao's help, will speak with the monks."

"What about me?" Fernanda asked, somewhat offended.

"You'll take part in the Taoist exercises for novices. What you learn about the Wudang martial arts may also help us with this problem."

As strange as it might seem, my niece didn't protest or fly into a rage, but her lips did turn white and her eyes filled with tears. The last thing she wanted was to be immersed in a culture and practices she completely rejected. But it certainly wouldn't hurt her. Now that she had such a lovely figure and her round face had slimmed and become so attractive, a little physical exercise would be quite good for her.

Each of us got to work the next morning after we'd done our tai chi, washed up, and had a bowl of rice flour with pickled vegetables and tea. Lao Jiang asked the servants for a stack of books that were brought to him in closed cases, and he shut himself up in the study on the second floor. Fernanda received a complete novice's outfit and went off looking despondent, accompanied by two young nuns who were barely able to hold back their laughter. Biao and I cheerfully set out to find a monk willing to chat, warmly greeting everyone we met along those grand cobbled paths. Unfortunately for us, no one seemed willing to converse in the pouring rain, enveloped in a darkness that was more suitable to night than first thing in the morning. Finally, tired and wet, we slipped into one of the temples, where an old master was teaching a group of monks and nuns who were sitting on brightly colored cushions on the floor, as still as statues.

"What's he saying?"

Biao wrinkled his forehead and shrugged his shoulders. "He's talking about the nature of the universe."

"All right, but what's he saying?"

"None of it makes any sense!" the boy protested.

An icy stare was enough to make him quickly start interpreting.

The old master with a little white beard was saying there is an energy that gives life to all things. There is an observable order to the universe, an order that is manifest in the regular cycles of the stars, the planets, and the seasons. The original force of the universe can be seen in such order, and that force is the Tao.

It really was quite complicated, although I attributed a good deal of the complexity to Little Tiger's halfhearted translation.

The Tao gave birth to chi, or vital breath, and that vital breath condensed into the Five Elements: Metal, Water, Wood, Earth, and Fire. These elements represent different transformations of energy and are organized under a duality known as yin and yang, complementary opposites that reciprocally balance and oppose one another, generating movement, evolution, and therefore change, which is the only constant in the universe. Yin is associated with passivity, peace, broken line, Earth, the female, and flexibility; yang with hardness, power, solid line, heaven, the male, and activity. We can become part of the original force of the universe by studying the Tao, but, the master said, since not all people are the same, nor do they all have the same needs and destinies, there are hundreds of ways of achieving this.

Despite my interest I found the ideas very hard to grasp, and I still didn't see the relationship between Metal, Water, Wood, Earth, and Fire, and yin and yang. There is no doubt that everything in life has its yin and yang—its heads or tails, that is—even though the master didn't seem to be making a simplistic assessment in terms of good and bad. Instead he merely asserted that opposites generate movement and change through their relationship with one another.

"It is very important that you learn the relationships between the Five Elements," he was saying, "because the harmony of the universe is based on these, and it is harmony that allows life. Therefore, remember that Fire is associated with light, heat, summer, ascending movement, and triangular shapes; Water with dark, cold, winter, wavy shapes, and descending movement; Metal with autumn, round shapes, and movement inward; Wood with spring, rectangular shapes, and movement outward; and, finally, Earth with square shapes and revolv-ing movement. Yang is born as wood, in spring, and culminates in Fire, in summer. Then it stops, and by stopping, it becomes yin, which appears in autumn, as metal, and in turn reaches its zenith in winter, as Water, putting it into motion again to become yang. The Earth ele-ment balances yin and yang. The Five Elements are also associated with the five directions. Since beneficial energy comes from the south, its element is Fire and it is represented by a red raven; north belongs to the Water element, and its figure is the black tortoise; west corre-sponds to Metal and is symbolized by a white tiger; east is associated with Wood, and its image is that of a green dragon; finally, the center corresponds to the element of earth, and its shape is that of a yellow snake."

Now, that was too much. As quick as a wink, I pulled my Moleskine notebook out of my pocket and made notes by way of little drawings and symbols, using my colored pencils. Biao, still repeating the lesson in Spanish and French, whichever he happened to feel most comfortable with, stared at me as if I were the green dragon or the white tiger.

Although the master spoke quite slowly and Biao had to think hard about some of the words, I don't believe I've ever drawn, scribbled, and covered a page as fast as I did during that class in Wudang. I was actu-ally fascinated by the theory; it opened up a world of possibilities to paint, create, and use in my future compositions, and I couldn't let a sin-gle detail slip past. However, as incredible as it might seem, the speech about the Five Elements wasn't over yet, because not only did they have an intense, complicated life of their own, they were also related to one another in the most original ways.

"The Five Elements are subject to the creative and destructive cycles of yin and yang," the master calmly explained. "Each one can nourish another if they are similar and obliterate it if they are different. In the creative cycle, Metal creates Water, Water creates Wood, Wood creates Fire, Fire creates Earth, and Earth creates Metal. In the destructive,

Metal destroys Wood, Wood destroys Earth, Earth destroys Water, Water destroys Fire, and Fire destroys Metal."

I had such a mishmash of concepts in my head that I could no longer understand anything Biao was translating, but I could go over my notes later. One day, in Paris, all this would bear fruit, and people would never know the source of my inspiration. Just as few knew that the cubism invented by my fellow countryman Picasso was born out of an African mask exhibit he went to several times at the Museum of Mankind in Paris. All you had to do was look at his famous painting *The Girls of Avignon* to know just how much Pablo owed to African art.

In any event, seeing the pained look of boredom on poor Biao's face, I decided that was enough of Taoist philosophy for one day. It was time to head out again in search of a monk who'd be willing to chat with a young boy and a foreign woman about the objective of his life. I put my notebook—now my most treasured possession—in one of the many pockets in my Chinese pants, and with wet feet we picked up our drip-ping, oiled-paper umbrellas off the stone floor. The weather was abso-lutely dismal, and it looked as if the rain wouldn't stop for days.

Unsurprisingly perhaps, we didn't have much better luck. Near mid-day the boy and I sat down next to a little old nun contemplating the nearby mountain peaks, sitting with her legs crossed on a pretty satin cushion at the entrance to a temple. She was so tiny and old that her eyes were barely visible among the wrinkles on her face. Her gray hair was pulled back into a bun, and her fingernails were extraordinarily long. The poor woman was delirious. She said she was born during the heavenly mandate of Emperor Jiaqing[35] and that she was 112 years old. She wanted to know where we were from but couldn't understand what Biao told her about me. To her there was nothing beyond the Middle Kingdom, and therefore I couldn't be from such a place. She waved her hand in con-tempt as if to tell me I was a liar and she wasn't about to listen to my tall tales. Before the conversation went completely downhill, I wanted Biao to ask her, with absolute respect and emphasizing that at her age, with all her experience, surely she could help resolve my doubt, whether it was more important to attain longevity or good health.

The old woman turned on her cushion, revealing milky eyes before snapping, "You don't understand a thing, poor fool! What a question! The most important thing in life is happiness! What's the use of health or longevity if you're unhappy? Aspire always and above all to happiness. Whether your life is long or short, healthy or ill, try to be happy. Now, leave me be. I'm tired of all this talking."

She dismissed us with a flick of her hand and concentrated again on those nearby mountains she mustn't have been able to see at all: It was plain that the white curtain pulled across her eyes had blinded her long ago. Nevertheless, she was smiling as Biao and I walked away toward our house. She truly did seem happy. Might happiness be the first ideogram we could put in its place?

I found Lao Jiang in the study upstairs, reading next to the heat from a brazier. We both agreed it was a good place to start. The principal aspiration of all humans was undoubtedly happiness, and however difficult it might be for us to understand, that was what the monks of Wudang wanted with their quiet, withdrawn life, too.

"The trouble is, we have only one chance," I commented. "There'll be no way to get the third piece of the *jiance* if we're wrong."

"No need to remind me of the obvious," the antiquarian grumbled.

"If you were truly happy, what would you want next? Health, peace, or longevity?"

The antiquarian groaned, letting a hand fall on one of the volumes open on the table. "Look, Elvira, it's not just about discovering what the Taoists of Wudang consider vital priorities. That old nun may indeed have given you the first of the four ideograms, but what matters most is that we have proof to support that position. There is no room for error. The abbot will not allow a single mistake. We need proof, do you understand? Proof that the characters go in a certain order."

For lunch, which Fernanda missed, we had chickpea noodles, vegetables, and a type of bread that looked and tasted very unusual. The little novices came midafternoon to collect our bowls and sweep the house again (they swept twice a day), as well as to fumigate the study using glasses of water perfumed with herbs that supposedly helped protect the books from being eaten by worms. Biao and I didn't go out that afternoon because of the torrential downpour, so Lao Jiang told us a little about one of the classical texts he was reading. It was called the *Qin Lang Jin*, written during the Qin dynasty, the time of the First Emperor, and it spoke of something called *K'an-yu*. This very important thousand-year-old philosophy had changed names over the centuries and became known as "wind and water," or feng shui, and dealt with the harmony between man, nature, and his environment. Lao Jiang hadn't had time to finish reading it, of course, because, apart from its being difficult to understand given the book's archaic, obscure language, he also wanted to make sure he read it very carefully. He was certain he'd find some clues, since the four concepts were mentioned many times.

Fernanda still wasn't back by the time we left the study, so I worriedly sent Biao to find her and bring her straight home. It was late, and the girl had been out all day. Besides, she'd been angry and sad when she left, and I didn't want her to do anything silly. Biao ran off in search of his Young Mistress, and I was left on my own on the covered porch, listening to the hammering rain and watching as it soaked the plants and flowers. Suddenly my heart leaped in my chest and my palpitations went wild. It had been so long since I'd had any cardiac trouble that I was terribly afraid. I began to pace back and forth like a madwoman, fighting the notion that I was going to die that very instant, struck down by a massive heart attack. I tried telling myself it was just one of my spells, but I already knew that, and knowing didn't help a bit. The healthy effects of our journey certainly hadn't lasted long! No sooner had I set myself up in a house than my hypochondria took hold once again. Silenced by the distractions of the last few months, my old enemy rose up full force at the first opportunity. Luckily, Biao and Fernanda soon came through the door, causing a commotion and distracting me from my dark thoughts.

"It was wonderful, Auntie!" Fernanda exclaimed, shaking off water like a dog. The girl was absolutely drenched, and her cheeks and ears were flushed. Little Tiger was looking at her enviously. "I spent the whole day in a huge patio with all the other novices, doing exercises quite similar to tai chi!"

Lao Jiang leaned over the second-floor balcony, a sour look on his face. "What exactly is going on?"

"Fernanda was thrilled with her first day as a novice at Wudang," I commented jokingly, still looking at my niece. It was good to see her so happy; this certainly wasn't the norm.

The antiquarian, suddenly quite pleased, came down to join us. "That's marvelous," he said, smiling.

"It *will be* marvelous," I interjected quite seriously, speaking to my niece, "but right now you'll go dry off and change before you catch pneumonia."

A shadow fell over Fernanda's face. "Now?"

"Right now," I ordered, pointing to our room.

The rain was quite loud so we moved into Biao's room, where visitors were received, and sat on beautifully embroidered satin cushions to wait for Fernanda. Lao Jiang was smiling at me.

"I think you and your niece will find this journey quite enriching," he said.

"Do you know what I learned today?" I replied. "I learned about the theory of yin and yang, and the Five Elements."

He smiled from ear to ear, obviously proud. "You're both learning many important aspects of Chinese culture, the main ideas that gave rise to our major philosophies and served as the basis for our medicine, music, mathematics—"

Fernanda burst through the door like a whirlwind, drying her hair with a fine cotton cloth.

"So," she said as she came in and took a seat, "I obviously wasn't going to understand a thing, right? All of them were Chinese and spoke Chinese, and I thought the whole thing was stupid. Plus, it was pouring rain, and I just wanted to come back here. But then the teacher, the *shifu*, came over and patiently repeated the names and the movements until I could copy them quite well. The rest of the novices followed along, laughing at me at first, but they got down to work when the *shifu* ignored them and only paid attention to me."

She threw the long towel on a little tea table and jumped up to stand in the middle of the room.

"You're not going to give us a demonstration, are you?" I asked, horrified. A look of fury crossed her face, but the antiquarian's presence kept her in check.

"I want to go with Young Mistress tomorrow," Biao then remarked.

"What did you say?" Lao Jiang asked, staring harshly at the boy.

"I said I want to go with Young Mistress tomorrow. Why can't I learn the martial arts, too?"

He might have been tall, but the boy was only thirteen years old, and he'd been terribly bored on our outing that day.

"Absolutely not. Your job is to interpret for your Mistress Elvira."

"But I want to learn to fight," Little Tiger protested, so angrily that I was taken aback.

"Well?" the antiquarian bellowed as he stared at me. "Are you going to let a servant take such liberties?"

"No, of course not," I stuttered, not quite sure what I should do. Lao Jiang stood up and walked over to a lovely vase on the floor in a corner and pulled out a long stick of bamboo.

"Shall I proceed on your behalf?" he asked when he saw the apprehensive look on my face.

"You're going to cane him?" I asked, shocked. "Most certainly not! Put that bamboo down!"

"You are not Chinese, Elvira, and do not know how things work here. Even the highest officers in the imperial court admit there's nothing wrong with a few lashes when deserved. It's an honorable punishment that is to be accepted with dignity. I beg you not to intervene."

It goes without saying that Fernanda and I cried our eyes out as we listened to the whistle of bamboo as it sliced the air out in the patio before smacking Little Tiger's behind. Every crack pained us through and through. The boy certainly deserved to be punished, but sending him to bed without any supper would have been sufficient. In China, however, it was a long-established tradition for servants who overstepped their bounds to receive a good thrashing. Fortunately, the consequences of that calamity were simply that Biao had trouble sitting for a few days. As for the rest, he came into our room the next morning to open the windows and air out the k'angs as if nothing had happened.

The rain continued to pour down, and it was impossible not to feel just a little melancholic in such unpleasant weather. Things only got worse when Fernanda wasn't able to get up for breakfast and I found she had a raging fever. Lao Jiang immediately sent Biao for one of the monastery doctors, who quickly came with all his strange Chinese instruments. Fernanda was shivering under the mountain of blankets we had piled on her, and my worry went through the roof when I saw the monk crush some (not terribly clean) herbs that he dissolved in water and had her drink. I was about to shriek and rail against the witch who was trying to kill my niece with his poisonous, alchemical concoctions, but Lao Jiang held me back, gripping my arms mercilessly as he whispered that the doctors in Wudang were the best in China and that the most respected physicians purchased their herbs from here on the Mysterious Mountain. I still wasn't convinced. I was overcome with guilt that I hadn't thought to bring Western medicine. I'd never be able to forgive myself if anything happened to Fernanda. She had no one else in the world but me, and now that Rémy had died, she was all I had. At my age and with my heart condition, losing the two most important people in my life in less than a year would undoubtedly be the end of me. I simply wouldn't be able to stand it.

I spent the whole morning sitting by Fernanda's side, watching her sleep and listening to her moan as she tossed restlessly. Lao Jiang and Biao had to take care of both of us. They brought me cup after cup of steaming hot tea—I didn't want anything to eat—and gave Fernanda the herbal infusion the doctor from Wudang had prescribed for her. Once, when I couldn't stop the tears streaming down my face, the antiquarian pulled a cushion over and sat next to me.

"Your niece will be fine," he declared.

"But what if she caught that pulmonary bug that's killing millions of your countrymen?" I objected desperately. I was finding it hard to talk, because I could barely breathe.

"Remember the abbot's words from the *Tao Te Ching*?"

"No. No, I don't," I blurted out angrily.

" 'Because one is moderate, one may be said to follow the way from the start. / Following the way from the start, one may be said to accumulate an abundance of virtue. / Accumulating an abundance of virtue, there is nothing one cannot overcome. / When there is nothing one cannot overcome, no one knows his own limits.' "

"So?"

"You, Elvira, need to work on moderation. The *Tao Te Ching* insists that the mind must always be still and at peace, emotions contained and controlled by our will, the body rested, and the feelings calm. Anything else is harmful to our health. A mind that is agitated by heightened emotions only leads to unhappiness and illness. Your objective should always be moderation, a happy medium. Fernandina isn't going to die. She simply has a cold. I don't deny that it could become serious if not treated properly, but she's in very good hands. She'll soon be back in class with the other novices."

"She will not; you can be sure of that! I will not allow her to go to another class!"

"Moderation, madame, please: moderation to face your niece's illness, moderation to confront your financial difficulties, and moderation to stand up to your own fears."

I received the blow he had just dealt with dignity and looked at him out of the corner of my eye, somewhat offended. "What are you talking about?"

"Throughout our trip here, whenever I saw you sitting quietly, gazing into the distance, the look on your face was always anxious and worried. Your tai chi movements are rigid; they don't flow. Your muscles and tendons are stiff. Your chi is blocked at several points along the meridians in your body. That's why the abbot advised moderation. You need to know you can overcome anything in life, because your strength is boundless. Don't be so afraid. Moderation is one of the secrets to health and longevity."

"Leave me alone!" I managed to say through my tears. There was my niece, horribly sick with heaven knows what, and the antiquarian thought he had the right to preach some bygone words written in an old book that was completely unknown in the civilized world.

"Should I go?" he asked quietly.

"Please!"

Still fuming, I fell asleep on the floor, my head resting on Fernanda's *k'ang*. Luckily, it wasn't long before my niece woke up (or I might have fallen ill myself from the damp and cold) and began squirming under the blankets.

"Get your head off my legs, Auntie! I'm boiling."

I opened my eyes, drowsy and disoriented.

"How are you?" I stammered.

"Just fine. Never better."

"Honestly?" I couldn't believe it. In the blink of an eye, she had gone from a near-delirious fever to the picture of health.

"Honestly," she replied, pulling back the covers and hopping out of her *k'ang*. "Where are my clothes?"

"You're not going anywhere today, young lady," I declared. "You have not fully recovered."

After a long—very long—look of indignation, came a never-ending stream of protests, condemnations, promises, and laments that left me absolutely cold. Under no circumstances would I let her out of the house that day. By the end of the afternoon, however, I was deeply regretting my decision: Fernanda's wails and complaints were so loud in the silence of the monastery that a crowd of monks and nuns had gathered outside to see what was happening. Still, I was happy: better loud and crying than her usual silent and taciturn.

We'd lost a full day of work, so after a good night's sleep and a session of tai chi in which I tried hard to show Lao Jiang just how flexible my tendons and muscles were, Biao and I left the house in high spirits, determined to achieve our goal. I had gotten it firmly into my head that the old woman from the temple would be a reliable source of information and told Biao we should head straight to where we saw her two days earlier. However, the old woman's cushion sat empty. A young nun was industriously scrubbing mud off the doors and the portico; her efforts seemed somewhat pointless given that it was still raining and anywhere you stepped off the paths that ran between the buildings, you sank into muck up to your ankles. Biao asked her about the alleged centenarian.

"Ming T'ien will be here later," she explained. "She's so old we don't let her get up until the hour of the Horse."

"Which is the hour of the Horse?" I asked Biao.

"I'm not sure, *tai-tai*, but I think it's midmorning."

A boy younger than Biao came running down the path carrying an umbrella. He was wearing the white outfit of a novice in the martial arts and not the blue cotton the servants who came to clean our house wore.

"Chang Cheng!" he shouted.

"It's so strange to see someone running!" I said to Biao as we left Ming T'ien's temple. "Everyone here walks as if they're in an Easter procession."

"Chang Cheng!" the boy repeated, waving his hand in the air to get our attention. Was he looking for us?

"What does 'Chang Cheng' mean?" I asked Biao.

"It's the Chinese name for the Great Wall," he replied. By now it was patently obvious the boy was coming for us.

"Chang Cheng!" the young runner yelled, not at all out of breath, as he stopped in front of me and bowed. "Chang Cheng, the abbot would like me to take you to Master Tzau's cave."

I looked at Biao in surprise.

"Did he really just call me 'Great Wall'?"

Biao nodded with a toothy grin.

I was outraged. "Ask him why he's calling me that."

The two boys exchanged a few words, and then Little Tiger, trying to remain serious, said, "Everyone in the monastery has been calling you Great Wall since yesterday, tai-tai, ever since Young Mistress' cries were heard all over Mount Wudang. They're calling you Chang Cheng and her Yu Hua Ping, or 'Pot of Rain.'"

Those poetic yet pompous-sounding Chinese names must have been an attempt at humor.

"We'd better go with the novice, tai-tai. Master Tzau is waiting."

Why would the abbot want me to visit this master who lived in a cave? The only way to find out was to follow the boy. So, trusting that the visit would be over before the hour of the Horse, we began a long walk in the pouring rain. On our way we passed many impressive temples, climbed up and down numerous sets of stairs, and came across several patios where monks and novices were practicing complicated martial arts, toiling in the rain wearing snow white outfits that contrasted beautifully with the dark gray stone and red temples. Some were working with extremely long lances, others with swords, sabers, fans—every weapon imaginable. In one of those open areas, several feet below a long bridge the two boys and I were crossing, a figure in white waved its arms to get our attention. It was Fernanda. I wondered how she'd known that it was us under the umbrellas when so many others were walking along that labyrinth of bridges, paths, and stone staircases decorated with thousands of carved caldrons, cranes, lions, tigers, tortoises, snakes, and dragons, some of which were truly frightening.

We finally reached the entrance to a cave after climbing one of the Mysterious Mountain peaks. The novice said something to Biao and, after bowing, ran off downhill.

"He said we're to go in and find the master."

"But it's as black as your hat in there," I protested.

Biao didn't say a word. I think he wanted us to leave as quickly as possible. Like me, he wasn't at all happy about going into a sinister-looking cave where who knows what kinds of bugs and animals might bite or attack us. However, we had no choice but to obey the abbot, so we swallowed our fear and, closing our umbrellas, went into the cave. There was a light way in the back, and we walked very slowly toward it. The silence was absolute; the sound of the downpour at our backs became fainter the farther in we went. We wound our way through passageways and galleries dimly lit by torches and oil lamps. The path was heading down into the mountain, and an oppressive sensation began to constrict my throat, especially when it became so narrow that we had to walk sideways. The air was thick and smelled of rock and humidity. Finally, after what seemed like an eternity, we came to a natural cavity that suddenly opened up at the end of a tight corridor. A monk so old he could've been a hundred or a thousand sat on a wide rock protuberance rising up out of the ground like a thick trunk cut low down. He was absolutely still, his eyes closed and his hands crossed in front of his stomach. At first I was afraid he might be dead, but upon hearing us approach he half opened his eyelids and looked at us with the strangest yellow eyes. I nearly screamed in terror. Biao quickly stepped back and hid behind me, so there I was, trying to be the bravest person in the world, acting as a shield between a devil and a frightened boy. The devil slowly lifted a hand tipped with nails so long they curled in on themselves and motioned for us to come closer. I wasn't sure what to do. Something inside stopped me from taking even one more tiny step toward that diabolical apparition, and it wasn't just the repugnant stench of filth and ox dung. He spoke, but Biao didn't translate. Nearly all of the old man's teeth were gone, and the few that remained were as yellow as his eyes and his fingernails.

I elbowed Biao and heard him gasp. "What did he say?" I managed to croak.

"He said he's Master Tzau and we shouldn't be afraid to come closer."

"Oh, certainly! Why not?" I replied without moving.

From somewhere behind him, the master pulled out a worn black leather tube and opened it by removing the top part. It wasn't very long, no more than the span of a hand, and not much wider than a bracelet. When he opened it, the bunch of little wooden sticks inside made a soothing sound that reverberated off the walls of the cavern. It was then I discovered that those walls were covered in strange signs and characters that had been carved into the rock. Someone had spent many years in that faint light, patiently chiseling long and short lines, like Morse code, and Chinese ideograms.

The spirit with yellow eyes spoke again, his voice like the screeching of train wheels along the tracks. I think every hair on my body stood on end.

"He insists we come closer. He says he has a lot to teach us by order of the abbot and doesn't have time to waste," Biao translated.

But of course! Why hadn't I thought of that? Naturally a thousand-year-old monk sitting on a rock all day inside an underground cave would have any number of things to do.

Frightened half to death, we moved toward the big rock as Master Tzau pulled the wooden sticks out of the leather cylinder as gingerly as would a woman whose nail polish has yet to dry.

"He says that's far enough," Biao whispered when we were about six feet away. "We're to stop here and sit on the ground."

"Just what I needed," I mumbled, obeying. From down there the master looked like the statute of an imposing, pestiferous god. Poor Biao still had trouble sitting, and it took a few seconds before he found a kneeling position that was more or less comfortable.

The yellow-eyed spirit lifted a dry old hand in the air to show us the sticks he was holding.

"Since you are a foreigner," he said, "there is no way you can understand the depth and meaning of the *I Ching*, also known as the Book of Changes. That is why the abbot has asked me to explain it to you. Using these sticks, I can tell you much about yourself, your current situation, your problems, and what course of action to take so matters can be resolved in the best way possible."

"The abbot wants you to speak to me about clairvoyance and fortune-telling?" The look on my face couldn't have expressed my opinion any more clearly, but surely it was as inscrutable to the Chinese as theirs was to me, because the master continued his lecture as if I hadn't spoken.

"It is not about clairvoyance or fortune-telling," the old man replied. "The *I Ching* is a book that is thousands of years old and contains the wisdom of the universe, nature, and mankind, as well as the changes they are subject to. Anything you want to know can be found in the *I Ching*."

"You said it was a book. . . ." I commented, looking around to see if there was a copy of this *I Ching* anywhere.

"Yes, it is a book, the Book of Changes." The devil with the yellow eyes let out a sinister little laugh. "You won't see it, because it is all in my head. I have studied it for so long that I know the sixty-four hexagrams by heart, as well as its rules, symbols, and interpretations, not to mention the Ten Wings, or commentaries, appended by Confucius, as well as the many treatises written over the millennia by more important scholars than I regarding this wise book.

"The *I Ching* describes both the internal order of the universe as well as the changes that occur within it, and it does so by means of the sixty-four hexagrams. The wise spirits use these to tell us of the different situations in which we humans can find ourselves and, according to the law of change, predict how such situations are going to evolve. Thus the spirits that speak through the *I Ching* can advise those who consult them about future events."

Good Lord, I thought. Why am I wasting my time? I have absolutely no interest in spirits!

"You'll find fortune-tellers you can pay to cast the *I Ching* on every street in China, *tai-tai*," Biao whispered to me. "But none of them are really worthy of respect. It's a great honor for Master Tzau to be your oracle."

"If you say so," I said doubtfully.

Biao glanced up at the master. "We should apologize for the interruption."

"Go on, then. Hurry up. I want to speak to that old nun Ming T'ien before lunch."

"The Book of Changes," Master Tzau continued, oblivious of my disinterest, "was one of few books that were saved when the First Emperor ordered that all books be burned. Thanks to the fact that he was a devout follower of the philosophies of yin and yang, the Five Elements, the K'an-yu or feng shui, and the I Ching, we can continue to consult the spirits today."

Now, this was a different matter, I thought, perking up my ears. I'd pay attention if he kept talking about the First Emperor. But he didn't, of course. It had been nothing more than a colorful anecdote.

"He told me to ask you what you want to know so he can cast the sticks," Biao said.

I didn't have to think twice. "Well, tell him I want to know, in order of importance, the four objectives for the life of a Taoist from Wudang. Make it clear I'm not talking about the objectives of any Chinese Taoist, but specifically Taoists from this monastery."

"Very well," the master replied once Biao had repeated my request. I didn't believe him, of course. Would the abbot really give us the answer to his own question through a medium—or whatever that strange old man was? He had already begun his odd ceremony, picking up the sticks and holding them out in front of him on the rock, like a gambler fanning a deck of cards on the table. First he took one out and set it aside. Then he grouped the rest in two parallel piles. He pulled one more out of the group on the right and put it between the pinkie and ring fingers of his left hand. Using that same hand, he picked up the pile closest to him and began to methodically pull out groups of four sticks. When he got down to fewer than four, he placed those between his ring and middle fingers, that hand beginning to resemble a pincushion or a cactus. Then he repeated the whole procedure with the pile on the right and put the final few between his middle and index fingers. After that he used a brush to note something on a piece of rice paper and, much to my dismay, began the whole ritual over again from the beginning until he had done it five more times. At that point he finally seemed satisfied, and I had to quickly come back from wherever my bored thoughts had taken me. Master Tzau's yellow eyes remained fixed on me as he pointed a curling nail at one of the etchings on the wall.

"There is your answer. That is your first figure, 'Duration.'"

I looked over, and this is what I saw:

"Since there is an Old Yin in the sixth line," he continued, "you also have a second figure, that one over there," he said, pointing in another direction. "'The Caldron.'"

I was completely confused. This oracle thing must have been intended solely for the Chinese, because I certainly didn't understand it. What was I supposed to do now, thank the master for that absurd prediction, according to which a very steadfast, long-lasting caldron was the answer to my question about the objectives of Wudang Taoists? The old man had pointed to two of the strange drawings on the walls, each consisting of six lines on top of one another, some of which were solid and others of which were broken in half, each with a Chinese ideogram on top that must have been its name. The ones that corresponded to me, thanks to that dance he had performed with the rods, was "Duration"—two broken lines, three solid lines, and finally another broken line—and "The Caldron"—one solid line, a broken line, three solid lines, and the last broken. That is, they were identical except for the top line. This led me to believe that must be the Old Yin on the sixth line the psychic had mentioned. Therefore, the hexagrams were read from bottom to top and not from top to bottom.

"You are one of those people," the old man began, "who lives in a permanent state of unease. This has brought and still brings you great misfortune. You are not happy, you are not at peace, and you cannot find relief. 'Duration' speaks of how thunder and wind obey the perpetual laws of nature, as well as of the benefits of perseverance and having somewhere to go. Furthermore, the Old Yin on the sixth line indicates that your perseverance is affected by your unease and that your mind and spirit suffer a great deal because of your agitation. However, 'The Caldron' says that if you change your attitude, if you always act in moderation with regard to everything, your destiny will lead you to find the meaning of your life and to follow the proper path, on which you will attain great fortune and success."

It wasn't exactly the answer to my question, but it came awfully close to a very good description of myself. Just as a river overflows as a result of torrential rains, I was beginning to slowly but unstoppably boil over as a result of this Chinese obsession with examining your soul and baring it all so you can make I don't know how many changes to your personality for I don't know what strange reasons. True, there was none of that horrible Christian morality I'd been raised with hidden behind their words, but I was far too proud to allow some white-haired Celestial to feel he had the right to tell me what I was doing wrong and what I should do to correct it. I had never allowed my family to do so, and I was not about to let strangers from another country do so now! Master Tzau, however, hadn't finished.

"The I Ching has told you things you should heed. The spiritual entities that speak through the Book of Changes only want to help us. The universe has a plan that is far too big for us to understand. We see only little, inexplicable bits and are essentially blind. It was the former kings Fu Hsi and Yu who discovered the signs made of combinations of solid yang lines and broken yin lines that make up the sixty-four hexa-grams of the *I Ching*, over five thousand years ago. King Fu Hsi discov-ered the signs that describe the internal order of the universe on the back of a horse that rose up out of the river Lo, while King Yu discov-ered the signs that explain how changes occur on the shell of a giant tortoise that emerged from the sea when the waters receded. King Yu was the only human who could control the rising waters and floods during the time of great rains that ravaged the earth. He often traveled to the stars to visit the heavenly spirits, and they were the ones who gave him the mythical *Book of Power Over the Waters* that allowed him to channel the waters and prevent the world from being inundated. Even today Taoist masters who practice the internal martial arts perform the supreme magic dance that took Yu to the heavens. It is a very powerful dance that should be interpreted with great care. Finally, I must tell you about King Wen, from the Shang[36] dynasty. It was he who joined and mathematically combined the signs that King Fu Hsi and King Yu found, composing the sixty-four hexagrams of the *I Ching* that you see chiseled into the walls of this cave."

Was it the hour of the Horse yet? I didn't want to seem rude and so pretended to be paying close attention to Master Tzau's speech, furrow-ing my brow and nodding my head. In reality, however, the only thing that concerned me just then was finding old Ming T'ien before lunch. I couldn't have cared less about those ancient Chinese kings and their universal floods. We in the West had had our flood, too, as well as our savior, Noah.

"And now you may go," the master unexpectedly declared, closing his eyes and assuming the same pose of absolute concentration as when we'd arrived. He placed one hand over the other in front of his stomach and looked as if he were asleep. It was the sign I'd been waiting for. Biao and I, still a little surprised at the sudden end to that conversation, stood up and took the same labyrinth of a path back out of the cave. When I could once again hear the lovely sound of the rain and the thundering skies in the distance, my heart felt much relieved, and I quickened my pace in order to get out into the fresh, clean mountain air. Enclosed spaces were so asphyxiating—especially when they reeked of filth.

Once we had our umbrellas in hand, Biao and I looked at one another, disoriented.

"Do we know how to get back to the monastery?" I asked.

"We'll get somewhere," Biao brilliantly deduced.

We wandered all over the mountain, at times taking trails that led to other caves or to springs where it was no wonder the water bubbled up in abundance. The mud stuck to our feet like heavy army boots. We could see the temple buildings off on the mountain slopes in front of us and tried to reach them but got lost time and time again. We finally came across a stretch of the Divine Corridor and followed it down, feeling immensely relieved. We washed our feet in puddles, but our canvas sandals were ruined, and we were barefoot by the time we reached the first of the palaces en route, a martial arts school for very young boys and girls. What looked like bags of sand and oddly shaped pieces of wood hung down from the roof for the children to use in their strange exercises, but we didn't stop to watch. I was anxious to speak with Ming T'ien. I was sure I'd be able to worm the second ideogram in the puzzle out of her. With two in our possession, the third would be as easy a pie, while the fourth and final, I thought with a smile, would be obvious through the process of elimination.

However, by the time we reached her temple, Ming T'ien was already resting after lunch. It turns out we'd been in the cave with Master Tzau and wandering on the mountainside for quite some time. A novice told us she wouldn't be back on her silk cushion until the hour of the Monkey.[37] Biao and I were thus left no choice but to go back to the house empty-handed.

Lao Jiang was sitting comfortably in a corner of the patio watching the rain when we arrived. Huge, deafening booms of thunder rang out as if the sky itself were splitting in two. Everything vibrated and shook, but the antiquarian had a satisfied look on his face and grinned as we came through the door.

"Wonderful news, Elvira!" he announced, standing and walking toward us with open arms. The hem of his tunic was wet from the water on the ground.

"Well, that's good, because all I got was my future told," I exclaimed desolately, leaning my umbrella up against the wall.

Lao Jiang seemed quite impressed. "Who did that?"

"The abbot wanted me to visit this Master Tzau who lives in an underground cave inside a mountain."

"What an honor!" he murmured. "If I may say so, take whatever the master said very seriously."

"You may, although oracles and mediums are not at all my cup of tea. Perhaps you'll be invited to visit his cave so the master can read your future."

The antiquarian's face changed for a few seconds. I thought I saw fear in his eyes, a strange fear that disappeared as quickly as it came and left me wondering whether it had simply been my overactive imagination.

"What I can tell you," I continued, perhaps a little too quickly, "is that the First Emperor ordered a great burning of books, and the *I Ching* was one of few that were saved."

Lao Jiang nodded. "That's right. Shi Huang Ti ordered that all the texts from the Hundred Schools, the chronicles from previous kingdoms, all poetry, and all documents from the old archives be burned. His intention was to eliminate any trace of previous government systems. After unifying Everything Under the Sky and creating the Middle Kingdom, he wanted the old ideas to disappear and, with them, any attempt to return to the old ways."

"That reminds me of your obsession with preventing an imperial restoration."

The antiquarian looked down at the floor. "Shi Huang Ti was right to suspect that whenever there is progress in the world, there are also always dangerous nostalgics capable of anything, madame. If you don't believe me, just look at the military coup in your country, Big Luzon. That's why the First Emperor ordered that all books and files be burned.

He wanted people to forget. However, we mustn't overlook the fact that he also ordered every citizen in his new empire to turn in his weapons to be destroyed. After smelting the bronze, the emperor had it made into enormous bells and twelve giant statues that he placed at the entrance to his palace in Xianyang. Ideas and weapons, Elvira. It makes sense, doesn't it?"

It was an odd question, especially because of the tone with which he'd asked it, but everything on that Mysterious Mountain was odd, and I was quite sure of my answer.

"Weapons, yes, Lao Jiang," I replied, realizing I was famished and walking toward the dining room, "but books, no. Weapons kill. Remember our recent war in Europe. Books, on the other hand, nourish our minds and set us free."

"But many of those minds get caught up in the web of dangerous ideas."

I sighed. "Well, that's the way the world is. We can always try to make it better without killing or destroying. I'm surprised that a Taoist like you, who spared the lives of the Green Gang assassins at Yuyuan Gardens in Shanghai, would say such things."

I sat down in front of my appetizing bowls of cold food, and Lao Jiang sat across from me. Biao had taken his into a corner, and Fernanda, naturally, wasn't there.

"I'm not defending weapons or death," Lao Jiang replied. "All I'm saying is that we need to prevent old ideas from strangling new ones, that the world changes and evolves, and going back to the past has never made a nation great."

"Look," I said, bringing some rice to my mouth, "I'm not all that fond of politics or big speeches. Why don't you tell me that good news you mentioned when I arrived?"

His face lit up. "You're right. I apologize. Let me go get the book, and I'll read what I found while you eat."

"Yes, please, do," I encouraged, gobbling my vegetables with gusto, but he wasn't gone more than a few minutes. Soon he was back, seated again, with an ancient Chinese tome open on his lap.

"Remember I once told you about Sima Qian, the most important Chinese historian of all times?"

I gestured in a way that meant nothing, because that's exactly what I remembered: nothing.

"When we were on the barge on the Yangtze," he carried on, unperturbed, "I told you that in his book, *Records of the Grand Historian*, Sima Qian says that everyone involved in building the First Emperor's mausoleum died along with him. Do you remember?"

I nodded and kept eating.

"Well, this is a marvelous copy of the *Shiji*, or *Records of the Grand Historian*, by Sima Qian, written over two thousand years ago, shortly after the First Emperor's death. I knew they'd have a copy in Wudang. Believe me, there aren't many. This would be worth an absolute fortune," he said, speaking like a true merchant now. "I asked for this particular book because I wanted to confirm the chronicler's information about the tomb, and it's the only documented source in existence. Listen to what I found in the part called The Basic Annals of the First Emperor of the Qin," he said with a heavy sigh, and then began to read. "'In the ninth month, the First Emperor was interred at Mount Li. When the emperor first came to the throne, he began digging and shaping Mount Li. Later, when he unified the empire, he had more than seven hundred thousand men from all over the empire transported to the spot. They dug down to the third layer of underground springs and poured in bronze to make the outer coffin. Replicas of palaces, scenic towers, and the hundred officials, as well as rare utensils and wonderful objects, were brought to fill up the tomb. Craftsmen were ordered to set up crossbows and arrows, rigged so they would immediately shoot down anyone attempting to break in. Mercury was used to fashion imitations of the hundred rivers, the Yellow River and the Yangtze, and the seas, constructed in such a way that they seemed to flow.'"

By this point I had stopped eating and was listening spellbound. Enough mercury to fashion rivers and seas? Replicas of palaces, towers, and officials, as well as wonderful objects and utensils? What exactly were we talking about here?

Lao Jiang continued reading:

"'Above were representations of all the heavenly bodies; below, the features of the earth. Whale oil was used for lamps, which were calculated to burn for a long time without going out. The Second Emperor said, "Of the women in the harem of the former ruler, it would be unfitting to have those who bore no sons sent elsewhere." All were accordingly ordered to accompany the dead man, which resulted in the death of many women. After the interment had been completed, someone pointed out that the artisans and craftsmen who had built the tomb knew what was buried there, and if they should leak word of the treasures, it would be a serious affair. Therefore, after the articles had been placed in the tomb, the inner gate was closed off and the outer gate lowered, so that all the artisans and craftsmen were shut in the tomb and were unable to get out. Trees and bushes were planted to give the appearance of a mountain.'"

He lifted his eyes from the text and looked at me triumphantly.

"What did I tell you?" he exclaimed. "It's full of treasures!"

"And death traps," I qualified. "According to that historian, there are any number of crossbows and arrows just waiting to fire automatically as soon as we set foot in the mausoleum—not to mention those mechanical devices we know nothing about, planned specifically for tomb raiders such as ourselves."

"As always, Elvira, you let negative thoughts carry you away. Don't you remember we have the map from Sai Wu, the foreman? He prepared it for his own son, Sai Shi Gu'er. The answers about to how to pass through the traps unscathed will undoubtedly be in the third piece of the *jiance*."

The Old Yin in my Enduring Caldron wouldn't allow me to just blindly trust whatever Lao Jiang said. Unease and agitation—weren't those the terms that defined my temperament according to the *I Ching?* Well, I couldn't calmly accept Sai Wu's instructions for avoiding the arrows, crossbows, and mechanical devices. No, sir, I could not. In any event, we still didn't have the third piece of the *jiance*, which reminded me I'd better not waste any more time eating if I didn't want Ming T'ien to slip away on me again.

"Is it the hour of the Monkey yet?" I asked in Chinese, wiping my mouth with a handkerchief and standing up.

The antiquarian smiled. "You're becoming a true daughter of Han, Elvira."

I smiled back. "I think not, Mr. Jiang. You treat your women too poorly for me to want that. I much prefer being European, but I don't deny that I'm becoming quite fond of your language and culture."

He seemed offended, but I didn't care. Wasn't he the one who said the world was changing and we had to keep old ideas from strangling new ones? Well, perhaps he should apply his big political ideas to the underprivileged other half of the population in this immense country.

"Yes, it's the hour of the Monkey," he grumbled.

"Thank you," I exclaimed, rushing out in search of a new pair of sandals. "Let's go, Biao!"

As Biao and I ran along the cobbled roads, up and down the endless staircases in Wudang, sheltered under our umbrellas, I felt happy. Without realizing it, I had revealed a great truth to Lao Jiang: I really was very fond of Chinese culture, art, and language. I simply could no longer be like the foreigners who live in international concessions, always ensconced in their little Western groups, never mixing with the locals, never learning their language, looking down on them as ignorant and inferior. That long journey through a crumbling nation divided among political parties, imperialists, mafia, and warlords was giving me much food for thought. I would need a good long while to assimilate and make the most of it all.

I was happier still when, in the distance, I saw tiny old Ming T'ien sitting on her cushion on the temple portico. As before, she was smiling as she looked out at the void, contemplating mountains she was unable to behold and an overcast, rainy sky her eyes could not see. Neverthe-less, she was obviously happy. She knew that it was us by the sound of our approach.

"*Ni hao*, Chang Cheng," she said in that cracked little voice she had used to call me "poor fool" the last time. It was clear just how quickly news traveled through the monastery given that she now called me by my new nickname, "Great Wall."

"*Ni hao*, Ming T'ien," I replied. "How are you today?"

"Well, my bones were aching a little this morning but feel much better after my tai chi. Thank you for asking."

Of course her bones ached! She was so hunched over, so bent and twisted with age, what was most surprising was that she could do tai chi at all.

"Do you remember getting angry at me the other day because I was so ignorant I didn't even know that happiness is the most important thing in life?"

"Certainly."

"Is happiness the most important thing for a Taoist from Wudang?"

"It is."

"Then what would be most important for a Taoist from Wudang *after* happiness?"

Ming T'ien,[38] living up to her name, beamed at the question. Per-haps she'd never had disciples and was thrilled by the very idea, or perhaps she'd had many and longed for those days. In any event, her wrinkled little face couldn't smile any wider.

"Imagine you're truly happy right now," she replied. "Feel it deep inside. You are so happy, Chang Cheng, that what you wish for most would be . . ."

What I wish for most? What would I want most if I were happy? I shook my head sadly. What did it mean to be happy? I couldn't just con-jure up a feeling I'd never experienced. There had been joyful, passion-ate, fun, exciting, euphoric times in my life—all of which could be considered happy, but I had no idea exactly what happiness was. Just as sadness and pain lasted only long enough for me to recognize and be able to define them, happiness was so ephemeral it was untraceable. I could imagine something similar if I combined feelings (joy and passion, for example), but this was only a temporary solution. Still, if I were very, very happy, most likely I'd want that feeling to last as long as possible, given that the main characteristic of happiness was precisely its fleeting nature.

"See, you've answered the question yourself," Ming T'ien replied once I'd summarized my deliberations. "When you're happy, you yearn for longevity, because a long life allows you to enjoy the happiness you've attained for a longer period of time. I'm a hundred and twelve, and I've been happy ever since I started on the path of Tao over a hundred years ago."

For the love of God! What on earth was the woman saying? For a moment I almost lost all respect for her.

"You likely think about death quite a lot," she added.

"Why do you say that?" I replied defiantly, barely keeping my frustration under control.

She let out a childish little laugh that I found exasperating. I studiously avoided looking at Biao, because I didn't want him to think this was any of his business.

"Leave me be now," Ming T'ien then ordered. "I'm tired of all this talking."

This abrupt end to conversations seemed to be customary. Since we Westerners were so ceremonious about saying a polite good-bye, it seemed I would need to get used to the jars of cold water they dumped on you from the temples, palaces, and caves of Wudang. It wasn't worth taking personally. I puffed a little wind back into my sails and stood up to leave.

"May I come back to visit you again?" I asked.

"You'll have to come at least once more, won't you?" she replied, closing her milky eyes and assuming the same pose of silence and impenetrable concentration as Master Tzau, seeming to indicate she was no longer there.

I was dumbfounded. Did Ming T'ien know why I was visiting her, why I was asking her those questions about the objectives of Taoists from Wudang? So why didn't she just give me the whole answer? Why was Ming T'ien so determined to give me just one ideogram with each conversation? It was unnecessarily prolonging our stay in Wudang, although leaving would be a little risky in this rain. Risky yes, but not impossible, so rationing the information was just wasting our time. I had to tell Lao Jiang.

When I did tell the antiquarian as we sat in the study, he didn't seem terribly interested. He had never put a lot of faith in Ming T'ien. He wanted tangible, irrefutable proof and thus persisted with his ancient Taoist volumes written during the time of the First Emperor—like the one about feng shui that spoke of the harmony between living beings and the energies of the earth. He was unaffected by both my worry and my happiness at having obtained the second ideogram in the abbot's puzzle. He thought it was a logical conclusion and agreed we might have solved half the problem: first happiness, then longevity. However, nothing he'd read thus far corroborated the accuracy of our suppositions, and he was therefore still skeptical.

"Doesn't it seem more logical," I asked him, "to read books written by monks who lived in this monastery and who might at some point mention the objectives of their lives?"

"You think I'm using the wrong criteria, is that it?"

"No, Lao Jiang, I simply think you should expand your criteria. You must have your reasons to read about feng shui, I have no doubt of that. I just doubt you'll find what we're looking for there."

"Do you want to know why I'm studying it?" he replied sardonically. "You see, the First Emperor believed in K'an-yu as much as any self-respecting Chinese person. All sons of Han, especially those of us who are Taoists, believe we must live in harmony with our environment and the energies of the universe. We're convinced that things will go either well or poorly depending on where we build our houses or place our tombs. Health, longevity, peace, and happiness depend in good measure on our relationship with the energies where we choose to live and those that circulate through our houses, our businesses, or our tombs. You see, even the dead need to be buried somewhere with beneficial energy so their existence in the great beyond can be placid and happy. How do you think all the temples and palaces in Wudang were built? Ancient master geomancers studied the mountain in minute detail to find the very best locations."

Now I understood! Feng shui was the reason all the buildings in China seemed so exquisitely harmonious. The incredible thing was that there was a thousand-year-old science dedicated just to this. The Celestials were very odd indeed, but these peculiarities had brought them close to beauty in a way that was unknown to us in the West. Could this also be the reason their furniture was placed symmetrically in every room?

"However, there is yet another reason to study these old feng shui books," Lao Jiang continued. "The First Emperor had a veritable army of master geomancers working for him. According to Sima Qian," he said, placing his hand on the tome he'd read out loud from that afternoon, "every one of his palaces—and there were many—was built according to the laws of feng shui. Obviously his tomb was as well. Since the characteristics of correct placement are easily recognizable at first glance, I thought we should be clear on certain notions about feng shui for when the time comes to find Mount Li and the mausoleum."

"But that will all be in the third piece of the *jiance*."

"And what if we don't get it?" he rejoined. "We could make a mistake with the ideograms. Hadn't you thought of that? You put such faith in that old woman, Ming T'ien, that the very idea of failing hasn't even crossed your mind." He pulled the hem of his tunic into a pleat above his knees. "In any event, I will do as you suggest. The servant who brings me the books should be here soon. I'll ask him to take all these volumes on feng shui and bring me works written by Wudang monks."

Biao and I had some time before dinner, so I asked him to pose and quickly sketched a portrait of him that he adored. It didn't turn out as well as I would have liked, partly because the light was terrible but mostly because the boy wouldn't stop fidgeting, scratching his head or his ears, coming over to look, and asking me questions.

"I'd like to learn how to draw, *tai-tai*," he commented, turning his head toward the door where the light came in.

"You'll have to study hard," I warned as I let my wrist sweep to draw the part in his hair. "Tell Father Castrillo when we get back to Shanghai."

He looked at me worriedly.

"But . . . I don't ever want to go back to the orphanage!"

"What nonsense is this?"

"I don't like the orphanage," he grumbled. "Besides, I'm Chinese and should be learning about my own country, not about the *yang-kwei*."

"I don't like you using that expression, Biao," I protested. Lao Jiang's nationalist pride appeared to be bearing fruit. "I don't think Fernanda or I deserve to be called 'foreign devils.' We've never offended you in any way as far as I recall."

He blushed. "I wasn't talking about you, *tai-tai*. I was talking about the Augustines at the orphanage."

I changed the subject and kept drawing.

"By the way, Biao, what happened to your family? I've never asked you about them."

Biao's face contorted strangely and he began to nervously chew on his lower lip.

"I'm sorry," I said. "You don't have to tell me anything."

His lanky body seemed to want to fold in on itself until it disappeared.

"My grandmother died when I was eight," he began to explain, staring straight at the door. "I was born in Chengdu, in the province of

Szechwan. My parents and siblings were killed during the riots of 1911, when Dr. Sun Yat-sen overthrew the emperor. The neighbors took our lands and threw my grandmother out. She managed to save me by hiding me in a basket of clothing and boarding a sampan to Shanghai at night. We lived in Pudong. My grandmother begged, and as soon as I learned to walk, I . . ."

He paused for a moment, unsure. I couldn't imagine what he'd say next, and my hand hovered in the air, pencil in hand, above my sketchbook.

"Well, like all children in Pudong, as soon as I learned to walk . . . well, I had to work for the Green Gang, for Pockmarked Huang," he murmured. "I was one of his messengers until Father Castrillo found me."

I couldn't believe what I was hearing. In fact, I was speechless. What sort of life had the boy lived?

"We'd wait in the alley behind the teahouse[39] where Huang did business," he went on. "He'd call us when he needed something picked up or delivered. He paid well, and it was fun. But my grandmother died, and one day, when I was ten, I ran into this huge foreigner who asked me where I lived and if I was alone. When I told him, he grabbed me by the arm and dragged me across Shanghai to the orphanage run by the Spanish Augustines. It was Father Castrillo."

Images of Biao jumping like a monkey over the Green Gang assassins in Yuyuan Gardens flashed through my mind, as if this memory might somehow be important to the boy's history. Poor Little Tiger, I thought. What a difficult life.

"Don't be ashamed of having worked for the Green Gang," I said with a smile. "We've all done things that hurt to remember, but it's best to just carry on and not make the same mistakes again."

"Are you going to tell Lao Jiang?" he asked worriedly.

"No, I won't tell anyone anything."

The servants arrived with dinner not long after I had finished sketching Little Tiger's big eyes. The poor boy hadn't said another word while he posed but got quite excited when I showed him the drawing. That was when I realized that my niece wasn't back yet and that not only was it dinnertime, but it was pitch black outside. I gave Biao the drawing, which he accepted with a smile and put away, and sent him to find Fernanda. If we were going to stay in Wudang, I'd have to speak with her teachers about sending her home at a decent hour. It was obvious she didn't know when it was time to stop her marvelous exercises.

The two came back drenched, and Fernanda was covered in mud up to her ears. Who would've guessed two months ago that my prim, proper, snobbish niece would become a splendid, athletic young woman who wasn't afraid of a little dirt? The change in Fernanda was spectacular, and for the sheer fun of it, I so wished my mother and poor sister could have seen her right then.

That night turned out to be rather strange. Something woke me in the wee hours, and I couldn't determine what it was until I was fully awake: It had stopped raining. Total silence enveloped the house, as if nature had exhausted itself and sunk into a peaceful slumber. Since I didn't think I'd be able to fall back asleep, I got up quietly so as not to bother Fernanda, wrapped myself in a blanket, and went out to the patio to sit and look up at the sky for a while. Much to my surprise, I saw Biao coming out of Lao Jiang's study, carrying a lantern and walking sleepily toward the stairs.

"Where are you going, Biao?" I whispered.

The boy jumped and looked wide-eyed in every direction.

"Down here," I said.

"*Tai-tai?*" he asked fearfully.

"Of course! Who else? What are you doing up at this time of night?"

"Lao Jiang asked me to wake you. He wants to see you upstairs."

"Now?" I asked, perplexed. It must have been two or three in the morning. The only possible explanation was that the antiquarian had found something important in his texts.

Little Tiger waited for me at the top of the staircase, holding the light high so I could splash my way up the wet stairs in my sandals. He then lit the way to the study. I peered in cautiously to see what the antiquarian was doing and saw him in the candlelight, absorbed in whatever he was reading. He didn't even notice when I came into the room and stood behind him. It was only when I pulled the blanket tighter around my frozen shoulders that he lifted his head and turned around, startled.

"Elvira! That was quick! I'm glad you got here so fast."

"I'd already been woken up by the silence. Why haven't you gone to bed?"

He didn't reply. There was a look of contained excitement on his face.

"Let me read you this," he said, gesturing for me to sit down.

"You've found something important?"

"I've found the answer," he burst out with a nervous laugh, pulling one of the many candles on the table closer to the book in front of him. Biao brought a stool and set it next to Lao Jiang, then withdrew into a corner of the room. I sat down, my stomach in knots. "This book is a bibliographic gem that would be worth a mint on the market. It's called *The True Secrets of the Kingdom of Pure Enlightenment*, and it was written by a Master Hsien during the reign of the fourth Ming emperor in the mid–fourteenth century."

"Just tell me the answer to the abbot's puzzle!" I cried out impatiently.

"Your dear Ming T'ien has been telling you the truth. This book has only four chapters, and I bet you can guess what they're called."

"'Happiness,' 'Longevity,' 'Peace,' and 'Health'?" I ventured.

Lao Jiang laughed. "No. You would have failed the test."

"'Happiness,' 'Longevity,' 'Health,' and 'Peace'?"

"Exactly," he said. "Let me summarize: According to Master Hsien, Taoists are to be happy first and foremost. This happiness will lead them to wish for a long life in order to enjoy that well-being and satisfaction for a very long time. Using Taoist techniques to attain longevity, some of which you already know, they also attain good health. This is very important, because they can't be happy if they're in poor health. Therefore, when they're happy and they know that they're going to live a long, healthy life, thanks to their daily efforts to develop certain physical and mental qualities, then and only then do they aspire to peace, an inner peace that allows them to cultivate the Taoist virtue of *wu wei*."

"*Wu wei?*"

"Inaction. It's a difficult concept for you Westerners to grasp. It means not acting in the face of life events." He softly stroked his forehead, searching for a way to explain that wasn't as simple as just calling it idleness. "*Wu wei* isn't the same as passivity, although it might seem that way to you now. Given that his mind is at peace, a wise Taoist lets things happen as they will, without interfering. By renouncing the use of force, heightened emotions, and ambition for material things, he discovers that trying to affect destiny is like stirring up the water in a pond and muddying it. If, on the other hand, his action consists of not stirring up the pond, leaving it be, the water will remain clear or will clear up on its own. The inaction of *wu wei* doesn't mean not acting, but rather always doing so with Taoist moderation, withdrawing discreetly once the job has been done."

"That bit about moderation, did you throw that in for any particular reason?"

He looked at me, amused, and shook his head. "The extent of your distrust is truly amazing, Chang Cheng," he said, using the nickname I'd been given on the Mysterious Mountain. How had he heard it when he'd been shut up in the study all day long? "So says the *Tao Te Ching*, as you know, in a beautiful piece that was offered to you as a gift. Well now, we'd better send word to the abbot and ask for a meeting to see whether or not we're correct."

"Do you have any idea what time it is?" I asked, horrified, realizing then that control over emotions and *wu wei* would never be a part of my life.

"It's nearly dawn," he replied. "The abbot will have been performing the morning ceremonies for hours already."

"I've had absolutely no sense of time since we arrived in Wudang," I admitted. "Those double Chinese hours with animal names just confuse me."

"That is the true Chinese way of telling time. The only place it's no longer used is in territory occupied by you Westerners," Lao Jiang replied as he got to his feet. "Biao, go to Purple Cloud Palace and ask for an audience with the abbot. Say we've solved the puzzle."

"Perhaps I should visit Ming T'ien to confirm the last two ideograms before we speak with the abbot," I proposed.

"Do," he agreed, stifling a yawn. "I think I'll be able to sleep for a while, knowing we have the answer. I wouldn't have been able to do it without your help. I'm glad you encouraged me to leave feng shui and look in Taoist texts from Wudang. Soon we'll have the third and final piece of the *jiance*."

Surprisingly, my niece was absolutely indifferent to the news. Perhaps, deep down, her transformation had merely been one of self-interest.

"So we'll be leaving Wudang soon?" she asked, furrowing her brow. "I'm not ready to leave my classes yet."

During breakfast the sun struggled to break through layers of thick clouds on that first morning without rain.

"Biao and I could stay here," she stubbornly proposed. The boy's eyes lit up, but he didn't dare say a word. He'd just come back from the abbot's palace with the news that a servant would come to accompany us to the meeting at the hour of the Snake.[40]

"You will go where I go, Fernanda," I declared, mustering patience. I was the one who had wanted her to stay in Shanghai with Father Castrillo to keep her out of harm's way, and she was the one who had fought not to leave my side. Now she was willing to watch me leave with Lao Jiang and the soldiers just so she could stay in Wudang. "How can

I leave you all alone in this Taoist monastery out in the middle of
China?"

"Well, I don't know why not, Auntie. We're safer here than anywhere else. Besides, you don't need Biao and me to find the tomb of that
darned Emperor Ti Huang . . . whatever."

"The case is closed, Fernanda," I said, raising my hand in the air. "I
will not allow you to stay here. Off you go to your classes, but you're to
return with Biao as soon as he comes to get you."

She didn't hesitate and strode out of the room without finishing her
breakfast. A sleepy-looking Lao Jiang appeared just then. That was the first
morning I'd done tai chi on my own, and although I'd made one mistake
after another, the solitude in those serene mountains was magnificent.

"*Ni hao*," the antiquarian said. "What news have you got?"

"In an hour—a Western hour, that is—one of the abbot's servants
will come to take us to Purple Cloud Palace."

"Ah, perfect!" he exclaimed happily, sitting down to breakfast.
"Didn't you want to visit Ming T'ien first?"

"We were just leaving, weren't we, Biao?" I replied as I got out of my
chair. I wasn't sure the old nun would be on her satin cushion that early,
but I had to try. It might be the last time I saw her.

We walked down the still-wet cobbled streets, puffs of steam coming out of our mouths. Monks dressed in long black tunics were sweeping the corridors, bridges, patios, palaces, and steps of Wudang, trying
to get rid of all the accumulated mud. The cold was revitalizing, and
the views after so many days of rain were positively intoxicating. As we
passed a path along a cliff, a carpet of white clouds lay several hundred
feet below us. Ming T'ien's temple was visible in the distance, across a
bridge, on a slope. Wudang was so enormous that the scenery changed
each day. This was a city, a mysterious city, in which peace filled your
lungs with every breath of fresh air. Deep down, my niece was right: I
wouldn't have minded staying awhile to reflect calmly on everything
I'd seen and heard, but above all to reconsider the things I'd learned

and dismissed perhaps a bit too quickly and with too many built-in prejudices.

Just then my heart leaped with happiness when I saw the little figure of the old nun sitting on the portico.

"Hurry!" I urged Biao, and we both quickened our pace.

As soon as we reached her, much to my surprise, Ming T'ien gave us a stern reprimand.

"Why are you always running from place to place?" she spit out angrily. Biao's soft tone when interpreting was far from the foul-tempered one she had used to address me.

"Forgive me, Ming T'ien," I replied, futilely bowing with my hands in front of my forehead. "Today is a very special day, and we're in a bit of a hurry."

"What does that matter? Do you think the sculptures of tortoises all over the monastery are just for decoration? The tortoise lives a long life because it isn't hurried. This is a lesson you need to learn. Repeat after me: Haste shortens your life."

"Haste shortens your life," I repeated in Chinese.

"That's better," she said, breaking into a wide smile. "I want you to remember that when you're far away from here, Chang Cheng. Will you do that?"

"I will, Ming T'ien," I promised, not entirely convinced.

"Good. That makes me very happy," she said, her white eyes turning back to the mountains. "I sense we won't have another opportunity to speak, but I'm glad you came to say good-bye."

How did she know?

"You must be on your way to Purple Cloud Palace," she added. "Little Xu will receive you soon."

"Little Xu?" I asked. She couldn't be speaking of Xu Benshan, the great abbot of Wudang, could she?

She laughed. "I still remember the day he came to these mountains," she explained. "Like me, he has never left, and he never will."

How did she know all this? How did she know we'd solved the puzzle? How did she know we had an audience with the abbot?

"I don't want you to be late, Chang Cheng," she admonished once again. "I know you need to confirm the order of the ideograms, so tell me, what's the correct answer?"

"'Happiness,' 'Longevity,' 'Health,' and 'Peace.'"

She smiled. "Go on," she said, waving her hand as if swatting a fly. "Your destiny awaits."

"But is that right?" I asked uncertainly.

"Of course it's right!" she snapped. "Now, go! I'm getting tired."

Biao and I turned and began to walk away. I was filled with sadness. I would have liked to stay and learn more from Ming T'ien.

"Remember me when you're my age!" she shouted, and then I heard her laugh. I turned to look at her and wave good-bye, even though I knew she couldn't see me. It was worth taking a few years off my life to hurry away before I couldn't see through my tears. *Remember me when you're my age,* she had said. I smiled. Was she trying to say I'd live to be 112, like her? In that case I'd die in far-off 1992 no less, almost at the end of the century that had just begun. I was laughing by the time we got back to the house and kept laughing as we headed to "Little Xu's" palace, accompanied by a richly dressed servant.

Purple Cloud Palace was even more impressive than the first time I saw it, the day we arrived in the downpour. The sky was still leaden, but, thankfully, not a drop of rain fell as we crossed the long bridge over the moat and climbed the magnificent staircase all the way up to the third level. The abbot received us once again in the Library Pavilion, sitting at the far end with the utmost dignity, flanked by the thousands of bamboo-slat *jiances* piled in rolls down both sides of the hall now illuminated by the light coming in through the windows covered in rice paper. There were no torches or fire this time, just the four big stone tiles set in front of the abbot, their smooth backs facing us.

After walking with the short steps required by protocol until we had gone as far as we were allowed, the monks who had accompanied us withdrew, bowing deeply. My eyes were again drawn to the enormous platform soles of the abbot's black velvet shoes, but now, in the natural light, the shine of his blue silk tunic caught my attention even more.

"Good news?" Xu Benshan asked softly.

"As if he doesn't know!" I mumbled quietly as Lao Jiang took a step toward the stone tiles. Pointing at them, the antiquarian said, "'Happiness,' 'Longevity,' 'Health,' and 'Peace.'"

"Little Xu" nodded his assent and placed his right hand in the wide left sleeve of his tunic. My heart raced when I saw him pull out an old roll of slats held together by green silk threads. It was the third piece of the *jiance.*

With great ceremony the abbot stood and walked down the three stairs while two monks dressed in purple turned the tiles so we could confirm our answer. There they were, in order: the ideogram *fu,* "Happiness," the one with the arrows and the squares; then *shou,* "Longevity," with its multiple horizontal lines; next *k'ang,* "Health," the trident piercing the little man; and finally *an,* "Peace," its protagonist dancing the fox-trot.

The abbot walked past the tiles and reached out to hand Lao Jiang the last piece of the *jiance* written by the architect and engineer Sai Wu over two thousand years earlier. Up close, Xu Benshan seemed very young, a boy almost, but my eyes left his face to follow the *jiance* as it passed from his hand to Lao Jiang's. It was ours. Now we'd know how to find the First Emperor's tomb.

"Thank you, Abbot," I heard the antiquarian say.

"You are welcome to enjoy our hospitality as long as you like. The most difficult part of your journey is about to begin. Do not hesitate to ask if there is anything you need."

We bowed deeply in thanks, and as the abbot stood watching, Lao Jiang, Biao, and I began the slow, interminable walk out of the palace, barely able to contain our desire to run and examine the anxiously awaited trophy outside. We finally had the third piece! And from what I could tell at a glance, it was identical to the two already in our possession.

"Let's not open it until we're at the house," Lao Jiang said, lifting the slats victoriously in the air. "I want to put all three together for a complete reading."

"Biao!" I said jubilantly. "Go find Fernanda, and the two of you get back as quick as you can."

Chapter

4

The table in the study was now completely cleared of books, and for the first time since that night in 1662 when the Prince of Gui severed the silk threads that held the bamboo slats together, separating it into three pieces that he instructed his most trusted friends to hide all along the Yangtze, those pieces of the old letter written by the architect Sai Wu were once again reunited. As we suspected, the last piece indicated the location of the First Emperor's tomb, as well as how to enter without setting off what we now knew were automatic crossbows and dangerous mechanical traps placed to keep tomb raiders out (to keep us out, that is). A full reading of the *jiance* was thus very important. Even Fernanda, who hurried back as soon as Biao found her, was visibly nervous, leaning over the slats as if she could understand what she was looking at. Lao Jiang was forced to order her to move back before sitting down and placing his glasses on his nose. The rest of us gathered behind him in complete silence and peered over his shoulder.

"What does the new piece say?" I asked after quite some time.

The antiquarian slowly shook his head. "These ideograms are a little smaller than the others, and some I can't read at all because the ink has smudged," he finally replied.

"Just what we needed," I murmured, inching a bit closer. "Read what you can."

He grunted something unintelligible and reached a hand out toward Biao. "Pass me the magnifying glass that's over there on those books."

The boy raced to get it and was back before the antiquarian had even finished his sentence.

"Let's see, then. . . . Here it says, 'When you, my son, arrive at the mausoleum, all of us who worked on it will have been sacrificed, and no one will remember its location.'"

"How old did Sai Wu think his orphan son would be when he went to the tomb?" Fernanda asked, surprised at how quickly the architect thought a work of that magnitude and importance would be forgotten.

"I imagine after he'd come of age, as it says in the first piece," Lao Jiang replied, taking his glasses off to look at her. "Somewhere between eighteen and twenty years after he sent the boy to live with his friend in . . . where was it? Chaoxian? Yes, Chaoxian," he confirmed by looking at the first piece. "But it's not surprising no one could recall where the First Emperor's tomb was after such a short time. Remember, only those condemned to forced labor and their bosses, the architects and engineers, were ever on that site, and all of them died with Shi Huang Ti when they were buried alive. The common people—or 'black-headed ones,' as free men were called—never knew where the construction site was. The only ones who did know the secret were the ministers and the imperial family, who had to perform the funeral rites. However, they all died within three years after Shi Huang Ti, as a result of court conspiracies, peasant revolts, and uprisings by former feudal lords. The dynasty our First Emperor founded for ten thousand years barely lasted three."

"Could you continue reading, please?" I asked, bringing my hands to my waist in a very Spanish gesture that took me by surprise.

"Of course," the antiquarian said, putting his glasses back on and holding the magnifying glass over the slats. "Where was I? Ah, yes, here. 'Look at the map, Sai Shi Gu'er. The secret entrance is in the artificial lake formed by the dam on the Shahe River. Dive in where I have indicated and descend four *ren*—'"

"Hold on! Hold on!" I exclaimed, pulling one of the stools over so I could sit comfortably. "We'd better take a closer look at this map. I haven't been able to make heads or tails of it no matter how hard I try. Perhaps now, with Sai Wu's directions, we'll actually be able to understand these blotches of ink."

Lao Jiang turned to look at me, smiling. "But it's perfectly clear, Elvira. Look, take a good look at this square here," he said, pointing to a tiny mark in the upper left-hand corner of the map. "Inside, it says 'Xianyang,' former capital of the first Chinese empire, Shi Huang Ti's city. It's only logical to assume that the mausoleum would be relatively nearby, no more than sixty miles in any direction. Xianyang is likely nothing more than a pile of ruins today, if anything's left at all. However, not far away is the metropolis of Xi'an, which is erroneously assumed to be the old capital. As you can see, Xi'an doesn't appear on this map, and that proves its authenticity, because the city wasn't founded until years after Shi Huang Ti died."

"And is Xi'an very far from here, from Wudang?"

Lao Jiang tilted his head pensively. "I estimate it's about the same distance as from Hankow, heading westnorth," he finally said. "Xi'an is the capital of neighboring Shensi[41] province to the north, and Wudang is on the border, so it's likely . . . about two hundred forty miles, maybe less. The hardest part will be the mountains. You see, the Qin Ling mountain range divides Wudang and Shensi, so we'll need another month or month and a half to get there."

It wasn't going to be easy, I thought desolately. In the middle of the rainy season, with winter coming on, we'd have to cross a mountain range that would surely be even more fearsome than Wudang with its seventy-two high, sheer peaks.

"Don't be discouraged, Elvira," I heard the antiquarian say. "Xi'an was the starting point for the famous Silk Road that linked East and West, so it's easily accessible. There are good roads and mountain trails."

"But what about the war? And the Green Gang?"

"Shall we get back to the map? So we've now located the First Emperor's capital, old Xianyang. This dotted line down below, running from one end of the slats to the other, is the river Wei," he said, pointing to another couple of illegible characters. Surely I'd have seen it better if he'd been able to point it out with those gold fingernails he'd had in Shanghai. "If we follow it to the east, we can see many effluents to the north and south, but this one," he emphasized, placing his finger on the last line that went down toward the lower right-hand corner of the map, "this is definitely the Shahe, which Sai Wu referred to in his letter. See? Here's the name. And this elongated wide bit is undoubtedly the artificial lake formed as a result of the dam. It's simply marvelous!" he exclaimed, opening his arms as if to embrace that unlucky foreman who'd died two thousand years earlier. "Note this little red mark at one end of the reservoir. It's barely visible, but it's there."

He passed me the magnifying glass and moved over so I could examine this red mark. When I looked at it in light of his explanation, the strange map did become comprehensible. If I followed the Shahe's vertical descent from the Wei to a mountain chain along the bottom of the bamboo slats, near the end there was an elongated wide bit angled slightly northeast that had a tiny red spot on the end closest to the mountains. So that red spot indicated where to dive into the water? Oh, please!

After Fernanda and even Biao had examined the map, the magnifying glass was passed back to Lao Jiang, who continued reading.

"'Dive in where I have indicated and descend four *ren*—'" he repeated.

"How far is a *ren*?" my niece asked.

The antiquarian seemed taken aback by the question.

"That's an ancient measurement," he explained after giving it some thought, "and many of them have changed over time. However, I'd say four *ren* is about twenty-five feet."

"Twenty-five feet!" I wailed. "But I hardly know how to swim!"

"Don't worry, *tai-tai*," Biao encouraged, "we'll help you. It's not hard."

Lao Jiang, fed up with the interruptions, continued reading:

"'. . . four *ren* until you come to the mouth of a pentagonal pipe that forms part of the funeral chamber's drainage system.'"

"Pentagonal?" Biao whispered.

"It has five sides," Fernanda quickly clarified.

"'Move through it for twenty *chi*—'"

"Not again!" my niece complained. "Now how far is a *chi*?"

"A *chi* equals approximately eight inches," Lao Jiang explained, keeping his eyes on the *jiance*. "If I'm not mistaken, twenty *chi* would be a little over thirteen feet."

"You're not mistaken," Biao the know-it-all said. There was no doubt the boy was good at math.

"May I continue reading, please?" Lao Jiang pleaded grumpily.

"Carry on," I said. If we kept interrupting him, he really never would finish.

"'Move through the pipe for twenty *chi*, then go up into a ventilation shaft. There is one every twenty *chi*. The last shaft is at the bottom of a pit that will take you directly into the burial mound. You will come out in front of the big doors to the main hall leading into the funeral palace. You should know that the tomb has six levels, six being the sacred number of the Original Dragon's reign.'"

"Six levels?" I asked.

"Sacred number?" Fernanda asked simultaneously.

Lao Jiang wearily pulled his glasses off once again. "Could you ask just one question at a time?" he begged with a sigh.

"Fine. Me first," I hurried to say, before my niece. "How is it the tomb can have six levels? The historian who wrote about the mausoleum never said anything about that."

"True, Sima Qian doesn't mention this, but remember, Sima Qian wrote his history a hundred years after the emperor's death. He'd never been there or never even knew where it was located. All he did was copy what he found in old historical records from the Qin dynasty."

"Why was six the First Emperor's sacred number?" interjected Fernanda, who could not have cared less about anyone's history or chronicles.

"Shi Huang Ti was influenced by master geomancers of the time and adopted the philosophy of the Five Elements. I'm not going to explain what that is right now," he said, and I nodded in agreement. I knew what he was talking about and was certainly glad he wasn't about to explain that complex theory. I was happy enough to have it noted down in my sketchbook. "However, according to Taoism, there is a harmonious relationship between nature and human beings, a relationship that is made material in the Five Elements: Fire, Wood, Earth, Metal, and Water. According to these Five Elements, Shi Huang Ti's reign was governed by Water, because the previous kingdoms belonged to the period of Fire and he had conquered and dominated them. Since Water corresponds to the color black, the entire imperial court dressed in black, and all the buildings, banners, clothing, hats, and decorations were also black."

"How sinister!" I blurted out.

"That's why the common people were also called 'black-headed ones.' Further, according to the theory of the Elements, Water is associated not only with the color black but also with the number six. This, then, is the answer to your question, Elvira: The tomb has six levels because that's what was required by the emperor. It was his geomantic number."

"That, and who would ever expect an underground mausoleum to have six levels, right?"

"Right," he confirmed, wearily putting his glasses back on again. "Well, as I was reading. . . . Here we are. '. . . the sacred number for the Original Dragon's reign. Each of the levels is a death trap designed to protect the true tomb, which is on the last level, the lowest, and safe from those who would desecrate and rob it. That is the level you must reach, Sai Shi Gu'er. I will now give you all the information I have gathered, with great difficulty, over the last few years. Those who belong to the secret . . . *Shaofu*?" Lao Jiang stopped. "I don't know what that word means. I've never heard it before. '. . . to the secret *Shaofu*[42] in charge of security work in complete isolation, and I have built only what they ordered me to. I can, however, tell you a few things that will help. I know that on the first level hundreds of crossbows will fire when you enter the palace, but you can avoid them by studying the founder of the Xia dynasty's achievements.'"

"This is mad!" I couldn't help but exclaim, overwhelmed.

" 'I know even less about the second level, but do not use fire to light the way. Move forward in darkness, or you will die. I know what I have done on the third level: There are ten thousand bridges that seem to lead nowhere, but there is one route that leads to the exit. On the fourth level is the chamber with the *Bian Zhong*' "—Lao Jiang stopped again, pensive. "I don't know what these *Bian Zhong* are. '. . . the chamber with the *Bian Zhong*, which are related to the Five Elements.'"

"Well, we know what those are," I bubbled, but no one seconded my assertion.

" 'On the fifth there is a special lock that opens only by use of magic. And on the sixth, the Original Dragon's true burial place, you will have to cross a wide river of mercury to reach the treasures.'" The antiquarian paused and ran a hand over his forehead. " 'My son, I beg you to come and do what I ask. Bowing twice, Sai Wu.'"

"Do you think we can do it?" I asked.

The confidence that had filled the air at the start of the reading had vanished. Like bedridden invalids, we remained silent, immobile, frozen by doubt.

"This text is very old," Lao Jiang muttered after giving my question some thought. "What was advanced science then isn't now. We also no longer believe in magic and certainly have enough copies of manuscripts that were accessible only to court scholars and emperors in those days. I don't think we need to worry," he concluded. "Yes, I'm sure we can do it."

No one said anything for a few minutes as we all became lost in thought. As Lao Jiang said, the real danger might not be that combination of old traps, which perhaps didn't even work. No, the real danger was that we'd be descending deep into the earth inside a ridiculously ancient structure. The entire mausoleum could come crashing down, and we'd be caught inside, like rats in a burrow. We could wind up buried under layers and layers of rubble; the very idea literally took my breath away. We had to consider the children: How could we put them in such peril? It would undoubtedly be best to leave them in Wudang. I had no choice because of the enormous debt Rémy had left me, but there was no need for Fernanda to die at just seventeen years of age, and Biao didn't have to come to such a sad end either.

"The children will stay in Wudang," I announced.

My niece turned to look at me with furious incredulity.

"It was your idea, Fernanda," I warned, before she could even begin to protest. "This very morning you were quite annoyed at having to leave the monastery. I'm going to allow you to stay and continue with your exercises."

"But now I want to go!" she fumed.

"Well, I don't care what you want now," I calmly replied. "You and Biao will stay in Wudang until we come back for you."

"I agree," Lao Jiang murmured. "Fernanda and Biao will stay in Wudang under the monks' care."

Biao's face had lit up like a blaze. Two vermilion circles appeared on his coppery cheeks, and his ears were about to burst into flames as he held back the angry protests boiling inside. Like Fernanda, he'd have given anything to go with us to the First Emperor's tomb.

My niece left the study, stalking out proud and offended. She was followed not far behind by lanky Biao, who, fearing the rod, hid his anger as best he could. I was sure my ears would soon begin burning.

Once alone, Lao Jiang and I looked at one another.

"We're really going to miss Paddy," the antiquarian commented.

"True. This is quite an undertaking for just the two of us."

"What can we do? Ask our soldiers for help? Involve them to that extent?"

"I don't think that's a good idea," I said.

"Neither do I, but we're going to need them. Think about it."

"I don't need to think about it. They'll do more harm than good."

"I know, I know. . . ." he admitted sadly. "But what else can we do?"

I desperately tried to think of a solution and suddenly had an idea.

"What if we ask the abbot for help? He said to be sure and ask if we needed anything."

"And what 'thing' would we ask him for?" Lao Jiang asked sarcastically.

"A monk," I proposed. "Or two."

"Monks?"

"Look around! We're surrounded by Taoist experts in the martial arts, ancient history, fortune-telling, astrology, magic, geomantics, philosophy. . . ." I said excitedly.

Lao Jiang looked at me with a furrowed brow. "But then we'd have to share the treasure with the monastery."

"Don't be so greedy!" I cried out indignantly. I knew that his share was really going to the Kuomintang, but what did I care? "Wouldn't it be magnificent for the First Emperor's riches to be distributed among a drunken journalist, a poor widow, the Nationalists, the Communists, and a Taoist monastery? Would you rather they fell into the hands of Puyi and his kind or, worse still, the Japanese?"

My questions gave him pause.

"You're right," he admitted, visibly annoyed. "I'll send a letter to the abbot explaining what we need. I'll also tell him the children will be staying here, and I'll offer a portion of the wealth from the mausoleum. We'll see what he says."

After a lunch at which Fernanda and Biao were conspicuously absent, two strange characters came to our door with a letter from the abbot in answer to Lao Jiang's. They were monks, and it was odd how much they looked alike: same height, same body, same face. While the antiquarian was engrossed in his reading, I studied the twins who waited stock-still on the portico. Both were slender, and their hair was still black, if thinning. They had bushy eyebrows, eyes spaced wide apart, and each had such a prominent chin it was almost disfiguring. After a careful examination (which was easy, because neither one looked anywhere but at Lao Jiang), I was astonished to find just one small difference between them, and that was a faint dark spot on the left one's cheek.

"The abbot has sent us these brothers, Daiyu and Hongyu," the antiquarian said as he looked up from the paper. Both monks bowed as soon as they heard their names. "One is Master Daiyu, or 'Black Jade,' an expert in martial arts." The one with the nearly imperceptible spot on his face bowed politely again. "The other is his brother, Master Hongyu, or 'Red Jade,' one of the most learned monks in Wudang." He bowed as well. "Both are from Hankow and speak French, so we'll have no trouble communicating. Masters Black Jade and Red Jade, Mme De Poulain and I, Jiang Longyan, are honored to have your assistance on this journey. We are very appreciative that the abbot has placed two such illustrious advisers at our disposal."

We all bowed several times, but I grew rather annoyed because the two Jades were ignoring me just as Lao Jiang had previously ignored my niece. I thought a comment might be in order.

"Perhaps Masters Black Jade and Red Jade should receive my permission to look at me and address me in all confidence."

They both raised their eyebrows, and the antiquarian launched into a speech in Chinese, attempting to avert a diplomatic conflict. I couldn't understand what he said, but it seemed to work. As soon as he'd finished, the twins turned and, after glancing at me uncertainly, began another series of bows. That was better.

"We'll leave tomorrow at dawn," Lao Jiang announced. "I'll send word to have our soldiers in Junzhou head north, where we'll meet them in Shiyan. There's no sense in backtracking just to get them."

"Tomorrow is an auspicious day to leave," Master Red Jade remarked. "The journey will be a good one."

"I hope so," I murmured skeptically.

It was a very sad dinner that night. Fernanda was still angry and refused to speak. She picked at her tofu, mushrooms, and vegetables, then went to bed with tears in her eyes. She was lying with her face to the wall when I went into our room.

"Are you awake?" I whispered, sitting on the edge of her *k'ang*. She didn't reply. "We won't be gone long, Fernanda. Study hard, take advantage of your time in Wudang. I'm going to leave a letter for the Spanish consul in Shanghai, Don Julio Palencia. If anything happens to me . . . If anything were to happen to me, make your way to Shanghai with Biao and give the letter to the consul. He'll see that you get back to Spain."

A heavy sigh was her only reply. Perhaps she really was asleep. I stood and went up to the study to write that letter.

Before dawn on that Tuesday, October 30, while it was still pitch black outside and the children lay sleeping, Lao Jiang, the twin monks, and I set out from the monastery at a swift pace, our bundles slung over our shoulders. It was horribly cold, but thankfully it wasn't raining; the last thing we wanted was to descend the Mysterious Mountain in the pouring rain. As the sun rose higher in a cloudless sky, Master Red Jade's prophecy of an auspicious day seemed to come true.

Walking in silence, we left behind the beautiful peaks of Wudang, the temples, the palaces, the long staircases, the statues of tigers and cranes, the oceans of clouds, and the thick, impenetrable forest hued such beautiful greens and ochers. We'd been there for only five days, but I felt it was a sort of home I'd always like to return to. Once I was back in Paris, surrounded by car noises, streetlights, people's voices, and the daily hustle and bustle of a big Western city, I'd remember Wudang as a secret paradise where life was unfolding in a different way, at a different pace. Even the monkeys seemed to be screeching good-bye. All I could think about was coming back soon for Fernanda—not because I was afraid of what awaited us, though I was, but because I actually missed her and wanted the whole matter to be behind us.

Close to nightfall we passed through another of those exotic gates that lead to the Mysterious Mountain. This one was a little different, smaller than the one we came through near Junzhou, less ornate, but just as ancient and impressive. We spent the night in a *lü kuan* for pilgrims, and I had a room to myself for the first time in ages. I wondered how my niece was doing, how she and Biao had spent the day. Unfortunately, Lao Jiang and Masters Red and Black—I'd begun to call them that after Stendhal's famous novel *The Red and the Black*—weren't very good company. I slept poorly but still managed to get up in time to join the three of them doing tai chi in the patio.

We walked all day, stopping for just a moment to eat. We didn't speak much then either, simply ate and got moving once again. The weather improved as we got farther from the mountains; the blackest clouds, the rain clouds, seemed stuck on the peaks of Wudang, unable to move in any direction. Once again on those Chinese trails, with ink slanting the shape of my eyes, I had the most overwhelming sense of déjà vu. It only intensified by midafternoon, once we'd crossed a small river and could finally see the town of Shiyan, where the five Kuomintang soldiers and the seven members of the Communist revolutionary army were waiting for us on the outskirts, gathered around a fire in an apparent atmosphere of camaraderie, our horses and mules grazing peacefully nearby.

That night over dinner, the soldiers told us that they hadn't seen anything suspicious, and no one had told them about anyone other than pilgrims coming or going from the monastery. They seemed content, too content, as if this had become a vacation and they were having a lovely time, laughing boorishly and drinking sorghum liquor a little too euphorically for my taste. It appeared they'd stocked up in Junzhou, so there was plenty of it with our provisions. I was particularly happy I'd left Fernanda at the monastery, safe from all that. I couldn't imagine her sitting next to me witnessing such a scene. We filled the entire, miserable *lü kuan* that night and set out in the morning for Yunxian, "a mere forty-eight *li* away," according to Master Red. Of the two brothers, he was the more inclined to converse—and *he* hardly opened his mouth.

The trails we took were no worse than the ones from Hankow to Wudang. I might even say it was better traveling, because we didn't meet all those sad caravans of peasants fleeing the wars en masse. The worst was yet to come once the snow fell, but for the time being we'd moved away from the most dangerous areas of conflict as we headed into mountainous regions that didn't interest the warlords. I could well understand why, once I saw the humble mountain village of Yunxian, located at a crossroads, circled by a river, and the awful paths that led there. It took us so long to walk those "mere forty-eight *li*" that it was well past dark when we arrived, without a hope of finding any lodging. We were forced to spend the night outdoors, battling freezing temperatures with huge bonfires and all the blankets we had. I had just managed to fall asleep when there was a terrible racket: the sound of shouting, banging, voices raising the alarm. I jumped up off the straw mat, my heart in my throat.

"What's going on?" I shouted repeatedly. Given the commotion and my fear, I hadn't realized I was speaking Spanish, which of course no one understood. Lao Jiang was standing beside me, along with the monks Red and Black, as the soldiers ran here and there with their weapons drawn. It had to be another attack by the Green Gang. I tugged on Lao Jiang's sleeve to get his attention, saying (in French), "We should hide, Lao Jiang. We're too exposed like this."

But instead of listening to me, he turned toward the soldier who had taken the first shift on guard duty that night. The young man was happily striding toward us, holding Fernanda and Biao by the scruff of their necks. I let out an astonished gasp, unable to believe my eyes.

"What in God's name . . . ?" I began to shout angrily.

"Don't get mad, Auntie. Please don't get mad!" my nitwit of a niece implored, bawling. I had never seen her so dirty or shabby-looking, and my heart stopped. Had something happened to them? How had they gotten this far?

The uproar in camp was quieting down, and all that could be heard were bursts of laughter. Out of the corner of my eye, I saw a few soldiers trying to calm the animals.

"What happened?" I asked, struggling to get my nerves under control. "Are you all right?"

Biao nodded, as taciturn and grimy as could be. Fernanda dried her tears on the wide sleeve of her Chinese coat and inhaled noisily, choking back her sobs.

"What on earth are you two doing here? I want an explanation! Now!"

"We wanted to come," Biao murmured solemnly, staring at the ground. He was so tall that I had to lift my chin a little to look him in the face.

"I can't hear you!" I shouted, to the delight of the audience that had begun to sit down around us as if enjoying a wonderful show. It was no wonder: My shrieks could easily have passed for operatic Chinese caterwauling.

"I said we wanted to come," the boy repeated.

"You did not have permission! We left you in the abbot's care!"

Neither of them said a word.

"Leave it be, Elvira," Lao Jiang suggested. "Tomorrow I'll give Biao the punishment he deserves."

"You will not cane him!" I exploded, shouting at the antiquarian in the same tone I was using to yell at the children.

"Please, *tai-tai*. I deserve it!" Biao pleaded.

"Everyone in this country is crazy!" I screamed like a madwoman, hearing more laughter behind me. "That's it! To bed! We'll talk about this tomorrow."

"We're hungry," my niece then confessed in an absolutely normal tone of voice. She was over being upset, and now she was making demands. Incredible! That filthy face of hers aroused no compassion in me.

"No dinner for the two of you today!" I declared with my hands on my hips. "To bed!"

"But we haven't eaten since yesterday!" she protested angrily.

"I don't care. You're not going to expire after a two-day fast! Now, where are your bags?"

"Over where the sentry found us," Biao hurried to say.

"Well, go on and get them!" I ordered, turning to walk away. "Tomorrow's another day, and I won't be as inclined to kill anyone then. Hurry up!"

I crawled into my *k'ang* and refused to open my eyes even when I heard those two wayward teens prepare their beds next to mine. I could hear them whispering for a while, and then, slowly, everything became silent again. I pretended to sleep, because I had no other choice, when in fact I was awake all night worrying about how to make them go back to Wudang the next morning.

However, by the time the last soldier on guard duty woke us up and I saw them lying there fast asleep, I decided they might as well accompany us to Xi'an. They could stay in the city while Lao Jiang, the monks, and I went into the mausoleum. My first obligation was to look after my niece, to keep her by my side as long as she wasn't in any danger. She was better off with me than in a Taoist monastery, and no good Western citizen would disagree with me. It was funny to see that there were now six of us doing tai chi in the mornings. Fernanda and Biao enthusiastically joined in the exercise, no matter how cold or even how much snow there might be. By the end of November, when we reached a city called Shang-hsien,[43] after nearly a month of hard journeying over terrible mountain passes in the frigid wind, battling snow squalls and landslides, we offered a magnificent display of harmony and coordinated movements.

The town of Shang-hsien, located in the very heart of the mountain range, in a small valley formed by the Danjiang River and the slope of

Mount Shangshan, was a historically dangerous area. After Lao Jiang spoke with one of the locals, he explained that numerous battles had taken place there. Remnants of the ancient walls and a few cobblestone streets could still be seen. Over the past two thousand years, armies and peasant rebellions had gone through Shang-hsien to reach the great Xi'an (just sixty-two miles away), since it was located in the only pass through the Qin Ling Mountains from the south. The city even had an old *lü kuan* that, after we'd spent all that time in the mountains, seemed the height of luxury, when in fact it was nothing more than a squalid shelter. But I didn't mind: I was willing to kill or die for a nice hot bath.

After we ate a good dinner, Fernanda and Biao began a game of Wei-ch'i. The brothers Red and Black started off watching enthusiastically but soon joined in the game. The soldiers were drinking heavily and making a racket over in a corner of the large dining hall. Meanwhile, Lao Jiang and I examined our copy of the map from the *jiance* (I had used my colored pencils to draw it on a page of my sketchbook) and speculated on how little the architect Sai Wu had told his son about the traps inside the tomb. I often wondered why Sai Wu's son never received that letter. It was clear from the text that the slats were to accompany the boy and that his father's friend was to look after them until young Sai Shi Gu'er came of age. If the *jiance* and the boy were together and the *jiance* had never reached its destination, clearly the boy never reached Chaoxian either. I felt so much compassion for that newborn whose father had such ambitious plans for him and who likely died with the rest of the Sai clan. If that were the case, there'd been a weak link somewhere in the chain, and it could only have been the "trusted" servant with whom Sai Wu had sent his son and the letter. But how had the slats survived? We would probably never know.

We went to bed clean and satisfied—I might even say happy, knowing we were about to sleep on lovely, warm *k'angs* placed on top of bricks that channeled heat from the ovens. This heavenly pleasure was an absolute Oriental luxury. However, my next memory of that night is of a voice whispering strange, violent words in my ear as something cold and metallic pressed against my throat. My eyes flew open, and I was instantly wide awake, only to discover I couldn't see a thing in the darkness and that a stranger was holding me with his hand over my mouth and nose so I couldn't move or even breathe. I wanted to scream but couldn't, and as soon as I began to struggle, the metal pressed deeper into my throat and a stream of warm blood trickled down toward my shoulder. I could tell by the smothered noises nearby that my niece was in trouble as well. We were about to die, and I didn't know what to do. As had happened in Nanking, the nearness of death, of which I was so afraid, actually made me feel stronger, even more alive. A flash went off in my head, and I remembered that there was a little table up against the warm bricks, not right at my feet but quite nearby, and on it was a large clay pitcher that would make quite a noise if it were to fall. However, if I stretched out to kick the pitcher, the knife would slice into my throat, severing the arteries. Then I heard my niece groan furiously and didn't hesitate another second: In a single motion, I moved my neck away by pushing my head back and to the left, into the assassin's chest, and stretched out my legs—my whole body—with such force that when my feet kicked the vessel, it flew through the air. The assassin holding on to me was surprised and angry, and he bashed me on the temple, but by then the loud crash as the pitcher hit the stone floor had been heard throughout the *lü kuan.* As I tried in vain to recover from the blow that had left me nearly unconscious, I heard a stifled exclamation and felt the assassin's arms go limp and release me. I collapsed onto the *k'ang,* but I heard a sharp, anguished scream from my niece, and I struggled to get up and help her.

"Don't move," whispered the voice of Master Red (or it might have been Master Black, I never knew). "Your niece is fine."

"Fernanda. Fernanda . . ." I called. The poor girl cried like a baby and held on tight to me, shaking like a leaf. I held her just as close while trying to make sense of what was happening, but I couldn't think. I was stunned. My head hurt like the devil, and the buzzing noise inside combined with the sound of shots being fired and shouting, banging coming from outside. The big dining hall had become a battlefield. It must be an attack by the Green Gang. These were their usual tactics, and this time they had come very close to making sure my niece and I weren't alive to tell the tale. Although we were still in danger, I thought with a start. We needed to move, get out of there, hide somewhere safe until the fighting was over. I was dizzier than a top and on the verge of vomiting as soon as my feet hit the floor, but Fernanda helped me stand, and with my arm around her neck I dragged myself to the door. In truth, I had no idea where to go; I was behaving irrationally. In order to leave the room, we'd have to go out into the dining hall, and that's where the shots were coming from.

"Oh, God, I hope Biao's all right!" I heard my niece say in a strangled whisper. My thoughts of escape had been ridiculous. I held on to Fernanda again or, rather, I leaned on her completely, and we went back into the dark, empty room, stepping on pieces of the shattered pitcher in our bare feet.

"What are you trying to do?" she asked in confusion.

"We have to hide," I whispered. "It's the Green Gang."

"But there's nowhere to hide!" she exclaimed.

A bullet whistled in through the door and slammed straight into the wall, sending bits of stone flying all around us. My niece screamed.

"Shut up!" I ordered, my mouth right next to her ear. "Do you want them to know we're here so they can come after us?"

She shook her head emphatically and took my hand, leading me to a corner of the room. On our way we had to step over the dead bodies of the two assassins who'd attacked us. I heard my niece move the blankets and bamboo mats off the k'angs and come toward me. Still reeling, I realized she was wrapping me in one of the blankets, then in one of the mats until I was completely rolled up. She then leaned me casually against the wall. I had to admit it was a good idea, the best one available to us.

"What about you?" I asked from inside my suffocating refuge.

"I'm hiding, too," she replied.

We didn't speak again until much later, when the struggle in the patio was over. I'd had a horrible time of it, and not only because of the fear. I don't know what that blasted assassin did to me, but the pain in my head, the anxiety, the dizziness, and worst of all the feeling of being about to lose consciousness at any second made the minutes I spent rolled up in those mats absolute heroics on my part. Just when I couldn't stand another moment, I thought I heard Biao's voice.

"*Tai-tai!* Young Mistress!" He sounded very far away, as if he were calling out to us from another world, though he was surely nearby. "Young Mistress! *Tai-tai!*"

"Biao!" I heard my niece reply. I tried to speak, but all I remember is vomiting inside my narrow hiding place, and then nothing more.

I opened my eyes and saw a white adobe ceiling. My first thought was that I'd slept for a long time and, then, that there was too much light. I half closed my eyes and thought it was strange we hadn't gotten up at dawn to do our tai chi. Where was Biao? Why hadn't Fernanda woken me up?

"Tell Lao Jiang," someone said. "She opened her eyes."

Of course I opened my eyes. How ridiculous. Or had someone else opened her eyes? I had no idea what was happening.

"Auntie? How are you?"

My niece's sad face, all swollen and teary, appeared in my reduced field of vision. I was about to ask rudely what in heaven's name had brought on all those tears, when I realized it was extremely difficult for me to speak. I couldn't move my jaw; it refused to open.

"Auntie . . . ? Can you see me, Auntie? Do you see me?"

Something was seriously wrong, and I couldn't understand what it was or why. I began to feel frightened. Finally, after an incredible effort, I was able to part my lips.

"Of course I see you," I croaked.

"She can see me!" Fernanda rejoiced. "Don't move, Auntie. You've got a bump on your head as big as a bullring, and half your face is black and blue."

"What?" I asked, trying to sit up but failing.

"Don't you remember what happened last night?"

Last night? What happened last night? Hadn't we gone to bed after dinner? Speaking of which, where were we?

"The Green Gang attacked," my niece said.

The Green Gang? Oh, right, the Green Gang! Yes, of course, they had attacked. Suddenly I remembered everything. The assassin had a knife to my throat, I kicked the pitcher over, there was a horrific blow to my temple—and then little bits of a dream: a blanket, a straw mat. . . .

"Yes, now I remember," I murmured.

"Good," Lao Jiang's voice said from nearby. "That's a good sign. How are you, Elvira? Or should I call you Chang Cheng?"

I heard Biao laugh somewhere nearby, and my niece did, too.

"Don't call me Chang Cheng," I grumbled.

"She's back!" the antiquarian exclaimed.

One of the identical twins, Red or Black (I still couldn't see well enough to make out whether he had a mark on his cheek), appeared before me and examined me carefully, touching the left side of my head. It hurt so much I screamed.

"You were hit very hard," the master explained, "most likely with an 'Iron Fist.' Some of the attackers knew secret Shaolin techniques. It could have killed you."

"It was quite a fight," Lao Jiang declared.

"What happened?" I asked.

"It was a surprise attack. They snuck into our rooms without the soldiers' noticing."

"Too much sorghum liquor," I growled angrily.

"Don't worry," he said somberly. "They paid a high price. Not one of them survived."

"What?" I asked, alarmed, trying to sit up again. My entire body hurt, so I didn't persist.

"Masters Red Jade and Black Jade were the first to get out of their room. The assassins attacked all of us at once. There were over twenty of them. I think Biao counted twenty-three bodies, didn't you, Biao?"

"Yes, Lao Jiang. Plus the twelve soldiers."

What a pointless massacre, I thought. Why do men always resolve problems by means of war, slaughter, or assassination? If the Green Gang wanted the *jiance* or the entire contents of the blasted hundred-treasure chest, then all they had to do was capture us, make us give it to them, and let us go. But no, they had to attack, kill, and be killed. Such absurd violence.

"We came here as soon as you knocked the *lien p'en* on the floor," the monk said. "We knew you must be in danger. The noise woke the soldiers, and the fight began."

"At first," Lao Jiang continued, "we shot several of the attackers, but those who remained at the end, when our soldiers were on their last legs, were trained in Shaolin like the one that attacked you. Masters Red Jade, Black Jade, and I managed to eliminate four or five of them, but there were still others who, even though they were hurt, finished off the last of the men in Shao's group. It was a strong, well-organized attack. They didn't want to take any risks this time. They came fully prepared to seize the *jiance*, but thanks to you we didn't give them time to even look for it. Master Black Jade has several serious injuries, and I've got quite a bit of bruising and some cuts. Master Red Jade fared the best; he has only a few cuts on his hands and back, none of them serious."

"What about Biao?" I asked worriedly.

"I'm fine, *tai-tai*," I heard him say. "Nothing happened to me."

"How did they know we were here? Did they follow us?"

"Undoubtedly," Lao Jiang agreed. "Wudang Monastery was the last reference they had with respect to the three pieces of the *jiance*. Remember, they'd already visited the abbot. This was their last chance to find us."

"So why here? Why in this city?"

"We don't know. They may have been late finding out we left the monastery. The martial-arts experts who attacked us most likely come from the Shaolin temple in Songshan, in the nearby province of Henan, to the west. It's the most important place for Shaolin in all of China. I don't think they were monks, but you never know. This city, Shang-hsien, is the best place for a group of assassins from the south to meet up with fighters from Henan. The Green Gang must have spent a for-tune organizing this attack."

"Now what?"

"Now we rest. You're in no shape to move for at least a couple of days, and we have to arrange for Master Black Jade to return to Wu-dang. He won't be able to accompany us on the remainder of our jour-ney, and we can't leave him here."

"Is he that bad?"

"Both arms are broken, and he has a very deep gash on his right leg. He fought courageously and took the worst of it, but he'll certainly re-cover.

"Now that we've no soldiers," Lao Jiang went on, "and Master Black Jade is going back to Wudang, we'll never survive another attack like last night's."

"Can't you ask the Kuomintang or the Communists here for help?"

"Kuomintang in this part of China? No, Elvira. There are no Kuo-mintang or Communists here. We're at the top of the Qin Ling massif, remember? It's essentially cut off from the rest of the world, except for a steep, narrow mountain trail covered in snow. However, the good news is that if we stay off that trail and take another route, they won't be able to catch up to us, and if they lose our trail now, they won't be able to find us again. They don't know where we're going."

"We're going to Xi'an," Fernanda replied.

"Xi'an is very big, young Fernanda, as big as Shanghai, and we're not actually going to the city," Lao Jiang said, ruining my plan to leave the children there. "The Green Gang has no idea what our destination is. Why do you think they wanted the *jiance*? They don't know where the mausoleum is."

"But, Lao Jiang," I objected—without blinking, so my head wouldn't explode—"how are we going to cross the mountains alone? Don't you remember what it took to get here? How will we survive if we don't follow the trail?"

"It's not far now, Elvira. Even in the worst possible weather, we're a week away from Xi'an at most, and it's all downhill from here. We have to prevent them from following us no matter what. It's all they can do, their only way of finding the tomb. I'm sure they've left spies in Shang-hsien, people willing to follow us to the very entrance of the mausoleum. Do you want them to attack us there? Can you imagine? We have to take every possible precaution."

"So there's someone out there waiting for us to set off once again," I said. A strange exhaustion was closing my eyes, but I was afraid to fall asleep.

"This final stretch is the most important for them, because they don't have any other references. It's all over if they lose sight of us now, and I don't think they're that stupid. On the other hand, I don't suppose they thought last night's assault would fail, but we'd better watch ourselves very carefully just in case."

"And how will we do that?" I asked. I was falling fast asleep and couldn't do anything to stop it.

"Well, we thought we'd do the following. . . ."

I don't remember another thing.

I awoke that afternoon but didn't feel any better. I was barely able to take a sip of water. My niece told me Lao Jiang had paid the owner of the *lü kuan* for our lodging as well as for all the damage and had hired six expert porters to take Master Black Jade back to Wudang. In order to avoid problems with the Chinese authorities in Shang-hsien, he had also purchased a small plot of land on the outskirts and made arrangements with some peasants to bury the dead there as soon as it was possible—the ground was still frozen at this time of year. Meanwhile, the bodies would be kept on Mount Shangshan, in caves, which Lao Jiang also had to rent.

While she spoke, Fernanda tried to feed me as if I were a small child, but I simply couldn't swallow a thing. Out of curiosity I passed my hand lightly over the bandage that covered the swelling on my head, and not only did I see stars, but I got quite a fright when I discovered that the bump was exactly as big as the broad side of an egg. What a knock that beast of a Shaolin, mandarin, or whatever he was had given me. He had, of course, paid a high price for being an idiot. Well, too bad for him. If he'd only chosen a more peaceful profession he would still be alive.

The next morning, however, I woke feeling much better. My head still throbbed, but I was able to get up out of the k'ang. I had to be extremely careful washing my face, because the whole left side hurt, and then at breakfast every mouthful caused me to cry out in pain. Later I wandered through the lü kuan, watching the servants try to repair all the damage that had been caused during the battle—it was a great deal. It looked as if a tornado had blown through or, worse, as if there'd been an earthquake like the one that had destroyed Japan three months earlier, when Fernanda and I arrived in Shanghai. It was amazing to think we'd been traveling through China in search of the lost tomb of some ancient emperor for that amount of time, but as hard as it was to believe, my callused feet and strong legs left no doubt. I continued to wander around the lü kuan until, unexpectedly, I found myself in front of a large octagonal mirror with a trigram carved on each side of the frame—the I Ching hexagrams consisted of six lines, while these had only three, but they seemed closely related. I couldn't help but yelp in horror when I saw my reflection. The bandage made me look just like the wounded soldiers who came back to Paris during the war, but even worse was the blue-black swelling that distorted the left half of my face (eye, lips, and ear included). I'd become a monster. If the much-talked-about Taoist moderation was ever going to do me good, it was undoubtedly now. It had nothing to do with being ugly, beautiful, or deformed: It was the realization that he could have killed me with that blow called an "Iron Fist." My face was absolute proof of it. I could be dead, I kept repeating to myself as I examined myself carefully. I knew that as long as that enormous bruise was still there, I'd best make use of moderation, *wu wei*, and moderation again.

New guests started arriving at the *lü kuan* that afternoon. At first it was just two or three men, but within a short while entire families streamed in as if it were a celebration. By night the inn was full; in fact, there weren't enough tables for everyone and hardly enough chairs. It must have been an avalanche of unexpected visitors or a large group of merchants traveling with their wives and children.

As soon as the servants had brought us our dinner, Lao Jiang cast a satisfied look around the dining room and exclaimed, "Well then, here are our protectors. I don't think anyone's missing."

Fernanda and Master Red seemed to know what was going on, be-cause they smiled and kept eating, but I didn't have the faintest idea what Lao Jiang was talking about.

"You fell asleep when I started to tell you our plan," he said, div-ing heartily into his rice soup. "We invited all these peasants from the surrounding areas for dinner. Do you see that man there?" he asked, pointing to a tall, thin, elderly man. "He'll be me, and that woman over there is you, Elvira. The innkeeper's daughter will cut her hair to look like yours. That man will be Master Red Jade, and the tall boy on his right will be Biao. I still haven't decided which of those two girls will be Fernanda. Who do you think looks more like her? Don't pay any attention to their faces; that's the least of it. Look at body shape and height. They'll all leave Shang-hsien in about three hours, in the middle of the night, heading toward Xi'an, with a few of our horses."

"So that's the plan. Doubles will take our place while we remain safe inside the *lü kuan*."

"No, we won't stay in the *lü kuan*. We'll leave as soon as Biao tells us the spies have followed that group or, if that doesn't happen, a few hours after they've gone."

"But what if these people have talked? What if the supposed spies already know what we're planning?"

"How could they?" he replied happily. "Our own doubles don't even know yet!"

The man never ceased to amaze me. I must have had a blank look on my face, although because of my swelling, you might not have been able to tell the difference.

"All these people are very poor," the antiquarian explained. "Master Red Jade and I invited the neediest of the peasants. There's no chance they'll refuse when I show them what we're willing to pay."

And indeed they did not refuse. While Fernanda and I finished our dinner and Biao came back from the kitchen, Lao Jiang and Master Red went from table to table closing deals and making payments. They also gave money to everyone else who was present, so no arguments would arise and no one would decide to rob us. Our impersonators followed us to our rooms, and less than half an hour later they were dressed in our clothing, had their hair combed like ours, and were wearing our hats, sheepskin coats, and boots (magnificent leather boots we'd been given in Wudang, lined with heavy wool and a thick leather sole for the snow). Luckily, we had extras of almost everything. Our doubles looked so good that even I might not have noticed the difference if I didn't look at their faces. They seemed very willing to do their well-paid work: to walk all night long and all the next day, not even stopping to eat. Then they could go back to their homes. By that time we'd have gotten far enough away that the Green Gang wouldn't be able to catch up to us.

I made sure Biao dressed warmly before he left the lü kuan through the woodshed. He was going to spend the next few hours hiding beside the trail that led to Xi'an, in the middle of the night and in the snow, and I didn't want him to freeze to death. Then our doubles left. The woman who was pretending to be me had protested loudly, because, she said, I had such a strange walk that it was hard for her to imitate. It wasn't because she had "Golden Lilies" (it was rare for girls from poor families to suffer that monstrous deformity, because they'd have to work in the fields with the men when they were older), but because I moved my whole body when I walked, especially my hips, and she'd never seen such a thing. The woman practiced in our room until she was satisfied. So did the young girl who was playing Fernanda.

Biao returned less than an hour later, nervous and shivering from the cold, with the news that a couple of men had indeed followed our doubles as soon as they left Shang-hsien.

"It's time!" the antiquarian exclaimed, quickly putting on his coat. "Let's go!"

We mounted the remaining horses and left Shang-hsien. Those of us who didn't know how to ride had to swallow our fear, keep our balance, and hold on to the reins as best we could. The mules loaded with the rest of the boxes and bags followed meekly behind, and one of the locals who'd been paid at the *lü kuan* led the way. The good man took us along a narrow trail that encircled the city, along the Danjiang River and slightly up the side of Shangshan Mountain. After a few hours, Lao Jiang stopped his horse in the middle of a thick forest of pines, dismounted, and spoke with our guide. The children were holding up well despite the late hour and freezing temperatures. I was the one having the most trouble: The cold air on the left side of my face felt like a knife slicing my skin into thin ribbons.

The guide left us there, and Lao Jiang and Master Red conferred for quite a while. In the faint light of a waning moon, they consulted something the size and shape of a plate that looked like a compass. We then continued on through the forest, following a nonexistent path in an unknown direction. The sun rose, but we didn't stop for breakfast, nor did we stop for lunch; we simply ate without dismounting. When the sun began to set and I started to think we'd never get off those poor animals, the antiquarian finally ordered a rest. Nothing in the landscape had changed through the entire day. We were still surrounded by trees, with snow up to our ankles, but now that it was nightfall, a mysterious fog slid softly between the trunks. We made camp there, and the next day was identical, as was the next. Nothing differentiated the time: trees and more trees, scrub peeking through the snow, the horses' hooves sinking into it with a dry, insistent crunch; a fire at night to scare off wild animals—felines and bears—and to prepare the night's dinner and the morning's breakfast. We erased all signs of our passing before mounting and continuing on our way. Occasionally Master Red would stay behind for a while, crouching down in the trees to make sure no one was following us. The children were always sort of dazed, lulled almost to sleep by the monotonous swaying of the horses. The only time they woke a little was when we did tai chi, but they soon fell back into their torpor. By the end of our eight-day journey, we'd crossed four or five rivers, some not very deep and others so wide and with such swift currents that we had to rent rafts to reach the other side.

The first sign that we were reaching more "civilized" areas was the apocalyptic vision of villages that had been razed or burned to the ground with the unmistakable tracks in the snow of passing military troops and gangs of bandits. Things were getting more difficult. We didn't have much food left, just a little bread that we soaked in our tea and some dry crackers. Fernanda gave me the happy news that my bump was noticeably smaller and that the left half of my face had turned a lovely shade of green. At least I was beginning to heal. Since we were still hiding from people and didn't want to be seen, we continued to take absurd detours with the help of that strange compass called a *luo p'an*, made out of a broad wooden plate with a magnetic needle in the center that pointed south. It was the strangest Chinese artifact I had seen so far, and I was determined to draw it at the first opportunity. The plate contained between fifteen and twenty narrow, delicately carved concentric circles, each ring containing trigrams, Chinese characters, and strange symbols, some in red ink and others in black. It was very pretty, utterly original, and Master Red, who owned it, explained that it was used to discover the energies of the earth and calculate the forces of feng shui, although we were using it for a much more vulgar purpose: to guide us to the First Emperor's mausoleum.

Finally, toward the end of the first week of December, having left the mountains and the snow behind, we came to a one-horse town called

T'ieh-lu, where we stocked up on provisions in a little shop inside the railway station.

As soon as we'd left, Lao Jiang pointed to a mountain in the distance and announced, "There's Li Shan, the Mount Li that Sima Qian mentions in his chronicle regarding Shi Huang Ti's tomb. We'll be at the dam on the Shahe River in a few hours."

He sounded so optimistic and encouraging. The end of our long journey was approaching, and precisely for that reason my stomach flipped in fear: We'd reach the Shahe dam only if we'd managed to trick the Green Gang, and if we hadn't, the next few hours were going to be extremely dangerous. In any event, arriving at the dam wasn't exactly a panacea. An undesirable dive into frozen waters and arrows fired by Shi Huang Ti's phantom army awaited us there. No matter how you looked at it, it was going to be a perilous afternoon.

Master Red, who even at this point on our journey still didn't know exactly where we were headed, showed interest when he heard the bit about the dam on the Shahe River. As a precautionary measure (although I'd say it was more of a misguided sense of distrust), Lao Jiang had refused to show the *jiance* to the brothers Red and Black or tell them about the clues Sai Wu had left to help his son get into the mausoleum and guide him through it. All poor Master Red knew was what Sima Qian said in his Basic Annals, and he was the only one of us who knew nothing about the cold bath that lay ahead.

The children, on the other hand, couldn't have been happier. As far as they were concerned, the best, most exciting part of the past few months was drawing near. This was a fantastic adventure with a considerable treasure for a prize at the end. What more could you ask for at thirteen and seventeen years of age? It had always been my intention to keep them safe, but things kept going wrong. I felt terribly guilty about exposing them to the same risks and dangers we would face inside the tomb. If anything were to happen to Fernanda or Biao . . . I didn't want to even think about it. And all this was to pay debts that weren't even mine. The law that burdened me with Rémy's

financial problems was absolutely unfair. None of this would be happening if only he'd been responsible. Suddenly, I don't know why, I
thought of the advice Lao Jiang had given me when we were in Nanking
and learned that Paddy Tichborne's leg would have to be amputated:
"Let me give you your first lesson in Taoism, madame: Learn to see the
good in the bad and the bad in the good. They're both the same thing,
like yin and yang." What could have been the good in all that? I couldn't
see it, to be honest, and it was amid these dark thoughts that we passed
through great, empty fields that must have yielded rich crops for their
owners in more peaceful times but now lay abandoned. All the peasants
had fled, and a great loneliness hung over the land.

We still hadn't seen the Shahe River when Master Red pointed out a
verdant hill approximately 150 feet high, strangely alone in a vast stretch
of farmland, the five Siamese peaks of Mount Li silhouetted behind.

"We've done it!" Lao Jiang exclaimed, standing up in his stirrups to
get a better look from that distance. We all smiled happily, filled with
emotion.

"Trees and bushes were planted to give the appearance of a mountain," Sima Qian had written. The description was a little pretentious,
since it didn't exactly look like a mountain, but it was certainly impressive to think that the tomb of the First Emperor of China, lost for two
thousand years, was there, under that insignificant, low hillock. The
truly incredible part was that we were going to be the first to go inside.

Suddenly something seemed to infuriate Lao Jiang.

"We should already be alongside the Shahe," he said. "According to
the map, it flowed from Mount Li toward the river Wei, behind us. But
there's no water here."

"The Shahe River doesn't exist?" I asked, perplexed.

"It might have dried up over the last twenty-two hundred years," he
grumbled. "Who knows?"

Increasingly worried, we continued heading south, with the mausoleum on our right. Not a river could be seen anywhere in that vast space
and, what was worse, no dam, no artificial lake. . . . We should have

been looking right at it but weren't; only wasteland stretched between there and the slopes of Mount Li.

Devastated, we stopped a little while later at the spot Sai Wu had mentioned in the *jiance* as the place to dive in. After surveying the land for as long as we could, until the sun went down, Master Red, Lao Jiang, and I came to the conclusion that the dam had existed sometime in the past. We discovered slight elevations in the ground that coincided with the big oblong shape on the map and a depression in the middle that seemed to indicate that there had indeed been a lake there at some point. Time and nature had undoubtedly eroded and finally destroyed the dam and any other works or diversions the First Emperor's engineers may have made to the Shahe. Only after reluctantly admitting to this distressing situation did we prepare to spend the night, already enveloped in complete darkness. It was a new moon, and so we didn't light a fire to prepare dinner or warm ourselves; it would have been far too visible across that immense, empty plain. In silence we ate some of what we'd bought that morning at the small store in the train station, and though it was bitterly cold and there was nothing to do but go to sleep, none of us moved.

All those many months of struggle and danger, all the dead and wounded, all that suffering for nothing. That was my only thought; actually, it was more of a sensation, an image that encompassed the whole idea and remained fixed in my mind. I didn't notice the passing of time. I wasn't aware of anything. Inside, I'd come to a complete stop.

"What are we going to do now?" came Fernanda's voice from far away.

"We'll find an answer," I murmured.

"No! There is no answer!" Lao Jiang thundered furiously. "We'll give the *jiance* to the Green Gang so they can see for themselves that the entrance has disappeared. Then they'll leave us in peace and we can go back to our lives in Shanghai. This madness is finally over."

I was outraged. I hadn't expended all that energy and subjected my

niece to all these dangers just to admit such an absurd, humiliating defeat.

"I do not want to hear that again!" I shouted. The antiquarian
looked at me aghast, as did Fernanda, Biao, and Master Red. "You want
to give the *jiance* to the Green Gang? You're insane! We'd be handing
them the mausoleum on a silver platter. All they'll have to do is come
with a crew and start digging. We'll give them the First Emperor's tomb
and its incalculable riches in exchange for our little lives in Shanghai or
Paris, is that it? Oh, and don't forget to tell them how to avoid the traps
inside! We'll give it all to them just so they'll leave us in peace, is that
right? You seem to have forgotten that the Green Gang is nothing more
than the criminal arm of the imperialists and Japanese you despise and
fear so much. Think! Use your head if you don't want to bow to an
all-powerful Manchu emperor who'll force you to wear the Qing queue
again!"

"What do you want? Do you want us to start digging?" he mocked.

"I want us to do something, anything, to find some other way into
the mausoleum!" I shouted, leaving them dumbfounded. "If we have to
dig, we'll dig!"

I was getting fired up just listening to myself. I knew I was right,
that was what we had to do, but if anyone had asked me how to resolve
the problem, I'd have deflated like a popped balloon. However, my speech
unexpectedly seemed to wake Master Red as if from a dream.

"It might be possible," he said very quietly.

"What did you say?" I asked, feeling somewhat in command of the
situation.

He glanced at me, embarrassed (it was still difficult for him to address me directly), and looked down at the ground before repeating, "It
might be possible to find another way in."

"Don't be ridiculous!" Lao Jiang snapped.

"Please don't take offense," Master Red entreated. "I remember having read something, a long time ago, about some shafts that were dug by
bands of thieves who wanted to loot the mausoleum."

"The First Emperor's mausoleum?" I asked, bewildered. "*This* mausoleum?"

"Yes, madame."

"But, Master Red Jade, that's impossible," I reasoned. "To begin with, they had to know where it was, and no one has known anything about it for two thousand years."

"Exactly, madame," he agreed quite calmly. "There is a passage in the *Shui Jing Chu*—"

"*Commentary on the Waterways Classic* by the great Li Daoyuan?" the antiquarian asked, taken aback. "You've seen a copy of *Commentary on the Waterways Classic*?"

"Indeed," the monk admitted. "A copy as old as the work itself, which was written during the Northern Wei dynasty."[44]

"One day the abbot of Wudang and I will have to talk business," the antiquarian mused.

"And what did this passage in *Commentary on the Waterways Classic* say?" I interrupted, before it became a discussion about all the valuable books in the Mysterious Mountain libraries.

"Xiang Yu was founder of the Han dynasty, the one that came after that of the First Emperor. According to the text, Xiang Yu assassinated the Qin imperial family and razed Xianyang, the capital, then went to Shi Huang Ti's mausoleum and set it on fire after taking all of the treasures."

"That's impossible," Lao Jiang said calmly. "Li Daoyuan wrote his work seven hundred years after the Qin dynasty disappeared. If such a thing had occurred, Sima Qian would have mentioned it in his *Records of the Grand Historian*, written just a hundred years after the fall of Qin and very well documented."

"I agree with you," Master Red asserted. "That is also the opinion held by all the wise and learned men who wrote about this part of Li Daoyuan's work during the fourteen centuries after. However, I remember that one of them, an old feng shui master, told a strange story about an ancient treatise. He said that although Li Daoyuan's story was false, there had indeed been two serious attempts to loot the First Emperor's mausoleum in the two hundred years after his death. Both were organized by noble families in the Han court that were anxious to get hold of his immense riches. In both cases they bored very deep shafts in order to reach the underground palace."

"And were they successful?" Lao Jiang asked skeptically.

"The first attempt failed because although they had the financial resources, they didn't know the techniques required to bore that deep."

"Those Han engineers weren't as skilled as the Qin foremen," my niece commented.

"That's right," I agreed. The night was getting much colder, and despite my lined boots, my feet were two blocks of ice.

"The second attempt had better luck," Master Red continued to explain. "The thieves arrived at the mausoleum but were never heard from again. It seems they perished inside."

"The automatic crossbows," I murmured.

"Most likely," Lao Jiang admitted. "But unless Master Red Jade can tell us exactly where the thieves dug the shaft on the second attempt, this whole conversation is pointless."

"I *can* tell you that," Master Red announced, smiling broadly. "The wise man who referred to these events was a master in feng shui from the Three Kingdoms[45] period. He didn't know where the First Emperor's tomb was located, but as a feng shui master he did possess the geomantic information that today could lead us to the shaft that reached the mausoleum."

"And you can remember that geomantic information?" asked Biao, who hadn't said a word until then.

"Of course I can," the monk said, still smiling. "It's quite simple. All you have to do is find the Dragon's Nest."

Biao opened his mouth and eyes as if he'd just heard the most extraordinary words in the loveliest poem in the world.

"Dragons don't exist, Master Red Jade! So how would we find a nest?" Fernanda challenged.

"I'm not talking of real dragons," the monk said, laughing. "A Dragon's Nest is a concept in feng shui. For us Chinese the dragon symbolizes good luck. A Dragon's Nest is a place where there is a powerfully balanced and natural concentration of chi energy. It's very rare and hard to find. In antiquity a Dragon's Nest indicated the precise spot where an emperor was to be buried. If the geomantic location was also correct, as was the case here, then the burial was especially fortunate and the dead were assured a good life in the hereafter."

"That's true," Lao Jiang said. "This is the proper geomantic location for a burial: the Fire of red raven to the south, which is the crests of Mount Li; the Water of black tortoise to the north, the river Wei; the Metal of white tiger to the west, the Qin Ling mountain range we crossed from Wudang; and to the east . . . What is there to the east?" he asked perplexed. "There's nothing there."

"Nothing we can see," the master replied. "The area to the east, that of the green dragon, will most certainly be protected in some way.[46] Shi Huang Ti's master geomancers were the best of their time."

"I've heard of this white tiger, red raven, black tortoise, and green dragon," I commented, surprised. "I think they explained it in a class about the Five Elements I went to at the monastery."

"You're right." The monk nodded. "The science of chi, the Five Elements, feng shui, the *I Ching*, the martial arts, and all of our culture's other ancestral knowledge are related."

"So, getting back to the Dragon's Nest," I said, taking up the conversation before we went off on another tangent. "Was the shaft that got down as far as the mausoleum in a Dragon's Nest or just the First Emperor's tomb?"

"I'm certain the tomb was built in a Dragon's Nest, but what that great scholar from the Three Kingdoms period emphasized as being special was that the shaft down to the mausoleum had been dug in a second nest very near the first. This is highly unusual."

"Then it would have been destroyed when it was dug up."

"A Dragon's Nest isn't destroyed, madame," he replied patiently. "It's not a piece of earth that, once turned, is never the same again. It's a place where the concentration of the earth's chi is particularly strong and in the best possible conditions. That energy alters the ground, creating a characteristic pattern, which is how nests are found."

"A pattern?" Biao asked.

"A Dragon's Nest tends to be more or less circular in shape, and within it the ground is two different colors: dark brown and light brown, separated by a white line. The dark earth is viscous, and the light earth is loose, like sand. The two colors form a pattern inside the nest that can be concentric circles, spirals, waning moons, or even the whirl of *t'ai-chi.*"

"Tai chi?" I asked, amazed. What did our morning exercise have to do with a Dragon's Nest?

"No. *T'ai-chi.* It's different. *T'ai-chi* is a pattern that represents yin and yang in the colors black and white in a small circular whirl, each side containing a dot of the other color. Dragon's Nests can sometimes also present this image." Master Red pulled up the collar of his coat. "Two thousand years ago, a wealthy, noble Han family ordered that a deep shaft be dug down to the mausoleum. Their master geomancers found the best place to do this: an unexpected Dragon's Nest. This ensured the project's success. However, all the servants who went down the shaft and reached the bottom died. Surely this would have frightened them enough that they'd have ordered it be filled in and then forgotten all about the matter. But a shaft that deep couldn't be just a simple hole, especially because this was a well-financed project. The shaft had to be wide enough for them to easily remove the treasures, with reinforced walls in order to prevent a collapse, some sort of pulley system to lower workers and pull up baskets of earth or, more likely, steps dug into the walls. When the attempt failed and they closed the shaft, the chi energy would emerge once again over the centuries and re-create the Dragon's Nest. Now that you know what it looks like, all we have to do is find it."

"Tomorrow morning at first light," Lao Jiang declared, "we'll divide up the area around the burial mound and begin our search."

"And now let's please get some sleep," I pleaded. "I'm exhausted and frozen."

However, I couldn't sleep a wink, and the night felt particularly long. We were all nervous and impatient. I heard the children rustle around for hours and Lao Jiang and Master Red whisper until early morning. Our blankets were covered in frost when dawn began to brighten the sky at last, and we got up to do our tai chi (not t'ai-chi). We finally warmed up after the exercise and the hot tea we had for breakfast once dawn broke so that we could light a fire.

Biao timidly proposed we divide up the four points of the compass. Fernanda and he would go together, he said, but my niece flatly refused. She was perfectly capable of finding a Dragon's Nest on her own, without anyone's help, so I teamed up with poor Biao, and we would cover red raven, the south. Lao Jiang took white tiger, the west; Fernanda took green dragon, the east; and Master Red took black turtle, the north. This last area was the most extensive, since it went as far as the river Wei, but Master Red was well versed in feng shui and had his *luo p'an* to study the terrain—in other words, if the Dragon's Nest was in his section, he'd walk straight to it following the chi energy lines. Since the areas that had to be covered were so vast, we took our lunch with us. First we went by horse to the mound Sima Qian said covered the mausoleum. Then we placed stones on top of the horses' reins so they wouldn't escape while we were gone. Finally we all set off to the side we'd been assigned around that verdant pyramid of earth.

"We'll walk up and down parallel to the mound, Biao. What do you say?"

"Sounds good, *tai-tai*, but to cover our territory as far as the base of Mount Li a bit faster we could walk from opposite directions and meet in the middle. That way we'll do double the work in half the time."

"That's a marvelous idea. Remember, each line has to be a little longer the farther we get from here."

"We could count the number of steps and take one more each time."

I lifted my hand and ran it over his wiry hair. "You'll go far in this world, Little Tiger."

His ears blazed red, and he smiled modestly. It was amazing to think how much he'd grown during our journey. I recalled seeing him for the first time in the garden at the house in Shanghai, standing next to Fernanda. I thought he looked like a crafty street urchin and wasn't impressed by what I took to be willfulness. How wrong first impressions can sometimes be.

We walked up and down that stretch of land all morning without finding a thing, stopping to eat at midday after the boy had complained of being hungry the three previous times we'd met in the middle. We'd barely taken a bite of our rice balls wrapped in mulberry leaves when a shout that seemed to come from the other side of the planet made us look at one another in surprise.

"Is someone calling, or did I imagine it?" I asked Biao, who was voraciously chewing a mouthful. He gave a nasal grunt that seemed to indicate he wasn't sure, and then we heard the shout again. "They're calling us, Biao! Someone has found the Dragon's Nest!"

He gobbled down his rice and, sputtering, stood up at the same time I did.

"Where's it coming from?" I asked, trying to get my bearings.

Since we couldn't tell, we waited quietly.

"Over there!" Biao exclaimed as soon as the shout was heard again, running off to the east, toward Fernanda's area. That's when I saw her. I thought I could make out several horses galloping but just one rider, and I could tell by the clothes that it was my niece. As I ran toward her, I realized she was one of those people who isn't proficient at anything quite simply because no one has ever encouraged them to try anything new. When she arrived in China, she was overweight and dressed in mourning—oh, that horrid bonnet! She had an unpleasant nature and a foul temper. But when she started to eat with chopsticks, she quickly became adept at it. She learned to play Wei-ch'i and was soon as good as Biao (and the boy was a genius); she had begun tai chi less than a month earlier and already excelled; she had refused to learn Chinese, but once she put her mind to it, she was at my level within a week; and now, in the middle of this Chinese prairie, I watched her gallop on a horse as if she'd taken lessons and ridden along the promenades in Madrid's Retiro Park her whole life. I would have to do something with that girl once we got back to Europe—*if* we got back.

Biao and I stopped running.

"Auntie!" she shouted, reining in her horse when she reached us. "Master Red Jade found the Dragon's Nest over an hour ago! I was nearby so he told me first, and then he went to find Lao Jiang. I've brought your horses so we don't waste any time. It's quite far."

"Wonderful!" I exclaimed. "Let's go!"

The only problem was how to make a horse gallop when you barely know how to get it to walk and, on top of that, felt a certain . . . shall we say respect for an animal of that size. This is no time to be cowardly, Elvira, I said to myself, mounting with verve. Surely all you had to do was use the stirrups to kick it in the belly a little more quickly and firmly than when encouraging it to walk. Feeling a bit frightened, that's what I did, and indeed I set off for the burial mound at top speed, followed not far behind by the children. Luckily, no one I knew back in Paris could see me bouncing around, leaning this way and that in the saddle.

We rode for a good while and went past the mound without stopping. The river Wei was still quite far off, but its sparkling waters could be seen in the distance beyond the small, upright figures of Lao Jiang and Master Red, who seemed to be waiting for us. It didn't take long to reach them. Hauling firmly on the reins, we stopped next to their horses and dismounted. The two men were smiling broadly.

"Look at the Dragon's Nest," Lao Jiang said. I was still somewhat unsteady on my feet but walked over to where he was pointing, my eyes fixed on a light-colored oval shape with strange zigzags of dark mud inside. It wasn't very big, perhaps two feet in length. It wouldn't have caught my eye if I'd never heard of a Dragon's Nest, and yet it really was quite unusual-looking.

"It's likely been planted over many times," Master Red remarked, "and this land must have always produced a good crop."

"What do we do now?" I asked. "Dig? Let me remind you that we don't have shovels."

"Yes, I had thought of that, and it's a bit of a setback," Lao Jiang murmured.

"We could go to that little town by the train station," Biao proposed, "but we wouldn't get back here until tomorrow."

"I have a solution to propose," the antiquarian announced mysteriously. "I have a small amount of dynamite in my bag that we could use to open the shaft."

As had happened in Nanking when the first battalion of Kuomintang soldiers saved us from the Green Gang and I found out that the antiquarian had been hiding the fact he was a member of that party, I felt myself slowly fuming at having been deceived once again. He was carrying explosives? With the children there? Since when? Ever since Shanghai? What did he plan on using them for? Any old weapon was a better means of defense, and he had his steel fan. So why was he carrying explosives from one place to the next, over thousands of miles, across China, knowing how dangerous that was?

"By the look on your face, Elvira, I gather you're upset," he noted.

"What do you think?" I muttered, trying not to lose control. "Didn't you ever consider the children? The risk we all faced traveling with you?"

"I don't know what danger you're talking about," he replied. "Dynamite is stable and safe no matter how much you move it or bang it around. It becomes dangerous only when you connect the detonator to the fuse and fuse to the sticks. I don't think I put you in danger at any time."

"So why did you bring it? We didn't need it on this journey!"

Fernanda, Biao, and Master Red looked at us with their heads lowered. The children seemed frightened.

"I brought it for this," the antiquarian replied, pointing to the Dragon's Nest. "I thought we might need it in the mausoleum or, in the worst case, to save us from the Green Gang."

"But we had protection from the Green Gang! Don't you remember? The Kuomintang soldiers followed us from Shanghai without anyone but you knowing. And then the Communists joined them."

"I don't know why you're so angry, Elvira. Why is it that a few little sticks of dynamite make you react like this? They're going to come in quite handy to open up the entrance, just as I knew they would. I honestly don't understand you."

Well, I didn't understand him either. It seemed the height of absurdity—it was ridiculous to carry explosives around for months in case you "might" need them at some point. We'd been very fortunate there hadn't been an accident. We could have been killed.

"You'd better get as far back as possible," he advised as he walked over to the bag hanging from his saddle. "Go on."

I took the children by the arms and began to walk swiftly away. Master Red followed in silence. I don't think he was particularly happy about the explosives either. We kept walking until we heard the detonation. I was expecting something different, but much to my surprise it sounded just like fireworks. We stopped then and turned back to look. A small column of smoke rose up into the cloudless sky as the animals pranced nervously, trying to break free. The antiquarian was lying on the ground halfway between us and the obliterated Dragon's Nest.

The column of smoke slowly dissipated before our eyes, becoming a cloud of dust and earth that rained down in a circle several feet around the hole. As soon as Lao Jiang stood up, we began walking back.

"Do you think they heard the explosion in Xi'an?" Fernanda asked worriedly.

"Xi'an is seventy *li* away," Master Red explained. "They didn't hear a thing."

The cloud of dust floating in the air slowly settled, and we were finally able to peer into the cavity that had opened up in the ground. It was cone-shaped, the mouth being wider than the bottom, about ten feet deep. It would be easy to fall down that bank, and, unfortunately, the hole still seemed blocked.

"I'd say that hole isn't deep enough," I commented.

"Should I use more explosives?" Lao Jiang asked.

"Let me go down first, Lao Jiang!" Biao said anxiously. "It might not be necessary."

"Go on," I urged, "but be careful."

The boy sat on the edge and turned to crawl down on all fours. I didn't call out any warnings, because he was obviously being very careful, making sure one foot was firmly planted before moving the other and gripping firmly with both hands. He was soon at the bottom. We watched him stand and dust off his padded pants. He looked a little unsure, tapping around with his foot, not daring to take a step.

"What are you doing?"

"It seems hollow underneath, and the ground's shaking."

"Get up here right now, Biao!" I yelled, but instead of obeying he got down on all fours again and began to dig in the earth with his hands.

"There are coins here," he noted, and held one in the air so we could see it.

"Throw it up to me!" Fernanda said.

The boy sat on his knees and wound up. No sooner had he thrown it than his expression changed, and in a split second I saw him lie flat on the ground and hang on tight with his eyes squeezed shut. The very same instant the coin landed in my niece's hand, you could hear a strange crunch, and a puff of dust rose up from the middle of the ground where Biao had been digging just moments before. None of us had time to react: The bottom of the opening split in two, and both pieces fell down into the void, sucking the earth Biao had been grasping. All of us screamed at once. The hole had become a hopper, and Biao was lost down it. As he fell, we saw his face turn to look up at us. I thought I might die. Then, in less than two heartbeats, we could hear a dry thud, followed by a wail of pain.

"Biao! Biao!" we called.

The wail intensified.

"Someone had better go down," one of us said, but I was already on my way. Braking with my boots and my hands, I slid down the loose soil right where Biao had gone. I'd be either dead in a few seconds or down there with the boy. Where the bank ended, I felt myself fall into the void, and a minute later my feet slammed into a hard surface. If it hadn't been for the tai chi that had strengthened my ankles and the treks that had firmed up my legs, I would certainly have broken something. The impact reverberated through every bone in my body. The boy was whimpering to my right; it was a good thing I hadn't landed on top of him. The dust made me cough.

"Biao, are you okay?" I asked, blinded.

"I hurt my foot!" he moaned. The image of Paddy Tichborne and his amputated leg came to mind. I knelt beside him and, patting around, took his head in my hands.

"We'll get you out of here, and you'll be fine," I assured him. Just then I came to the horrific realization of what I'd done. Had I really thrown myself down a hole like some suicidal maniac? My hands began to tremble. Had I gone insane? What in God's name had just happened? Had I, Elvira Aranda, a Spanish painter residing in Paris, the aunt and guardian of a young orphan who had no one else in the world, nearly killed myself in a thoughtless, completely unusual leap I never would have taken if I'd been in my right mind? My heart raced.

"Are you all right?" Lao Jiang called out. I couldn't reply. I was so shocked by what I'd just done that not a sound came from my throat. "Answer me, Elvira!"

Petrified. I had become petrified.

"We're fine!" Biao finally shouted. My trembling hands must have told him that something strange was happening to me. He struggled out of my grasp and dragged himself back, breaking free of me. Moving slowly, he was able to stand by leaning against the wall. Then, bending over and pulling on my arm, it was he who helped me to stand. "Come on, *tai-tai*, we have to move."

"Did you see what I just did?" I managed to say.

He smiled shyly. "Thank you," he whispered, putting my right arm around his neck and standing up to his full height.

"Auntie! Biao!" my niece yelled from above. The dirt I'd brought down with me had dissipated, and the midday light streamed in. I looked around. It was extraordinary. The boy and I were standing on a platform six feet long by about two and a half feet wide, carved into the ground and paved with white baked-clay bricks. The shaft was perfectly cylindrical, about sixteen feet across, paneled with wooden boards and beams that had seen better days. The sturdiest thing was the step we were standing on, as well as the ramp that led down to it and the next that led down to another platform and another ramp, and so on, swirling to the bottom of the shaft that was actually out of sight.

"How's your foot?" I asked the boy.

"I don't think it's broken," he assured me. "It doesn't hurt as much anymore."

"We'll see how it is after you've been still for a while."

"Yes, but I can walk on it now."

"Auntie . . . ! Biao . . . !"

"Just a minute!" I shouted. "How do we get them down here?" I asked the boy.

"I don't think there's any other way," he replied, looking around us. "They'll have to slide down."

"But they might hurt themselves."

"They can throw their bags down first and we'll arrange them like *k'angs*."

"Except for Lao Jiang's!" I replied, alarmed.

"Right," he agreed very seriously, "except for Lao Jiang's."

My niece sounded terrified when she said she didn't think she could slide down that bank. I replied, quite honestly, that I thought it was perfect if she wanted to stay up there and look after the horses. She quickly changed her mind and jumped bravely when it was her turn after Master Red. Everyone made it down without any trouble. After Fernanda came that damn bag of Lao Jiang's with the explosives. He kept repeating from up above that there was nothing to be afraid of, that nothing was going to happen, but the children and I went down the ramp to the next plat- form just in case. Master Red caught the disagreeable bundle in his arms and then carefully set it to one side in order to help Lao Jiang. Soon we were all safe and sound inside that Han-dynasty shaft, where a strange, rotten smell rose up from below. It was calming—though not entirely—to know that we were standing on solid ground reinforced by boards and beams that, however bad they might look, were definitely doing their job Everything felt as steady as a rock.

I don't know how far we descended until the light became just a white dot up high and no longer illuminated anything. I hadn't counted on this eventuality, but of course Lao Jiang had. He pulled from his pocket a silver cigarette lighter and a thick piece of bamboo that he fid- dled with until he was able to remove a very small piece. When he held it up to the flame, it lit just like a torch.

"An old Chinese lighting system for traveling," he explained. "It's so efficient that it's still in use today after many centuries."

"And what sort of fuel does it use?" Fernanda asked.

"Methane. A magnificent text by Chang Qu[47] from the fourth cen- tury describes how bamboo pipes caulked with asphalt were built and conducted methane to cities to be used in public lighting. You in the West didn't light up your big capitals until less than a century ago, isn't that right? Well, not only did we do that over fifteen hundred years ago, but we also learned to store methane in bamboo tubes like this one to use as torches or fuel reserves. Methane has been used in China since before the time of the First Emperor."

Master Red and Little Tiger smiled proudly. Indeed, the wealth of the Chinese people's valuable ancient knowledge was amazing and worthy of admiration, but their constant boasting about it wore a little thin. I had taken a suicidal leap after Biao, and yet I didn't go around mentioning it so they'd remind me how brave I'd been (although, let's be honest, I wouldn't have minded at all).

After that, our descent down the ramps was much easier and more secure. Every step took us deeper into the earth, and I wondered, frightened, when the first crossbow would fire. I walked warily, although after my leap I felt a renewed energy that made me a little braver, a little more intrepid. It was a sweet sensation, as if I were twenty years old again and ready to take on the world.

"We're reaching the end," Master Red said, and we all stopped. There were only two platforms and three ramps left. Oddly enough, it wasn't any colder way down at that depth than it was outside; I might even say the temperature was warmer. The only difficulty was the smell, but after three months in China even that had ceased to be such a problem for me.

"What should we do?" I asked. "The crossbows could begin firing at any moment now."

"We'll have to take that chance," the antiquarian replied.

I didn't move an inch.

"Remember the *jiance*," he snarled. "The foreman told his son that if he went into the shaft after diving in the water, he'd come out directly inside the burial mound, in front of the doors to the main hall leading into the funeral palace, and that's where hundreds of crossbows would fire on him. This shaft is a long way from the burial mound. The crossbows aren't here."

"But in the story Master Red Jade told," I insisted, "the thieves who came down these very same ramps never went back up again."

"But they didn't necessarily die right here, madame," Master Red replied. "We Chinese are very superstitious, even more so two thousand years ago. Given that this is the tomb of such a powerful emperor, it's only logical to assume that the first servants to go inside would have been terrified. They were probably prisoners, like those who built the mausoleum, and the foremen and nobles would have remained up on the surface waiting to see what happened."

"What did happen?" Biao asked, as if he'd never heard the story before.

"Those that went down never came back up again." The master smiled. "That was all the chronicle I read had to say. But those who were waiting became so frightened that they filled in the shaft, as if they were afraid something horrible might escape."

"It must be quite terrible to defile a tomb in China," I commented, "where ancestors are so revered and respected."

"Even more so if it's the tomb of an emperor that the Han themselves left without a single descendant to carry out the funeral rites required by tradition."

"Let's do this," I proposed. "We'll throw our bags in front of us, and that way we'll know whether it's clear."

"That's a very good idea, Elvira."

"But not your bag, Lao Jiang."

We descended the last bit and began throwing our bundles as far as possible from the shaft and clumps of earth that had given way under Biao's weight. Nothing happened.

"The trap's not here," Master Red said.

"Let's carry on, then."

The last step we took off the last ramp was the beginning of many disconcerting visions that left us agape: A long, seemingly empty stretch opened up in front of us, punctuated by columns without capitals or bases, lacquered black and decorated with dragons and clouds. The inlaid ceramic ceiling was some ten feet high and supported by thick wooden beams that didn't inspire a great deal of confidence. Many of the ceramics had come loose and lay smashed on the tile floor.

"Where are we?" my niece asked.

"I'd say we're on the outer edge of the funeral palace," Lao Jiang ventured, pointing to something hidden behind one of the columns. I took a few steps forward and got the fright of my life when I discovered a man kneeling, his body resting on his heels and his hands hidden inside his "sleeves that stop the wind." He was very large, and his hair was neatly combed, parted straight down the middle and pulled into a ponytail at the nape of his neck.

"Is it a statue?" I asked. It was a silly question, because it obviously couldn't be a human being, but it seemed terribly real, as real as any of us.

My niece laughed. "Of course it's a statue, Auntie!"

"Yes, but not just any old statue. It's magnificent," Lao Jiang affirmed, truly impressed. He moved closer and called Biao over. The boy took a few hesitant steps. The antiquarian passed him the torch and held Biao's arm up as high as he wanted it. Then he set his glasses on his nose and bent over to study the piece. "It's a young servant in the Qin dynasty, made of baked clay. It's extraordinary; you can still see the paint. Look at the color of his face and the red scarf tied around his neck. Incredible."

"He was placed looking south," Master Red noted, "toward the burial mound."

"We'd better keep going," I proposed. I'd never been fond of statues, especially ones in human form like that, so realistic. Whenever I went to a museum in Paris, I always felt as if the sculptures were looking at me and that those were human eyes that followed me.

But that young servant wasn't the only statue we came across. Every few columns there was another, all facing south, the same direction we were heading. There were also imperial officers, standing tall, dressed in thick jackets and wide black pants, their writing instruments hanging from eye-catching ribbons around their necks. We found skeletons of animals that could have been deer or some other wild species next to ceramic troughs, the rings that held them to the columns still around the vertebrae of their necks. They were only bones and skulls, but quite a sight in that darkness. We discovered many other equally strange things as well. There were compartments with ornately decorated stone altars containing a variety of bronze receptacles (pitchers, vases, kettles, three-legged caldrons) covered in verdigris; rooms that must have housed beautiful silk curtains and cushions; a few large repositories of weapons; others containing thousands of *jiances*; kitchens filled with clay animals such as game birds, pigs, or hares next to a wide variety of butcher's implements; even stables where the floor was littered with the bones of horses, practically reduced to dust. But by far the most beautiful of all were the chambers filled with sumptuous ceremonial outfits made of silk and pieces of jade. We didn't dare go into those rooms, afraid our mere presence would damage the delicate, two-thousand-year-old fabrics. We walked for a good while, impressed and also a little shocked by the things we were seeing. The closer we got to the burial mound, the higher the ceiling rose up over our heads, until it was disproportionately high. We soon discovered the reason for this: a long, earthen wall, plastered and painted red, prevented us from going any farther. The wall was so high that we couldn't see the top (although it must be said that Lao Jiang's torch wasn't exactly the best, casting a circle of light no more than ten or twelve feet).

"Now what?" I asked. "Left or right?"

Master Red pulled his *luo p'an* out of his pocket and consulted it. I don't know what those strange calculations were, but he kept running the nail of his index finger over the signs and characters on the wooden plate. He was extremely focused.

"The 'Dragon's Veins'—" he finally murmured, lifting his head, satisfied.

"Chi energy lines," Lao Jiang interrupted by way of explanation.

"—flow toward the south, but there is another, much weaker, that flows from east to west. If my Nine Star calculations are correct," Master Red said, "we'll get to the main entrance sooner if we go to the right."

"Don't ask me about the Nine Stars," Lao Jiang warned the rest of us when he saw us all open our mouths to draw a breath and speak. "It has to do with feng shui and is so complicated that only the great experts can understand it."

We thus continued walking and reached the corner of the wall about ten minutes later. We turned and continued our descent. There were large chips in the wall that exposed the packed earth behind. Much to my delight, we were stepping on pieces of red plaster as we walked, creating an ominous rasping noise in that dark solitude.

After quite some time—half an hour or a bit more, perhaps—we reached the end and turned left again. It couldn't be much farther to the door. My senses heightened: with a little good luck (or bad luck, depending on how you looked at it), we might see the remains of those servants who'd been speared by the crossbows, warning us of the danger. But when we finally got there, we saw nothing to indicate that an arrow had ever flown through that air. It was obvious, however, that someone had been there before us, because the doors of the monumental entrance were wide open. Nearly fifteen feet high, each door was adorned with an enormous rusted iron ring that hung from a door knocker in the shape of a tiger's head. We passed through them carefully, looking in all directions, entering a sort of vaulted tunnel some thirty feet long that looked like the ideal place for a surprise attack. It was a massive building of colossal proportions. No European king had ever had such a grandiose burial. Not even the pyramids in Egypt could compare.

The other end of the tunnel opened up onto a patio, or rather a huge corridor, white and gray tiles forming spiral and geometric patterns on the floor. By this point I was wishing there were some of those lamps with great quantities of whale oil that Sima Qian's Basic Annals said would never burn out. I was growing tired of the dark that filled the spaces around us, and I couldn't picture the magnitude of the structure with any clarity.

After crossing the enormous patio, we arrived in front of another wall identical to the first. The mausoleum was protected, it seemed, by two barriers capable of stopping any army in the world, however large it might be, even a modern army with its tanks and Big Bertha cannons. All that to protect a dead man? The First Emperor had undeniably been an extreme megalomaniac. There was another door of gigantic proportions in the second wall, although this one was a sliding door and the entire surface was covered in dangerous spikes. It had been left propped open with heavy bronze bars that the servants of Han must have put there; it was a wonder they'd withstood all that pressure for such a long time. Passing between the two, we came into another vaulted tunnel at the end of which were stairs leading up to an enormous black space. We walked up slowly, paying attention to every sound or sign of danger. Once we reached the top, quite simply, we saw nothing. The light from our torch was lost in the most lugubrious, empty silence.

"What do we do now?" my niece asked, her voice melting into that vast space.

No one spoke.

After a moment's hesitation, Lao Jiang walked over to the wall on the left and lifted the torch as high as he could. Then he walked over to the right and searched for something there, finally seeming to find what he was looking for.

"Come here, Biao," he called.

The boy walked over to him, and the antiquarian knelt down.

"Get up on my shoulders."

Biao looked puzzled but obeyed, and before standing, Lao Jiang passed him the torch.

"Hold on tight," the antiquarian said. "Master Red Jade, help me stand up, please."

Master Red walked over and took him under the arm, pulling up as Lao Jiang struggled to rise with the boy on his shoulders, balancing precariously.

"Do you see a receptacle attached to the wall?"

"Yes."

"Put your hand inside and tell me what you feel."

Biao's face contorted on hearing those instructions, and he looked toward Fernanda and me in search of help but couldn't see us in the pitch black. Horrified, I watched him reach into that receptacle as if it were a snake pit.

"It's like . . . I don't know, Lao Jiang. There's a little metal stick stuck in something. It might be dried wood or something else that's grooved."

"Smell the wood."

"What?" the boy asked, appalled.

"Bring your hand up to your nose and tell me what the wood smells like." The antiquarian's legs were shaking. He wouldn't be able to hold Biao much longer.

I was absolutely revolted as I watched the poor boy sniff whatever he had touched with his fingertips. Who knows how much filth had collected there over two thousand years?

"It doesn't smell like anything, Lao Jiang."

"Put your hand back in!"

Biao obeyed. "I don't know. . . ." He hesitated. "A bit rancid, I guess. Like rancid butter. I'm not sure, though. It's dry."

"Put the flame up to the little metal stick."[48]

"Put the flame where?"

"Bring the flame to the whale oil!" Lao Jiang shouted, unable to take any more. He was leaning heavily on Master Red, whose face grimaced with the effort.

Biao tipped the torch over the receptacle and, after what seemed like an eternity, lifted it back up and jumped down off poor Lao Jiang's shoulders. Fernanda and I watched the scene intently, in part because we couldn't see anything else. Our jaws dropped when a little gleam appeared in the receptacle and grew brighter until, with a splutter, a beautiful light appeared. Our eyes being so used to the dark, it was as if a powerful electric bulb had been turned on. We all let out a few oohs and aahs of admiration watching the fire run along a little channel on the wall, lighting other wicks every thirty or forty feet. We turned around, following the path of the flame with our eyes, when our gaze suddenly came upon the silhouette of an enormous building, a gigantic palace that blocked our view of the flame's advance. An interminable esplanade opened up before it, with a grandiose stone staircase divided into three levels and defended by two huge tigers sitting on pedestals. Somewhere out of our sight, the flame's path must have split into several branches, because as we looked at what was still the vague shape of a palace, two tongues of fire crept up on the left and right of the building, turned toward the tigers, and, once there, ran back toward us along the gray tiles that outlined a wide avenue bordered by pilasters.

We were spellbound, to put it mildly. The tops of the pilasters also lit up as the flames licked past, illuminating the middle and sides of the plaza, where there were two giant ponds. Both were so deep you couldn't see the bottom and must once have been filled with water and fish, undoubtedly connecting to the pentagonal pipes in the funeral chamber's drainage system. As soon as I saw them, I knew that's where we'd have come out if the dam on the Shahe River had still existed. The crossbows couldn't be far away. As the esplanade lit up like a fair, the flame returned to its starting place on the left side of the wall, having circled the entire area. It was an explosion of light, and now the palace was perfectly defined and lay stunning before us, with its three tiers of yellow walls and brown ceramic roof tiles. The only problem was the horrible smell of the whale oil as it burned. However, I did have to acknowledge the merit of its burning smoke-free.

Various other buildings stretched out on both sides of the palace almost as far as the eye could see. If the First Emperor had intended to fool everyone about the truth of his real burial place, he had undeniably achieved his aim. It went far beyond the scope of anyone's imagination.

Without uttering a word, we began the long trek down the gray-tiled avenue toward the palace. If anyone had been watching us from the roof, they'd have thought we were a row of ants marching down the middle of a great ballroom. Indeed, it took us quite a long time to cover the distance up to the terrifying gold tigers that guarded the staircase. Each was as big as a house and had enormous sharp nails and exotic scales down its back, making them rather repulsive-looking. From down below you had to tilt your head far back in order to see the building at the top of the last set of stairs.

"Are we going to climb up now?" Fernanda asked. Biao and Master

Red startled at the sound of her voice; we'd been quiet for so long that it sounded like cannon fire.

"Is anything wrong?" I asked in concern.

Fernanda frowned. "I'm tired. It must be late. Why don't we have dinner here, where it's light, and sleep for a while before we go any farther?"

"I'd like nothing better, Fernanda," I said, putting my arm around her shoulders. "But this is no place to sleep, next to these horrible animals. We'll find somewhere better soon, I promise."

Out of the corner of my eye, I thought I saw a mocking look on Biao's face. How mean adolescents can be, I thought, gathering patience. In any event, if we must reach the top of all those stairs, we needed to get started as soon as possible, so I walked over and led the pack. In order to boast about the incredible feat later, I decided to count each step: one, two, three, four . . . fifty, fifty-one, fifty-two . . . seventy-three, seventy-four . . . one hundred. First set completed. Everything was fine to that point, although my calf muscles did ache a little.

"Shall we carry on?" Lao Jiang encouraged, starting up the second set of stairs. Come on, let's go, I said to myself, and began to count again. But by the time we were nearing the end of that Chinese torture, I was ready to drop. It's one thing to walk and quite another to climb stairs carrying the weight of a travel bag. I was too old for this sort of thing. However proud I might have been of my renewed strength and new-found agility, my forty-something years were taking their toll: I sank down on the floor as soon as I reached the next landing.

"Are you all right, Auntie?"

"Aren't you *not* all right?" I groaned from that humiliating position. "You said you were tired before we started climbing."

"Yes, well . . ." she replied. Her kind heart (in a manner of speaking) didn't want to hurt my pride.

"I'm fine. Just give me a minute to catch my breath, and I'll get up."

"Will you be able to make it to the top?" Lao Jiang asked nervously.

So I was the only one who thought I was going to die, is that it? All the others, including that old man with a white beard, were as fresh as spring daisies.

"I can help if you'll let me, madame," Master Red murmured as he knelt in front of me.

"You can? How?"

"Allow me," he said, taking one of my arms and pushing up the sleeve. With both thumbs he began applying light pressure to various areas. Then he moved over to the other arm and did the same thing. The pain in my legs disappeared completely. He continued, pressing spots near my eyes, on my cheeks, and finally he applied a slightly firmer pressure to my ears, using his thumbs and index fingers. By the time he stood up with a courteous bow, I was the freshest daisy in that garden.

"What did you do to me?" I asked in astonishment, standing with the greatest of ease. I felt wonderful.

"I got rid of your pain," he replied, picking up his bundle, "and helped you release your own energy. It's traditional medicine."

I looked at Lao Jiang in search of an explanation, but upon seeing that all-too-familiar look of pride in his eyes, I promptly refrained and ran up the last set of stairs. The Chinese possessed a wealth of ancient knowledge and knew things we Westerners couldn't even imagine, entrenched as we were in our colonialist superiority. Oh, how we lacked the humility to be able to learn and respect the good things others had to offer!

I was the first to reach the top and threw my arms up in victory. Before me were six large openings in the yellow wall that led into the palace. They had evidently been covered by elegant wooden doors when it was built, but now only the rotten remains lay scattered on the floor. The bright light from the esplanade hung softly through the openings in the walls and gradually disappeared inside until it was completely extinguished, swallowed up by the black ceilings, floors, and columns. Black, symbolizing the Water element, was Shi Huang Ti's color, and, like the man of excess he was, he took even that to an extreme. For the Chinese, white is the color of mourning, but to me that enormous throne room seemed very funereal. According to what Lao Jiang had

once told us, a chronicler who knew the First Emperor had written that
he was a man with a hooked nose, the chest of a bird of prey, the voice of
a jackal, and the heart of a tiger. Well, that room in the funeral palace
couldn't have been more suited to someone like him: It must have been
over sixteen hundred feet from one side to the other, and it couldn't have
been any less than five hundred feet from the other end to where we
stood, in the south. The room was divided into three distinct levels by
two sets of stairs. Rows of thick black-laquered columns marked the
path to the throne, which in this case, instead of an opulent seat whence
to preside over important events, was a sarcophagus placed on an enormous altar. On either side of this altar, two imposing sculptures of gold
dragons with open jaws stretched from floor to ceiling.

"Look," Master Red said, pointing in front of us.

Straining my eyes a little, because I was tired and because the tall
timber doorframe cast a long shadow that made it difficult to see, I
could just make out some sticks and shapeless silhouettes on the floor a
few feet away from the entrance.

"The Han servants," the antiquarian murmured.

I grew alarmed. There? That was where the crossbows fired? But I
couldn't see a single one anywhere.

"We'd better not go any farther," Master Red pronounced.

"Will we spend the night here?" Fernanda asked.

I looked at Lao Jiang, and he gave a slight nod of his head.

"Right here," I replied, letting my bag fall to the floor. It must have
been quite late, possibly close to midnight, and we were exhausted. It
had been a very long day. We ate hard-boiled eggs and balls of rice that
we dunked in our hot tea. A full belly is the best of all soporifics, and so,
despite the light and the extraordinary things surrounding us, we all
fell fast asleep as soon as our heads hit the k'angs.

There was no way to know if it was morning or not. I opened my eyes.
That light, that strange eave, that far-off ceiling . . . The First Emperor

of China's mausoleum! We were finally inside. So much had happened, but we were finally inside! And we were near where the crossbows fired: exactly as the architect Sai Wu had warned his son, once he was inside the main hall of the funeral palace.

I heard something nearby and turned to look. Four pairs of eyes were smiling down at me; everyone was awake and waiting.

"Good morning, Auntie."

Good morning indeed; as good as if it weren't the most dangerous one of our lives. Still, despite my fears, I enjoyed doing my tai chi on that balcony in front of the palace, contemplating the distant red walls, the grand esplanade with flames on top of the pilasters, and the empty ponds. If this was going to be the last time, then we might as well do it in style.

I was still savoring my tea when Lao Jiang gave the order to get moving.

"Where do you suppose you're going?" I mocked, taking the last sip.

"Not far." He smiled. "How about the throne room?"

"Do you want us to die?" I joked.

"No. I want us to pick up our things and start studying the terrain. First, we'll use our bundles to see if the old crossbows still work. If they do, we'll try to find where the arrows come from in order to avoid them."

"Here, use mine," I said, tossing it to him. "Yours had better stay right here."

The children hurried to gather their things as soon as they saw Lao Jiang, Master Red, and me approach one of the doors and stop, kneeling just in front of the wooden sill. That great hall was impressive. If it had been a real administrative palace, thousands would easily have been able to gather there. Nearby we could see what was left of a handful of ancient skeletons. In among the virtually disintegrated bones and tattered clothing were fifteen or twenty bronze arrows as long as my forearm.

"Are you sure we can use your bag?" Lao Jiang asked, glancing at me suspiciously.

"I have a hunch the crossbows aren't going to work," I replied optimistically. Even if worse came to worst, my passport and Fernanda's, as well as my sketchbook and pencils, were safe in my pockets.

Why do I always speak too soon? The moment my belongings touched the ground on the other side of the sill, you could hear the sound of chains, and before we knew it, a single arrow came from the north wall, somewhere between the coffin and the gold dragons, and speared the bag as if it were a pincushion.

"Well, your hunch was wrong," Master Red noted very seriously.

"I see that," I replied.

"Now we know everything we needed to know," Lao Jiang said. "First, the crossbows still work, and second, they're very precise and a great distance away. There's no way we can get to the firing mecha-nism."

"The problem's with the floor," I added pensively. "When some-thing touches it, the arrows fire."

"Well, we can't fly to the other side," Fernanda joked.

"It's time, Master Red Jade, for you to hear what the third piece of the *jiance* says regarding this trap," Lao Jiang said. "Your vast knowledge has already helped us once. I hope it will be able to help us again."

Master Red, who was already kneeling, bowed so deeply before the antiquarian that his prominent chin nearly dug into his throat.

"It would be a great honor for me to be able to help you again, Da Teh."

The monk called Lao Jiang by his courtesy name, Da Teh, the one Fernanda and I were supposed to have been using.

"The architect Sai Wu wrote to his son, 'On the first level, hun-dreds of crossbows will fire when you enter the palace, but you can avoid them by studying the founder of the Xia[49] dynasty's achieve-ments.'"

Master Red crossed his arms, burying his hands in his "sleeves that stop the wind," and slipped into a state of deep meditation (although, rather than meditation it must have been thought, because Taoist medi-tation consists of emptying the mind and thinking of nothing, the exact opposite of what he had to do). I began to ponder as well. Something in what Lao Jiang had read of Sai Wu's words caught my attention.

"In reality, hundreds of crossbows didn't fire," I commented in surprise, "just one."

Why just one? Would Sai Wu mislead his son, especially to warn him of a danger far beyond what was real? I didn't think so. Therefore, he truly believed that hundreds of arrows would be fired when Sai Shi Gu'er stepped on the black floor of the palace. If he believed that, then he had actually ordered that hundreds of crossbows be placed behind the walls, even if he didn't know how they would work.

"What would happen if we threw the bag somewhere else?" I asked out loud.

"What do you mean?"

"Pass me my bag," I said to Lao Jiang, because he was closer. He reached out carefully and got it. I rashly pulled the arrow out and threw my bag on the tiles again, this time to the right. An arrow appeared from the far east wall and plunged in with the same precision and force as the first, but, surprisingly, this time it had been fired from eight hundred to a thousand feet away and at another angle. After hesitating for a few seconds, I stood up, took my niece's bag out of her arms and Biao's as well. Using both hands, I threw one to each side, at different distances away from us. It was incredible: two bronze arrows appeared from the east and west walls and again hit the center of their targets. That thousand-year-old mechanism against tomb raiders not only had extraordinary aim, but it behaved exactly as if it had the eyes of a great archer.

Seeing what happened, Lao Jiang brought his hands to his head as if struggling to remember something important. He brushed his white hair back off his forehead again and again.

"It could be . . ." he finally said. "It could be a combination of earthquake detectors and automatic crossbows. I'm not entirely sure, but that's the most logical explanation. The detectors would register both vibrations in the ground as well as the point of origin and would activate the corresponding crossbow."

"Lao Jiang, please," I entreated. "What are you talking about? Earthquake detectors?"

"The dragons," he asserted.

I didn't understand a word, and by the look on Biao's and Fernanda's faces, neither did they.

"What dragons? Those?" I asked, pointing to the two enormous dragons that flanked the altar where the coffin lay.

"Yes. We in China learned to detect earthquakes a long time ago. A few old seismoscopes can still be seen in Peking and even Shanghai. The first reference to such an invention is from the second century, although scholars have always suspected that a similar device had existed much further back. I think we have the proof of that here, in those dragons."

"Why in the dragons?" Biao asked.

"Seismoscopes have always been built in the shape of a dragon. It may be because of the superstition around good luck, I'm not sure. The earthquake detector works by means of little metal balls in the animal's mouth. These vibrate in a certain way and in a certain number depending on the intensity of the tremor and where it occurred. They say the dragon in the Peking observatory could tell of earthquakes that occurred anywhere in China, so why couldn't an older mechanism detect simple footsteps inside a room?"

"You mean to say that . . . seismoscope," I asked, "registers our steps on the black tiles and sets off the precise crossbow aimed at the place where the vibration occurred?"

"That's exactly what I'm saying."

"And how many arrows could each crossbow fire?"

"Perhaps twenty or thirty, I'm not sure. The largest ones, for war, had to be transported by four men. They were used to hit targets at great distances, firing on a far-off enemy who could even be hidden behind walls or mountains. Every machine was equipped with twenty or thirty arrows placed on a horizontal bar underneath the bow so the crossbowmen could reload quickly."

"Hundreds of those huge crossbows intended for war won't fit behind these walls. Weren't there other, smaller ones?"

"Yes, of course. You're right: The ones hidden behind these walls can't be that big. That would be absurd. They're probably small crossbows, the ones carried by a single bowman, and in that case they were equipped with no more than ten bronze arrows. That was the most a man could carry."

"But there are no men here, Lao Jiang," my niece objected. "It's just some sort of automatic mechanism."

"Let's not complicate matters," he said dismissively. "Wars then weren't like they are today, and machines weren't as sophisticated either. Most likely there'd have been a limited number of arrows per crossbow in an imperial mausoleum. How many attempts could be expected on a place like this? How many have there been over the last two thousand years?"

"I think I have the answer!" Master Red then exclaimed. We all turned to look at him. He was still sitting in the same position but had opened his small, wide-spaced eyes, and his head was tilted to look up at us.

"Really?" Biao asked admiringly.

Meanwhile, being a woman of little faith, I picked up the first arrow that had hit my bag and resolutely threw it at the bones of the Han servants, resulting in what could be considered a dusty sacrilege. Some of the remains and cloth flew into the air and fell on nearby tiles. The interesting part of this experiment was that only two arrows were fired from the north wall and another from the west. It was hard to know, but intuition told me that surely there should have been more. If I was right, it must indicate that the crossbows were emptied after firing only two or three times. I wasn't about to go and test my theory, but it was a point that could come in handy if Master Red, contrary to his assertions, really hadn't solved the problem.

"Have you had quite enough fun, Elvira?"

"Yes, Lao Jiang. I'm very sorry, Master Red Jade. Please, tell us what you've found."

"You told me, Da Teh," he began explaining, "that you could avoid the arrows by studying the founder of the Xia dynasty's achievements. I began thinking about the Xia dynasty and its founder, Emperor Yu, who carried out great works and innumerable feats such as being born of a father dead three years earlier, speaking with animals, knowing their secrets, raising mountains, becoming a bear at will, or, much more important, discovering on the shell of a giant tortoise the signs that explain how the changes in the universe occur."

That was beginning to sound familiar. Wasn't it that Master Tzau, the old man in that cave in the heart of a mountain in Wudang, who told me about this Yu? Yes, yes, it was him. He told me that bit about the solid yang lines and broken yin lines that form the symbols of the *I Ching* and were discovered by Yu on the shell of a tortoise.

"None of this has any apparent relationship to the crossbows," Master Red continued. "However, one of Emperor Yu's most important achievements does: containing and controlling the overflowing waters. He lived during the time of the great floods that ravaged the earth. The rains and rising water levels resulted in many deaths and destroyed crops. According to the *Shanhai Jing, The Book of Mountains and Seas*—"

"You also have a copy of—"

"Lao Jiang, please!" I cut him off. Was there a single ancient book that didn't interest him?

"—the emperors of heaven and the celestial spirits ordered Yu to save the world from the dangerous waters. Why did they order Yu? Well, they knew him; he had often traveled up to heaven to visit them."

"And how did he travel up to heaven?" Fernanda asked, intrigued.

"By means of a dance," I said, remembering what Master Tzau had told me. Master Red smiled and nodded. "Yu had a magic dance that would take him up to the stars."

"A dance that only a few of us who practice the internal arts know and is called the 'Dance of Yu' or the 'Steps of Yu.'"

"I still don't see the connection," the antiquarian protested.

"A dance, Lao Jiang!" I exclaimed, turning to face him. "Dance, steps . . ." He looked at me as if I'd gone crazy. "Steps, footsteps, tiles, crossbows, dragons . . . !"

His eyes grew wide, indicating that he had finally grasped what I was trying to say.

"Now I understand," he murmured. "But you're the only one who knows the steps to this dance, Master Red Jade. The rest of us can't start learning it now."

"True, it is rather difficult," Master Red admitted, "but you could follow me. You can step where I step, copying my gestures."

"The gestures won't be necessary," I noted.

"Will we be able to get our bags back?" Fernanda asked.

"That may be a problem," I admitted remorsefully. If we didn't dance anywhere near them, they'd be lost forever, and it was my fault for tossing them so blithely.

"Shall we begin?" Master Red Jade encouraged.

"But what if that dance isn't the answer?" Biao asked worriedly. In addition to Lao Jiang's theories, the boy was picking up my neuroses.

"Then we'll think of something else," I said, putting a hand on his back and pushing him toward the doors. "What worries me now is that we don't know where the starting point is, which tile to step on first."

But Master Red had already thought of that. He bent over and calmly picked up a long bone from one of the Han servants that had fallen near the doorframe after I'd scattered them with the arrow.

"Get up against the walls, away from the doors," Master Red Jade instructed. Any arrow that came out of the north wall and didn't find a target would fly out into the esplanade below, spearing whoever happened to be in its way. Master Red was the one who would be in danger, even though he lay on the ground, hidden behind the doorframe and also took cover behind his bundle, just in case. With the bone in his right hand, he hit every tile in the first row one after the other, slithering along like a snake from the first door on the right to the last one on the left, nearest us. The first tap filled our hearts with gladness: No arrows flew, but that's because Master Red had been unsure of how strong the bone was and tapped it too softly. The second tile set off an arrow from the north wall as expected. It flew out the door and over the stone balustrade on the terrace. The same thing happened with the next tile, and the next, and the next. . . . We didn't get discouraged no matter how slim our opportunities were becoming; we knew we were on the right track. Thus, when Master Red hit the same tile twice without an arrow's being fired from the other end, we all let out a happy whoop.

"It's here," he said confidently. "The next one should be safe as well."

And indeed he gave it a good knock, and no arrow flew through the air.

"This is where the dance begins," he announced as he got to his feet.

"Shouldn't you test the remaining tiles just to make sure you're right?" I suggested as we all stood behind him.

"The remaining tiles, madame, will set off arrows," he said.

"Are you sure? Then how do you plan to move forward?"

"Just be patient, Auntie. Let's see what happens."

Master Red, in a surprising show of bravery, lifted one leg and then the other, setting one foot on each of the two contiguous tiles that hadn't rattled the little metallic balls in the dragons' mouths. He had done it. He was inside and apparently safe.

"Get down on the floor, children," I ordered as I lay flat and watched Lao Jiang follow suit. "Master Red, first test the next tile you're going to step on, and try to get out of the line of fire, please."

Since none of us dared lift our heads, we couldn't see what was happening. All we heard were Master Red's steps and, so far, not a single whistling arrow. His footsteps moved farther away as he continued through the hall.

"Are you all right, Master Red Jade?" I shouted.

"Fine, thank you," he replied. "I'm almost at the first set of stairs."

"How are we going to follow him?" my niece asked worriedly.

"I suppose he'll tell us what to do once he's at the other end."

"But it'll be so easy to make a mistake," she objected. "One wrong tile and it's all over."

She was right. We had to change our strategy.

"Master Red Jade!" I shouted. "Could you come back?"

"Come back?" he asked. His voice sounded very far away.

"Yes, please," I asked. We waited patiently, without moving, until we heard him arrive. Only then did we stand up with a sigh of relief.

"That went well, didn't it?" Lao Jiang asked, satisfied.

"Very well." Master Red nodded. "The Steps of Yu work."

"Here, Master Red Jade," I said, handing him my box of pencils. "Mark the tiles that are safe with a colored X so we'll know where to step."

"But you can just follow me," he objected. "You're not in any danger. Come with me now."

I didn't like the idea. I didn't like it at all.

"Master Red Jade is right," the antiquarian said. "Let's just go with him."

"I'll mark the tiles in any event," I said stubbornly, refusing to admit that this was going to be impossible, "in case we have to turn around and run out."

That's how we had the great honor of learning to follow the Steps of Yu, a four-thousand-year-old magic dance that was capable of taking ancient Chinese shamans up to heaven.

Lao Jiang followed Master Red, I went next, then Fernanda, and finally Biao. When my turn came, I was shaking from head to toe as I stepped on the first two tiles. The next step was diagonally to the left on just one foot and then hopping on the same foot two tiles ahead. Next was another diagonal step to the right and three more hops on the right foot; another three on the left; three more on the right; another three on the left; and at last, both feet next to one another, like at the beginning. Master Red told us this first sequence was called "Steps on the

Heavenly Scale" and the next was "Pacing the Big Dipper," which consisted of one jump diagonally to the right, one more ahead, another to the left, and three ahead, as if drawing the shape of a ladle.

Basically, those were the Steps of Yu, and repeating both series, we reached the first staircase, where we were relieved to find no crossbows aimed at us. By this time we'd retrieved my bag and Biao's, but not Fernanda's. It had fallen too far from where our dance had taken us. The girl was sulking and looked at me so insistently that I knew I had to somehow get that bag or put up with her reproaches for the rest of my life. Since this would clearly have been harmful to my health, I madly tried to think of a way to rescue that lost bundle. I consulted with Lao Jing in a whisper. After assuring me that such an effort was ridiculous, he grudgingly said he'd take care of it. The antiquarian opened up his bag of tricks and pulled out the hundred-treasure chest as well as a very thin, extremely long line of some sort. He tied a knot around one of the gold pieces from the chest, a pendant earring on what looked like a fish-hook.

"If you catch it with that," I warned, "you'll set off all the crossbows when you drag the bag across the tiles."

"Do you have a better idea?"

"We'd better lie flat on the stairs," I said, turning to address the others. Everyone hurried to obey me. There were only three stairs, but since they were so long, we all fit on the first and safest one. Lao Jiang moved to the left of the bag and onto the second stair, so that when he tossed the line, it was nearly horizontal. He made his first attempt. Luckily, the earring didn't weigh enough to cause the balls of the seismoscope to vibrate, because the antiquarian's aim left a lot to be desired. When he finally hooked Fernanda's bag, we heard the unpleasant sound of chains and the sharp whistling of arrows just above our heads.

We reached the second set of stairs and rested. The light wasn't as good there as it had been at the start. That final stretch was an absolute nightmare. I sweated buckets from the effort, the nerves, and the very reasonable fear of making a mistake. The lines between the tiles were hard to distinguish, and we took each step guided purely by intuition, but we made it. Everyone arrived safe and sound, and I don't remember a nicer sensation than putting my foot on the first of many stairs leading up to the altar and the coffin. I was overjoyed. The children were fine, Master Red and Lao Jiang were fine, and I was fine. It had been the longest, most exhausting dance of my life.

The children shouted enthusiastically and ran up the stairs to look at the coffin. For a moment I was afraid something might happen to them, that there would be some other death trap on that first level of the mausoleum, but Sai Wu hadn't mentioned anything of the sort in the *jiance*, so I decided not to worry. The adults followed the children, just as pleased but more restrained. "Haste shortens your life," Ming T'ien had said. Master Red, Lao Jiang, and I were the very embodiment of moderation at this thrilling time.

The stone altar on which the coffin lay was shaped like a double bed, only three times as big. There was not only a black-lacquered rectangular casket finely decorated with dragons, tigers, and clouds of gold, but also fifteen or twenty medium-size coffins separated by those little tea tables that sit on Chinese sofas. Around the coffin, beautiful brocade cloths covered pyramids of something, and several dozen jade soldiers and fantastic animals were lined up all over the surface. There were also ceramic vessels, mother-of-pearl brushes and ornamental combs, lovely burnished bronze mirrors, cups, and knives inlaid with turquoise. Everything was covered in just a thin layer of dust, as if it had been cleaned a week earlier.

Taking great care not to break anything, Lao Jiang leaped nimbly onto the altar to open the coffin. He undid the latch, but the lid was too heavy for him to lift on his own. Biao jumped up beside him, and although the two of them were able to lift it an inch or so, they finally had to let it go. Master Red, Fernanda, and I climbed up onto the altar as well, and this time, between the five of us, we were able to open the stubborn sarcophagus, only to discover that it contained just an impressive set of armor. Made of small stone plates joined together like fish scales, it was complete with shoulder guards, breast and back plates, and a long skirt. There was even a helmet with an opening for the face and a neck guard. It may well have been a funeral offering of great worth, a unique display of Qin-dynasty imperial armor, as Lao Jiang asserted, but I got the distinct impression that the First Emperor was playing a joke, thumbing his nose at whoever opened this false sarcophagus.

We let the lid fall before it broke our arms and got down off the altar, ready to examine the rest of the treasures. Lao Jiang seemed impatient to take a look at our find and was the first to remove the cloths and open the chests. The pyramid shapes were piles of little medallions, similar to the weights used on grocery-store scales (although these were made of pure gold), and the chests were filled with priceless jewel-studded pieces. There was an absolute fortune there.

"We've done it," I murmured.

"Do you know what these figures are made of?" the antiquarian asked as he picked up one of the little soldiers that dotted the altar.

"Jade," Fernanda replied.

"Yes and no. It is jade, but a magnificent type of jade called *yufu* that no longer exists. This soldier would be worth between fifteen and twenty thousand Mexican silver dollars."

"That's wonderful!" I exclaimed. "We've got what we need! We don't have to go any further. We can divide all this up and leave right away!"

It was over. The madness had come to an end. I now had the money I needed to pay Rémy's debts.

"It's not that much once it's divided into six, Elvira."

"Six?" I asked in surprise.

"You, Wudang Monastery, Paddy Tichborne, the Kuomintang, the Communist Party, and me. After all this effort, I might as well keep a few things for my antiquities shop. Let me warn you as well that the Kuomintang will want to recoup its expenses for our trip."

Well, Lao Jiang had set his political idealism aside and fallen into the grip of avarice. I could have sworn I saw it written all over his face.

"It's still plenty, even divided into six, Lao Jiang," I objected. "We have more than enough. Let's get out of here."

"It might be plenty to you, Elvira, but it's not much for two political parties that are struggling to build a new, modern nation on what's left of one that's famished and all but destroyed. And let's not forget that Wudang has so many mouths to feed and all those repairs that need doing. At least that's what Abbot Xu Benshan told me in the letter he sent with Masters Red Jade and Black Jade when he accepted my offer of a portion of the treasure in exchange for his help. Don't just think about yourself; try to think about everyone else's needs as well. What's more, it's our duty to tear these riches from imperialist claws."

"But we can't carry everything that's in this tomb!"

"True, but everything we take, which will be much more than just this, will pay for the excavations needed to get the rest. Shi Huang Ti will bring wealth to his people once again!" he exclaimed. Now there was no doubt in my mind that Lao Jiang had gone crazy. He made me so angry at times, especially that nasty, condescending display of generosity: "Don't just think about yourself; try to think about everyone else's needs as well." We had to keep risking our lives because there wasn't enough on that altar to pay for the rebirth of China. Well, wasn't China lucky? I thought. After all, *it* had the opportunity for rebirth, but if we died, *we* certainly wouldn't. And so, given that all those riches were insignificant and worthless, I decided they might as well be put to good use.

"Take cover," I warned, scooping up gold weights in my cupped hands.

"What are you going to do, Auntie?" my niece asked nervously when she saw the look on my face.

"I said take cover," I repeated. "Arrows are about to fly."

They all quickly lay flat on the floor, and, squatting in front of the altar, I threw the medallions against the tiles with all my might. As soon as they touched the floor, a cloud of arrows appeared in the air and slammed into the gold pieces, creating an awful din.

"What are you doing?" Lao Jiang yelled. "Are you crazy?"

"Not at all," I replied, throwing a second handful even farther. "I want to assure our escape. I'm going to empty the crossbows so there'll be a safe path to the exit. Later you can bend down to pick the treasure up off the floor if you like. Give me a hand, children! Throw the jewels from the chests straight out in front of us!"

Even Master Red enthusiastically joined in the fun of using those ancient treasures to empty the crossbows of arrows. We took big fistfuls of precious stones, earrings, charms, strange hair pendants, bar-rettes, necklaces, hairpins, bracelets, and more, throwing them on the tiles as if we were tossing stones into a lake. The best thing was when the arrows themselves bounced onto other tiles and set off yet more ar-rows that bounced, making the path to the doors safer and safer. They finally ceased, at about the same time we began to tire. It had been just like watching a beautiful fireworks display, only a little more dangerous, but now we could run to the exit if we wanted without risking our lives.

Lao Jiang had remained hidden behind the altar, safe from the ar-rows, and never said another word. He hadn't, of course, participated in the fun, and so he wasn't as jubilant or sweaty as we were, roaring with laughter and congratulating one another. Master Red and I bowed as if it were an affectionate handshake (it wasn't proper to touch, of course), and he looked as pleased as punch. Everyone had had a marvelous time. Everyone but Lao Jiang, who stood up with a face as dark as thunder and threw his dangerous bag over his shoulder with contempt.

A short distance behind the altar was a vertical black stone slab that came down from the ceiling and was about six feet long, lending an im-posing, solemn air to the place where a throne should have sat. Mag-nificent sculptors had carved two powerful tigers standing on their back legs, a whirl of clouds in their muzzles and columns of what might have been steam spilling out. Lao Jiang strode decisively behind the slab and disappeared, the rest of us still laughing and indifferent to his wounded pride, after stuffing big handfuls of precious stones into our bundles

(Fernanda and I also took two beautiful bronze mirrors). A trapdoor stood open on the floor behind the slab. Ignoring us, the antiquarian was already climbing down to the bottom of a dark pit on an iron ladder secured to the wall. I knotted the strings on my bag and slung it across my shoulders. Master Red went ahead, and the children came last so I could help them if they slipped or if a rung came loose. I couldn't for the life of me figure how Lao Jiang thought he was going to remove the huge treasures he seemed so willing to take in order to build a new, modern country.

It was horrifying to climb down in absolute darkness, listening to Fernanda and Biao huff and puff above me. My breathing was soon labored as well. Fortunately, the arduous descent didn't take long, and we were soon at the bottom, in what seemed like a cubicle with no exit.

"Why don't you light the torch, Lao Jiang?" I asked.

"Because the *jiance* forbids it, don't you remember?" he barked.

"We have to move about in the dark?" Master Red asked in disbelief.

"Sai Wu said, 'I know even less about the second level, but do not use fire to light the way. Move forward in darkness, or you will die.'"

"There must be some sort of door," Biao murmured as he moved around that hovel, feeling his way along the walls. "Here! There's something here!"

We all turned around, bumping into one another, as we let Lao Jiang through and heard him struggle with some sort of bolt. After a good deal of wrestling, the door finally opened with the most unpleasant creaking of hinges.

"Well, I don't know how we're going to get through this second level if we can't light the torch. Who knows where we go down to the third."

I was the one who made this optimistic comment, but it didn't arouse any response from the others. They were all crossing through the invisible door Lao Jiang had opened. So this is what it must be like to be completely blind, I thought, extending my arms so I wouldn't run into anyone. I thought back on Sunday mornings in the park when I was little and used to play Blind Man's Bluff with my friends. I told my-self to look at this the same way, to find the fun in it, as if it were a challenge—provided, of course, that the dangers awaiting us on the other side weren't so terrible that profound darkness became a hellish nightmare.

There was nothing on the other side of that door. The only thing we felt was absolute emptiness. Since it wouldn't do to just randomly wander about and wind up lost and disoriented, I had the idea that one of us should tie one end of Lao Jiang's long line around his or her waist and explore a little while the rest of us stayed where we were near the exit. Everyone agreed, and Biao quickly offered to be the one to explore, because he was quick and had good reflexes. He could react in an in-stant, he said, if he came up against anything or noticed a hole opening up under his feet.

"True," I commented. "Don't ever let anyone say it was you who fell to the bottom of that shaft where we came into the mausoleum."

"But that's how I survived!" he protested. "I quickly jumped onto the wall when the ground gave way!"

"That's exactly why you're not going to be the one to tie the line around your waist. That and because I can't take any more scares. I'll do it."

"No, Elvira, you won't," Lao Jiang's resonant voice declared emphati-cally. "Master Red Jade or I will go, not you."

"Why not?" I asked, offended.

"Because you are a woman."

So we were back to that, were we? Men seemed to think that being a woman meant you were crippled or maimed, even if they wrapped it in the guise of male gallantry.

"Don't I have arms and legs, too?"

"Don't insist. I'll go." We could hear him open his bag and close it again. "Please hold on to this line, Master Red Jade."

"What sort of line is this?" Master Red murmured. "It's not made of twine."

"Hold on tight," Lao Jiang said as he walked away. "It could slip out of your hands if I fall."

"Don't worry. I'm tying it around my wrist."

"Anything out there, Lao Jiang?" I asked, raising my voice.

"Not yet."

We all remained quiet, waiting for news. After a while Master Red told us that the antiquarian had gone as far as the line would allow and was tracing a sort of semicircle, like a compass, to see what he might find along the way. Unfortunately, he found me: I suddenly felt something touch my stomach, screamed, and jumped back. Though the shock had made me yell loudly, it came back as a faint, strange echo, as if we were in a cathedral of unimaginable proportions.

"Did you scream, Elvira?" the antiquarian asked.

"Yes," I admitted, a little embarrassed. "You scared the daylights out of me."

"Everyone please sit down on the floor and lower your heads so I can finish examining this area."

"How long is your line?" I asked as I sat cross-legged, noticing that Fernanda and Biao sat next to me. The floor felt like a mirror, cold and polished smooth, though it wasn't slippery.

"About eighty feet."

"Is that all? It seems like you're much farther away. In any event, it's too bad you didn't think to bring a longer one."

"Would you be so kind as to be quiet? You're distracting me."

"Oh, of course! Sorry."

The children, on the other hand, continued whispering. The pitch black made them nervous, and talking made them forget their fear a little. I was scared, too, though there was no logical reason to be: The foreman hadn't spoken of any special danger in this room. He had simply recommended that his son not use fire to find his way, because he'd die if he lit a torch.

Why? I suddenly asked myself. "Move forward in darkness, or

you will die." It didn't make any sense, unless . . . Coal miners died from
gas explosions. The gas would detonate when it came into contact with
the flames on their lamps. What kind of gas? Methane, the very gas the
Chinese had been using for thousands of years to illuminate their big
cities or make torches like the one Lao Jiang was carrying. He had
proudly assured us that Celestials had known how to use methane ever
since the time of the First Emperor. So were we breathing methane?
Nearly every day there was an article in our papers about a coal-mine
explosion. Although there'd been great technological advances such as
security lamps, methane didn't smell. Sometimes miners would be chip-
ping at a wall and gas would suddenly escape from a great pocket, ex-
ploding when it came into contact even with a nearly cold lamp wick.

I sniffed the air. It didn't smell of anything, of course. After one had
inhaled methane for a certain amount time, it caused symptoms such
as dizziness, nausea, headache, lack of coordination, loss of consciousness, and asphyxia. What I didn't know was how long it took for any of
that to begin.

The darkness drove me crazy. My old neuroses were back. How
could there be methane in an emperor's tomb? This wasn't a coal mine.
Either Lao Jiang got back with news soon, however bad it might be, or
my sick thoughts were going to consume me in that gloom. My heart
was pounding, and my hands were beginning to sweat. Calm down, Elvira. Calm down. The last thing I wanted was to have a severe attack of
panic in there.

"You're on your way back, Da Teh?" I heard Master Red ask.

"Yes."

"Did you find anything?"

"No."

"Well, there has to be something," Fernanda declared.

"The only thing I can think of is to move along the walls until we
find the exit," Lao Jiang said.

"But what if it's another trapdoor in the middle of the floor somewhere in here?"

"In that case, young Fernanda, it will take us a little longer, but we'll find it."

I did everything I could to force myself not to think about the ridiculous idea of death by methane.

"Let's start at the door and go clockwise around the room," I said, to scare off any other thoughts.

"And what direction is that?" Master Red inquired curiously.

"You speak French perfectly, and yet you've never seen a Western clock?" I asked, dumbfounded.

"There were none at the mission where my brother and I studied."

"Well, the hands turn in a circle from right to left."

"So we'll start where I'm standing," he observed, as if we could see him.

"We should leave something at this door so we recognize it on our way back," I suggested, always worried about the way back.

"What do you propose?"

"I'll leave one of my pencils."

We began walking. I ran my left hand along the surface of the wall, which, unlike the floor, was rough and uneven. Then I began grazing just my fingertips so as not to set my teeth on edge and, toward the end, using only my index finger. After a while I came to the conclusion that it was a much larger room than the funeral palace on the floor above. It must have been the size of the plastered walls on that level. By the time we turned the first corner, I was sure of it and prepared for a long, boring walk. Why not make it a little more pleasant? I could walk wherever I wanted. Since I couldn't see anything, I was free to imagine anywhere in the world, and I chose the Left Bank of the Seine in Paris, with its secondhand-book stalls and amateur painters. I pictured the lovely bridges, the water, the sun. . . . I could hear the sound of the cars and buses, the shouts of the sweet vendors. . . . My house! I saw my house, the gate, the stairs, the door. . . . And inside, my living room, my bedroom, my kitchen, my studio. . . . Oh, the smell of my house! I had forgotten what the wood furniture smelled like, the flowers I always had in vases, the burners I cooked on, the starched clothes in my drawers, and of course the brand-new, unused canvases, the oil paints, the turpentine. . . . It had been so long since I left home! I became desperately homesick, and I wanted to cry. I was too old for such silliness.

It might have been the sadness that made me feel a bit dizzy, as if the wall or the floor were moving, like on the *André Lebon*. It couldn't be much farther until we were back at the beginning. We'd already turned four corners, so the door where I'd left a pencil had to be nearby. Perhaps the rocking sensation was simply because I was hungry. You shouldn't walk long distances on an empty stomach. I didn't want to think of the other possibility.

Ten minutes later I had my pencil back in my hand.

"I don't think we got very far," Fernanda said sulkily. "We're back where we started."

"Yes, but we've also eliminated one possibility. Now we have to try others."

"I'm feeling a little dizzy," my niece protested, alarming me.

"What about you, Biao?"

"I'm also dizzy, *tai-tai*. But it's not too bad."

"What about you two?" There was no need for me to say their names; they simply responded.

"I'm fine," Lao Jiang said. "We've just been groping around in the dark for too long, that's all."

"I'm also fine," Master Red said. "What about you, madame?"

"Yes, fine," I lied. Either we found our way down to the third level right away or I was hurrying the children back up to the funeral palace. "Does anyone have any quick ideas?"

"We should examine the floor." Master Red hesitated. "But if the children aren't feeling well—"

"We know we're in a big rectangular space," Lao Jiang interrupted. "Let's divide it into strips that we'll mark using Elvira's pencils and then search the floor for the trapdoor."

That would take forever, and we didn't have that long.

"I propose we go up to the palace and eat. There's light up there, and we need to recover a bit of energy. Then we can come back down and check the floor. What do you say?"

"Not yet," Lao Jiang disapproved. "Let's do at least one section before we go up."

"One section's too much," I protested, without knowing exactly how big a piece the antiquarian was referring to, but he ignored me.

"Biao, take five big steps forward and stay there while the rest of us search the floor between the wall and the line you represent. If we get lost, we'll call out so you can guide us with your voice. Understood?"

"Yes, Lao Jiang, but may I say something?"

"Don't tell me again that you're not feeling well," the antiquarian warned.

"No, no. . . . What I wanted to say was there's something strange under my feet. It's not a trapdoor, but it must be important, because it's like one of those hexagrams from the *I Ching*."

"Are you sure?" Lao Jiang spit this out as if he'd been stung by a wasp.

"Let me check," Master Red said. "Biao?"

"Yes, that's me. Crouch down. It's right here. See?"

"No, I can't see"—Master Red Jade laughed—"but I can feel it, and it is indeed a hexagram. The floor must be made of polished bronze, and the hexagram is engraved in relief."

"Bas-relief," I confirmed as I touched it with my own hands, noting how smooth the shapes were: six horizontal lines, some solid and others broken, forming a perfect square a little more than two and a half feet on each side.

"How odd!" Master Red said. "The hexagram is Ming I, 'Darkening of the Light.' It would be quite meaningful if it weren't just a simple decoration."

"What sort of decoration would they put in a place that's pitch black?" Fernanda snapped. "It's there for a reason."

"Do you know the *I Ching* by heart, Master Red Jade?" I asked.

"Yes, madame, though that's not unusual," he noted modestly.

"Master Tzau in Wudang knew it by heart as well."

"Master Tzau is a very wise man, madame. In fact, no one in China knows more about the I Ching than he. People come from all over to consult him. I'm glad you had the opportunity to meet him."

"Enough of the idle chitchat!" Lao Jiang interrupted. "Interpret the sign, Master Red Jade."

"Of course, Da Teh. I humbly beg your pardon."

"Hurry up!" Lao Jiang barked. I couldn't believe the radical change that had come over the antiquarian since we arrived inside the mausoleum. It was as if anything we said or did infuriated him. Indeed, he was nothing like the elegant, educated gentleman I had met in Paddy Tichborne's rooms at the Shanghai Club.

"The hexagram Ming I, 'Darkening of the Light,'" Master Red was saying, "alludes to the sun's having sunk beneath the earth, causing utter darkness. A sinister man is in a position of authority. Wise and able men suffer as a result, because although it is a burden, they must not abandon him. The judgment says that the light has disappeared, and in such situations one must persevere when faced with an emergency."

"I don't understand a thing, tai-tai," Biao whispered in my ear. I put my hand over his mouth to tell him to be quiet, not wanting to hear any more reprimands from Lao Jiang.

"Given the situation we're in," Master Red went on, "I suppose the interpretation would be that there's some risk we can't see, some emergency that requires us to move quickly. I think the hexagram is telling us to hurry and find the light, because we're in some sort of danger."

I knew it. I hadn't gone crazy after all. The air was filled with methane, and we had to get out of there as soon as possible.

"Here's another hexagram!" my niece then exclaimed.

"So close?" Lao Jiang asked in disbelief.

"Starting at the door and going in a straight line, first there's the one Biao found and then, about six feet farther on, this one that Fernanda just found," I explained, kneeling down by the engraving to examine it. All I actually did was touch it to ensure she hadn't made a mistake. It was Master Red who examined it carefully to see which hexagram it was.

"Sheng," he pronounced after studying it with his hands, " 'Pushing Upward.' It refers to a tree pushing up through the earth as it grows. In reality, it speaks of rising to success from a lowly position thanks to personal effort and determination. The judgment says you must set to work and not be afraid, because a departure to the south brings good fortune."

"Departure to the south?" Lao Jiang repeated. "We should head south from here?"

"I'd say so."

"How are we going to know which way is south?" I asked as I tried to map out the mausoleum in my head. The door we'd come through into that poisonous room was to the north, because it was in front of the iron rungs we climbed down at the back of the funeral palace. Going south, then, meant going farther into the darkness ahead, retracing the route we'd taken upstairs, walking into the depths of Mount Li.

"I can locate the eight cardinal points on my *luo p'an*, madame, because they're carved into the wood. Then, if I touch the needle lightly, I can see where it's pointing."

What would we have done without brilliant Master Red? I congratulated myself for having had the marvelous idea to ask the abbot to provide us with a monk who was an expert in the Chinese sciences. We were finally in a position to begin moving. The problem was, how would we know the way back? Just as I'd emptied the crossbows in the throne room, I wanted to mark the floor with something so that on our way back we'd simply have to follow the trail to the door, but I couldn't think clearly. I was terribly dizzy and beginning to feel a slight headache, which scared me a little.

"Hurry and find the south, Master Red Jade," the antiquarian ordered.

What did I have in my bag that I could use . . . ? The precious stones! That lovely handful of green turquoise I'd taken off the altar before following Lao Jiang. They were roughly the size of a chickpea and would be hard to find in the dark, but I didn't have anything else. As Master Red continued his calculations, I rummaged deep in my bag and found the stones, moving them into my jacket pockets. Since I didn't dare drop the first one because of the noise it would make, I discreetly knelt down and set it softly on the floor. Fairy tales had to be good for something. After all, didn't Hansel and Gretel leave a trail of bread crumbs in the forest so they could find their way home?

After a while Master Red finally said, "Hold on to my tunic and form a line. I'll lead the way."

It seemed ridiculous to walk like that, everyone holding hands (except when I let go to set a turquoise on the floor), but we were all so dizzy and afraid that no one made a single joke, not even when Master Red stopped and we all bumped into one another. Here was yet more proof that the effects of the gas were getting worse. Why hadn't I insisted we go back to the throne room in the funeral palace? I felt guilty, but I hadn't wanted to cause a panic, and I wasn't sure there really was methane.

"Three yin lines, one yang, another yin, and another yang," Master Red was saying. "Therefore, the hexagram is Chin, 'Progress.'"

"That means we're on the right track," I commented, trying to sound optimistic.

"The sun rises rapidly above the earth," our scholar explained. "The judgment for 'Progress' says that the powerful prince is honored with horses in large numbers. I'd say this sign means we should run, gallop as quickly as horses to the next hexagram."

"But do we keep going south?" I asked. The pain in my head was becoming more severe, and every time I bent over to set a turquoise down, it felt as if I left a piece of my brain on the floor as well.

"Yes, madame. Given that the hexagram doesn't mention another direction, we should keep going south. Hold on to one another again, and follow me as quickly as you can."

"Are you sure you feel all right, Master Red Jade?" I asked as I

grasped the children's frozen hands. If he became disoriented or lost consciousness, the rest of us were dead.

"Yes, madame. I'm just fine."

"I'm scared, Auntie," my niece whimpered. "And my head hurts."

"Nonsense!" Lao Jiang exclaimed harshly. "You'll be fine as soon as we get out of here. It's just the darkness."

"I don't feel well either, *tai-tai*," Biao murmured.

"Silence!" the antiquarian ordered.

He knew. Lao Jiang knew we were in a methane trap. He'd come to that conclusion when I had, and he'd decided on behalf of everyone that it was a risk we had to take. He probably thought no one else realized what was happening.

"Walk quickly, children," I said, pushing Biao's shoulder and pulling Fernanda's cold hand.

What was going on in the antiquarian's head? Something had happened to him, and I needed to know what. I set another turquoise on the floor, and as I stood up, struggling to keep my balance, I collided with Fernanda as she bent over to speak with me in private.

"Ow!" I exclaimed, reaching up to rub my head where her chin had nearly pierced my skull.

"Ouch!" she said at the same time.

"What's wrong with you two?" Lao Jiang grumbled.

"Nothing. Keep walking," I replied churlishly.

"Why do you keep letting go of my hand and bending down?" Fernanda whispered in my ear.

"Because I'm leaving a trail of crumbs, like Hansel and Gretel."

I don't know whether she believed me or thought I'd gone stark raving mad, but she didn't say a word, just held on tightly to my hand, and we kept going. After that, every time I let go of her hand and then took it again, her fingers squeezed mine affectionately, as if approving of my actions. The girl was an absolute pearl—an uncultured pearl, perhaps, but a pearl nonetheless.

"Another hexagram," Master Red announced. "Let me see which one it is."

We all remained quiet, waiting.

"K'un, 'The Receptive.' This is a complicated sign and usually interpreted in conjunction with the previous one, Ch'ien, 'The Creative.' They're like yin and yang."

"Get to the point, Master Red Jade," the antiquarian commanded.

"If we limit ourselves to the judgment," he said somewhat hurriedly, " 'The Receptive' implies that the nobleman who wants to lead may go astray but will be successful if he follows others with the perseverance of a mare, an animal that combines the strength and swiftness of a horse with the gentleness and devotion of the feminine."

"That's it?" Lao Jiang snarled. "We're to go from the swiftness of a horse to that of a mare? So this hexagram is just another reminder that we should continue south at full speed."

"No, not to the south now," Master Red said. "The judgment says, 'It is favorable to find friends in the west and south, / To forgo friends in the east and north.' "

"Why can't these hexagrams be a little clearer?" my niece complained.

"Because that's not their purpose, Fernanda," I explained. "It's actually an ancient text that's used by oracles."

"Very well then, we're to avoid the east and the north, which is where we came from," Lao Jiang summarized. "We're to head south and west, is that it? So let's head southwest."

"No, Da Teh, that's not the way to interpret it. When the *I Ching* wants to propose a direction, it clearly indicates it. If it wanted us to go southwest, it would have said so. However, it speaks of the south and the west separately. Since we came from the south, the direction it's indicating is the west. Of the sixty-four hexagrams in the *I Ching*, K'un, 'The Receptive,' is the only one that mentions the west. Whoever chose these hexagrams had only K'un to indicate that direction."

"If you say so, Master Red Jade. Take us west, then. Let's get on with it."

"Yes, Da Teh."

The next hexagram we found was Pi, "Holding Together," which said we should stay together and run, because "Those who are uncertain gradually join. / Whoever come too late / Meets with misfortune." It was yet another warning that time was of the essence. We didn't need to be reminded; Lao Jiang and I, knowing what we were dealing with, encouraged the group to hurry. Continuing in a straight line west, we came upon the sixth hexagram, Chien, "Obstruction," which may have indicated the presence of an obstacle in our path, though we didn't run across anything. That was when Biao vomited. An instant later so did Fernanda. I was about to be the third, because the pain in my head was excruciating. I couldn't believe that Lao Jiang and Master Red weren't affected by the methane. I was therefore not surprised when the antiquarian suddenly fell to the floor.

We heard a tremendous thud, and Biao, who'd been holding his hand, cried out.

"Lao Jiang's fallen down!" he yelled.

"I'm fine. I'm fine. . . ." the antiquarian muttered. We had all gathered around, and Master Red was examining him in the dark.

"This danger the hexagrams speak of . . ." Master Red began.

Violating protocol, I brought my mouth close to his ear and said, "This room is filled with methane, Master Red Jade. Don't let the children know. We've got to get out of here right away. There's not much time left."

He nodded without a word; I could tell by the way his hair brushed against my face. It smelled awful, like rancid oil, and I recalled Biao's complaint when he had to stick his hand in the whale-oil receptacles that now burned brightly on the floor above us.

Lao Jiang stood with everyone's help, repeatedly assuring us he was fine and telling us to let go of him.

"Interpret the sign, Master Red Jade," he said.

"Of course, Da Teh. This one is Chien, 'Obstruction.' The judgment assures it is wise to head southwest."

"Another change in direction."

"It can't be much farther," I said. "I could swear we've crossed the room in a diagonal."

"With a little zig in the middle," the antiquarian acknowledged. "Hurry, Master Red Jade. We're running out of time."

There was no doubt he was in terrible shape. He'd done his best to hide it, but he was actually worse than any of us.

Biao pulled on my hand and whispered, "Lao Jiang's walking as if he were drunk. What should I do?"

"Nothing," I replied. "Just try to make sure he doesn't fall."

"I'm still scared."

"I know, Biao, but think of your name. You're a little tiger, strong and powerful. You can overcome your fear."

"I should really change my name, *tai-tai*. I'm not so little anymore."

The boy could still think of things like that! Not me. My fear heightened as we spoke.

"Later, Biao. Once we get out of here," I murmured, trying to keep from vomiting.

Luckily, it didn't take Master Red long to find the next hexagram, one that had a lovely, hopeful name: Lin, "Approach." The judgment for this sign literally said, "Approach has supreme success."

"Auntie," Fernanda called out weakly. "Auntie, I can't go any farther. I think I'm going to collapse."

"No, Fernandina! Not yet!" I pleaded, using the name she preferred. "Hold on a little longer. Come on."

"I really don't think I can."

"You are an Aranda and a woman! Do you want Lao Jiang, Biao, and Master Red to think we're not up to this sort of thing, that we're weak? Keep walking, and don't you dare faint!"

"I'll try," she whimpered.

Ages—what seemed like a lifetime—later, Master Red announced that he'd found the eighth hexagram. No one was hurrying now. I don't know how, but Biao was holding Lao Jiang up by the shoulders to keep him from stumbling and falling. Meanwhile, I was barely able to take another step myself but had to haul Fernanda along by the waist, pulling on the arm she had slung around my neck. We weren't going to make it; we were minutes away from losing consciousness. I suppose all we had left was our survival instinct.

"Come on!" hardy Master Red exclaimed, his energetic voice like a beacon in the dark. "We've found the hexagram Hsieh, 'Deliverance.'"

That sounded so good. Deliverance.

"Do you know what the judgment says? 'Deliverance. / The southwest furthers. / If there is still something where one has to go, / Hastening brings good fortune.' Let's go! Hurry! We're not far from the exit."

None of us moved. I heard Master Red walk away and thought maybe Fernanda and I should just fall on the floor to rest and sleep. I was tired, so incredibly tired.

"Here! The trapdoor's here!" Master Red shouted. "I found it! Come on, everyone! We've got to get out of here!"

Yes, we had to get out of there, but we couldn't. I wanted to follow him, wanted to get out of that room, but I simply couldn't move, let alone drag my niece along with me.

"*Tai-tai,* are we going to die?"

"No, Biao. We'll get out of here. Walk toward Master Red Jade."

"I can't with Lao Jiang."

"Can you manage with Fernanda?"

"Maybe . . . I don't know."

"Come on, try."

"What about you, *tai-tai?*"

"Go get Master Red Jade and tell him to come back for Lao Jiang. Go on with Fernanda now. It's the air, Biao. There's poisonous gas in the air. The two of you get out of here as quick as you can."

I felt him take Fernanda from my arms and heard them stumble off. There was no need to say anything to Master Red. They met along the way and he told Biao how to get to the trapdoor.

"Come, madame," Master Red said next to me.

"What about Lao Jiang?"

"He's lost consciousness."

"Pick him up and get him out of here. I just need to hold on to your tunic so I don't get lost. I don't think I can follow a straight line on my own."

Where did I get the strength to walk, to hold Master Red's tunic between my frozen fingers and follow him to the trapdoor, dragging my feet, unconscious of my own movements? I honestly don't know. But once I was able to think clearly again, I realized I was much stronger than I had known. Just as it said in that phrase from the *Tao Te Ching* that the abbot of Wudang had given me, when there is nothing one cannot overcome, no one knows his own limits.

Though it might sound paradoxical, I opened my eyes when I was blinded by the light. I blinked and rubbed them until I was once again used to the glare. It was the flame on Lao Jiang's torch, as bright as the midday sun. I was lying on the floor but had no idea where I was, and my first thought was for Fernanda.

"My niece?" I asked out loud. "And Biao?"

"They're still asleep, madame," Master Red said, leaning over so I could see his face. He was the one holding the torch. I propped myself up on my elbows and raised my head to look around: We were on a broad platform similar to the ones in the Han shaft we'd descended to reach the mausoleum, but this one was tiled in black. It was also much bigger; apart from the four of us lying there, at least four or five more would have fit. We were in another deep shaft, as wide and circular as the first but the walls here were made of rock and seemed much more solid, sturdier.

Fernanda, Lao Jiang, and Biao were sleeping, completely still.

"Have you tried to wake them, Master Red Jade?"

"Yes, madame, it shouldn't be long now. I applied some herbs to each of your noses. The stimulant will soon bring them back to consciousness. It's extremely dangerous to breathe methane."

"Why weren't you poisoned?" I asked, using my hands to help me into a sitting position.

Master Red smiled. "That's a secret, madame, a secret of the internal martial arts."

"You're not saying you don't breathe," I joked, but something in his face made me blanch. "You do breathe, don't you, Master Red Jade?"

"Perhaps a little less than you do," he reluctantly admitted, "or perhaps in a different way. We learn to breathe from the abdomen. Control over the breath and the muscles that regulate it is one of our usual meditation practices, a technique we learn for health and longevity. While you inhale and exhale some fifteen or twenty times, and the children a little more, we do so only four times, like tortoises and they live to be over a hundred. That's why the methane didn't affect me: I inhaled much less of it."

The Celestials, and the Taoists in particular, never ceased to amaze me, but I didn't feel up to learning anything right then. My entire body ached. With supreme effort I managed to stand. As I turned, just behind me, I saw iron rungs in the wall that were undoubtedly the ladder we'd come down—though I don't remember how. The ceiling was some ten feet above me, and fortunately the trapdoor leading to that huge, gas-filled cathedral with the bronze floor was shut tight. I don't know how we made it out of there alive. At least I'd been able to drop pieces of turquoise right until the very end (the end of my memory, in any event, and I wasn't exactly sure where that had been). We would see if they were of any use at all.

My niece opened her eyes and moaned. I knelt by her side and ran my hand over her hair.

"How are you?" I asked affectionately.

"Could someone turn off the light?" she protested rudely. The hand I held on her head was tempted to rise up and give her a proper smack, but I didn't believe in such things. The desire, however, was most certainly there.

Biao also woke up complaining about the torchlight, although like a good servant he was a little more polite.

"Where are we?" he asked.

"I have no idea, Biao. We've left the second floor of the mausoleum, but we're not yet at the third. There are ramps similar to the ones in the shaft you fell into, although these are much bigger and more secure. Look," I said, pointing to the wall in front, where two of them could be seen going down. I'm sure we'd have seen more if we'd looked into the shaft, but I didn't feel like moving all that way.

I helped the children up, and it was then that Lao Jiang gave signs of life.

"How are you, Da Teh?" Master Red asked, bringing the torch closer.

"Move that away, please!" he exclaimed, putting his arm over his eyes.

"Well, we're all alive," I said happily, mostly to hide how furious I was with Lao Jiang. I didn't plan on saying anything, but I was going to keep a close eye on him and read his thoughts if necessary to prevent him from making another unilateral decision that could endanger all our lives. That would not happen again.

"Shall we eat before heading down?" Master Red asked shyly.

The children wrinkled their noses in disgust, and both Lao Jiang and I shook our heads. I couldn't even think about food without feeling sick all over again.

"Do you know what would do us good right now, Auntie?" Fernanda commented as she picked up her bundle. "One of those ginger infusions you used to drink on the ship."

"Eat something along the way, Master Red Jade," Lao Jiang said as he walked along the platform toward the first ramp. We all hurried behind; Master Red didn't even try to pull food out of his bag.

We started down into the pit, following the spiral of platforms and ramps built up against the wall. It wasn't difficult, and there was a wonderful, soft current of fresh air that rose up from the bottom, clearing the fog from our heads and the poison from our veins. It soon became cold, and shortly after that it was positively icy. We bundled up and hid our hands inside the big sleeves on our padded jackets. By then we'd reached the bottom of the shaft, where the last ramp ended abruptly. In front of us yawned the mouth of a tunnel; there was nowhere else to go.

"Where are the ten thousand bridges?" Lao Jiang muttered.

"The architect Sai Wu told his son he'd find ten thousand bridges on the third level that would seem to lead nowhere," I clarified for Master Red. "However, there would be one route that would lead to the only exit."

"Ten thousand bridges?" he repeated. "Well, ten thousand is a symbolic number for us. All it means is 'many.'"

"Yes, we know," I replied, watching the antiquarian stride over to a receptacle at the mouth of the tunnel, similar to the ones along the walls in the funeral palace. This one took somewhat longer to light when he held the torch up to it, perhaps because of the cold. Once it did, however, we again watched the fire advance down a groove along the wall, illuminating the tunnel.

We cautiously walked some fifty feet, all five senses alert. A strange iron structure was at the end and beyond it nothing but darkness. We headed over to examine the enormous rusted frame that seemed to rise mysteriously out of the floor. Three thick, rather short posts emerged from the rock (one on either side and one in the middle of the floor) with enormous iron chains attached. The chain in the middle headed straight into the dark on the other side; the two on the sides rose diagonally up to the top of two sturdy posts a little over three feet high and from there went straight off into the void as well.

"A bridge?" Fernanda asked, terrified.

"I'm afraid so," Lao Jiang confirmed.

Three chains, I said to myself, just three iron chains: one to walk along and the other two, about three and a half feet high, to hold on to. The links were as big around as my fist, but even so it didn't look like the safest way to cross a chasm.

The flame reached more and more receptacles, gradually illuminating the shadows. Standing at the end of the tunnel, we watched agape as the third level of the mausoleum was revealed. The iron bridge in front of us ended about a hundred feet away on a pedestal that must have been nine square feet. Two more bridges reached out from there, one to the far end and one to the side. Unfortunately, there were several pedestals just like it, all connected by iron bridges, and these pedestals were actually huge pillars that sank so deep into the earth we couldn't make out the bottoms of them. As far as the eye could see below us, thousands of bridges formed a labyrinth of horizontal and diagonal chains at varying heights and slopes, beginning and ending on top of pillars of different heights. Sai Wu hadn't lied or exaggerated when he said there were "ten thousand bridges that seem to lead nowhere."

Overwhelmed, we contemplated the labyrinth without a word, holding our breath as the fire moved down, expanding our field of view and confirming our fears. At some point the flames reached the bottom and started back up the pillars. Soon the entire place was perfectly illuminated, and there was once again the unpleasant smell of burning whale oil.

"This is very dangerous," Lao Jiang observed, in case the rest of us hadn't realized it. "We could end up right back where we started after walking for hours and hours along those unstable iron chains."

Very uplifting—made you want to get started right away.

"There must be some logic even if we don't see it," I said, adopting the Chinese way of thinking.

Master Red regarded the bridges and pillars, turning his head left and right, looking down every now and then.

"What are you looking at, Master Red Jade?" Fernanda asked curiously.

"As madame said, there must be some logic. If there's an exit, this can't simply be random. How many square columns do you see?"

I hadn't thought to count. On our level there were three rows of three giant pillars each. Down below, it was impossible to calculate.

"Nine columns," Master Red declared out loud. "And how many bridges begin and end at each one?"

"That's hard to say, Master Red Jade. They all cross at different points."

"I'm going to that column in front of us," he said, walking toward the bridge as he adjusted and secured the bag on his back. "I'll be able to see better from there."

My blood ran cold, and not because of the air temperature.

Holding on tightly to the chains, Master Red put one foot on the unsteady, rusted walkway that creaked and swayed as if it were about to collapse. I squeezed my eyes shut. I didn't want to watch him fall into the void or smash into one of the pillars or the ground far below. Luckily, all I heard was the creaking and squeaking of the iron as he moved forward. There would be no convincing me to let the children walk on those. Master Red finally reached the end after a few very long minutes of unbearable tension. You could hear a collective exhalation when he did, and Lao Jiang and the children gave a jubilant shout. I was too terrified to move, let alone openly rejoice. I just sighed and relaxed every muscle in my body that had contracted in fear. Master Red Jade waved to us from the other side.

"It's steady," he said, "but don't come just yet."

We watched him examine the labyrinth again, turning his head in every direction and leaning dangerously over the edge of the pillar. Then, unexpectedly, he sat down and pulled the *luo p'an* out of his bag.

"What's he doing?" Biao wanted to know.

"He's using feng shui to study the flow of energy and the arrangement of the bridges," Lao Jiang explained.

"And how will that help us?" the boy insisted.

"Remember, this tomb was designed by master geomancers."

Red Jade stood up and put the compass away.

"I'm going on to the next column," he announced.

"Why?" Lao Jiang asked.

"Because I need to confirm a few things."

"Please be careful," I begged. "These walkways are very old."

"As old as this mausoleum, madame, and as you can see, it's still standing."

The iron links creaked once again, and we watched him move away, putting one foot in front of the other and holding on to the pliant chain handrails. If his legs wobbled even a little, he'd be dead. Balance was fundamental, and I took good note of that for when it came time to risk my life.

Even though the posts anchoring the bridges stood between him and us, we saw that he arrived safe and sound at the second pillar. We could tell he had pulled the *luo p'an* back out to perform his energy calculations. Once again he leaned dangerously over the edge to examine the walkways below, then finally stood and beckoned us over.

"You two stay here," I said to Fernanda and Biao.

The boy looked up at Lao Jiang for help, but the antiquarian had already begun walking across the chain. My niece furrowed her brow like I'd never seen her furrow it before.

"I'm going," she declared, obstinate and defiant.

"No, you're staying."

"I want to go, too, *tai-tai*."

"Well, I'm sorry. The both of you will wait here until we come back."

"And what if you don't come back?" Fernanda asked, still glowering.

"Then leave and find help in Xi'an."

"We'll follow you as soon you're gone," she warned arrogantly, dropping her bag on the floor.

"You wouldn't dare."

"Yes we would. Wouldn't we, Biao? We already followed you from Wudang, remember?"

"Biao," I said, "I forbid you to follow Lao Jiang, and I mean even if Fernanda orders you to. Do you understand?"

The boy lowered his head sadly. "Yes, *tai-tai*."

"And you, Fernanda, you will stay with Biao. If you disobey me, I'll put you in the strictest Catholic boarding school there is as soon as we're back in Paris. Is that clear? I'm sure you've heard what French nuns are like. And I swear you will not come out, even for holidays."

Her expression changed from anger to surprise to rage, but I had gotten through to her. She stomped her foot and flopped down on her bag with her arms crossed, looking back along the tunnel.

Master Red was still beckoning to us.

"Here, Biao," I said, opening my bag and handing him my box of pencils and my sketchbook. "So you don't get too bored. Please be careful. Don't do anything silly. We'll be back soon."

"Thank you, *tai-tai*."

I secured my bag tightly so it wouldn't throw me off balance, moved one trembling foot forward, and grasped the rails with my cold, sweaty hands. Lao Jiang was nearing the other side.

"Shall I follow you or wait?" I asked.

"The walkways are very solid, madame!" Master Red shouted from afar. "Don't be afraid! They'll hold the both of you!"

And so, terrified, I started to walk. It was the hardest test of any so far. Death was just one false step away. I didn't want to look down, but nor did I want to place my feet incorrectly and lose my balance. If I kept sweating as I was, my hands would slip no matter how much rust coated those iron rings.

Lao Jiang reached the pillar and turned around.

"Keep coming," he said. "I assure you there's nothing to worry about."

No! Of course not! Nothing at all! Just a fall of I don't know how many hundreds of feet, but I had taken the first steps and had to keep going. It was best to carry on and not think about it. Hadn't I heard that bravery didn't mean you weren't scared, just that you faced and overcame your fear? I was brave. Yes, very brave. My legs might be shaking, but the very fact that I was even crossing that bridge proved it.

"Well done, Elvira!" Lao Jiang congratulated me as he reached out to help me with the last step. I was still dazed when I finally set foot on the pillar. Had I reached the end? Really? Was I on the pillar? Had I made it all the way across?

"Just look at the view from here," he said, reaching an arm down.

"No thank you. I'd rather not look if you don't mind."

He smiled. "Let's get on with the next," he said. "You go first, and I'll keep an eye on you."

Oh, no! Not again!

I took a deep breath and moved unsteadily toward the second walkway that continued straight ahead. It was crazy: There was absolutely no way to know which one led to the exit. A cold sweat broke out all over my body once more. No, you never get used to fear, and it never disappears; you just learn to live with it and not let it get the better of you.

So as not to offend the beaming Master Red, I resisted the impulse to hug him as soon as we reached the pillar he was on. I was very happy I'd lived to see him again.

"Do you know how to get out of here?" Lao Jiang asked with barely disguised impatience.

"Of course," the monk replied, holding up his *luo p'an* proudly. "We follow the path of energy along the Nine Stars of Later Heaven."

"Incredible!" Lao Jiang blurted out.

"Yes, incredible," I agreed quietly.

"You have no idea what we're talking about, do you, Elvira?"

"No, Lao Jiang, and I'm not sure I want to."

The antiquarian smiled, then laughed. "Remember Yu, the first emperor of the Xia dynasty, whose dance we followed on the first level?"

"Of course."

"Well, it was Yu who discovered the drawing of the Nine Stars of Later Heaven on the shell of a giant tortoise that emerged from the sea when he stopped the floods and saved the earth."

"No, hold on, that wasn't what happened. Master Tzau told me that some old kings named Fu Hsi and Yu had discovered signs consisting of solid and broken lines that then made up the hexagrams of the *I Ching*. King Fu Hsi discovered some on the back of a horse that rose up out of a river, and King Yu or Emperor Yu of the Xia dynasty discovered a few more on the shell of the tortoise that emerged from the sea. Later some king from a subsequent dynasty combined them to compose the sixty-four hexagrams of the *I Ching*. Master Tzau hadn't mentioned anything about any kind of star or heaven, much less 'later heaven.'"

Master Red looked at me admiringly. "Not many women know so much about these matters."

I refused to accept his apparent compliment. If not many women did, it was because no one encouraged or allowed them to study things that were considered exclusive to men. It was sad that I, a foreigner, could know more than 200 million Chinese women about their own culture.

"You see, madame, when Emperor Yu, under orders from the celestial spirits he visited in heaven thanks to the Steps of Yu, managed to finally save the world from the floods, he saw a giant tortoise come out of the sea with strange signs on its shell. These signs weren't the yin and yang lines of the hexagrams, however. Let's just say that Master Tzau told you a simplified version of the story so you would get the basic idea. Emperor Yu saw the Pa-k'ua of Later Heaven. *Pa-k'ua* literally means 'Eight Signs,' and 'Later Heaven' refers to the sky after the change, the universe in constant motion and not static like Early Heaven. But I don't want to confuse you. Suffice it to say that those Eight Signs represented a pattern of the variations in the flow of energy in the universe. They gave rise to the eight trigrams that were the basis for the sixty-four hexagrams of the *I Ching*, as well as the eight directions they pointed, the eight cardinal points (south, westsouth, west, westnorth, north, eastnorth, east, and eastsouth) plus the center. These, then, are the Nine Stars, the name they've been known by in feng shui for thousands of years. Thanks to the Nine Stars and the *luo p'an*, the compass, we can understand how chi energy circulates in a given place, whether a building, a tomb, or any other space."

Well, I didn't understand it all, but the basic idea was clear: The Nine Stars were the eight cardinal points plus the center, the nine spatial directions.

"You see this labyrinth of iron walkways?" he asked, glancing around. "Well, if I'm not mistaken, this labyrinth hides the path of chi energy through the Nine Stars of Later Heaven."

"It's so complicated!" I burst out after taking a quick look at the tangle of bridges filling that enormous space.

"No, madame, it's really not. As I told you, the labyrinth hides a pattern. The sheer number prevents you from seeing the simplicity of the route."

"Pass me your sketchbook and pencils, Elvira," Lao Jiang said.

I shook my head sadly. "I don't have them. I left them with the children so they'd have something to keep themselves busy."

"Well then, imagine a grid that's three by three, a square with nine boxes. All right?"

"All right."

"The eight boxes around the outside are the eight directions. The middle box in the top row represents the south; to its right, going clockwise, the box is southwest; beneath it the box is west; and so on until you're back at the top. Do you see?"

"Yes, that's easy. I'm picturing tic-tac-toe."

"What?"

"It doesn't matter. Go on."

"Well, chi energy would always circulate through these boxes following the same route. Once we find south, we can follow that route. What Master Red Jade was trying to say is that the path chi energy follows is here, laid out using some of these bridges."

"Do you remember that there are nine square columns?" Master Red asked me. "Well, those are the nine boxes Da Teh was talking about. Each one of these columns is a box, and only one of the bridges that connect them is correct. The First Emperor's master geomancers simply copied the outline of the Nine Stars. As you can see, it couldn't be simpler."

I was dying to make a sarcastic comment but refrained.

"In fact," Lao Jiang explained, "right now we're in the center box of the Nine Stars grid. The previous platform, the one we just came from, would be north."

"And that's also where the energy begins; though don't ask me why, because it's too complicated to explain in just a few minutes."

"Don't worry, Master Red Jade, I assure you I wasn't going to ask. The question is, where should we go now?"

"Well . . ." he faltered. "We should actually go back. The chi energy starts in the north and goes directly to the westsouth, but we can't get to the westsouth from here."

"On that bridge?" I said, staring horrified at a walkway that went clear from the first pillar we came in on to the one in front of us and then to the right. It was as long as two bridges plus a pedestal, only without the pedestal in the middle.

Crossing was going to be the death of me, not because I'd fall into the void (which could happen), but out of sheer nervous strain.

We went back to the pillar in front of the tunnel where the children were waiting. I waved, but only Biao waved back. After all those centuries without use, the iron chains had withstood the weight of one person, then two, and finally three at the same time without a problem. Would that blasted two-hundred-foot bridge stand up as well? It was best to not think about it. One thing was clear: If I had to die, I'd die. It was too late to go back now.

Placing one foot in front of the other, we moved toward the southwest. Master Red Jade went first, then I, and Lao Jiang brought up the rear. The scene was worth painting: two Chinese men and one European woman walking along an iron suspension bridge by the light of whale-oil lanterns, hundreds of feet underground and hundreds more above the floor. It would have been funny if it hadn't been so frightening. I did have to laugh when I thought of the treasures Lao Jiang wanted to take out of there. Perhaps others could after we'd paved the way, but none of us was taking anything other than what we could carry in our pockets. Thankfully, Chinese clothing had a lot of very big pockets.

We reached the southwest pillar and from there went toward the one in the east, passing right next to the central pillar we'd already been on. Two bridges that started and stopped on other pillars we had yet to reach crossed above and below us.

From the east to the southeast in a straight line and from there back

to the center, which we were already familiar with, and from the center
to the pillar in the westnorth, as they call it. I didn't understand why we
had to go back through the center if we'd already been there. Wouldn't
it have been simpler (and safer) to go directly to the northwest without
doing the whole route from the beginning, backtrack included?

"I had to confirm the flow of energy through the Nine Stars of Later
Heaven, madame," Master Red justified, making a strange face when I
asked him.

"Oh, come now, Master Red Jade!" I protested. "All you had to do
was take a look at the bridges. However complex the labyrinth might be,
it was ridiculous to go back to the beginning in order to end up in the
center again. Do you know how many of these walkways we could have
saved ourselves?"

"Leave it be, Elvira," Lao Jiang ordered.

"Leave it be?" I raged.

"You don't understand the way we think. You're a foreigner. We believe that things must be done well, fully, so their end will be as good as
their beginning, so everything is in harmony."

Harmony? That did it. We had unnecessarily risked our lives on
superfluous walkways for universal harmony?

"As Sun-tzu says, Elvira, 'The general who wins a battle makes
many calculations in his temple ere the battle is fought. The general
who loses a battle makes but few calculations beforehand.' One small
error could lead to enormous failure, so why not follow the proper route
if all it takes is a little extra effort?"

I wasn't going to reply to that.

"I had to confirm the *luo p'an* calculations, madame. I had to make
certain my theory was correct before we got lost on the bridges and
couldn't find our way out."

Next we went from the northwest to the west and from the west
to the eastnorth (or northeast). Finally, from the northeast we walked
along another of those two-hundred-foot walkways to the south, on a
lower level. This bridge suddenly descended to the top of a pillar some

sixty-five feet below. I had memorized the sequence of directions we'd taken, because I didn't know how else to mark the way out. All I was left with was my memory in case anything happened. I used the popular song "Por Ser la Virgen de la Paloma" to hum "north-southwest-east-southeast-center-northwest-west-northeast-south" over and over again. That line in the second verse about the "shawl from China" must have had something to do with my musical choice.

"Well," Master Red said, "I think it's time to follow the energy descending through the Nine Stars."

So much for my memory trick, and it was sounding so good.

"And until now it has been ascending?"

"*En effet,* madame."

All right, then. Once again we found ourselves walking along a very long bridge that went back toward the northeast. And from the northeast to the west, and . . . wait a minute. The sequence was the same but in reverse. Descending meant the energy traveled in the opposite direction, but since I wasn't interested in further explanations regarding why chi energy would suddenly decide to turn and go back through the starry universe, I didn't comment and simply played dumb, following Master Red as if nothing else were on my mind. Unfortunately, the music of *Por ser la Virgen de la Paloma* no longer worked. It didn't really matter, though, because all I had to remember was that the proper direction on the second level was the inverse of my musical sequence. After that, everything went as smooth as silk: I got the knack of those fussy little steps we were forced to take on the chains, and that feeling of security allowed us to move more quickly. Further, the energy lines were always the same, ascending on uneven levels and descending on even ones. The only thing that didn't repeat was that first bridge on the first level between north and center, placed there in order to confuse. It was indeed all very carefully thought out, and once I understood the general outline in plain language, I felt I could go back up to where Fernanda and Biao were waiting without getting lost. We finally reached the ground after descending eight levels, and I did a little happy dance in my hardy Chinese boots, thrilled to no longer be hanging in the air, walking like a trapeze artist. Lao Jiang and Master Red looked at me somewhat disconcertedly, but I didn't pay them any mind. We'd descended from a dizzying height, surely over five hundred feet, arriving safe and sound thanks to our prudence and, above all, thanks to those solid iron bridges it seemed the millennia hadn't touched. I thanked Sai Wu from the bottom of my heart for his good work.

Everything looked different from down here. I tilted my head as far back as I could, cupped my hands around my mouth, and called the children by name. I couldn't see them through that mesh of iron but heard them shout something indecipherable back. The important thing was that they were fine and had stayed put. I hadn't been so sure they would, knowing the sorts of tricks they'd gotten up to on our journey thus far. Now I could turn my attention to these mysterious Bian Zhong on the fourth level.

"Lao Jiang, why don't you tell Master Red Jade what Sai Wu said in the *jiance* about the Bian Zhong?"

"Master, do you know what Bian Zhong are?" the antiquarian asked. "Sai Wu told his son that there was a chamber with Bian Zhong on the fourth level and that they had something to do with the Five Elements."

"Bian Zhong are bells, Da Teh."

"Bells?"

"Yes, Da Teh, bells, magic bells made of bronze that can produce different tones: One is low when struck in the middle, and the other is high when struck on the edge. They're very complex to play and no longer used but are among our oldest musical instruments."

"How is it possible I've never heard of these bells before?" Lao Jiang wondered.

"Perhaps because there are only a few left in a few monasteries, and we'd know nothing of their existence if it weren't for the annotated scores in some libraries that reveal their great age. Also, they're not normal bells like the ones you're used to seeing. These are flatter. They almost look as if a rock fell on them."

"Very well," Lao Jiang said. "Let's go find these bells."

We walked along the walls for a while and finally found a trapdoor, some three hundred feet behind the last walkway.

"More descents?" I asked.

"So it would seem," Lao Jiang replied, holding on to the ring and hauling up on it. The door opened with ease, as had the others on previous levels, and we once again discovered those ubiquitous iron rungs attached to the wall as a sort of ladder. We climbed down, plunging into darkness, but thankfully it didn't take long. Lao Jiang went first and soon advised us he'd reached the bottom. Master Red came last, and by the time he put his foot on the ground, the antiquarian had already taken out his lovely silver lighter and lit his methane torch (the very word "methane" now made my stomach turn). Indeed, there were the Bian Zhong, imposing, impressive, hanging in front of us on a beautiful bronze frame that took up the entire back wall, from floor to ceiling and one side to the other. It was filled with those strange, squashed bells, a veritable plethora: six rows, to be exact, and I counted eleven in each row. The bells got bigger as you went from left to right, the small ones on the left being the size of a water glass and the huge ones on the right that could have been stood on end and used as trash cans.

Their undulating designs in gold still shone in the light of Lao Jiang's torch. We later discovered they also had designs in silver, but these had tarnished and didn't stand out as much. They looked like purses on display in a store window, the lovely pointed bottom corners making them even more fashionable. The handles hung from hooks spaced regularly along the six thick bars that stretched from one end to the other of that colossal frame covered in verdigris. In front of this beautiful Bian Zhong, which is what the full carillon was also called, was a little table and two hammers made of the same metal. Each hammer was at least two feet long and was undoubtedly used to strike those squashed bells.

"Is there a particular piece of music we have to play?" I asked somewhat sarcastically.

Master Red, with his usual penchant for analysis and concentration, was walking over to the Bian Zhong to examine it carefully, and since he needed light, he motioned for Lao Jiang to follow. The antiquarian, however, had found whale-oil receptacles on the walls and was in the process of lighting them so he could extinguish his torch. As soon as the room was illuminated, Master Red concentrated on the bells. Lao Jiang and I approached the frame to take a look as well, even though I wouldn't be much help. The bells were truly beautiful, with small raised knobs on the upper part and decorated with floating clouds, made of gold, down below. Both the top edge and the pointed bottom were trimmed in silver, similar to a frieze but with the spiral, flowing shape so particular to Chinese design.

"Here are the Five Elements," Master Red announced, placing a hooked finger on the middle of the bell that was right in front of him. I moved closer and saw that he was pointing to a Chinese ideogram inside an oval between the knobs and the clouds. It looked like a little man with his arms open wide. "This is the character for Fire, and this," he said, putting his index finger on the bell next to it, "is Metal. On this one you can see the element Earth, Wood is here, and Water is here."

I glanced at the Bian Zhong as a whole and said, "I hate to discourage you, Master Red Jade, but every one of these bells contains one of those five ideograms."

The character for Water was quite similar to the one for Fire, except the little man had three arms, two of them on the right. Earth looked like an upside-down letter *t*, Wood was a cross with three legs, and the ideogram for Metal could easily have passed for the drawing of a cute house with a gabled roof. That was most certainly my favorite character.

"I'm afraid this puzzle is going to be rather difficult to solve," Master Red lamented, glancing at the long hammers lying on the table. "First we have to figure out what we need to do: discover a musical sequence using the ideograms for the Five Elements?"

"Why don't we begin by striking those five bells in the middle and see what happens? Then we can try all the ones with the same character and continue with different combinations until something works."

Both men looked at me as if I'd gone crazy.

"Do you know how much noise these Bian Zhong make, Elvira?" Lao Jiang roared.

"What does that have to do with it?" I objected. "Isn't that why these hammers are here? How do you expect us to get to the fifth level if we don't uncover this musical score?"

"We'd better think," Master Red said, gathering his tunic and sitting on the floor in a meditative pose.

"Can't I at least try?" I insisted defiantly, picking up the hammers.

"Do what you like," Lao Jiang replied, covering his ears with his hands and moving closer to continue examining the bells.

That's what I wanted to hear. Without a second thought, I dove into the thrilling interpretive experience of striking (carefully, that is) sixty-six ancient bells in every order and way I could think of. They had a lovely sound, slightly muffled, as if you'd set a hand on them to stifle the vibration but they somehow continued to pulse. It was a very Chinese sound, quite unlike what I was used to but undeniably beautiful. Suddenly I felt a hand on my shoulder.

"Yes?" I asked in surprise, turning to find Lao Jiang.

"Stop, please. I beg you."

"Does the sound bother you?"

Master Red, who was still sitting on the floor, let out a spontaneous and completely uncharacteristic guffaw.

"It's unbearable, Elvira. Please stop."

Some things never change. When I was a girl, before I began studying those hateful scales, I used to love to bang away on the piano until I was pulled off the stool and punished. The same thing had just occurred over thirty years later, and in China of all places. It seemed to be my tragic destiny.

I set the hammers on the table and prepared to while away the time until Master Red came up with some brilliant idea that would enlighten us as to what we should do with those lovely bells. I pulled a ball of rice out of my bag and began to eat it. It was dry. A cup of hot tea would have done me a world of good, but at least the rice was appeasing my stomach. I decided to entertain myself by counting the bells while I ate. There were only five Bian Zhong with the ideogram for Metal, the little house, and there were nine with Earth, thirteen with Fire, seventeen with Wood, and twenty-two with Water. Biao would surely have found some numerical relationship among those numbers if he'd been there. It actually wasn't all that difficult: The sequence worked almost perfectly if you added four to the previous number. That is, if there were five little houses, five plus four meant nine bells with the ideogram for Earth. If you added four to the nine Earths, you got thirteen Fires. Thirteen Fires plus four equaled seventeen Woods. It stopped working with Water, however, because according to the sequence there should have been twenty-one bells with the character for Water, but there were twenty-two. There was one too many, and precisely of Water, Shi Huang Ti's ruling element and the one that had more bells than any other. Water was the most plentiful in that Bian Zhong, followed in descending order by Wood, Fire, Earth, and Metal. What had that master in Wudang said about the Five Elements? I vaguely recalled something about their being different manifestations of chi energy, that they were all related to one another and to other things like heat and cold, colors, shapes. . . . Oh, why had I left my sketchbook with the children? I tried to call up a visual memory, not of what that master in Wudang had said but of what I'd drawn. What sorts of notes had I taken using various animals? Ah, yes, I remembered: I'd sketched the four cardinal points with a black tortoise in the north representing Water, a red crow in the south that was Fire, a green dragon in the east for Wood, a white tiger in the west symbolizing Metal, and a yellow snake in the middle for the element Earth.

But none of that did me any good. There was still too much Water in that huge carillon that must have weighed several tons. I walked away to sit on the floor next to Master Red. Lao Jiang followed me.

"Well, Master Red Jade?" the antiquarian inquired.

"It could be some sort of musical composition based on either the creative or destructive cycles of the Elements."

Lao Jiang nodded his head. I didn't remember ever having heard anything about those two cycles, although maybe I had and just forgot.

"What cycles are those, Master Red Jade?" I asked.

"The Five Elements are closely related to one another, madame," he explained. "Their interaction can be either creative or destructive. If it's creative, Metal is nourished by Earth, Earth is nourished by Fire, Fire is nourished by Wood, Wood is nourished by Water, and Water is nourished by Metal, ending the cycle. If, on the other hand, their interaction is destructive, Metal is destroyed by Fire, Fire is destroyed by Water, Water is destroyed by Earth, Earth is destroyed by Wood, and Wood is destroyed by Metal."

A distant Bian Zhong rang in my head when I heard that string of elements mutually nourishing and destroying one another.

"Could you please repeat the first cycle, the creative one?" I asked Master Red.

He looked at me strangely but nodded. "Metal is nourished by Earth, Earth is nourished by Fire, Fire is nourished by Wood, Wood is nourished by Water, and Water is nourished by Metal."

"Do you start with Metal for any particular reason, or could you start with any of the other elements?"

"Well, that's the way I learned it and they way it usually appears in the ancient texts, but if you like I could give you the cycle starting with whichever element you want."

"No, that's not necessary. Thank you. Could you repeat it all one more time?"

"Again?" Lao Jiang cringed.

"Of course, madame," Master Red kindly agreed. "Metal is nourished by Earth . . ."

Five bells with the ideogram for Metal; five plus four, nine bells with the ideogram for Earth.

". . . Earth is nourished by Fire . . ."

Nine bells with the ideogram for Earth; nine plus four, thirteen bells with the ideogram for Fire.

". . . Fire is nourished by Wood . . ."

Thirteen bells with the ideogram for Fire; thirteen plus four, seventeen bells with the ideogram for Wood.

". . . Wood is nourished by Water . . ."

Seventeen bells with the ideogram for Wood, and here's where my addition fell apart, because seventeen plus four was twenty-one, but I had twenty-two bells with the ideogram for Water.

". . . and Water is nourished by Metal, thus closing the circle to begin again. Why are you so interested in the creative cycle of the Five Elements?"

I told them about the increasing number of bells according to the creative cycle and that there was one bell too many with Water, though I didn't know why.

Master Red Jade became very pensive. "The creative cycle . . ." he finally repeated in a whisper.

"Yes, the creative cycle," I confirmed. "What about it?"

"Nourishment, madame, a substance that invigorates and strengthens, one element feeding the next so that it can become stronger and more powerful, and can in turn feed the next, and it another, and so on until it comes back to the point of origin. There's something you didn't notice. Suppose this bell with the element Water isn't actually one too many but is the beginning, the origin of this chain of elements that reinforce one another. We would thus start with a bell that has the element Water, adding four each time as you discovered. What would we get? Five bells with the element Metal, the ones you put first, and in this way the twenty-one Bian Zhong that were a nuisance when they were twenty-two would fit perfectly. So what do we have? We have a creative design between the Five Elements that begins and ends with Water, the First Emperor's foundation and his emblem."

"But what does all this have to do with the bells?" Lao Jiang asked, bewildered.

"I still don't know, Da Teh," Master Red replied, standing and walking over to the Bian Zhong, "but it's not a coincidence. We've likely discovered the musical score even if we don't know how to play it."

The antiquarian and I followed and stood by his side in front of the huge bronze frame, but I didn't see anything. I couldn't imagine how to take that creative cycle to those sixty-six bells with gold and silver designs hanging quietly from their elegant handles.

"Shall we begin by striking the largest Water bell?" I ventured.

"Let's try," Lao Jiang agreed this time, reaching out to pick up the hammers before I could. He walked resolutely over to the right side where the largest Bian Zhong were, found the ideogram for Water, and struck it. The deep, hollow, stifled sound reverberated for a long while, but nothing happened.

"Should I hit the five Metal bells now?" Lao Jiang asked.

"Go ahead," Master Red said. "Do it according to size, from largest to smallest. If that doesn't work, we'll try the other way."

But nothing happened then either. Nor when he rang the nine Earth, the thirteen Fire, the seventeen Wood, and the twenty-one Water. Just a little while earlier, Lao Jiang had complained of the noise I was making by striking the bells, but now he was having a ball with the hammers: Seeing is believing, after all. The sound didn't bother him in the slightest when he was the one playing. He repeated the series in reverse, but to no effect, so we sat back down on the floor, completely disheartened and partially deaf.

"What are we missing?" I asked desolately. "Why can't we figure out this blasted score?"

"Because it's not a score, *tai-tai*, it's a combination of weights," came a timid voice from behind us.

Tai-tai? Biao . . . ? Fernanda!

"Fernanda!" I shouted, leaping to my feet and hurrying over to the iron rungs to look up through the trapdoor. "Fernanda! Biao! What the devil are you doing here?"

I could just make out their miserable little heads peering over the edge and received nothing but silence in reply to my question.

"Biao! What did I tell you? Hmm? What did I tell you?"

"Not to follow you and Lao Jiang even if Young Mistress ordered me to."

"And so what did you do? Hmm? What did you do?" I was furious. The very thought of their coming down those iron walkways made my blood boil.

"I followed Master Red Jade," he replied humbly.

"What?" I shrieked.

"Don't get so angry, Auntie," Fernanda said in a cavalier, condescending tone. "You ordered him not to follow you or Lao Jiang, and he obeyed. He followed Master Red Jade."

"And what about you, Miss Impertinent? I absolutely forbade you to move from there."

"No, Auntie. You ordered me to stay with Biao. You literally said, 'If you don't stay with Biao, I will put you in the strictest Catholic boarding school there is.' I only did what you told me to. I stayed with him every step of the way, I promise."

For the love of God! What was wrong with those two? Weren't they aware of the danger? Didn't they know what it meant to obey? Now that they were here, I couldn't order them to go back up. Besides, how had they managed to come down those bridges? How had they known what path to follow?

"We watched you come down," my niece explained, "and Biao drew the route in your sketchbook."

"Give me my sketchbook and pencils right this instant, Biao!"

The boy disappeared from view and reappeared feetfirst, slowly descending rung after rung. When he reached my side, I held out an imperious hand, and, frightened, he passed me my things. I took the sketchbook and opened it, finding his drawing. The route was correct, it was drawn well, and he had used arrows to indicate the change in direction of energy on the even levels. The two were clever indeed, but above all they were disobedient, and the more disobedient was my niece, the ringleader. It was no time to discuss what they'd done or think of a magisterial, unforgettable punishment, but that time would come, sooner or later that time would come, and Fernanda Olaso Aranda would remember her aunt for the rest of her life.

Enraged, I turned to put my things in my bag, leaving them stock-still with heads hung.

"Are you through being angry, Elvira?" Lao Jiang asked unpleasantly. That was all I needed.

"Do you have a problem with the way I treat my niece and my servant?"

"No. I couldn't care less. I simply want Biao to explain what he said about a combination of weights."

I had forgotten that. Fury had erased it from my mind. The boy walked toward the Bian Zhong very slowly (it must have been the burden of guilt he carried with him), then muttered something we could barely hear.

"Speak up!" Lao Jiang ordered the boy. What the devil was wrong with that man? He was unbearable.

"I asked if someone could help me pick up the big bell with the character for Water," Biao said more audibly.

The antiquarian hurried over, and between the two of them they lifted it a little and pulled it off. There was the squeaking of a spring, and the hook it had been hanging on rose up about an inch on the bar. They carefully set the bell on the floor.

"What now?" Lao Jiang asked.

"We have to remove that bell," the boy said, pointing to the medium-size Bian Zhong in the middle of the bottom row, the sixth one in from either side. Lao Jiang picked it up with a certain amount of effort and set it on the floor as well. "Now we've got to put the big one where that medium one was," Biao said, bending to help the antiquarian with the huge Bian Zhong containing the ideogram for Water. The squeaking of springs and the minor shifting of the hooks up or down when they were empty or full revealed that something was happening inside that frame, and therefore Biao was on the right track. With Master Red's help, they continued removing and replacing bells. After a while you could start to see the puzzle Biao had in mind. Every so often there was a distant metallic grumbling, like a bolt being pulled back. The men were sweating from the effort. Fernanda and I helped with the smallest bronze bells, the ones the size of water glasses, although they weren't so light either. Biao had a hard time keeping up with telling us which bells to remove and where to place others.

Finally just one very small bell with the Water element was left to be placed in the bottom left-hand corner of the frame and was in my hands, my unbelievably dirty hands. All the Bian Zhong went from smallest to largest, left to right. The enormous bell with the character for Water that we'd set in the middle of the lowest bar was now surrounded by the five containing the element Metal, the little house, because Metal was powerful nourishment for Water. The five Metal bells were surrounded in turn by the nine for Earth, which nourished Metal, which in turn nourished Water. The nine Earth bells were surrounded by the thirteen for Fire, the thirteen for Fire by the seventeen for Wood, and, ultimately, these by the twenty-one for Water (the last one still in my hands). It was a perfect cycle, a masterful arrangement of strength and energy. If Biao was right, Shi Huang Ti's master geomancers had made the emperor's reigning element the start and end of that combination, allowing the creative cycle of the Five Elements to reinforce Water with all their power, and it in turn would encompass them all.

There was a sense of anticipation in the air as I walked over to the last empty hook on the frame. Feeling like a prima donna before her audience, I placed the bell with a grandiose, theatrical gesture that made the children and Master Red Jade laugh. Lao Jiang was so desperate for it to work that he was indifferent to my antics.

There was a metallic click, the squeaking of springs, stone grinding on stone, and then a creak. The wall of Bian Zhong slowly slid back, causing the sixty-six bells to vibrate softly. It came to a dead stop after several feet. Large holes some twelve to fifteen inches apart were visible on the ends of both perpendicular walls and the parts of the floor and ceiling where that movable wall had once fit. The gap to walk through on either side was, as usual, in total darkness.

"Tell me, Biao," I heard Master Red whisper behind me, "how did you know it was the arrangement and weight of the bells, and not a musical score?"

"For two reasons," the boy replied quietly. "First, I thought it seemed strange that the architect Sai Wu didn't ever mention music in the *ji-ance* when he told his son that the chamber with the Bian Zhong was related to the Five Elements. After all, he was talking about bells. Second, you'd already struck them in every possible way without any results. It couldn't be a song. The only sure thing was that it had something to do with the Five Elements, with chi energy. Just then, Young Mistress Fernandina made a comment about how much that enormous musical instrument must weigh, how difficult it would be to move it to see if there were some sort of door behind. The idea suddenly came to me when I heard you talking about the number of bells and the creative cycle of the Five Elements. Plus, it was only logical to assume that there was some sort of hidden mechanism that would open the door Young Mistress was talking about, but the room was completely empty except for the Bian Zhong. The bells were hanging on hooks, so it was possible to move them. Also, if Water was the main element and there was one Water bell too many or, as you said, it was the first in the series, then I thought it had to be the biggest one and placed in its cardinal point, north. If you picture a Chinese map on top of the Bian Zhong, south is at the top, east and west on the sides, and north at the bottom. The big bell needed to go in the middle of the bottom row. That and what you said about the number of bells for each Element and the order of the creative cycle was what gave me the idea, Master Red Jade."

I was dumbfounded. I couldn't believe what I'd just heard. Biao was extraordinarily intelligent and had a marvelous capacity for analysis and deduction. It was simply unthinkable the boy could go back to Father Castrillo's orphanage to wind up becoming a carpenter, a shoemaker, or a tailor. He needed to study, take advantage of such exceptional qualities, to carve out a good future for himself. I suddenly had a magnificent idea: Why didn't Lao Jiang adopt him? The antiquarian didn't have children to inherit his business or carry out funeral rites in his honor when he died. It was a very delicate matter, and given how irritable he'd been lately, it was best not to say anything for the time being. As soon as we were out of the mausoleum with our pockets full of money, I'd speak with him to see if he thought it was as good an idea. Biao was not going back to the orphanage.

After picking up our bags, we prepared to cross through the opening made by the wall of Bian Zhong. Lao Jiang took out his lighter again and lit the torch, placing himself at the head of the line. I followed him, shielding my silly niece and Biao, who was walking next to Master Red Jade. I didn't know what we might find behind that wall, even though we hadn't had many unpleasant surprises so far. However, my fears immediately came true: The antiquarian exclaimed and jumped back, nearly falling into me. I instinctively stepped back as fast as I could, bumping into Fernanda, who in turn stumbled back into Biao and he into Master Red.

"What is it?" I asked.

Lao Jiang had miraculously kept his balance, and when he turned to look at us, I saw something black moving on the hem of his tunic, scurrying up between the pleats. Cockroaches? I was utterly disgusted.

"Beetles," Master Red said.

"And more," Lao Jiang added, brushing off his clothes. Little black things with legs fell onto the floor and moved. "I didn't get a good look. The walls and floor are covered in insects. There are thousands of them, millions: beetles, ants, cockroaches. You can't even see the trapdoor."

My niece let out a terrified shriek.

"Do they bite?" she asked, petrified, her hand over her mouth.

"I don't know. I don't think so," Lao Jiang replied, turning back toward the room and reaching in with his torch to light up the interior. I couldn't even think about leaning in to take a look. What's more, I couldn't go in there if it were the last place on earth.

"Come on, then," Biao said, walking over to Lao Jiang.

The three men peered in.

"It's infested!" Master Red exclaimed. "The light's making them move. Look at them fly and fall off the ceiling!"

"We'll never find the trapdoor," the boy agreed, brushing bugs off the arms of his jacket. Lao Jiang and Master Red ran their hands over their faces.

"I'll go look for it and call you once I've found it," Lao Jiang said.

"I'm sorry, Lao Jiang, but I can't go in there," I said.

"Stay here, then. Do whatever you like," he snarled, disappearing behind the wall. I was astonished.

"What are we going to do, Auntie?" my niece asked, looking at me anxiously.

I was tempted to give her an answer like the one the antiquarian had just given me (I was still furious that she'd disobeyed me), but I couldn't do it. Fear united us; I knew just how she felt. We would have to overcome it. I didn't want my niece to inherit my neuroses.

"We'll pluck up our courage and get through it, Fernanda."

"What are you saying?" she asked, horrified.

"Do you want the two of us to stay here like silly fools while they carry on to the treasure?"

"But there are millions of bugs!" she howled.

"So? We'll make it through. We'll close our eyes. We'll tell Biao to lead us by the hand as fast as he can. All right?"

Her eyes filled with tears, but she agreed. I was also terrified, and my skin crawled at the very thought of going into that room, but I had to teach my niece a lesson in bravery. I also had to prove to myself that my recovery was real, that I could face my fears.

Biao offered to lead us before we even had to ask. There was hardly time to prepare ourselves: Lao Jiang's shout exploded like a bomb in our heads. It was best not to think twice. Biao took my hand, I took my niece's, and we entered that mysterious hall rife with insects. I was immediately covered in little living things that landed on and crept all over me. I nearly died of repulsion and panic but couldn't let go of the children to brush myself off. I had to keep a firm grip on my nerves and especially on Fernanda's hand, which tried several times to wriggle out of mine to get rid of those horrible creatures. I didn't open my eyes until Biao told me the trapdoor was at my feet. That's when I looked and wished I hadn't: Floor, ceiling, walls—everything was black and moving; thousands of winged insects flew through the air. I pushed Fernanda to go down first and, as she did, noticed Lao Jiang. He stood motionless, holding the torch to light our way, and was covered from head to toe in the same layer of bugs that obliterated the walls. Biao looked similar, and though I didn't want to acknowledge it, I must have, too.

"Hurry, Fernanda!" I yelled as I started through the trapdoor. It was a miracle we didn't kill ourselves. Still covered in little living things, my niece and I swatted them off as we climbed down. I soon heard the dry thud of the hatch as it closed above our heads, and a shower of cockroaches and beetles rained down, grazing my hands and face. Lao Jiang had turned off the bamboo torch so we couldn't see a thing. It was better that way, to be honest. I had no desire to see the baggage I was carrying.

It wasn't very far to the bottom—thirty feet, perhaps. We were soon on the ground, and I heard Fernanda stomping, squashing everything under her feet, every footfall accompanied by crackles and crunches. Lao Jiang lit the torch as soon as he reached the bottom. We were overrun, they were everywhere: in our hair, on our faces and clothing, it was absolutely horrific. My niece and I brushed one another off as the men took care of themselves. The floor was littered with crushed bodies floating in a thick, yellowish puddle. Finally we were able to stop scratching and hitting ourselves as if we'd gone insane. We walked a few steps away from that disgusting stain, turning our backs so we wouldn't have to look at it.

"Are you finished?" Lao Jiang asked.

Fernanda hiccupped by my side, drying the tears brought on by nerves, while Biao's face was frozen in a look of disgust. I was compulsively brushing off my arms, getting rid of insects that weren't there.

"Let's inspect this new level," he suggested.

I couldn't see well because the place was quite large and we didn't have much light, but I thought I could make out tables that were set as if for a banquet.

"Take a look for whale-oil receptacles, Lao Jiang," I urged.

"Give me a hand, Biao," the antiquarian said, and the two of them walked over to the walls. When Lao Jiang moved away, Fernanda, Master Red, and I were left in the dark, but as our eyes adjusted, we were able to see a bit more of that enormous room where there were indeed three tables placed in the shape of a horseshoe with the opening facing us. When the antiquarian and Biao finally lit the vessels, the area took on a new dimension and appeared to be an impressive, sumptuous banquet hall. The walls were decorated with gold dragons and whirls of jade clouds, and the floor was tiled black, like in the funeral palace. Also as in the palace, a huge black stone slab some six feet long came straight down from the ceiling to the floor just behind the head table. A large grid was carved into it, the lines inlaid with gold. Near the lanterns were impressive baked-clay sculptures like the ones we'd seen outside the palace, but these didn't depict humble servants or elegant officers. Instead they looked like performers ready to begin some sort of show. They all had their hair pulled back into ponytails, were barefoot and naked except for short skirts that showed off great muscled chests, arms, and legs. They looked like acrobats or fighters of some sort. Their faces, so serious and impassive, were frightening. I ignored them and for the next while repeated to myself that they were nothing more than a pile of mud in human form; mud, not people, lifeless clay.

What really caught my eye were the three tables, still covered in luxurious brocade cloths and a vast array of trays, plates, bowls, curvaceous bottles, mugs, jars, jugs, fruit bowls, spoons, chopsticks, and more. Everything was made of gold and precious stones. It was an absolute wonder. We approached very carefully, intimidated as if we were a band of beggars trying to sneak into the emperor's grand funeral banquet. I had the impression that it was a celebration for ghosts, a fete for the dead condemned to participate in that macabre gathering for eternity. An icy shiver ran down my spine, and every hair on my body stood on end. Once we got closer, when we were about fifteen or twenty feet away, we discovered that the plates weren't empty. There was no food, of course, but a strange stone cylinder made to look like a napkin for each guest. Perhaps they were a sort of place card, although they were as thick as my arm and made of a rough, gray stone that stood out against the fine gold surfaces. I counted twenty-seven chairs per table. Multiplied by three, that gave a total of eighty-one of those cylinders. Master Red walked straight over to pick up the closest one.

"Be careful!" Lao Jiang warned.

"Careful of what?" I asked timidly. Master Red, who already had the piece in his hand, looked at the antiquarian curiously as well.

"I'm just saying we should be careful. We're right above the First Emperor's true mausoleum, and I think we need to be particularly cautious. That's all."

"But there's no mention of unexpected danger in the *jiance*," I reminded him. "The only thing it says about this fifth level is that there's a special lock that can be opened only by using magic."

"A special lock that can be opened only by using magic?" Master Red Jade repeated inquisitively.

"Exactly," I confirmed, walking quickly to pick up another of those stone rolls.

"That must be what this is," Fernanda announced, pointing to the floor. She was right in the center of the room, in the middle of the three tables. I walked over to her, and the others followed.

I had seen that design before. It was the same as the one on the slab behind the seat of honor. I lifted my eyes to compare the two: They were identical except that the one on the floor was much larger and there was a hole in each box, holes that were the exact size of the gray

cylinders. I studied the one in my hand and discovered a Chinese ideogram carved in relief on the bottom.

"It's a nine-by-nine grid," Lao Jiang commented, "so there are
eighty-one holes in the floor and eighty-one stone rolls on the tables.
We've found the lock. Now all we have to do is find the magic."

I wasn't capable of finding anything by this point. I was hungry and
tired, and my body still itched as if it were covered in bugs. We'd spent
all day passing tests, descending from one level to another. It had to be
quite late, dinnertime at least, and I couldn't go on. Besides, weren't
there exquisitely laid tables and a magnificent dinner service we could
take advantage of in order to feel like royalty as we ate our humble provisions? It was the perfect place for a rest.

Not even Lao Jiang could refuse, though a flicker of annoyance did
cross his face. We used the torch to boil water and were finally able to
drink a cup of hot tea—nectar of the gods—and the balls of seasoned
rice tasted heavenly. In Paris, I would have refused both with disgust,
sickened by look of them and the dirt on our hands. I would have worried about germs and digestive illnesses. Here, I didn't care. I just wanted
to eat off those beautiful dishes—the layer of thousand-year-old dust
would simply be a little added protein. Sometimes I couldn't believe I
was the same person.

The children began to yawn and nod off as soon as dinner was over,
but Lao Jiang was adamant. We were just one level away from the First
Emperor's mausoleum, and we weren't going to sleep now. If the children were tired, they should have another cup of tea and splash a little
water on their faces. No sleeping. It was time to think. It was time to
find the magic that would open the lock so we could reach Shi Huang
Ti's true burial place that very night.

"Do you know what'll happen when we arrive, Lao Jiang?" I asked
defiantly. "We'll fall asleep right there, next to the desiccated body of
that old emperor. We're tired, and there's no sense in continuing our
search tonight. Today we've made it through the crossbows by dancing
the Steps of Yu, discovered the hexagrams from the *I Ching* that marked

the route to the exit on the second level while being poisoned by methane, followed the path of energy through the Nine Stars of Later Heaven, risking our lives on those awful ten thousand bridges, arranged the sixty-six bronze bells of the Bian Zhong according to the theory of the Five Elements, and finally we're here after passing through a room filled with horrible insects that nearly devoured us. This was our first decent meal of the day, and you want us to carry on and solve a new puzzle without getting at least a few hours of sleep?"

I felt a wave of solidarity from the children and Master Red, who were looking at me and nodding their heads as they stifled yawns.

"I don't understand," Lao Jiang objected coldly, "why you want to stop now, Elvira. We're so close to achieving our goal; it is literally within our grasp. Sleeping in front of the door to the treasure is the most absurd thing I've ever heard. It's no time to rest. It's time to discover the combination for this damn lock so we can obtain everything we left Shanghai for and risked our lives for a thousand times over these last few months. Don't you understand?"

He turned to look at Master Red and asked, "Are you with me?"

Master Red Jade closed his eyes and didn't move, but after a few seconds of hesitation I watched him slowly stand. Lao Jiang was the devil himself, taking pity on no one.

Turning toward the children, he asked, "And you two?"

Fernanda and Biao looked at me in search of the answer. I truly wanted to kill the antiquarian, but it was no time to get blood on my hands or start an argument. We could last a while longer. Once our trek was finished, we could sleep for hours.

"I'll make more tea," I said, getting up from my seat and nodding to the children to follow Lao Jiang and Master Red.

I listened to them talk as I boiled water. Fernanda and Biao had gathered the cylinders off the table, and the two men sat on the floor examining them.

"Their bases are numbered from one to eighty-one," Lao Jiang said.

"True, true . . ." Master Red murmured sleepily.

"Why don't you study the design that's on the floor and the slab first?" I asked as I dropped tea leaves into the water.

"The design is quite clear, Elvira," Lao Jiang said. "It's a nine-by-nine grid, each square the same size and each with a hole in the center where these eighty-one cylinders fit. The problem is the arrangement, the order in which they should be placed."

"Ask Biao," I advised, pulling the tea leaves out of the cups.

The two men looked at each other, and very slowly, with cold determination, Lao Jiang stood and grabbed the boy by the scruff of the neck, leading him over to the large grid and the cylinders. Biao was exhausted, barely able to keep his eyes open, and I didn't think he would be much help.

"We'd better start at the beginning," he mused, drawing out his words. "With the *jiance*. What exactly did the architect say?"

"Again?" Lao Jiang barked.

"He said that on the fifth level there is a special lock that only opens by using magic," I recalled as I held out a cup of tea for the poor boy.

"Using magic," he repeated. "That's the key. Magic."

"This boy is an idiot!" Lao Jiang shouted, releasing him roughly.

"Don't you dare insult him!" I snarled. "Biao is no idiot. He's much more intelligent than you, me, or all of us put together. If you say one more word like that, you can solve the puzzle on your own. The children and I have more than enough with the jewels from the funeral palace."

A bolt of rage flew from the antiquarian's eyes, piercing me through and through, but I wasn't scared. I was not going to allow him to humiliate Biao just because he was impatient to reach the treasure.

"Da Teh," Master Red intervened, still studying the board on the floor as if nothing else were happening around him, "Biao might be right. The key to this puzzle might be magic."

The antiquarian remained silent. He didn't dare insult Master Red, but from the look on his face it was clear he was thinking the same thing he'd thought of Biao.

"Do you remember Magic Squares?" the monk asked, and Lao Jiang's expression changed, a light spreading over his face.

"It's a Magic Square?" he asked, incredulous.

"It might be. I'm not sure."

"What's a Magic Square?" I wanted to know, leaning in to take a look.

"One in which the numbers in the grid add up to the same amount vertically, horizontally, and diagonally. It's a symbolic Chinese exercise that is thousands of years old," Master Red explained. "There's a very ancient tradition in China that relates magic with numbers. The earliest legend says that the first Magic Square was discovered by . . ." Master Red laughed. "You'll never guess."

"Who?" I asked impatiently.

"Emperor Yu, of the Steps of Yu. Legend says that what Yu saw on the shell of a giant tortoise that emerged from the sea was actually a Magic Square."

How many versions were there of what Yu had seen on that blasted tortoise shell? Master Tzau had told me it was the signs that gave rise to the hexagrams for the *I Ching*, while Master Red Jade said it was the path of energy through the Nine Stars of Later Heaven, and now he was telling me it was actually a Magic Square on the animal's shell.

"Now, Master Red Jade," I protested, "don't you think that poor tortoise had too many things on its shell to be able to emerge from the sea at all? I've heard three different versions of the same story."

"No, no, madame. In reality they all say the same thing. It's hard to explain, but believe me, there's no difference between them. Do you remember the path of chi energy we followed along the suspension bridges?"

The music for "Por Ser la Virgen de la Paloma" began to sound in my head.

"Of course I remember," I replied. "North-southwest-east-southeast-center-northwest-west-northeast-south."

Everyone looked at me in surprise.

"What's the matter?" I said. "Can't I have a good memory?"

"Of course, madame. In any event, that's exactly the path the energy follows." He stopped for a moment, still taken aback. "What was I going to say? Oh, yes! You see, if we take that path and number the square columns we pass through from one to nine, the north would be one, the westsouth two, the east three, and so on until we reach the south, which would be nine (and remember, south is at the top and north at the bottom according to the Chinese way). If you now consider those columns to be squares inside a three-by-three grid, you'll have the first Magic Square in history, over five thousand years old. That is the one Emperor Yu found on the tortoise's shell. If you do the same but follow the descending path of energy, you'll create a different Magic Square."

I tried to picture what Master Red was saying and saw, with some difficulty through my exhaustion, three lines of numbers: The top line consisted of four, nine, and two; the middle contained three, five, and seven; and the bottom had eight, one, and six. All the rows added up to fifteen. All the columns also came to fifteen, as did the diagonals. So this was a Magic Square. It seemed a little silly to waste time on such mathematical games. Who would invent such a thing?

"So this is a Magic Square?" I asked.

"It's the only answer I can come up with," the monk said sadly. "During the First Emperor's time, it was a noble mathematical exercise, and only a few master geomancers knew of its relationship to feng shui. Remember, feng shui was a secret science available only to emperors and their families."

"So then, do we really have to place those eighty-one cylinders such that all the rows, columns, and diagonals add up to the same amount?" I asked, appalled. It was sheer madness.

"If that's the case, madame, we might as well give up. There is nothing more complicated in the world than a Magic Square, especially if it's as big as this, nine by nine. If it were three by three, like the path of energy, or four by four, we might have a chance, but this is an impossible problem. I'm afraid we're looking at the securest lock in the world."

"No wonder, considering what it protects," Lao Jiang grumbled.

"Well, what can we do?"

"Nothing, madame. We'll try, of course, but what are the chances we can correctly align eighty-one stone rolls at random?"

"Don't be so pessimistic, Master Red Jade!" Lao Jiang burst forth, pacing to and fro like a caged animal. "I assure you we aren't leaving until we figure it out!"

"Then let us sleep!" I snapped. "We'll all think better after a few hours of rest."

The antiquarian looked at me as if he didn't know me and continued his desperate pacing from one corner of the board to the other.

"Let's sleep," he finally conceded. "We'll solve this tomorrow."

Thus we were finally able to unroll our *k'angs* and rest after such a bizarre, exhausting day. I had strange dreams that combined all sorts of things: the Bian Zhong with the bright carp in Yuyuan Gardens; the old nun Ming T'ien with the path of turquoises I'd left on the second level of the mausoleum; the arrows from the crossbows with Rémy's lawyer, Monsieur Julliard; Fernanda falling into an enormous shaft and me unable to get her out; Lao Jiang using the cane he had in Shanghai to break all the statues of the First Emperor's servants; Master Red and Biao dragging themselves over that board on the floor consisting of eighty-one squares. . . . I didn't know where I was when I opened my eyes. As usual, the others were already up, having breakfast, and so I had missed our tai chi.

"Good morning, Auntie," my niece said when she saw I was awake. "Did you have a good rest? You were sleeping so soundly we didn't want to wake you."

"Thank you," I said, getting out of my *k'ang*. "Could I have some tea?"

Fernanda held out my cup and a piece of bread.

"That's all there is," she said by way of apology. I shook my head to indicate it didn't matter and thirstily drank my tea. My head hurt a little.

That was when I saw Biao and Master Red bent over my Moleskine sketchbook. The boy was drawing something with one of my pencils. Fernanda noticed and nudged him in the ribs. Biao lifted his head, stunned, and looked in all directions until he was caught in my gaze.

"What are you doing, Biao?" If my voice had been a knife, Biao would have been sliced in two. He opened his mouth, squinted, made strange faces, and finally mumbled a series of incoherent words. "What did you say?"

"I said I needed your sketchbook, *tai-tai*, and since you were sleeping . . ."

"And why did you need my sketchbook?"

"Because I had a dream last night and wanted to make sure—"

"So you took my sketchbook because you dreamed something you wanted to make sure of?"

"Yes, *tai-tai*. It was an important dream. I dreamed I'd discovered how to do a Magic Square."

He looked at me in the hopes my expression would change, but I didn't move a single muscle.

"Not the big Magic Square, of course," he quickly clarified. "The small one, the path-of-energy one that appeared on the tortoise shell."

"And when you woke up, you knew how to do it?" I asked coldly.

"No, *tai-tai*. It was just a dream. But it gave me an idea: If we can discover the mathematical trick for the small Magic Square, the three-by-three one we already know, then we can use that to solve the big one, the nine-by-nine."

"And how many pages of my sketchbook have you ruined trying to decipher that puzzle?" I asked pointedly, having noticed a handful of crumpled pages on the floor.

"Don't be so harsh, Auntie," Fernanda reprimanded. "We don't have anything else to write on. You can buy more sketchbooks in Shanghai."

"But that one's from Paris," I objected, "and my drawings from the trip are in it."

"I haven't touched your drawings, *tai-tai*! I only used new sheets."

I got out of bed, angry with myself. Who cared about a blasted sketchbook? Enough of this ridiculous possessiveness! All I wanted was another cup of tea.

"Carry on," I told Biao without looking at him. "I just slept poorly."

"You should do tai chi," the antiquarian recommended.

"I certainly hope *you* did enough to improve your mood," I retorted. "You've been unbearable ever since we reached the mausoleum. Aren't you moderate and Taoist? That's not how you've been behaving, Lao Jiang, believe me."

He pursed his lips and lowered his gaze. My niece looked wildly around, and the other two pretended to be engrossed in their mathematical calculations. How awful it is when you don't sleep well! My head hurt.

"Yes, could be . . ." Master Red said, "but I don't see how you're going to place the numbers that are left over."

"They're not left over, Master Red Jade," Biao explained. "Since we already have the result, we know where they go. We need to see if there's any sort of rule that determines where they're placed."

"Very well then, move the first number down."

"Yes, but I'll use another color to see if a pattern appears," the boy said, taking the red pencil out of the open box.

"Now move number nine up."

"Yes, that's right," Biao murmured. "Now I'll take the three over to the left and I'll put the seven in the empty box on the right."

I was curious, and so, a cup of hot tea in hand, I came up behind the boy and looked over his shoulder. He had drawn a rhombus using the nine numbers that made up the Magic Square. That is, he had put number one at the top; underneath were four and two; on the next line, the middle and longest one, were seven, five, and three; on the fourth line were eight and six; and, finally, nine was at the bottom.

"Why did you arrange the numbers like that, Biao?" I asked, not expecting to understand but hoping to get an idea.

"Well, I noticed that in the Magic Square the diagonal that goes from the eastsouth to the westnorth consisted of the four, five, and six. So, following that guideline, I put the one above the two in the westsouth corner and the three below it. I now had two diagonal rows of consecutive numbers, so then I did the same with the seven and nine, putting them above and below the eight in the eastnorth corner. Now I had three diagonal lines of numbers from one to nine. Once I took away the numbers that repeated on the inside of the Magic Square, I was left with this shape—"

"It's a rhombus."

"—this rhombus that Master Red Jade and I have been studying. We've come to a few conclusions. When you asked, we were putting the numbers back in the Magic Square to see where they came from and whether there's a common rule for this movement."

"And is there?" I asked, taking a sip of my tea.

"It seems there is, madame," Master Red replied, "and the most admirable thing of all is its simplicity. If the reverse flow of energy fits, then I think Biao has found the formula for creating Magic Squares, one of the most complicated mathematical exercises there is."

With a false modesty betrayed by his red ears, Biao drew the rhombus again so I could see the whole process. I smiled at Lao Jiang, thinking I'd find him calm because things were going well. Instead his face was wrinkled in displeasure, his eyes were blank, and his fingers were twirling the silver lighter. I felt a strange, undefined fear. That image of Lao Jiang set off my old neuroses, and my pulse quickened. But the poor antiquarian wasn't doing anything unusual; he was just standing there lost in thought, far away from us all. There was no reason for me to be so afraid. I'd never be free of these sick apprehensions. I'd always have to fight the ghosts called up by my irrational fears.

With every ounce of will, I focused instead on the rhombus of numbers Biao had just drawn.

"Can you see it clearly, *tai-tai?*" he asked.

"Yes, perfectly."

"Now I'll draw the borders of the Magic Square over the rhombus. Do you see that?"

Indeed, he enclosed the five middle numbers in a square, as if it were a die: four and two up top, five alone in the middle, and eight and six below. He then added the two vertical and two horizontal lines needed to make a grid with nine squares.

"Do you see what's happening?" he asked nervously.

"Yes, yes. Of course," I replied kindly.

"Well, now we have to take the numbers that are outside the grid and put them in the empty squares."

Using the red pencil, he crossed out the one on its own up top and wrote it in the space below the five. Then he crossed out the nine down below and scribbled it in the top space. The three that was on the right he placed on the left, and the seven on the left he moved to the right. There was the completed Magic Square, fully restored and absolutely perfect.

"You see?"

"Certainly, Biao. That's fascinating."

"The rule is that you move the leftover numbers into boxes along the same line but on the other side of the five, which is the center."

"Do it again using the Magic Square for the descending path of energy," Master Red said.

Biao quickly noticed that the diagonal from southeast to northwest, which previously contained the four, five, and six, now consisted of the six, five, and four. That little clue led him to reverse the layout of the numbers in the rhombus, and after that the rest of the process was exactly the same. When he was finished, he had another perfect Magic Square.

"Will you be able to apply that to a square as big as the one on the floor, Biao?" I asked.

"I don't know, *tai-tai*," he said nervously. "I hope so. It should work, but we won't know until we do it on paper. There'll be many more numbers from the rhombus that fall outside the borders of the square, and we won't be able to refer to the finished Magic Square to confirm that we're doing it right."

"Just get on with it," Lao Jiang ordered as he continued to fiddle with his lighter.

The boy began to write tiny little numbers so they'd all fit on the sheet of paper.

"In the three-by-three Magic Square, the diagonal rows in the rhombus consisted of three numbers. Since this one has eighty-one squares, I'm using nine," he explained as he continued to write numbers in diagonal lines.

Finally he wrote the number eighty-one in the bottom vertex.

"The middle number obviously isn't five," he muttered to himself. "It's forty-one. So . . . if this is the middle, then the borders of the Magic Square would be here, here, here, and here," he sang softly as he drew the square. "Done!"

He proudly held the sketchbook in the air, and we all smiled. He had enclosed the eighty-one squares in a nine-by-nine grid, with many of the boxes still empty. The absurd idea that Lao Jiang adopt Biao no longer entered my mind. The antiquarian would be a terrible father, even if he could pass on his deep cultural values. Still, it was clear to me that Biao shouldn't go back to the orphanage. Would Wudang Monastery be a good place for him when all this was over? Would they give him what he needed to develop his talent, which, like painting, required long, hard years of study? I'd have to give it some thought. I couldn't take him back to Father Castrillo, nor could I take him with me to Paris, so far from his roots. He would be a second-class citizen there; they'd always look at him as if he were an exotic Chinese souvenir. Maybe Wudang was the best option for him.

"Now you've got to take all the numbers left outside and put them in the Magic Square," Master Red said to Biao.

The boy became visibly distressed, anxious.

"Yes, that's going to be the hard part. I'll use the red pencil again."

A pyramid of four rows of numbers was left above the square, as well as others below, to the left and right of it. In theory, all those numbers had to go back into the square following the rule Biao had found earlier: Place them in boxes along the same row or column but on the opposite side of center, which was now the number forty-one.

Each of these leftover pyramids consisted of ten numbers, which meant there was a total of forty that had to be put back in the grid. Biao began with one, which was at the vertex of the pyramid on the top: He crossed it out and wrote it underneath forty-one. He then repeated the same operation with the vertex of the pyramid on the bottom: He crossed out eighty-one and wrote it in the square right above center. He did the same with the nine located at the vertex on the right, placing it to the left of forty-one, and took seventy-three from the vertex on the left and wrote it on the right of forty-one. The little square consisting of the nine middle boxes was complete. Now he had to do the rest.

"I'll start putting those cylinders in their holes," Lao Jiang said impatiently as he got to his feet.

"No, Da Teh, please," Master Red begged, hurriedly trying to stop him. "Wait until we've finished. We'll put the stone rolls in their places once we've added up the lines, columns, and diagonals, making sure they come to the same amount. If we make a mistake with one number, just one, the lock won't work. What Biao's doing is not easy. He could make a tiny mistake without even realizing it."

The antiquarian grudgingly sat back down and once again became absorbed in contemplating his lighter.

Meanwhile, Biao continued to move numbers from outside the Magic Square to the inside. He was surprisingly determined and meticulous, following his own rule with the utmost care.

"There!" he exclaimed once he'd put the last number in its place.

"Let's add them up," Master Red proposed. "You do the rows and I'll do the columns. I wish I had an abacus!" He sighed.

Biao and Master Red Jade squeezed their eyelids shut at the same time, opening them every now and then to look at the numbers and then closing them again. Biao was the first to finish.

"All the rows add up to three hundred sixty-nine, except for the third," he lamented.

"Do that one again," I recommended.

He looked back at the numbers and closed his eyes. Master Red finished just then.

"All the columns add up to three hundred sixty-nine," he announced.

"Add the diagonals while Biao double-checks the rows," I told him.

"There can't be a mistake, madame," Master Red said in surprise. "If the columns are fine, then the rows have to be fine. If there was an error in a row, I'd have found an error in a column."

Biao finished in the meantime and smiled from ear to ear.

"I must have misread some numbers," he explained in relief. "This time I got three hundred sixty-nine."

"Do the diagonals," I encouraged.

Lao Jiang couldn't wait any longer. Seeing that we had the solution in hand, he quickly stood and walked over to the pile of stone cylinders.

"Master Red Jade," he called. "Since you and I are the only ones who know how to read Chinese numbers, you pass me the cylinders and I'll put them in their place. You, Elvira and Fernanda, stand them all up so Master Red Jade can find them quickly. Biao, take your book and read the numbers aloud."

"Could you hold on just a second?" I spit out. "We haven't finished yet."

"Yes we have," he parried. "The Magic Square is complete, and as an old Chinese saying goes, 'An inch of time is an inch of gold.' We have to get down to the First Emperor's mausoleum right away."

Please! It's not as if we were being chased by the Green Gang! What was his hurry? And yet we all obeyed like simpletons. Biao and Master Red rose and walked over into the middle of the tables. The boy stationed himself in front of the board with his book open as if he were an altar boy ready to recite psalms in a church. Meanwhile, Fernanda and I stood the stone tubes so that the Chinese characters were visible.

"Read the numbers by row, starting at the top," the antiquarian ordered.

"Thirty-seven," Biao began.

Master Red found that cylinder and handed it to the antiquarian, but Lao Jiang didn't move.

"What's wrong now?" I asked.

"Where should I put it?"

"What do you mean, where should you put it?" I asked. "Put it in the first square in the first row of the grid."

"Yes, but which is the first row?" he replied uncomfortably. "There are four sides, and not one of them is marked with anything that says 'Top' or 'Start here.'"

Well, that was a conundrum. However, as with everything else, there had to be a logical solution. Staying within the area flanked by the tables, I walked over until I was in front of the seat of honor, with the identically carved stone slab hanging behind it. Vertically, it was quite clear which was the top row and which the first square in that row. I began to walk backward, careful not to run into the cylinders, and kept going until the square on the floor was in front of me. I then pointed to the top line.

"There. Facing the seat of honor, that must be the proper orientation."

Lao Jiang did as I said, placing the cylinder marked with the number thirty-seven in the top right-hand corner.

"Seventy-eight," Biao intoned, reminding me of the children from San Ildefonso school in Madrid who'd been singing the winning national lottery numbers for two centuries.

Fernanda and I stood the cylinders on end as fast as possible so Master Red could find the one Lao Jiang needed. The antiquarian grew impatient. Master Red was going too slowly, and Biao wasn't speaking clearly, and the two of us, who weren't doing anything, were getting in the way. It was impossible to please him. Everything was wrong as far as he was concerned.

After some time we reached number forty-one in the middle of the square; all that work, and we'd gotten through only four and a half lines. I consoled myself with the thought that things would go much faster as we went on, because Master Red would have fewer and fewer cylinders to look through.

And indeed we made up for our slow start during the second half. My niece and I formed a chain to pass the cylinder with the number that Biao sang out from Master Red to Lao Jiang. Before we realized it, the last stone roll had passed from my hands into the antiquarian's.

"There," I said with a triumphant smile. "We've done it."

He smiled, too; hard to believe, but he'd actually smiled. It was the first time in a long time, and so I smiled happily back. Lao Jiang, however, was determined to finish the job and turned indifferently around, dropping the cylinder in the last hole.

As had happened in the chamber with the Bian Zhong, there was a metallic click followed by the grinding of stone on stone. The floor shuddered, and we all looked at one another a little frightened. We knew where the sound was coming from but couldn't see any means of access to the next level. Then the floor behind the stone slab began slowly, gently lowering, becoming a ramp that landed with a thud on the floor below, shaking the entire banquet hall.

We all walked over, tentatively, expectantly, after silently picking up our bags. Some mysterious mechanism had already lit the lamps on the lower level, because light shone up through the enormous hole without our having done anything.

We descended cautiously, ready for whatever might happen, but nothing did. We reached the bottom of the ramp and found ourselves in a huge, frigid esplanade, even bigger than the one we'd seen up above and best described as gleaming. Everything glowed as if the servants had just finished cleaning or, better yet, as if a speck of dust had never found its way in there. The floor was made of forged, polished bronze, like the mirrors Fernanda and I had taken. Thick, black-lacquered columns held not only receptacles that were already lit but a ceiling as well, also made of bronze that stretched away from our heads the farther we walked. The floor was on a slight incline, barely perceptible, causing the space to expand until it was colossal, truly magnificent. We continued walking, following an imaginary straight line. The air was very cold. At some point I turned back to look at the ramp, but couldn't see it anymore. I did, however, discover a town, or something that looked like a town, on our right, with its walls, towers, flagpoles, and the roofs of its houses and palaces. It was just like a real one, only smaller, as if little people or children lived there. A bit farther on, to the left, I saw another, and then many more. After a while we crossed one of those arched Chinese bridges over a small river whose waters were actually liquid mercury, brilliant silver, flowing smoothly within its banks. The children rushed to reach into the current and touch the strange, fascinating metal that slipped through their fingers, forming little silver balls in the palms of their hands, but I wouldn't let them dawdle, and they reluctantly rejoined the group.

Lao Jiang bent over a small stone stela on the floor to read the inscription.

"We've just left the province of Nanyang and are entering Xianyang," he said, chuckling. "It can't be far, then, to the prefecture of Hanzhong."

"We've crossed Everything Under the Sky already?" Master Red asked, using the expression commonly used among the Chinese to refer to their country.

"Well," Lao Jiang said quite enthusiastically, "they likely put the ramp near the capital, the center of power for both the real empire above as well as this little Zhongguo, Tianxia or Everything Under the Sky. This is an exact replica. It's like a giant map with magnificent models and these astonishing rivers of mercury."

"It's missing the mountains," my niece replied.

"Perhaps they didn't think they were necessary," the antiquarian commented, passing through the walls of the town across the bridge in front of us. He suddenly let out a hearty laugh. "All that traveling for nothing! Do you know where we are? We're back in Shang-hsien!"

I couldn't help but break into a big smile.

"So will tiny little assassins from the Green Gang attack us here?" my niece joked.

"Lao Jiang," I begged, "please don't make us cross the Qin Ling mountain range to get to the mausoleum. Could we take the main road to Xi'an?"

"Of course," he replied.

We crossed through little Shang-hsien, which, despite its size, was more elegant and lavish than the actual town, and left through the western gate to follow the route to Hongmenhe, a scant hundred and fifty feet away. We walked along enthusiastically, noting every detail in that marvelous reconstruction. Along the shiny bronze paths were scale statues of carters pulling their oxen, peasants with hoes raised in an eternal gesture of cultivation, covered wagons filled with fruits and vegetables heading to the capital, lone gentlemen on their mounts, and farmyard animals such as chickens and pigs. It was a country in miniature, industrious and full of life, a life that became increasingly intense the closer we got to the heart of that world: imperial Xianyang. None of us could believe our eyes. You couldn't imagine a place like that even in your wildest dreams.

"Shouldn't we head toward Mount Li and find the hill that marks the mausoleum?" Biao suddenly asked.

"I don't think the emperor would reproduce the funeral palace inside his burial mound," Lao Jiang said. "Logically, he'd have wanted to be buried in his imperial palace at Xianyang. If he's not there, then we'll look where you suggested."

We passed through beautiful cities, crossed bridges over streams that sparkled like silver in the light of the whale-oil lamps, and had to swerve around the increasing numbers of statues that were incredible representations of everyday life in that long-lost empire. Finally, when we were beginning to feel as if we were part of a strange world where everyone and everything had been frozen in time, we found ourselves in front of huge walls that protected what Lao Jiang said was Shanglin

Park. This was an exceptional place built south of the river Wei for the Qin kings' enjoyment and was later enlarged by the First Emperor.

"In fact," Lao Jiang said, "shortly before Shi Huang Ti died, he decided he was tired of the noise, filth, and crowds in Xianyang, north of the river Wei, and ordered that a new imperial palace be built inside this park, amid the lovely gardens. Sima Qian said that the new palace of Epang, which was never finished, would have been the biggest of any palace ever built, and yet it was simply the entrance to a monumental complex that, according to the project, would have covered hundreds and hundreds of miles. However, work stopped when Shi Huang Ti died, and the only part that had been completed was the great front hall, which could hold ten thousand men and flagpoles that were sixty feet high. If I'm not mistaken, Sima Qian said there was a path in the lower part of this great hall that led directly to the top of a nearby mountain and an elevated, covered walkway that went from Epang to Xianyang, over the river Wei. The First Emperor had several palaces in the capital, so many that the exact number isn't known. All his residences were connected by tunnels and elevated walkways that allowed him to move from one place to another without being seen. Epang was his last palace, his great dream, and he put hundreds of thousands of convicts to work on it. I think he would have ordered that a replica of Epang be built down here so it could be his final resting place."

"But if the one up above wasn't finished . . ." I commented.

"The one down here wasn't either," Lao Jiang agreed. "Both Epang and the mausoleum were being built at the same time, so I suppose the two also stopped at the same point. If I'm right, the First Emperor's real tomb has to be in the underground copy of that magnificent front hall."

We crossed through a great bronze door richly tooled and decorated with what I didn't dare think were enormous precious stones and found ourselves in a splendid garden where the trees were normal size, as well as the paths and small rivers of quicksilver. The bronze sky was now blue—painted, undoubtedly—and no longer reflected the light from what were now lanterns hanging from branches or set on stone pillars alongside the path.

"How can the mercury still flow after two thousand years?" Biao asked, truly perplexed by the question.

None of us knew the answer. Lao Jiang and Master Red wove a thousand and one explanations, each one as far-fetched as the last, about the possible types of automatic mechanisms that could operate the rivers from some hidden part of the mausoleum. Meanwhile, we continued walking through those incredibly beautiful gardens that would have put Yuyuan Gardens in Shanghai to shame even at their height during the Ming era. All the trees and other vegetation were made of baked clay, like the statues we'd found throughout the mausoleum, but the colors remained vibrant and strong. I couldn't understand how certain much more recent artistic works (various Renaissance frescoes, for example) could be in such terrible condition while the pigments in this clay were as fresh as the day they were painted. Perhaps it was because they'd been enclosed down here with no changes in humidity, out of the wind, and safe from passersby. Surely if any of these statues were taken outside, they'd lose their color forever. The bronze floor was engraved to give it the texture of earth, sand, or grass, and the natural stones that decorated every nook and cranny had the strangest, most elegant shapes imaginable. It was my niece who discovered something else in the rivers of mercury.

"Good Lord, look at this!" she exclaimed, leaning over the handrail on a bridge, pointing straight down with her arm.

We all hurried over to examine that liquid silver surface transporting strange floating fish that seemed to be made of iron. In reality, the actual shape of a fish had been lost long ago, and they now looked like the frames of sunken ships: deformed, eroded by rust, wrecked.

"They must have been lovely aquatics made of high-quality steel when they were placed in the mercury," the antiquarian commented.

All right, then: first historical error, and one I was not about to let pass unnoticed.

"I believe, Lao Jiang, that steel was invented by an American in the nineteenth century."

"I'm sorry, Elvira, but steel was invented in China during the Warring States Period, prior to unification by the First Emperor. We discovered cast iron in the fourth century B.C., although you Westerners insist on claiming these advances for your own many centuries later. We've always had good clay for building ovens and foundries."

"It's true, madame."

"So why did they make these fish out of steel and not gold or silver?" Fernanda asked, watching the sad remains float away downriver.

"Gold and silver would have alloyed with the mercury and disappeared, while iron is resistant, and steel is nothing but tempered iron."

We continued through the gardens, discovering ever-more-amazing things—beautiful birds lined up on tree branches, geese and cranes pecking on the ground amid flower beds and stands of bamboo, deer, dogs, strange winged lions, lambs, and, appropriately, a large number of those ugly animals called *tianlu*s, mythical beasts with magical powers whose mission, like that of the winged lions, is to protect the soul of the dead, defending it from devils and evil spirits. There were also buildings with the typical upturned eaves in the middle of little rivers, tables of refreshment and orchestras of musicians with ancient instruments. We passed a small dock with rusted steel skiffs moored to it. An army of life-size servants was all along the way; you'd turn a corner and suddenly come upon someone, nearly jumping out of your skin until you realized it was a statue, and then nearly jump out of your skin again. There were pavilions where groups of acrobats or athletes like the ones we'd seen in the banquet hall were performing, trays with exquisite jade glasses and jugs to satiate the emperor's thirst, baskets of fruit made of pearls, rubies, emeralds, turquoises, topazes, and so much more. I couldn't take my eyes off that immense wealth, that exaggerated opulence. True, everything here would pay off my debts and give me back my freedom, but why, for what purpose, would the First Emperor have accumulated so much? It had to be some sort of sickness, because once you have everything you want and need, what's the use in accumulating, for example, baskets of fruit made of precious stones or innumerable palaces where you live in hiding from the world?

All of us but Lao Jiang picked up what we liked along the way and put it in our bags. The antiquarian said that these were just trinkets and that the real treasure was in the emperor's true funeral palace. Still, it took us quite a while to get through the gardens before we came upon the largest building any of us had ever seen: a huge pavilion with red walls and several tiered black roofs as well as numerous staircases rising up from the middle of another esplanade that stretched as far as the eye could see. The pillars there burned incessantly, reflecting brightly off the giant bronze statues of warriors guarding the approach, the shiny floor, and an incredible ceiling studded with colossal heavenly constellations that sparkled with every imaginable color. Up above, the figure of a magnificent red crow that could only have been made of rubies or agates was visible in the south; a black tortoise fashioned out of opals or quartzes was to the north; to the west was a white jade tiger; to the east was an amazingly beautiful green dragon undoubtedly made of turquoises or emeralds; and in the center, above the gigantic front hall of the underground palace of Epang, was an exquisite yellow snake fashioned from topazes.

Such beauty and such excess! We were spellbound, staring at the image that lay before our astonished eyes, as if it were some fantastical place that couldn't be real. But it was, it was real, and we were there to see it.

"I believe we have a problem," I thought I heard Master Red say.

"What's wrong now?" Lao Jiang asked, his voice also sounding unreal.

"We can't get there," Master Red replied. I had to tear my eyes off that amazing ceiling to look at him and saw he was pointing toward the set of stairs in the middle of that enormous front hall. A wide river of mercury some fifteen feet across encircled that never-ending esplanade like a medieval moat, cutting off access.

"Isn't there a bridge anywhere?" I asked unnecessarily, because I could see there wasn't.

" 'And on the sixth, the Original Dragon's true burial place, you will have to cross a wide river of mercury to reach the treasures,' " Lao Jiang recited from memory. "How could we have forgotten?" he moaned.

"Why don't we use those iron boats we saw near the pavilions in the garden?" Fernanda proposed.

"They weigh too much," Master Red replied, shaking his head. "We wouldn't even be able to carry one between the five of us. Besides, we'd have to break so many of those lovely clay trees to get them here."

"But there's no other way," Lao Jiang objected angrily. Flushed and sweating, he was running out of patience.

"Let's use the trees," I said without thinking. "We could cut—I mean, we could break some off at the bottom and use that line of yours to make a raft."

"No, we'll not use my line," he refused, slicing his hand categorically through the air.

"Why not?" I asked, confused.

"We might need it on the way out."

"That's not true!" I retorted. "All six levels are open. The hardest part will be climbing those bridges and getting through the methane. We're not going to need your line for anything."

"Just a moment," Master Red interrupted. "Please don't argue. If Da Teh doesn't want to ruin his line in the quicksilver, we won't use it. I have another idea. Remember the steel fish we saw floating in that stream?"

We all nodded.

"Well, why don't we try to swim across?"

"Swim in mercury?" I asked in disbelief.

"It's a very dense liquid, Master Red Jade," Lao Jiang objected. "I don't think that's possible. We'll tire out before we get halfway across, if we get that far."

"You're right," the monk admitted, "but the fish floated, so we will, too. If we use poles to propel ourselves, we could easily get to the other side."

"And where do we get poles?" I asked.

"The bamboo in the garden!" Fernanda exclaimed. "We can use that to push ourselves. We'll be like gondoliers in Venice!"

Master Red and Biao looked at her blankly. Gondoliers in Venice must have been as incomprehensible to them as *tianlus* were to us.

Any silliness aside, I wasn't the least bit sure about us going into the mercury. After all, immersing yourself in a metal seemed a little danger-ous, not to mention how incredibly cold it was. What if we accidentally swallowed some and poisoned ourselves? I knew that mercury was an ingredient in many medicines, especially purgatives, deworming treat-ments, and some antiseptics,[50] but I was afraid it might be harmful in amounts higher than those prescribed by doctors.

The children were already running toward the garden in search of clay bamboo. Though he hadn't complained about the foot he'd hurt when he fell into the Han shaft, Biao was limping some. He didn't seem to be in serious pain, however. I heard a loud knock, and then it sounded as if an earthenware pot had hit the ground.

"Get it, Biao!" my niece shouted.

Master Red, Lao Jiang, and I went to get our own poles. Master Red Jade picked up a crane with a long beak and used it to chop at the bam-boo. Soon enough we all looked like penitent Nazarenes keeping time with the shafts of their tall candles. We were ready to wade into that river of quicksilver.

Lao Jiang went first, after he'd tested the depth of the river. It was only about six feet and therefore perfect for pushing himself along. He smiled happily as soon as he was in.

"I'm floating just fine," he said, and, digging one end of his bamboo into the riverbed, began to propel himself toward the other bank.

"Fernanda, Biao," I called. "Come here. I want you to promise me you'll keep your mouths closed when you're in the mercury and not put your heads in under any circumstances. Do you hear me?"

"I can't dive?" whined Biao, who had evidently already been plan-ning to.

"No, Biao, you cannot dive, you cannot take a drink of that quicksilver, you cannot get your face wet, and, if at all possible, don't put your hands in either."

"But that's ridiculous, Auntie!"

"No it's not. Mercury is a metal, and it could be toxic. I don't want to hear any arguments. Is that clear?"

They nodded unhappily. No doubt they'd been picturing many exciting tricks and experiments in the mercury.

Lao Jiang had already reached the other side and, after struggling to get the pole out of the moat and set it on the ground without breaking it, tried to haul himself out by pushing down on his hands. Although his clothes looked dry, they must have been soaked with mercury and made it hard for him to move. Finally, with a great deal of effort, he managed to get one leg up on the bank and crawl out. Puffing, he shook himself off like a poodle, creating a cloud of quicksilver that fell onto the ground.

"Throw me my bag, Master Red Jade," he called out, and my stomach knotted. Yes, I'd been told that dynamite was the safest thing in the world, but hearing it didn't mean I believed it. The bag of explosives flew through the air, clean across the river thanks to Master Red's strength.

"Your turn, madame."

"I'd rather the children crossed first."

Fernanda and Biao didn't hesitate. I watched them like a hawk the whole way, but apart from a little messing around and laughing, they obeyed my orders to a tee, and I was able to breathe freely once I saw them safe and sound beside Lao Jiang. I prepared to head in while Master Red threw the children's bags.

At first the icy mercury took my breath away, but then it was rather nice to float along, bobbing in the thick liquid without having to move arms or legs. All you had to do was push the bamboo against the bottom, and inertia moved you in the desired direction as if you were a

Venetian gondola. I now understood the children's silly laughter, because it was really quite a lot of fun.

Soon I was on the other side, where Lao Jiang and Biao had to help
me out; my clothes did indeed weigh as much as if they were made of
lead. Master Red threw my bag over and then his own before wading in.
I turned to examine the amazing esplanade with its bronze giants.
There were twelve in total, six on either side of the main avenue, and
each one must have been over thirty feet high. They were all different
and seemed to represent real human beings with fierce eyes and a martial stance. They were certainly imposing. If their objective was to ter-
rify the First Emperor's visitors, they were successful.

We walked toward them along the avenue, intensely emotional and
nervous now that we were so close to what was undeniably the First
Emperor of China's true tomb. We reached the stairs and started to
climb. Fortunately, there were only fifty, so no one fell behind, and
before we knew it, we were standing in front of the open doors to the
great front hall of Epang. The hair-raising sight that lay before us
wasn't something we could ever have prepared for: millions of human
skeletons scattered on the floor, countless piles stretching into the
distance, bare bones heaped against walls with old bits of dresses, jewelry, or hair ornaments still visible. Women, there were so many
women: the concubines who'd never given Shi Huang Ti children.
The rest were the poor slave laborers who'd built that mausoleum. Sai
Wu, our guide on that long journey, would be among the remains
in that vast graveyard. A lump formed in my throat at the same time
the terrified children drew close on either side of me. No one could
look at that deplorable sight without feeling tremendously sorry or
imagining the horrible deaths those thousands and thousands of people must have suffered to satisfy the megalomania of one man, a king
who thought he was all-powerful. So many lives wasted for nothing, so
much suffering and anguish just to punish the supposed infertility of
young girls married to an old egomaniac and to keep that tomb a secret!

I could understand Sai Wu's fury and desire for revenge. As admirable as the First Emperor's construction was, he had no right to take the lives of so many innocent people with him. I knew that it had been another time and that one shouldn't criticize the past from such a distant perspective, but even so, I thought it odious that one man could have had so much power over others.

"Come on," Lao Jiang said firmly, lifting a foot to cross the threshold and setting it down among the human remains.

I don't remember a more horrific walk than the one that day through that sea of corpses; it was worse than the swarms of beetles. The children were terrified; they jumped or let out a choked cry whenever they inadvertently stepped on bones or when a little pile of remains tumbled down on their feet. The last ones alive had obviously piled up the bodies of those who had already died. I shuddered at the superstitious thought of all that pain impregnating the walls of this magnificent, solemn hall.

Finally, after an eternity, we reached a long red wall with a little doorway and two sliding doors.

"The funeral chamber?" Master Red asked.

"The outer sarcophagus," Lao Jiang specified. "According to the customs of that time, an emperor's coffin was placed in a room surrounded by compartments containing his funeral possessions. These are the treasures we've been looking for."

"Will it be locked?" I asked, trying to open the door. Not only did it open, but it disintegrated in my hands, scaring me half to death. Another red wall was in front, with a narrow hallway to walk along, but there was no light in here. It was pitch black, and so Lao Jiang had to ignite his torch again. He went in first, and the rest of us followed. Although the passageway was very long, as soon as we turned the first corner, we saw the entrance to one of the compartments Lao Jiang had mentioned.

The light from the torch didn't properly illuminate all the fabulous riches piled in that huge room the size of a warehouse: thousands of chests overflowing with gold pieces that littered the floor, along with hundreds of elegant outfits embroidered in gold and silver and covered in precious stones. There were also countless beautiful cases containing spices and medicinal herbs, stunning jade objects of all shapes and kinds, and long, ornately decorated cylinders that contained marvelous maps of Everything Under the Sky painted on exquisite, delicate silk. The next compartment seemed to be devoted to the art of war. All the pieces—there must have been fifteen or twenty thousand—were made of pure gold: Swords, shields, lances, crossbows, arrows, and a variety of completely unknown weapons seemed to stand guard around an enormous case in the middle. It was also made of gold, decorated with silver and bronze spiraling clouds, lightning, tigers, and dragons, and it held the First Emperor's incredible armor, identical to the set we had seen upstairs, but this time the little plates joined together like fish scales were made of gold. Each piece was trimmed in precious stones, separating one from another: the breastplate from the back, these from the skirt, the arm pieces from the shoulder guards, and the throat piece from the neck guard. It was made for an average-size man, and only the helmet indicated that he'd had a very large head. Judging from that armor, the First Emperor must have been very strong. Wearing that suit—which surely weighed at least forty-five or fifty pounds—during an entire battle was a feat in itself.

It goes without saying that we didn't take anything from that compartment, because all the objects were too big to fit into our already full bags. The third wasn't terribly appropriate for plundering either. It was an absolute wonder, housing millions of everyday items such as ladles, incense holders, bronze mirrors, buckets, trowels, vases, knives, measuring cups, bowls, stoves—some even with an outlet for the smoke—bottles of essences for the bath, water heaters, ceramic toilets for the dead to use in the afterlife, and more. According to Lao Jiang, any one of those objects would fetch an astronomical price on the antiquities market. Oddly enough, he didn't take a thing. Actually, he hadn't put a single thing from the other compartments in his bag either. Once

I realized this, I again felt that strange sense of unease, morbid and absurd. I forced it out of my mind, because I didn't want to drive myself
crazy with outrageous suspicions. The fourth compartment was dedicated
to literature and music. Countless huge chests, the size of houses, held
thousands and thousands of valuable *jiances*; delicate animal-hair
brushes of varying sizes, only slightly the worse for wear, hung on the
walls next to bars of red and black ink stamped with the imperial seal;
and there were beautiful jade stands, exquisite jars for the water, and, on
a long, low table, small knives with curved blades that Lao Jiang said
were used to smooth the bamboo or erase poorly written characters.
Huge quantities of whetstones, bamboo slats, and sheets of silk sat waiting to be used. The variety of musical instruments was endless: long
zithers, flutes, drums, a small Bian Zhong, syrinxes, strange lutes, upright violins, a lithophone, and gongs. In short, there was a full orches-
tra to make a powerful dead man's eternity more enjoyable.

The fifth and final compartment, the smallest of them all, contained
nothing but an enormous, stunning chariot made of equal parts bronze,
silver, and gold. It had a huge round canopy, like a gigantic parasol, underneath which sat a clay charioteer holding tightly to the reins from
six massive horses made entirely of silver, with blankets on their backs
and long black plumes on their foreheads, ready to take the First Emperor's soul to any part of his private estate, known as Everything Under the Sky. The charioteer, who wasn't as impressive as the terrifying
horses, was elegantly dressed and wore one of those lacquered cloth
hats that slope back.

Shi Huang Ti had everything he needed to confront death. It was
hard to believe he'd worried so much about his wealth in the great beyond when he'd spent his life in search of immortality. As we walked
toward the main room, Lao Jiang told us that during the many years of
his long reign, hundreds of alchemists had tried to find a magic pill or
elixir that would tear him from the jaws of death. He even sent marine
expeditions in search of an island called Penglai, where the immortals

lived, to find the secret to eternal life. It was also said that those expeditions, in which the emperor sent hundreds of young men and women as gifts, were what populated Japan, since none ever returned.

Nothing more than a small opening now separated us from the funeral chamber where the First Emperor's real coffin was to be found. The children were nervous. We were all nervous. We'd done it! It was hard to believe after everything we'd been through. My bag was so full I couldn't have squeezed another thing into it, and I hoped I wouldn't come across any more of those treasures you just can't leave behind without crying bitter tears. The important thing was that we were in front of that entrance, only a few feet away from Shi Huang Ti, the First Emperor.

It was pitch black inside. Lao Jiang slowly reached in with the torch, and we could see that it was a big room, seemingly empty, with stone walls and an incredibly high ceiling.

"Where is it?" the antiquarian asked nervously.

We all walked in and looked disconcertedly around us. There was nothing here, not a single visible crack or joint anywhere in the solid gray stone floor and walls.

"Could I have the torch for a moment?" Master Red asked.

Lao Jiang turned furiously around. "What do you want it for?" he snapped.

"I thought I saw something. . . . I don't know. I'm not sure."

The antiquarian held out his arm to pass him the torch, but Master Red gestured for Biao to take it.

"Get up on my shoulders," he said to the boy.

We hadn't taken more than ten steps into the room, but there was only emptiness as far as we could see in that poor light. I couldn't imagine what Master Red must have spied.

With everyone's help, Master Red stood with the boy on his shoulders.

"Lift your arm as high as you can and illuminate the ceiling."

When Biao did and the vault became visible, I couldn't believe my eyes: A great iron coffin some ten feet long, six feet wide, and one foot high hung motionless in the air without, at first glance, any chains or scaffolding holding it there.

"What's the sarcophagus doing there?" Lao Jiang bellowed, incredulous. "How can it stay in the air like that?"

We had no answer. How would we know what sort of ancient magic kept that iron coffin floating as if it were a zeppelin? Biao jumped off Master Red's shoulders and stood still, holding the torch.

The antiquarian roared and began pacing.

"We don't need to reach the sarcophagus, Lao Jiang," I said, knowing full well he would just snap at me. "We got what we wanted. Let's get out of here."

He stopped cold and looked at me with wild eyes.

"Go! Get out of here!" he yelled. "I'm staying! I've got things to do!"

What was he talking about? What was wrong with him? Out of the corner of my eye, I saw Master Red, who was looking for something in his bag, lift his head in astonishment and stare at Lao Jiang.

"Didn't you hear me?" the antiquarian continued to shout. "Go, get up to the surface!"

I was tired of his bad manners and the unbearable attitude he'd adopted over the last few days. I wasn't about to let him shout at us like that, as if he'd gone crazy and wanted to kill us.

"Stop!" I screamed with every ounce of air in my lungs. "Be quiet! I've had enough of you!"

He stood, surprised, looking at me for a moment.

"Listen," I said, glaring at him. "There's no need to behave like that. Why do you want to stay behind on your own? Haven't we been a team since we left Shanghai? If you have something to do in here, as you say, why don't you just do it, and then we'll all go? You wouldn't have been able to get here on your own, Lao Jiang. Calm down and tell us how we can help you."

A strange smile was playing on his pursed lips.

"Three humble shoemakers make a wise Zhuge Liang," he replied.

"I have no idea what you're trying to say," I spit out in frustration.

"It's a Chinese proverb, madame," Master Red murmured from the floor where he was still crouching with his hands frozen inside his bag. "It means the more people there are, the greater your chance of success."

"'Four eyes see better than two,' isn't that what you say?" the antiquarian clarified, his face serious once again. "That's why I brought you with me. That and because you provided a good cover."

I didn't understand him. I was upset and confused. It seemed absurd to have this conversation in this situation, in this place. I'd often been moved over the course of our journey when I thought about how those people I hadn't known at all a few months earlier (including my niece) had become so important to me. Everything we'd been through had brought us closer, and I'd come to place a great deal of trust in Fernanda, Biao, Lao Jiang, Master Red, even Paddy Tichborne. I would even have included old Ming T'ien, who was still very much in my thoughts. That's why the change Lao Jiang had undergone distressed me so.

"Do you remember what I told you in Shanghai about how important this place is for my country?" the antiquarian asked me darkly. "This," he said, throwing his arms wide to encompass the entire room, coffin included, "is as important for the future as it was for the past. China is a country colonized by foreign imperialist governments that are bleeding us dry and subjugating us with their thievery and demands. Anywhere that imperialism doesn't reach, only because it doesn't want to go there, you'll find the feudal remains of a dying country dominated by warlords. Do you know that the Soviet Union is the only power ever to give back the concessions and privileges that were stolen from us by its former czarist regime, without asking for anything in return? No other power has done that. The Soviets have also promised to support our fight to regain our freedom. Last summer twelve of us met at a secret location in Shanghai to hold the second Chinese Communist Party Conference."

Lao Jiang was in the Communist Party? Wasn't he Kuomintang?

"At that meeting we resolved to bring an end to foreign imperialist oppression, to expel you *yang-kwei,* your countries, your missionaries, your merchants and companies. But above all to create a united front against those who want to restore the old monarchy, against those who want China to go back to its feudal system. And do you know why we Communists have had to gather strength, accept help from the Soviet Union, and take up the flag of freedom? Because Dr. Sun Yat-sen has failed: In the twelve years since his revolution, he hasn't given the Chinese people back their dignity, he hasn't reunified this fragmented country. He hasn't gotten rid of the feudal warlords with their private armies paid for by the Dwarf Invaders, nor has he made your kind leave or done away with the abusive, humiliating economic agreements. Dr. Sun Yat-sen is weak, and out of fear he continues to allow the Chinese people to die of hunger and you, with your democracies and your colonial paternalism, to keep burying us ever deeper in ignorance and desperation."

Without my realizing it, Lao Jiang's impassioned speech had transported me out of the First Emperor's mausoleum and back to Paddy Tichborne's rooms in the Shanghai Club. His words hadn't actually changed; his contempt for Dr. Sun Yat-sen and his Communist affiliation were all that was new in this unexpected situation.

"Keeping my ties to the party a secret over the last two years allowed me to advise Moscow of the Kuomintang's movements as well as foreign commercial and political activity in Shanghai. When the imperial eunuchs and later the Green Gang and the Japanese diplomats came to my store on Nanking Road, I guessed at the importance of that hundred-treasure chest I'd sold to Rémy, and I alerted the party. However, after your late husband and my old friend refused to return the chest, after his death at the hands of the Green Gang, we were as anxious for your arrival and what you might find in the house as the imperialists were. We used my old friendship with Rémy to unearth what was shaking the foundations of the imperial court in Peking. When you sent me the chest and I was finally able to examine it, I was shocked to discover that it contained the original version of the legend of the Prince of Gui and the clues needed to find the *jiance* that could lead us to this, Shi Huang Ti's mausoleum. I immediately advised the Central Committee, and while they decided what type of action we were going to take, they ordered me to tell Sun Yat-sen. You know what happened then. Dr. Sun considers me a close friend and a loyal partisan, and therefore I always have access to a great deal of information. No one in the Kuomintang knows I'm a member of the Communist Party, because, as I explained to you one day, the two currently work together, if only on the surface, but sooner or later we'll wind up in conflict. Dr. Sun, as you know, offered to finance our journey for the purpose I already told you: to fund the Kuomintang and prevent an imperial restoration. The Central Committee of my party, on the other hand, gave me a clear and categorical order: Under cover of Dr. Sun's mission, my real task is to destroy this mausoleum."

"Destroy the mausoleum?" I exclaimed, horrified.

"Don't look so surprised," he said to me, and then looked at the others. "You either, Master Red Jade. After its being lost for two thousand years, too many people now know that this place exists. Not only the Manchus from the last dynasty and the Japanese Mikado's people but the Green Gang and the Kuomintang. How long do you think it'll take any one of them to make use of what's here, especially that strange, floating coffin above our heads? Do you know what this would mean to the people of China? We Communists don't care about the riches in here. They don't interest us. However, the others, apart from profiting from all of these treasures, will use this discovery to take over a China that's tired of power struggles, hungry, and sick. Hundreds of millions of impoverished peasants will be manipulated into going back to their former situation as slaves, instead of fighting for freedom and equality. That despicable Puyi isn't the only one who wants to become emperor.

What do you think Dr. Sun Yat-sen would do? And what would the foreign powers do if it fell into Sun Yat-sen's hands? How much blood would be spilled if the warlords decided to come here and take these treasures? How many of them would want to be emperor of a new, truly Chinese, not Manchu, dynasty? Whoever gains possession of this," he said, pointing up, "will be blessed by the founder of this nation to take control of Everything Under the Sky in his name, and believe me, we will not allow that to happen. China isn't prepared to assimilate this place without dire consequences."

"But do you really have to destroy the mausoleum?" I asked skeptically.

"Most certainly. Without a doubt. That's what I was ordered to do. I'm going to allow you to leave with everything you've taken. It's my way of thanking you for what you've done. I had to use you to get here and to deceive both the Kuomintang and the Green Gang."

"And what about Paddy Tichborne?" I asked. "Is he a Communist like you? Did he know all this?"

"Not in the least, Elvira. Paddy is simply a good friend who was very useful for gathering information in Shanghai in order to get to you."

"What will he say when he hears of this?"

The antiquarian roared with laughter. "As I've said, I hope one day he'll write a good adventure novel about it! That would go a long way to making this whole thing just a fantastic legend. I, of course, will deny ever having been here. If anyone wants to come and prove that there's any truth to whatever any of you might say after today, they won't be able to, because I'm going to destroy this place."

He bent over to pick up his bag and slung it over his shoulder.

"Don't even think about trying to stop me, Master Red Jade, or I'll blow this place up with the lot of you inside. Help Elvira and the children get out of here quickly."

"Are you going to die, Lao Jiang?" a frightened Biao asked, on the verge of tears.

"No, I'm not going to die," the antiquarian coldly assured him, seemingly offended by the question, "but I don't want you here while I prepare the explosives. I don't have all the material I need to blow the entire place, so I'm going to have to set charges such that the structure will come down and destroy the whole complex. That line we used on the second level, Elvira, is one of the fuses I brought for this mission. I'm sure you can appreciate that I need every inch of it so I can get out of here as well. They're slow-burning, but even so, the complexity of the mausoleum is going to make it very hard for me to reach the surface in time. I expect that it will take an hour or an hour and a half to prepare the detonation, and I'll have approximately one more hour to get out of here. That's why I'm begging you to leave now. You have two and a half hours to reach the top, climb out of the shaft, and get away, so go! Now!"

"Two and a half hours!" I exclaimed frantically. "Don't do this to us, Lao Jiang! We won't make it! What's your hurry? Give us more time!"

He smiled sadly. "I can't, Elvira. You've been convinced that we escaped the Green Gang once and for all when we left Shang-hsien, but they have assassins and resources everywhere. Think about it: The day after we left the village, when our doubles stopped and turned back, the Gang knew we'd tricked them. They either abandoned the search, which is highly unlikely, or went back to Shang-hsien and interrogated everyone until they found out what happened and where we went. By then we may still have had a two-day lead, but they undoubtedly got the information they needed from the guide who led us out of the village and into the pine forest or the boatmen who helped us cross the rivers between Shang-hsien and T'ieh-lu. Even though we cleaned everything up before riding again each day, it's not hard to imagine they'd find some indication of our nightly fires or our refuse. In any event, even that wasn't necessary. There's a straight line from Shang-hsien to T'ieh-lu that's very easy to follow. Our horses up top will be the last clue they need to find the mouth of the shaft. If we still had a two-day advantage, or even if we add one more day for the time they spent interrogating people in Shang-hsien and following our trail, the Green Gang assassins are already here, inside the mausoleum."

In other words, we were jumping out of the frying pan and into the fire.

"Don't waste any more time, and don't make me waste it either," he urged. "Leave. I have much to do. We'll see one another outside in a few hours."

It had been so long since I'd used a watch that to a certain extent I'd learned how to calculate the passing of time intuitively. I knew that if we were barely going to make it out of the mausoleum, even counting on all the good fortune possible, there was no way Lao Jiang was going to make it out unless he had some unknown and unlikely resource. I'm sure he knew it, too.

"Good-bye, Lao Jiang," I said.

"Good-bye, Elvira," he replied with a ceremonious bow. "Good-bye, everyone."

Fernanda and Biao remained motionless. My niece had an indignant look on her face, and Biao's eyes were red, his head hung.

"Come on," I ordered. The clock had started to count down, and if we knew what was good for us, we had to try to beat it. No one moved, so I grabbed the children by the arms and pulled them out of the room. "Let's go, Master Red Jade!"

Lao Jiang had kept the only torch, so our flight was going to be in darkness, at least through that outer sarcophagus. Luckily, we remembered the way and were soon in the front hall with that sea of skeletons before us. I stopped.

"Master," I said hurriedly, "I think it would be best to leave our bags here. We'll take what's most valuable and run."

Master Red nodded, and the children pulled out great handfuls of precious stones, gold coins, and jade figurines, stuffing them into their many big pockets.

"Fernanda, make sure you take the mirror. Put it inside your jacket."

"The mirror?" she asked in disbelief. "That's the last thing I was going to take. It's big and awkward," she said contemptuously. She was angry, not at me but at Lao Jiang.

Apart from filling his pockets with treasures, Master Red placed his cherished *luo p'an* inside his coat. Biao did the same with the sketchbook and box of pencils he had appropriated from me.

"Don't look at where you're putting your feet," I warned them. "And don't stop for any reason. Run!"

I took off through the piles of bones as fast as I could, trying not to lose my balance whenever I stepped on one. I ran as if my life depended on it, because it did. I was so happy that I'd gotten in such good shape through tai chi and months of long treks in the mountains! It was a blessing.

We left the stairs of Epang and the bronze giants behind, reaching the river of mercury where we picked up the canes of bamboo we'd also left behind. All of us crossed at once, pushing with every ounce of strength in order to move more quickly through that liquid, which seemed to want to slow us down, not let us pass. Once on the other bank, we ran through the garden like greased lightning. Anxiety must heighten your senses, because we didn't get lost even once; certain animals, a few stones, and the pavilions on the little rivers led us directly to the great bronze door in the walls encircling Shanglin Park. We veered around the many statues in the path leading to the ramp up to the fifth level. I don't remember a single bridge or any of the cities except the cobbled streets of small, elegant Shang-hsien. Then we came to the enormous, bright esplanade with its thick, black-lacquered columns. The exit was somewhere at the other end, and I hoped we wouldn't get lost. We sped along without stopping, and when the ceiling got closer to our heads, we knew we were on the right track.

"There!" my niece shouted, turning a little to the left. A short while later, we were sprinting up toward the big black slab in the banquet hall. We didn't stop. We flew past the tables with their brocade cloths and gold objects, heading toward the iron rungs on the wall behind the enormous puddle thick with the bodies of dead insects. Fernanda hesitated.

"Keep going!" I shouted breathlessly. I was beginning to tire. How long had we been running nonstop? Perhaps twenty or twenty-five minutes.

Master Red took the lead, and I was thankful to him for that. As the first one to face the millions of repugnant bugs infesting that room up there, he helped us to get through it more quickly. The idea of once again having my hair, face, and clothes covered in those writhing black things was almost more than I could bear, but there was no time to waste. They didn't have long to live, and if the price I had to pay for the next fifty years of life (it's best to be optimistic with such calculations) was to pass through that little piece of hell once more, then I would do it.

Biao followed Master Red, then Fernanda, and I went last, receiving the least number of insects on my head. Master Red Jade had left the trapdoor to the chamber with the Bian Zhong open and repeatedly called out to us, guiding Biao, who in turn guided Fernanda and me as well. It didn't matter if my eyes were open or closed, because I already knew that it was cockroaches, beetles, and ants all over me, crawling on my face.

We lost more time than we should have because of those insects. Unfortunately, they'd been irresistibly drawn to the light coming in through the openings on either side of the movable wall and invaded the room with the Bian Zhong. By then they'd taken over the beautiful bells and the iron ladder that led up to the next level. Not only that: Since we hadn't closed the trapdoor the previous day (when the children had taken us by surprise), the most daring insects had decided to explore the mysterious space beyond that strange opening in the ceiling and flown up into the vast area with the ten thousand bridges.

There we were again, in that incredible place. I lifted my eyes and was overcome by fear. We wouldn't be able to run along those iron chains suspended in the air without falling.

"Please, Master Red Jade," I begged. "Don't make a mistake. One tiny error means we'll get lost in the labyrinth."

"I assure you, madame, that I will pay close attention and take the utmost care," he replied as he walked onto the first footbridge.

"How much longer do we have?" my niece asked, following him.

"I estimate about an hour and forty-five minutes," I replied.

"We're not going to make it," she whined.

"Everyone, listen to me," Master Red said. "I want you to concentrate and pay close attention to what I'm about to say. Forget that you're walking on an iron chain and imagine it's a wide white line painted on the floor of a large room. The chain is a secure, stable line, a line that presents no danger. All right?"

"What's he saying?" Biao turned to whisper so that only I could hear him.

"Look, Biao, I don't have the faintest idea what Master Red is trying to do," I replied out loud, "but if he says this quivering chain is a white line painted on the floor, then you believe him, and that's that."

"Yes, *tai-tai*."

"You, too, Fernanda. Do you hear me?"

"Yes, Auntie."

"And hold on tight."

"Repeat to yourself that you're walking on a very wide line painted on the floor of a big room," Master Red insisted.

I, of course, tried with all my might several times during that endless walk along those horrid bridges, but I lost concentration every time an insect flew in front of me. My feet would become unsteady, and I would unwittingly shake the entire footbridge. When that happened, I was terrified that one of the children would fall and it would be my fault. Not a Taoist master in the world or even a circus magician could then convince me I was walking on a white line. It was a mistake to let myself get carried away by panic, because at a certain point I lost any concept of time. I couldn't calculate how long it was taking us to make that climb.

However, the practice acquired the day before and Master Red's mental game seemed to put wings on our feet. Once we reached the top, standing on solid ground, we each agreed that the climb had taken us only an hour. I didn't want to mention it as we ran through the tunnel toward the shaft up to the second level, but that meant we had just forty-five minutes—at most—to get out of the mausoleum.

Before starting up the ramps, I told everyone to stop.

"What's wrong?" Master Red asked in confusion.

"Take out your mirror, Fernanda, and give it to Biao."

"What do *I* want it for?" the boy wondered.

"You see that whale-oil lamp, the one at the entrance to the tunnel?"

"Yes."

"Stay here and use the mirror to direct the light so we can find our way up."

Biao remained pensive. "Can I move up the ramp a little as long as I still light the way?"

"Of course," I replied as the rest of us set off at a run.

"Auntie! You're not planning on leaving him behind, are you?" my niece reproached.

"Don't be ridiculous. Run."

The icy air grew warmer as we sprinted up that wide shaft toward the trapdoor leading into the enormous methane-filled hall with the bronze floor. We were out of breath by the time we reached the last platform and stopped in front of the iron rungs below the door in the ceiling.

"Are you all right, Biao?" I shouted.

"Yes, *tai-tai*." The point of light he had aimed at us shone brightly right next to Master Red.

"Master," I said, "I want you to open the trapdoor, please, and go up."

While he did as I asked, I took out my own mirror and asked Fernanda to climb up after Master Red.

"What are you going to do?" she inquired suspiciously.

"I'm going to light the way so you can run."

I followed her and stood half inside and half outside the poisonous room.

"Biao!" I yelled. "Move your mirror to the right!"

The boy did as he was told.

"Now a bit toward the wall."

As soon as he did, the gleam of light reflected off my mirror. I aimed it straight at the floor of that immense chamber, and it set off sparks of greenish light from a little trail of turquoises that some very intelligent person had left.

"Run, Master Red. Take Fernanda, and tell me once you've opened the door on the other side."

"Very well, madame."

I watched their feet race away following the path of light that was amplified by the polished bronze floor. It wouldn't take them more than a few minutes to reach the other side at that speed. It would have been so good to have been able to run like that the day before! We wouldn't have suffered, being poisoned by gas to the point of losing conscious-ness as we wandered blindly. A few moments later, I heard Master Red call out that Fernanda and he had reached the door. I asked him to get Fernanda up into the throne room in the funeral palace, and he replied that she was already on her way. I breathed a sigh of relief. Now I had to turn my attention to the boy.

"Listen to me, Biao," I said, descending a few rungs so that my head was once again in the shaft. "Have you moved up a little already?"

"Yes, *tai-tai*."

"Good. Now I want you to lean your back against the wall and get up here as fast as you can."

"Okay, *tai-tai*," he replied, suddenly leaving me in absolute darkness. My mirror had served its purpose so I put it back inside my jacket and prepared to wait for Biao, who might be a while. However, in no time I heard his labored breathing getting closer, and then something touched my foot.

"How did you get here so quickly?" I asked in disbelief.

"I couldn't run with my back up against the wall, but if I used just my elbow, I wasn't in danger of falling into the shaft."

What a clever boy! And brave! I wouldn't have dared.

"Up we go, Biao."

The two of us were soon at the top, and I called out to Master Red again. I asked him to keep talking so his voice would guide Biao and me toward him.

How strange it is to run in the dark! At first you're afraid of falling. Your steps are unsure, because when you lose your sight, you also lose your balance. But being aware of the danger, of how little time we had left before the whole place exploded thanks to that old madman Lao Jiang, forced us to adapt to the situation. Following Master Red Jade's voice as he bellowed some dreadful chant in Chinese, we crossed the enormous basilica like a shot and were soon at the door.

"You can stop singing now," I begged. "We're here."

"As you wish, madame."

We crossed into the small cubicle with the ladder and climbed up, once again guided by a diffuse light shining in from above. Fernanda was waiting for us next to the trapdoor, behind the huge black stone slab. I was so happy to be back in the light! We passed next to the enormous stone altar where the First Emperor's ersatz coffin lay and started running toward the exit along the path where we'd had such fun setting off all of the arrows. I was worried that one of the crossbows might still be armed, but we had no trouble reaching the big stairs that led outside.

We descended the steps two at a time, three at a time, taking the chance that we might fall and crack our heads, but I suppose by this point we felt we didn't have much to lose, and we managed to stay in one piece on our suicidal descent down that great imperial staircase. I didn't want to ask how much time we had left so as not to worry the children, but I was sure it couldn't have been more than twenty or twenty-five minutes. We were still far enough from the exit that we wouldn't make it even if we had twice that much time. I quickened my pace, and, unconsciously, the others did the same. We crossed the esplanade, ran through the tunnel outside the first wall, leaped over the thick bronze bars that held the gigantic spike-studded door open, made it through the corridor in the middle, passed through the second tunnel outside the other wall as well, and finally left behind the immense door with its tiger-head knockers. We were out of the burial palace. Now all we had to do was run like mad to reach the shaft.

Unfortunately, a large group of Green Gang assassins holding torches in one hand and knives in the other didn't agree with that plan.

"Oh, no, no!" I moaned desperately. We were done. The four of us bunched together as if this would save our lives. I put an arm around my niece's shoulder and pulled her close.

The stupid assassins stared at us aggressively. The one who seemed to be in charge, a tall man with a shaved forehead and features that were more Mongolian than Chinese, said something threatening. Master Red Jade replied, and I watched the leader's expression change. Master Red continued speaking, repeating the words "*cha tan*" and "*bao cha*" over and over again. I don't know what they meant, but they seemed to have an effect because some of the thugs looked at one another uneasily. Master Red kept repeating *cha tan* and *bao cha*, getting more and more upset, as well as the full version of the antiquarian's name, Jiang Long-yan, and his courtesy name, Da Teh. Several times I also heard the word "Kungchantang," the name of the Chinese Communist Party. I gathered he was telling them that the place was going to explode in a few minutes, that the antiquarian was a Communist who'd been ordered to destroy the First Emperor's mausoleum, that we would all certainly die if we stayed there, and that there wasn't much time left. The boss seemed doubtful, but some of the others looked nervous. Master Red kept talking. Now it was if he were pleading, then explaining, then pleading again, and finally the leader brusquely waved his arm to indicate that we could go. Some of his men were visibly distressed and began shouting. We still hadn't moved. The leader yelled, screamed, and then suddenly said something emphatic and walked toward the door. The only thing that interested him was the mausoleum; thankfully, he didn't care about us at all.

"Let's go!" Master Red exclaimed as he started to run.

Without a word we took off after him at full speed. Strangely enough, a small group of assassins followed. I was terrified. Were they going to kill us? Then some of them started passing us, even leaving us behind.

We reached the end of the red wall and turned to the right. We ran and ran. Now there was a large group of us racing toward the shaft. It's not as if I felt sorry for the ones who stayed behind, but I would always be thankful to their boss for sparing our lives. The sole objective of the hunt that had begun in Shanghai and appeared to have just ended had been to find the mausoleum; the Green Gang's two employers, the im-perial family in Peking and the Japanese, had wanted nothing more. All we had to worry about now was getting out of there. We were some-what lucky the thugs had decided to flee with us, because their torches lit the way and we were able to move more confidently. Even though Master Red had his *luo p'an* and would have gotten us to the shaft, I knew what it was like to run in the dark and was thankful I could see the floor in front of me and not be running into those thick black col-umns that were everywhere.

We passed the walls that circled the palace at the precise moment I would have sworn that the two and a half hours the antiquarian had given us were up. As soon as I realized this, I grew weak with fear. We were escaping on borrowed time, and I hoped the antiquarian's dyna-mite and fuses had failed, that his plan had fallen through. I was puffing like a bellows and began to feel a twinge of pain in my right side. I wouldn't last much longer. If the shaft didn't appear soon, I was going to drop right there. No air was reaching my lungs, and that sensation had always been my worst nightmare, the horrible end to one of my anxiety attacks.

"Come on, Auntie, keep going!" my niece said, taking me by the arm and pulling.

Fernanda. I had to keep going for Fernanda. Who was going to look after her if I stayed behind? And then there was Biao. I had to take care of Biao. I couldn't give up.

That's when we reached the ramp. That beautiful ramp made of white clay bricks made me dream of living to see another day, and another, and another. . . . Something had obviously gone wrong on the sixth level. Something had failed, and the Green Gang assassins were going to find Lao Jiang and his explosives. I didn't know if I felt sorry about that or not. All I could think of was the lovely, lovely ramp I was setting foot on. I was so tired and yet so optimistic, so happy!

We charged up the ramps. The thugs escaping with us had no qualms about pushing and elbowing to get past us, even in the middle of those narrow platforms. The way we were running had clearly convinced them that Master Red's story was true, and they were desperate to reach the surface now that the exit was in sight. We only hoped they wouldn't toss us into the shaft as they raced past, so it was best to get out of the way, up against the wall, and let them pass. They were the first to reach a sturdy rope ladder hanging down from up above to the platform where Biao and I had fallen. The assassins began to climb, punching, pulling, and pushing one another. Looking up at that piece of sky and the golden midafternoon light coming in through the circle that signified salvation, I realized that those brutes could attack us without mercy as soon as we were at the top and they discovered that the mausoleum wasn't going to explode. The antiquarian's failure—and it did seem as if his plan had failed—meant we were once again in danger. We had to find some way to defend ourselves, and I whispered this to Master Red. He nodded and tried to allay my fears.

"There are only seven of them, madame," he murmured confidently, "and they don't have firearms. Don't worry. I can handle them."

I only half believed him, but it was enough to make me feel somewhat better. The four of us were finally able to climb the ladder.

Fernanda and Biao went first. As I waited, I thought back on the explosion that had opened up that funnel where the Dragon's Nest used to be and smiled bitterly. At the time I hadn't been able to understand why Lao Jiang, a respectable old antiquarian from Shanghai, was carrying explosives in his bag. How blind we had been!

When I reached the top, the children were sprawled exhausted on the ground.

"Get up!" I shouted. "This isn't over yet. We've got to move away from here."

Our animals were right where we'd left them. The Green Gang assassins rushed past them toward their own mounts grazing quietly nearby.

That's when it happened. At first we felt a slight tremor in the ground, barely noticeable, but it kept increasing in intensity until it was an earthquake that made us stumble and fall. The horses reared up and whinnied in fright as the mules brayed madly, kicking their feet in the air and jumping as I'd never seen a quadruped jump before. One of them broke its reins and, dropping the bit, galloped off, only to fall hard a moment later. The ground was rocking like a stormy sea. Several waves—that's exactly what they were—rose up over the countryside and shook us like little boats adrift, rolling us from side to side as we screamed desperately. Suddenly there was a dull roar, a thundering from deep inside the earth. Volcanoes must sound like that when they erupt. The ground seemed to be made of rubber, sinking down as if it were about to form a giant funnel, then rising again into a slight hill, and finally leveling out. Everything ceased. All of us, assassins included, stopped yelling at the same time. Only the animals continued making a racket but gradually calmed down until they stood still and silent. A terrible calm fell over the place. It was as if death had passed through, brushing each of us with its cloak, then moved off and disappeared. The entire world had fallen quiet.

I looked around in search of my niece and found her beside me, face-down with her arms stretched out above her head, shaken by silent convulsions that could have been either stifled sobs or spasms of pain. I moved closer and turned her over. Her face was covered in dirt and sticky with tears that formed a white paste around her eyes. I held her tightly.

"Is everyone all right?" Master Red asked.

"The two of us are fine," I replied, the last words I spoke before bursting into tears. "What about Biao?" I sobbed after a minute, letting go of Fernanda and looking to see if the boy was okay.

There he was, getting up off the ground, filthy dirty but alive.

"I'm fine, *tai-tai*," he murmured weakly.

The Green Gang assassins were slowly getting to their feet a certain distance away. They seemed frightened.

"Master Red," I whimpered, trying to speak coherently, "tell those men that the First Emperor's mausoleum has been destroyed. Ask them to tell their boss in Shanghai, that damned Pockmarked Huang or whatever the hell he's called, that it's over, that Lao Jiang is dead, and the *jiance* and the hundred-treasure chest have disappeared. Tell them."

Raising his voice in that heavy silence, Master Red started into a long speech. You'd think the assassins would have been grateful we saved their lives and shown at least a little gratitude by paying some attention, but they simply got on their horses and rode away.

"Are we free of them?" my niece asked through hiccups and tears.

"I think so," I replied, rubbing to clear my eyes and watching happily as they moved off into the distance, leaving a cloud of dust behind.

"What do we do now?" Biao asked. "Where do we go?"

Master Red Jade and I looked at one another and then at the solitary verdant mound in the middle of that great plain, encircled by the river Wei and the five peaks of Mount Li. It continued to mark the impressive mausoleum of Shi Hang Ti, the First Emperor of China, as it had for the last two thousand years. Nothing appeared to have changed up top; everything was just the same.

"Master Red Jade," I said. "How would you like to spend a few days in Peking?"

"In Peking?" he asked in surprise.

I reached into the outer pockets of my jacket and pulled out handfuls of precious stones and little jade objects that sparkled in the twilight.

"As I understand it," I explained, "there is a large antiquities market around the Forbidden City, and since it's the great capital of this enormous country, I'm sure we'll find buyers willing to pay a good price for these lovely jewels."

Chapter

5

When we reached Peking on the express from Xi'an, the city was in the midst of one of its usual yellow dust storms from the Gobi Desert, and the wind, a wind that never stopped the entire time we were there, stirred up nasty whirls on all the streets, avenues, and alleyways. Yellow sawdust covered everything—it got in your eyes, your mouth, your clothes, your food, even your bed. It was also very, very cold. People went about in fuzzy earmuffs and wrapped in enormous fur coats that made them look like polar bears. That and the leafless trees, branches bare, lent a sad, ghostly air to the imperial capital.

Once again Fernanda and I were able to look and dress like Europeans. Using what was left of the money I'd brought with me from Shanghai, we went shopping at the stores in the Legations Quarter. This small foreign city within the larger Chinese one was strongly protected by armies from every country with a diplomatic presence (the fifty-five days of terror they'd lived through during the famous Boxer Rebellion of 1900 was still very present in their minds). Wearing pretty new clothes and with our hair done, we were able to find lodging at the stately old French-style Grand Hôtel des Wagons-Lits, with bathrooms, hot water, and room service. In order for Biao and Master Red to be allowed into the Legations Quarter, where they were safer, they had to pose as our servants and sleep on the floor in the hallway outside our room. So as not to call attention to ourselves in public, Fernanda and I were forced to follow colonial customs and treat them in a despotic, contemptuous manner that felt terrible. Thankfully, we didn't plan on staying in Peking any longer than necessary. We would leave just as soon as we'd sold the valuables from the mausoleum.

Not all of us would return to Shanghai, however. Master Red yearned to go back to his quiet life of study at Wudang and could do so only by returning to Xi'an, picking up the horses and mules we'd left with the owner of the store at that little station in T'ieh-lu, and once again crossing the Qin Ling Mountains heading south. As soon as we had the money, we'd divide it into three equal parts: one for the monastery, another for Paddy Tichborne, and the last for the children and me. We still had to come up with a plausible story for Paddy, to justify the money we were giving him without disclosing the dangerous secret surrounding Lao Jiang's death.

On our first day, we went to the most important gold merchants in Peking and negotiated until we obtained a fair price. Not one of them seemed surprised to see two European women with such valuable Chinese pieces, nor did they ask where we got them. The next day we called on the most reputable dealers in precious stones with the same results. Finally, on our last day, we visited the antiquarians on "Gate of Earthly Peace" Street who'd been recommended as being very discreet and reliable. Everything Lao Jiang had said about the sale of antiquities from the Forbidden City was absolutely true: Furniture, calligraphies, rolls of paintings, and decorative objects were sold in surprising numbers and at ridiculous prices. All of it was obviously too valuable to have come from anywhere but the other side of the high wall between Peking and

Puyi's palace. It was hard to believe that the young, ambitious Puyi we'd been running from all those months was right there, so nearby. The overthrown emperor had never once left the Forbidden City, and it was rumored in the Legations Quarter that if he ever did, it would be to go into exile.

We obtained such an absolutely shameful amount of money that we had to quickly open several bank accounts at various entities in order not to draw too much attention to ourselves. This strategy proved useless, however. The Banque de l'Indo-Chine, Crédit Lyonnais, and Hongkong and Shanghai Banking Corp. branch managers simply had to pay their respects as soon as they were told how much I was depositing at their banks. All of them offered me unlimited letters of credit; presents and invitations to dinners and parties began arriving at the hotel as well.

Once the French ambassador and the minister plenipotentiary for Spain, Marqués de Dosfuentes, learned that the rich Spanish Parisian whom all the bankers were talking about was staying at the Grand Hôtel des Wagons-Lits, they insisted on organizing official receptions to introduce me to the most prominent members of both communities. I had to repeatedly send my regrets. Apart from wanting to stay out of the social pages in the international press, our luggage was already in the car we'd hired to take us to the station, where we were to board a luxury express train to Shanghai. In an effort to protect the security of the foreign and affluent Chinese passengers traveling south, our train would be guarded by soldiers in the Republic of the North's army.

We were so absurdly rich we could have bought the train or the very Legations Quarter itself if we'd wanted. Some of the pieces had been so valuable—especially those made of that magnificent and virtually nonexistent variety of jade known as *yufu*—that a bidding war had ensued between merchants, and we were able to obtain exorbitant prices. Wudang monastery could now afford to be completely renovated, and Paddy Tichborne would be able to buy Scotland's entire production of whiskey. As far as I was concerned, apart from paying off Rémy's debts and taking care of Fernanda and Biao until they came of age, I hadn't any specific ideas about what I wanted. My only desires were to go home, continue painting, and show my work—oh, and buy beautiful clothes, expensive shoes, and pretty hats, of course.

During the few days we spent in Peking, we scoured both the Chinese and foreign papers each morning to make certain that no one—not the Kuomintang, the Kungchantang, the Chinese imperialists or the Japanese—mentioned the mausoleum *affaire*. There was no room for error in China's political situation, so everyone kept the matter quiet and let it run its course. Some did so fearing how the foreign imperialist powers, as they called them, would react, while others didn't want to suffer the condemnation and disrepute of world opinion. After all, the First Emperor could no longer play the part that those who had sought restoration wanted for him. As for those who had wanted to prevent the restoration, now that they'd achieved their goal, why sully themselves by publicly confessing to having destroyed a colossal, historical work such as Shi Huang Ti's mausoleum?

Once we reached the crowded station, we looked for a quiet place to say good-bye to Master Red. The date was Sunday, December 16, and, as hard as it was to believe, we had therefore spent only a month and a half together. It had been such an intense time, so fraught with danger, that it could just as easily have been a lifetime. None of us wanted to admit that we were going our separate ways and, worse still, might never see one another again. Fernanda, wearing a beautiful fur coat and a lovely sable hat like mine, had tears in her eyes and sadness written all over her face. Biao was shockingly handsome in a three-piece English tweed suit, his hair cut short and lacquered with brilliantine. He looked magnificent—and he needed to in order to be allowed onto that train and into the first-class cars.

"Master Red Jade, what will you do when you get back to Xi'an?" I asked with a lump in my throat.

The monk, who was carrying his share of the money in heavy bags cautiously hidden underneath his loose, worn tunic, blinked his small, wide-spaced eyes.

"I'll pick up the animals and return to Wudang, madame." He smiled. "I'm anxious to unload all this wealth onto the mules."

"You run a great risk traveling alone on those paths."

"Don't worry, I'll send word to the monastery, and they'll have people come meet me."

"Will we see you again, Master Red Jade?" my niece whimpered.

"Will you ever come back to Wudang?" the scholar asked, with a touch of nostalgia in his voice.

"When you least expect it," I confirmed, "someone will tell you that three strange visitors have hurried through Xuanyue Men, the Gate to the Mysterious Mountain, and are running up the Divine Corridor calling out your name."

Master Red blushed and, with a shy smile, lowered his head in that characteristic gesture that always made me worry he'd drive his dangerously pointed chin into his throat.

"Have you never wondered, madame, how the First Emperor's heavy coffin floated in the air?"

The mention of that funeral chamber, which now seemed so far away, was a discordant note that ruptured the emotion of the moment. That place would forever be connected to the last image I had of Lao Jiang in those horrible circumstances. I was suddenly conscious of all the Westerners who were looking at us strangely, the many families from the Legations Quarter who'd come to the station to send off relatives or friends.

"How did it float?" Biao asked, immediately interested.

"It was made of iron," Master Red emphasized, as if that were the key to it all.

"Yes, we saw that," I replied.

"And the walls were made of stone," he continued. How could we fail to see when the answer was so obvious? he seemed to be saying.

"That's right, Master Red Jade. Stone," I repeated. "The entire room was made of stone."

"When I opened my bag, I noticed that the needle on my *luo p'an* was spinning wildly."

"Stop playing games, Master Red Jade," Fernanda snapped, unconsciously holding her bag as if she were about to hit him over the head with it.

"Magnets?" Biao timidly suggested.

"Exactly!" Master Red exclaimed. "Magnetic stones! That's why my *luo p'an* didn't work. The entire chamber was built using magnetic stones that exerted a proportionately equal pull on the coffin and kept it floating in place."

I was completely flabbergasted. Could magnets be that strong? Evidently they could.

"But, Master," Biao objected, "the slightest movement of the sarcophagus would have unbalanced those forces and made it fall."

"That's why they put it up so high. Don't you remember? It was impossible to reach, and at that distance from the floor and the entrance nothing affected it, not air or human presence. Everything was carefully planned so that great iron coffin would remain in the center of those magnetic forces forever."

"Not forever, Master Red Jade," I murmured. "It's gone now."

The four of us were silent, saddened by the irretrievable loss of all the marvelous things we'd discovered and that no one would ever see again. The engine whistle blew in the large station building.

"Our train!" I said, alarmed. We had to go.

Completely unconcerned about my regained Western appearance or whoever might be watching, I closed my right hand into a fist and wrapped my left hand around it, held them up in front of my forehead, then bowed long and low before Master Red Jade.

"Thank you, Master. I will never forget you."

The children, who had followed my lead and still had their heads bowed when I straightened up, murmured their thanks as well.

Master Red was extremely moved and bowed to the three of us. Then, smiling warmly, he turned and walked toward the station door.

"We'll miss our train," Fernanda suddenly declared, pragmatic as always.

Over the next thirty-six hours, we crossed China from north to south inside deluxe sleeping compartments, lovely club cars with pianos and dance floors, and magnificent dining cars where Chinese waiters served exquisite meals. The dishes made with duck or pheasant, which were as common in China as chickens, were by far the best. Before being roasted, the meat was painted with a fine coat of lacquer—the same kind used on buildings, furniture, and columns—to make lacquered ducks or pheasants, a delicacy that was once reserved for emperors.

The soldiers who guarded the train were an uncomfortable presence, rough and brutish, but they allowed us to pass without incident through truly dangerous areas controlled by warlords or bandit armies. The weather improved during our second day of travel, and while still cold, it wasn't the glacial cold of Peking, so we were able to spend time on the balconies enjoying the scenery. We neared the Yangtze, and though it might sound absurd, I felt connected to that river after so many days traveling on it to Hankow. If our lovely, cultured travel companions had even suspected that the children and I had journeyed upriver aboard filthy barges and sampans, dressed like beggars and escaping something called the Green Gang, they'd have avoided us as if we'd had the plague. How long ago those days were, and how wonderful they'd been!

Immense, water-filled rice paddies flew past for hours on end before we reached Nanking, the former Southern Capital founded by the first Ming emperor, a city I recalled as dilapidated and where Lao Jiang had walked the filthy streets happily recalling his student days. I'll never forget Nanking's immense Jubao Gate, or Zhonghua Men as it was now called, and the underground tunnel containing a Wei-ch'i problem on the floor. Known as "The Legend of Lanke Mountain," it was over twenty-five hundred years old, and our intelligent Biao had solved it. That was where the Green Gang had attacked us for the second time, resulting in the loss of Paddy Tichborne's leg when he boldly stepped in front to protect the children and me. I would be eternally grateful for that gesture, and although I wouldn't be able to tell him the whole truth, I would of course give him his full share of the treasure.

We disembarked once we reached Nanking and were ferried across the immense, interminable Blue River on lovely steamers that agilely dodged the little junks, sampans, and numerous seagoing vessels with apparent ease. Back on the train by nightfall, we carried on to Shanghai, just a few hours away. The stations became more plentiful, and we could see crowds waiting in the light of red paper lanterns as we sped through.

Our convoy finally stopped near midnight at one of the platforms in the Shanghai North Railway Station, the very station we'd departed from three and a half months earlier, when Fernanda and I were newly arrived in China, carrying our bags and dressed as poor peasants. We were now returning in first class, looking so refined it would have been impossible to recognize us.

Although we'd left Shanghai in the stifling heat of summer and it was now the middle of winter, it still wasn't cold enough for fur coats and sable hats. Nevertheless, we left them on so as to stay warm on that late-night rickshaw ride. Since I was certain that Monsieur Julliard, Rémy's lawyer, would have sold the house and auctioned off the furniture and artwork as I had instructed, I decided we should stay at a hotel in the International Concession, far from the French Concession, controlled by Pockmarked Huang's police. One of our travel companions had recommended the Astor House Hotel, and that's where we spent our first night. Thanks to his imposing height, elegant Western clothing, and a considerable sum of money paid to the manager, Biao was allowed to stay in a small room in the servants' quarters. We'd been granted a very special favor; giving lodging to a yellow could seriously damage the hotel's good reputation.

I soon realized that getting around in areas reserved for Westerners was going to be a serious problem with Little Tiger. Outside the pretty public gardens near the Astor was an English sign that read "No dogs or Chinese allowed." The next morning I left the children at the hotel with the solemn promise from them that they were not to leave under

any circumstances and took a rickshaw to see M. Julliard at his office on
rue Millot in the French Concession.

It was a pleasure to ride through that city. Christmas was approaching, and some of the buildings had already been decorated for the season. I didn't recognize any of the well-known sites or places, because I
hadn't had time to visit them when I was first in Shanghai, but I was
thrilled to be traveling along the famous Bund, that great avenue on the
west bank of the dirty, yellow Huang Pu River that we'd sailed up on
board the *André Lebon* as far as the Compagnie des Messageries Maritimes docks on the day we arrived in China. There were so many cars,
trams, rickshaws, and bicycles! So many people! The wealth and opulence were unlike anything I'd seen anywhere else in that enormous
country. People from all over the world had found in Shanghai a place to
work and live, revel and die—like Rémy. If not for the corruption that
reigned in that city, if not for the gangs, the mafia, and the opium,
Shanghai would have been a wonderful place to live.

We passed through the wire fence that separated the concessions
without being stopped by the gendarmes. I was profoundly relieved,
fearing that my name might set off alarms with Pockmarked Huang's
Sécurité. I was no longer afraid of the Green Gang after what happened
in the mausoleum, but I didn't want to stir up already turbulent waters
before leaving Shanghai.

Nothing had changed in André Julliard's office on rue Millot: the
same smell of must and rotting wood, the same glassed-in office, and the
same Chinese clerks milling around the young typists' desks. M. Julliard
was even wearing the same sorry, wrinkled linen jacket as last time. He
was pleasantly surprised to see me, greeting me warmly and asking
what I'd been doing those last few months, as it had been impossible to
locate me. I gave him a vague story about a sightseeing trip into the interior of China, which he didn't appear to believe. Over a cup of tea, he
pulled the thick file containing Rémy's documents out of a drawer and
explained that he had indeed sold the house and auctioned off the other
effects. He'd obtained nearly 150,000 francs, enough to cover half the

debt, but the other half was still outstanding. Creditors were growing impatient, and more than one lawsuit had been decided against me, making me practically an outlaw.

"Oh, but don't worry about that!" he commented in his strong ac-cent from the south of France, smiling widely. "It's quite normal in Shanghai!"

"I'm not worried, M. Julliard," I replied. "I have the money. I'm going to write you a check for the full amount, plus a little more should some other unforeseen debt arise and to cover your services." His eyes grew wide behind the dirty lenses of his small, round, wire-rimmed glasses, and a question he never managed to ask formed on his lips.

"No need to worry, M. Julliard. The check won't bounce. Here's a copy of a letter of credit from the Hongkong and Shanghai Bank, and here," I said, pulling out a brand-new checkbook and taking the pen he offered, "are the two hundred thousand francs that will put an end to this nightmare."

The poor lawyer didn't know how to thank me for such a generous honorarium and launched into a thousand courtesies and niceties. At the door to his office on my way out, I asked him to please be discreet with respect to payment, not to pay all the debts at once, but little by little in order not to draw attention.

"Don't worry, madame," he replied with a complicit gesture I didn't quite know how to interpret, "I completely understand. Rest assured that's what I'll do. If you want or need anything, if I can be of service to you in any way, please don't hesitate to ask. I would be delighted to do what I can."

"Well, I do have one favor to ask," I replied with a beguiling smile. "Would you purchase three first-class tickets on the next ship to set sail for Marseille or Cherbourg?"

He once again looked at me in surprise but nodded his head.

"Even if it were to leave tomorrow?" he asked.

"Even better if it leaves tomorrow," I answered, handing him a thousand silver dollars. "Please send them to my hotel as soon as you have them. I'm at the Astor House."

We said good-bye, exchanging pleasantries and mutual gratitude, and I left with the lovely sensation of being debt-free for the first time in ages. It felt good to be rich; it was a sort of protective shield that kept any unexpected setback or mishap at bay.

My next stop that morning was the Shanghai Club. I hoped Paddy Tichborne would be fully recovered and hadn't been drinking too much. I was quite surprised when the concierge told me he no longer lived there, that he'd moved to other lodgings in the Hong Kew area—and from the look on his face, I presumed it must be somewhere cheap and shabby.

It turned out that the neighborhood of Hong Kew was between the railway station and my hotel; we'd been past it, but it had nothing in common with the Shanghai I knew. It was a miserable, filthy place where the people seemed extremely dangerous. Everyone on the street looked like a criminal, and I trembled as if I were seeing the Green Gang assassins again with knives in their hands. I ignored the curious stares and hurried out of the rickshaw as soon as my coolie stopped in a narrow Chinese alley in front of a brick building with the darkest entranceway I'd ever seen. There, on the second floor, was where Tichborne lived. Something very serious must have happened for this to be his new home.

I worriedly knocked on the door, unsure what to expect on the other side, but it was the same fat, gray-haired Paddy Tichborne who opened it. After he'd stared disconcertedly at me for a few seconds, a bright gleam lit up his eyes and an enormous smile came over his face.

"Mme De Poulain!" he nearly shouted.

"Mr. Tichborne! It's so good to see you!"

It was true. Hard to believe, but true: I was happy, very happy to see him again. Then I noticed his crutches, and my eyes traveled down to his right leg, which was gone below the knee. His pant leg was pinned back.

"Come in. Please, come in," he invited, struggling to move out of the way on his crutches.

It was a sorry-looking hovel, consisting of only one room. On one side was a dirty, unmade bed; on the other, a tiny kitchen stacked with unwashed dishes; in the middle were a couple of chairs and an armchair around a rickety table covered, of course, in empty whiskey bottles. At the back, next to a small bookshelf, was a door that likely led to the communal patio and washrooms. It smelled terrible, and not just because the house was filthy: It had been some time since Paddy had seen soap or water either. He was unshaven, generally slovenly, and unkempt.

"How are you, Mme De Poulain? And how are the others? Lao Jiang? Your niece? The Chinese boy?"

I laughed as we slowly walked toward the seats and didn't make a fuss when I had to sit on one of the greasy, stained chairs.

"Ah, Mr. Tichborne, I have a very long story to tell you."

"Did you reach the First Emperor's mausoleum?" he asked anxiously, falling like dead weight into the poor armchair, which creaked dangerously.

"I see you're impatient, Mr. Tichborne, and I do understand—"

"Call me Paddy, please. It's so good to see you!"

"Then call me Elvira and we'll be equal."

"Would you like a drink of . . ." He paused, glancing around the miserable, dirty little room. "I'm afraid I don't have anything to offer you, madame . . . Elvira. I don't have anything to offer you, Elvira."

"Don't worry, Paddy. I'm fine."

"Do you mind if I pour myself a little whiskey?" he asked, filling a dirty glass on the table.

"No, not at all. Please, go ahead," I replied, though he was already taking a long drink, nearly emptying the entire glass. "But tell me, why did you leave the Shanghai Club?"

He avoided my eyes. "They threw me out."

"They threw you out?" I asked, feigning surprise.

"When I lost my leg, you remember, I wasn't able to work as a jour-nalist or for the Royal Geographic Society any longer."

"But losing a leg is no reason to fire you," I objected. "You could still write, you could get around Shanghai by rickshaw, you could—"

"No, no, Elvira," he interrupted. "They didn't fire me because I lost a leg; they fired me because I started drinking too much when I got out of hospital and wasn't able to fulfill my obligations. And as you can see . . ." he said, refilling his glass to the rim and taking another long drink. "As you can see, I still drink too much. Now then, tell me, where is Lao Jiang? Why didn't he come with you?"

The most difficult part of our meeting had arrived.

"Lao Jiang's dead, Paddy."

His face fell. "What?" he burst out, completely stunned.

"Let me tell you the whole story, starting from when you were wounded in Nanking."

I explained that luckily a detachment of Kuomintang soldiers was passing through Zhonghua Men at the exact time we were being at-tacked by the Green Gang. They saved our lives that day and took him to their barracks, providing him with medical attention.

"Yes, I know," he commented. "I was feverish and don't remember all the details, but there was something about an argument with a Kuo-mintang officer. I wanted to be transferred to a hospital in Shanghai when they said my leg would have to be amputated."

"Exactly. The Kuomintang took charge because you were a foreigner and a journalist. As soon as we told them, they offered to take care of everything."

There was the first part of the new story. Not bad. As he drank glass after glass of whiskey, I told Paddy about our trip by sampan to Han-kow, our time in Wudang, how we got the third piece of the *jiance*, more attacks by the Green Gang, our trek through the mountains to the mausoleum at Mount Li, how we managed to get in, thanks to Mas-ter Red Jade and his Dragon's Nest, and everything else. I spoke for a long while, giving him all sorts of details—thinking about the book he might write one day—but deliberately omitted all political details. I never mentioned the Kuomintang again, nor did I tell him about the young Communist militiamen or Lao Jiang's revelation in the room with the First Emperor's coffin. Instead I told him that the five of us left together and that when we were on the third level, going up the ten thousand bridges, one of the old walkways came loose and Lao Jiang fell over three hundred feet. There was nothing we could do; on the contrary, we had to run for lives because the gigantic pillars had started to come down, smashing into one another, causing a quake that shook the entire funeral complex. I described my trick with the mirrors on the level with the methane gas as well as our run-in with the Green Gang as we were leaving the throne room. I explained how they tried to stop us but then, seeing how the whole mausoleum was collapsing, they escaped with us and galloped away as soon as we were outside, leaving us there.

"All they wanted was the First Emperor's tomb," Paddy muttered, slurring his words. The death of his old friend Lao Jiang, the antiquarian from Nanking Road, was obviously very painful.

"Which brings us to the conclusion of this story," I replied happily, trying to cheer him up. "The Green Gang is no longer after us. However, since they're aware of everything, if you or I were to go about Shanghai with this," I said, taking the check I had filled out at the hotel before leaving that morning and setting it on the table in front of him, "they might want to make life difficult for us."

Paddy reached out, picked up the check, unfolded it very slowly, and read the figure I had written on it. He turned deathly pale and started to sweat so profusely that he had to pull a filthy handkerchief from his pocket and wipe it, trembling, across his brow.

"That's . . . that's not . . . that's not possible," he stammered.

"Oh, but it is. We sold everything we took from the mausoleum in Peking and divided the money into three equal parts: one for Wudang, one for you, and one for me."

"What about the children?"

"The children will stay with me."

"But I didn't run all the risks you did. I didn't even get to the mauso-leum. I—"

"Would you be quiet, Paddy? You lost a leg saving our lives. We'll never be able to thank you enough, so not another word."

He smiled widely and put the check in the pocket with his handker-chief.

"I'll have to go to the bank," he murmured.

"You'll have to wash up first," I recommended. "And listen to me, Paddy: Don't stay in China. We can't trust the Green Gang, and you're too well known in Shanghai. Get on a ship and go back to Ireland. You don't need to work anymore. Buy yourself a castle and write books. I'd like nothing more than to go to one of my favorite bookstores in Paris and buy a great novel about the First Emperor's treasures. The children and I could visit you, and you could come to our house and stay as long as you like."

He furrowed his brow. He had stopped drinking; a full glass sat abandoned on the table.

"You'll have to get Biao's papers," he commented worriedly, "if he has any. He won't be able to leave China without documentation."

"I'm speaking with Father Castrillo, superior of the Augustinian mission, this afternoon," I told him, "but it doesn't matter what he says. Biao has certain contacts and could get forged papers within a few hours. Money's not an issue."

"How you've changed, Elvira!" he exclaimed, letting out a laugh. "You used to be so fussy, so prudish—" He suddenly realized how in-sulting that was and came to a full stop. "I'm sorry. I didn't mean to of-fend you."

"You didn't, Paddy," I said. That was a lie, of course, but the polite thing to say. "You're right. I have changed a great deal, more than you can imagine, and for the better. I'm happy. There's only one thing that worries me."

"Anything I can help with?"

"No," I replied sadly, "not unless you can change the world and make sure Biao isn't ostracized in Paris because he's Chinese."

"Oh, that's going to be difficult!" he exclaimed, remaining pensive.

"I don't know what I'll do, but Biao has to study. He's incredibly intelligent. Any sort of specialty in the sciences would be perfect for him."

"Do you know what just came to mind?" Paddy murmured. "The Lyon Incident."

"Lyon Incident?"

"Yes, don't you remember? It happened a few years ago, toward the end of 1921. After the war in Europe, France called on its colonies in China to cover the labor shortage in its factories. A hundred and forty thousand coolies were sent. At the same time, the best students from Chinese universities were invited to continue their studies in France as a means of propaganda. The intention, they said, was to promote good relations between the two cultures. You don't want to know how the story ended." He grunted, leaning back in his chair. "A few months after the first students arrived, the Sino-French Educational Association went bankrupt; there wasn't a single franc to pay their school or boarding fees. These young students, almost all of whom were from good families or particularly intelligent, like Biao, had to go to work in factories alongside the coolies just to survive. Others who were luckier found work as dishwashers, and the rest became beggars on the streets of Paris, Montargis, Fontainebleu, and Le Cresot. The Chinese ambassador in France, Tcheng Lou, washed his hands like Pontius Pilate and announced that he didn't intend to take responsibility for such wretches. You see, the French Communist Party had begun circulating Communist ideals among them when it found such a fertile field ready to be sown."

I listened in horror, imagining Biao in such a situation. How would the boy be regarded in France? Like a Chinese coolie, a dishwasher, a factory worker, a Communist revolutionary?

"At the end of September 1921," Paddy continued, "the students organized a demonstration in front of the Sino-French Institute of Lyon, located in Fort Saint-Irénée. Ambassador Tcheng made that statement about the Middle Kingdom washing its hands of such agitators, and so, after a harsh police attack in which dozens were hurt, some of the students were deported. Others were able to get their families to send money and buy a ticket home."

"Are you trying to say it would be better to leave Biao in Shanghai?" I asked in distress.

"No, Elvira. I'm simply telling you what the boy will encounter in Europe, not only France. The European colonial mentality is a very high wall that Biao will have to climb. It doesn't matter how smart, good, or honest he is, or how rich. It doesn't matter. He's Chinese, a yellow with slanted eyes. He's different, inferior. People will stop and stare, point at him when he walks down the street anywhere in Europe."

"You're too pessimistic, Paddy," I retorted. "Yes, he'll be different, but they'll get used to him. There will come a time when the people closest to him—his classmates, his teachers, his friends—won't even notice he is Asian. He'll just be Biao."

"He'll need a last name, too," Paddy pointed out. "Will you adopt him? Are you prepared to become the legal mother of a Chinese boy?"

I knew that this time would come.

"If necessary, yes," I replied.

He looked at me for a long while, whether with pity or admiration I'm not sure. Then, with a great deal of effort, he stood and picked up his crutches. I stood as well.

"You can count on my help," he declared. "Now I'm going to shower, as you suggested, and go to the bank. I'll buy new clothes and a ticket to England. Then I'll come by your hotel, though you haven't yet told me where you're staying. . . ."

"Astor House."

"Then I'll go by Astor House and . . . No, better yet, I'll stay at Astor House as well, and we'll talk about this again. Thank you, Elvira," he said, holding out his hand. I shook it warmly and walked to the door, followed by the rhythmic clicking of his crutches.

"We'll see you at the hotel," I said by way of good-bye.

He smiled. "See you then."

But we never did see him again. That afternoon, once I'd arranged Biao's documentation with Father Castrillo at the orphanage and returned to the hotel, the concierge handed me an envelope containing the first-class tickets that M. Julliard had bought for us on the *Dumont d'Urville*, a packet boat leaving for Marseille at seven the next morning, Wednesday, December 19. There was another envelope with a note signed by Patrick Tichborne, apologizing for his absence: He'd been lucky enough to find passage on a steamer leaving that very night for Yokohama. After a great deal of thought, he'd decided to go to the United States, to New York, where he could arrange for the best prosthetic leg in the world. He promised to look me up in Paris as soon as he got back to Europe.

He never did. We never heard news of Paddy again, never knew what had happened to him. I suppose he got his prosthetic leg and lived like a king, drinking to excess somewhere in the world with the fortune from the First Emperor's mausoleum.

The children and I returned to my house in Paris. After everything she'd learned in China, and no doubt due to a certain family propensity, Fernanda developed a sharp sense of independence over the years that made her a woman to be reckoned with. When young, brilliant Biao was accepted to the famous Lycée Condorcet, my niece decided she wanted to study as well. While our splendid house was being built on the outskirts of Paris, I was forced to hire private tutors for her in the same courses Biao was taking at the lycée. She continued her studies after we moved, and when Biao was accepted to the Sorbonne at the University of Paris to study physics, she became the first foreign woman ever to enroll—with some help from influential friends and acquaintances—at the L'École Libre de Sciences Politiques. There she met and became engaged to a young, forward-thinking diplomat who knew how to handle her as no one else did.

Biao courageously handled the difficulties he faced in Paris as an Oriental. Never discouraged by the bad jokes or obstacles some stupid fools placed in his way, he charged ahead, unstoppable, graduating with a doctorate, at the top of his class, winning every award in existence. Unable to find work in France, he accepted a contract with an American company in California that made him an offer fit for an emperor. Shortly after he arrived in the United States, he met and married a woman named Gladys (that was my first trip across the Atlantic). A year later Fernanda married André, the diplomat, and they left for some unpronounceable country on the African continent.

What did I do? Well, while the children were still at home, I painted and invested in art, spending a considerable amount on works by my favorite painters, becoming a renowned collector. I also opened several art galleries and a splendid painting school on rue Saint-Guillaume. When Fernanda and Biao left home, I traveled through Europe visiting museums and art exhibits. A short while later, in 1936, a group of fascist soldiers staged a coup d'état in Spain, and the Civil War began. I moved to southern France, near the border, where I collaborated personally and financially with the Republican refugees fleeing the country. It was an interminable, exhausting task. Thousands crossed the Pyrenees every day, escaping the enemy army, arriving lost, without money, without food, and without knowing the language. They were dirty, sick, wounded, and demoralized. It was grueling work, and then, just when it seemed about to end, came the Second World War. By that time I was sixty, and Biao, who had two young children, categorically ordered me to leave Europe and come to California to live with him and his family. Fernanda, still in that unpronounceable African country, encouraged me to go, saying it was the safest course of action, that France would soon fall into the hands of the Nazis, and assuring me that she and her two small children would follow shortly.

Thus, in 1941, my collection of paintings and I boarded an ocean liner to New York and then crossed that enormous country from coast to coast by special train, finally arriving in the city of Los Angeles.

Three months later my niece arrived with her little ones. Since there wasn't room for us all in Biao's house, I bought a car and a lovely villa in Santa Monica, where the majority of L.A. art galleries are located.

After the war André left the diplomatic corps and came to California as an executive with a citrus export company, where he did very well for himself. But the one who really prospered was Fernanda. By sheer coincidence she found work in the Business and Legal Affairs office of Paramount Picture Studios and today strikes terror into the hearts of agents representing Hollywood's most important actors. The studios love her, and it's no wonder why.

Nowadays I like to sit in the sun and paint. I never became a famous artist, but I did become a renowned collector and an important patron to great painters. I'm old now, so old. But that doesn't prevent me from going to the beach with my grandchildren, swimming in my pool, or driving my car. My doctor tells me I have an iron constitution and that I'll surely live to be a hundred.

I always reply, "Doctor, you've got to live life learning to see the good in the bad and the bad in the good."

He laughs and says I have some strange ideas, like doing tai chi every morning. I laugh, too, but then I remember old Ming T'ien looking up at the lovely mountains she could no longer see.

"Haste shortens your life," she repeats over and over again, smiling all the while.

"Yes, Ming T'ien," I reply.

"Remember me when you're my age!" she shouts before disappearing.

And so I keep moving my chi energy out in the garden with the sun shining on me, slowly, with my hair down as the Yellow Emperor recommended.

Notes

1 The official name of the last emperor of China was Hsuan Tung of the Great Qing. However, he is better known in the West by his nickname, Puyi, thanks to Bernardo Bertolucci's movie *The Last Emperor*.

2 Title used by Chinese servants to address their mistresses.

3 As Spain's ambassador to Bulgaria, Julio Palencia (1884–1952) bravely faced Nazi authorities during the Second World War in order to prevent the country's Jews from being exterminated. Thanks to his efforts, over six hundred people were saved.

4 Given the extent of her work, it would be impossible to give a biography of Isabel de Oyarzábal (Málaga 1878–Mexico 1974), a journalist, writer, and the second female and first Spanish diplomat in the world as ambassador to Sweden.

5 Chinese greeting equivalent to "Hello," "Good morning," "How are you?"

6 Pronounced *Ching*. The *Q* is equivalent to our *Ch* sound.

7 Important dynasties in Chinese history: Tang (A.D. 618–907), Song (A.D. 960–1279), Ming (A.D. 1368–1644).

8 Over 450 miles per hour.

9 *Chin*. It is believed the name China derives from this kingdom.

10 In 1645 the Manchus ordered that all adult Chinese males shave their foreheads and braid their hair (the famous Chinese queue) in the Manchu style.

11 "Beautiful country."

12 "The country of law."

13 The current way to write Nanking is Nanjing.

14 Zhejiang.

15 Sun Tzu is the author of the famous treatise *The Art of War* from the fourth century B.C.

16 *Bu* means "No."

17 Now the city of Liaoyang, in the province of Liaoning, north of Beijing.

18 Sima Qian (145–90 B.C.) authored the great work *Records of the Grand Historian (Shi ji)* and greatly influenced subsequent Chinese historians.

19 Said to put an end to a matter. "Case closed."

20 A Chinese measure of length. One *li* is equal to about a third of a mile.

21 It is also written as Weichi, Weiqi, Wei Qi, or Weiki, but Wei-ch'i is the most correct.

22 First recorded in *Shu Yi Zhi*, written by Ren Fong (Southern and Northern dynasties, A.D. 420–589).

23 This diagram is better known by Go players as Ranka, its Japanese name.

24 This is the Japanese expression used by Go players in the West.

25 The Kuomintang flag.

26 Along with Hanyang and Wuchang, Hankow forms part of what is now a single city called Wuhan, capital of Hubei province.

27 Contrary to the way it is done in the West, the Chinese mention east or west before north or south. Thus, we would say "northwest" while they say "west-north," or "eastsouth" for southeast.

28 *Shan* means "mountain."

29 Zhang Zuolin, 1873–1928.

30 Now the city of Danjiangkou.

31 Reign name Yonle (1403–24).

32 *Gong* means "temple" or "palace."

33 Famous martial-arts master and abbot of Wudang (1860–1932).

34 *Tao Te Ching / TaoTe King / Dao De Jing,* fourth century B.C., a fundamental philosophical treatise on Taoism attributed to Lao-tzu (Lao Tsé / Lao Zi).

35 Seventh Qing Emperor of China, from 1796 to 1820.

36 1766–1121 B.C.

37 Chinese hours are double. The hour of the Monkey is from 3:00 to 4:59 P.M.

38 *Ming t'ien* means "bright heavens."

39 The famous Cornucopia Tea House, located at the lower end of the Bund in Shanghai.

40 Between 9:00 and 10:59 A.M.

41 Now the province of Shaanxi Sheng.

42 Department in the First Emperor's employ responsible for the mausoleum projects.

43 Now called Shangxian or Shangzhou.

44 A.D. 386–534

45 A.D. 220–65

46 To the east, buried in an enormous tomb, is the well-known and impressive Terra-Cotta Army, not discovered until 1974.

47 Historian (A.D. 291–361), author of *Records of the States South of Mount Hua*, better known as the *Chronicles of Huayang*.

48 It is believed that the Chinese used asbestos to make wicks several centuries B.C. These wicks never had to be replaced, because they were never consumed.

49 Mythological dynasty, approximately 2100–1600 B.C.

51 The highly toxic nature of mercury was discovered only a few years ago.